THREE COURSES
AND A DESSERT

THREE COURSES AND A DESSERT

William Clarke

Illustrated by George Cruikshank

"Sit down and feed, and welcome to our table."
AS YOU LIKE IT

NONSUCH

First published 1830
Copyright © in this edition 2005
Nonsuch Publishing Ltd

Nonsuch Publishing Limited
The Mill, Brimscombe Port, Stroud, Gloucestershire, GL5 2QG
www.nonsuch–publishing.com

British Library Cataloguing in Publication Data.
A catalogue record for this book is available from the British Library.

ISBN 1–84588–072–2

Typesetting and origination by Nonsuch Publishing Limited
Printed in Great Britain by Oaklands Book Services Limited

INTRODUCTION
TO THE MODERN EDITION

WILLIAM Clarke, who wrote the stories contained in *Three Courses and a Dessert*, was born in 1800. Little is known about his comparatively short life, apart from the fact that he also wrote *The Boys' Own Book: A Complete Encyclopedia of All the Diversions, Athletic, Scientific, and Recreative, of Boyhood and Youth* (1829), edited the *Monthly Magazine* and brought out a humorous periodical entitled *The Cigar*. During the last three or four years of his life he was apparently writing a work of natural history, but it was unfinished when he died of an apoplexy in 1838 and was never published. *Three Courses and a Dessert* is all that remains of Clarke's contribution to nineteenth–century literature and the only reminder of his satirical wit. In the eyes of posterity, he is overshadowed by his illustrator.

In contrast, far more is known about George Cruikshank, whose style of illustration will be familiar to a modern audience, in particular his engravings for Charles Dickens' *Oliver Twist*. The son and brother of caricaturists, he was born in London in 1792, and, despite having had no formal artistic education (and very little of any other kind), he began drawing at an early age. When he was twenty years old he began his career as a political caricaturist, and he produced a series of pamphlets with William Hone, one engraving for which, the 'Bank Restriction Note' of 1818, Cruikshank believed contributed towards the cessation of hanging for minor offences. In 1824–26 he designed two volumes of etchings for Grimm's *Popular Stories,* in 1831 he illustrated an edition of Defoe's *Robinson Crusoe* and in 1835 the same author's *Journal of the Plague Year.*

1836 was an important year in Cruikshank's career: he began his long association with the novelist Harrison Ainsworth by illustrating *Rookwood*, as well as the first series of Dickens' *Sketches by Boz*. He also illustrated the second series, which appeared the following year. In 1837 he supplied the cover for the first issue of *Bentley's Miscellany*, the first of 126 plates which he provided for the magazine over the years, and, in the same year, the illustrations for *Oliver Twist*. He later claimed that he came up with the ideas for the story. Two years later Ainsworth's *Jack Sheppard* was also published in *Bentley's Miscellany* with engravings by Cruikshank, and when Ainsworth retired from the editorship of the *Miscellany* to start *Ainsworth's Magazine* Cruikshank continued to collaborate with him.

Late in life Cruikshank came to espouse the cause of teetotalism, which he strove to promote in *The Bottle* (1847) and *The Drunkard's Children* (1848), both of which threw into stark relief the ill effects of alcohol abuse. Unfortunately, his moral crusade was not universally appreciated and his popularity declined. He also took up painting in oils, and produced a number of pictures, but they were not received in the same way as his earlier works. He died in 1878, and, after a temporary interment in Kensal Green, he was buried in St Paul's Cathedral.

Three Courses and a Dessert was first published in 1830, when George Cruikshank was still regarded more as a political caricaturist than as a book illustrator. The book, however, is concerned not so much with politics but with society itself, and, in particular, West Country and Irish society, as viewed through the eyes of Clarke and Cruikshank. Mainly satirical, but sometimes moving, these short stories are full of allegories and allusions and they are populated by a varied cast of characters who come vividly to life in the mind of the reader. Author and illustrator gleefully expose the follies of human nature and poke fun both at individuals and at society itself, but they also treat some of the more poignant stories with the sympathetic dignity that they deserve. From Habakkuk Bullwrinkle's ridiculous efforts to find love to Dick and Giles Orrod's struggles with the English language, Clarke and Cruikshank find humour in all sorts of unlikely places. The characters are not drawn solely from the West Country and from Ireland, but form a cross–section of society, all of whom are treated equally irreverently by the satirist and caricaturist. Although society has changed a great deal since 1830, *Three Courses and a Dessert* remains as sharp and satirical as it was then, an illustration of how little human nature changes over time.

THREE COURSES AND A DESSERT

INDUCTION

THE purveyor of the ensuing apology for a "feast of reason," takes leave to greet his guests with a hearty, but respectful, welcome. It would be in bad taste for him to dilate at his threshold upon what he has provided for their entertainment: his brief bill of fare will presently be laid before them.

He ventures to indulge a hope, that his repast will prove obnoxious to none, and, in some degree, gratifying to many; that those who may discover nothing to their taste in one course, will meet with something piquant in another; that no one

"Will drag, at *each* REMOVE, a lengthening chain;"

and, that even if the *dishes* be disliked, the *plates*, at least, will please: but he feels bound to state, that whatever faults the decorations may be chargeable with, on the score of invention, he, alone, is to blame, and not Mr. George Cruikshank; to whom he is deeply indebted for having embellished his rude sketches in their transfer to wood, and translated them into a proper pictorial state, to make their appearance in public they have necessarily acquired a value, which they did not intrinsically possess, in passing through the hands of that distinguished artist; of whom it may truly, and on this occasion especially, be said, QUOD TETIGIT, ORNAVIT.

Having thus, perhaps rashly, presented himself at the bar of public opinion, conscious as he feels of his own demerits, he can only throw himself on the liberality of his judges, and plead for a lenient sentence.

BILL OF FARE

FIRST COURSE:

WEST COUNTRY CHRONICLES

WEST COUNTRY CHRONICLES

INTRODUCTION

THE true old English squire is now nearly extinct: a few admirable specimens of the class flourished a few years ago in the western counties; from the discourse and memoranda of one of the most excellent of these, the substance of the following narratives was gleaned. For my introduction to, and subsequent acquaintance with, the worthy old gentleman, I was indebted to the delinquency of a dog. Carlo was most exemplary in his punctuation; he would quarter and back in the finest style imaginable; no dog could be more staunch, steady, and obedient to hand and voice, while there was no living mutton at hand: but no sooner did he cross a sheep–track, break into view of a fleece, or even hear the tinkling bell (a dinner bell to him) of a distant flock, than he would bolt away, as rectilinearly as the crow flies, towards his favourite prey, in spite of the most peremptory commands, or the smack of a whip, with the flavour of which his back was intimately acquainted. I had been allowed a very fair trial of the dog; but, unfortunately, no opportunity occurred, previously to his becoming my property, of shooting over him near a sheep walk. His behaviour was so excellent in Kent, that I never was more astonished in my life, than when I beheld him severely shaking a sheep by the haunch, the first time we went out together in Somerset. Unable to obtain a substitute, and hoping that his vice would not prove incurable, I was compelled, most indignantly and unwillingly, to put up with his offences for three days. On the morning of the fourth, he suddenly broke forward from heel, and went off at full speed before me: aware, by experience, of what was about to take place, I lifted the piece to my shoulder, and should, most assuredly, have tickled his stern, had he not dashed over the brow of a little hillock, so rapidly, that it was impossible to cover him with my Manton. On reaching the brow of the acclivity, I saw him, in the valley below, with his teeth entangled in the wool of a wether; and a sturdy old person, in the garb of a sportsman, belabouring him over the back with an enormous cudgel. The individual, who inflicted this wholesome castigation on the delinquent, offered to cure him for me of his propensity. I gratefully accepted the offer; and thus became acquainted with that fine specimen of the old–fashioned gentlemen of England, Sir Mathew Ale, of Little Redland Hall, Baronet,— (whose grounds I was crossing, on my way to a manor over which I had the privilege of shooting,)—by means of a rascally dog, that had a fancy for killing his own mutton.

SIR MATTHEW ALE

IT was a question, even with my friend the Baronet himself, whether, as some of the genealogists asserted, his respectable ancestors were related to the illustrious judge, who, with the exception of an aspirate, was his namesake: but if, as the old gentleman said, he had none of the eminent lawyer's blood flowing in his veins, a fact of much greater importance was indisputable;—he possessed, without the shadow of a doubt, that great man's mug,—the capacious vessel from which he was wont to quaff huge and inspiring draughts of the king of all manly beverages, "nut–brown ale." The pitcher,—to which appellation its size entitled it,—"filled with the foaming blood of Barleycorn" from ten to fifteen years of age, invariably graced my friend's old oaken table, during our frequent festive meetings. There was a strong likeness, in the outline of Sir Mathew's mug, when full of the frothing liquor in which he delighted, to his "good round belly," his ruddy face, and his flowing wig. It was highly valued by the old gentleman, while he lived; and is looked upon with a kind of reverential love, by those to whom he endeared himself by his good qualities, as the only likeness of him extant, now that he is dead.

Sir Mathew was an enthusiastic admirer of the customs of merry old England, and especially attached to those of "the West–Countrie." Born in Devon, and living, as he said, with one foot in Gloucester and the other in Somerset, he had acquired a greater knowledge of the qualities, habits, and feelings of the people who dwelt in two or three of the "down–a–long" shires, than most men of his day. He was well versed in their superstitions, their quaint customs, and their oddities;—an adept in their traditionary lore, and acquainted with most of the heroes who had figured in their little modern romances of real life. A large portion of his time had been absorbed in making collections for a System of Rustic Mythology, a Calendar of West Country Customs, and in perfecting his favourite work,—the Apotheosis of John Barleycorn. The ensuing pages are devoted merely to a few circumstances which fell under his own observation; with the characters in the narratives, he was, personally, more or less acquainted: the auto–biography of the obese attorney, Habakkuk Bullwrinkle, is faithfully transcribed from the original manuscript, in Sir Mathew's possession.

Sir Mathew frequently declared, that nearly all the superstitions of the people, relating to charms and tokens, were, as he knew by experience, founded in truth. He had, at one time, been a staunch believer in the power of the "dead man's candle" to prevent those, who are sleeping in the house where it is lighted, from waking until it is burned out, or extinguished: but latterly Sir Mathew thought proper to intimate that his belief in the efficacy of the charm had been, in some degree, staggered. A malicious wag, in the neighbourhood, propagated a tale, which, if true, accounts naturally enough for the change in Sir Mathew's opinion upon this point. Whenever an eminent burglar happened to be imprisoned in either of the neighbouring gaols, it was the Baronet's custom, for a number of years past, as the story went, to consult the criminal, as a high authority, on the virtue of the mystic light in house–breaking. The result of his inquiries induced him to repose so much faith in the charm, that, in order to set the question beyond a doubt, he determined on making a midnight entry into the house of a dear friend; who, he knew, neither kept fire–arms, nor would, for a moment, suspect him, even if discovered and taken in the fact, of being actuated by burglarious motives. With the assistance of a lecturer on anatomy, who lived in a neighbouring town, and a clever journeyman–tallow–chandler, Sir Mathew made "a dead man's candle," *secundum artem*; armed with which, he penetrated into his friend's pantry, regaled himself very heartily on some cold beef, and a bottle of stout ale, and finding that his proceedings had not caused the least alarm, he daringly made a great deal of unnecessary noise. His friend and the servants were at length roused: in his hurry to get off undetected, Sir Mathew's candle was extinguished; and during the darkness, his dear friend, and Jacob, his dear friend's butler, thrashed him so unmercifully, that, although his fears endowed him with sufficient agility to effect a retreat, he could scarcely crawl home; and was confined to his bed, by a very mysterious indisposition, for more than a week.

Sir Matthew stoutly denied the truth of this impeachment: he admitted that he was a practical man,—an experimentalist in such matters; but he indignantly pleaded "not guilty" to being so enthusiastic a simpleton as his jocose calumniator had represented him. The wag, in reply, said "that it was very natural, right or wrong, for Sir Mathew to deny the correctness of the story. Although the old gentleman is certainly quite simple enough to do the deed," added he, "I must needs own, I never suspected him of being such a blockhead as to confess it."

After this, Sir Mathew treated the tale as an ingenious and venial invention, and always enjoyed it highly whenever it was subsequently related in his hearing. He would have laughed heartily at it, perhaps, if he could; but he had long been compelled to drill his features, periodically, into a state of almost in flexible gravity. "People who know but little of me," he would say, "call me 'the man without a smile;' I pass, with many, for a very surly fellow; unfortunately, I am often misrepresented, and my real character is mistaken, through, what others would deem, a trifling affliction: the bane of my life is, that, very frequently, for a month together, I can't laugh, and don't dare even to indulge in my habitual smirk, because I have an apparently incurable and terrifically susceptible little crack in my lip."

Sir Mathew was a most zealous supporter of the ancient customs of the country. He patronised the sports of a neighbouring village fair, at a considerable expense, until its frequenters almost abused him for not giving two pigs with greasy tails to be caught, instead of one. He entertained the cobblers of the surrounding villages, annually, with a barrel of strong ale, in order to keep up the good old custom of Crispin's sons draining a horn of malt liquor, in which a lighted candle was placed,—without singeing their faces, if they could,—on the feast of their patron saint: nor did he discontinue this practice, even after some of them had despoiled him of a favourite pair of boots; until a party of the gentle craft, on one occasion, emboldened by beer, stormed his inmost cellar, tapped a barrel which he did not intend to have broached for half a score of years, and, as he asserted, thickened the beet in three others, by their tremendous uproar! Sir Mathew's housekeeper, whose two sons were cordwainers, ventured to hint that the beer in those barrels had never been fine; and that, even after the fatal feast day, although certainly a little thick, it was far from ropy. Sir Mathew vowed, on the contrary, that it was ropy enough to hang the whole scoundrelly squad; and that he only wished they would give him an opportunity of making the experiment.

Sir Mathew was a decided enemy to duelling; and most vehemently abused the practice of two people popping at each other with pistols. "If gentlemen must fight," he would exclaim, "in the name of all that's old English and manly, why not make use of the national quarter–staff,—as I did, when Peppercorn Vowler called me out, and gave me my choice of weapons?"

According to tradition, Sir Mathew was almost a stranger to his opponent when the bout between them took place; and much to his astonishment, Peppercorn Vowler gave him an elaborate cudgelling. It was whispered, that the Baronet felt so indignant at the result of the quarter–staff conflict, that he sent his adversary an invitation, which was politely declined, to renew the fight with pistols. Peppercorn Vowler, it appears, felt even a greater aversion to fire–arms than Sir Mathew, and had given the latter his choice of weapons, because he was sure, from the inquiries he had made, that Sir Mathew would most certainly choose the quarter–staff; in the exercise of which Peppercorn Vowler was quite a proficient.

The Baronet adopted the old rustic mode of curing my dog of his propensity to mutton: he turned him into a barn, with a couple of very powerful and evil–disposed rams. "I warrant," said he, as he closed the door, "that the animal will never look a sheep in the face again." He was certainly right in his prediction; for half an hour afterwards, the dog died under the extra ordinary discipline of the battering rams to which Sir Mathew had zealously subjected him.

THE COUNTERPART COUSINS

ALMOST every house, in a little village situate in the lower part of Somersetshire, near the borders of Devon, was tenanted, two or three generations back, either by a Blake or a Hickory. Individuals, of one or the other of these names, occupied all the best farms, and all the minor lucrative posts, in the parish. The shoemaker, the carpenter, the thatcher, and the landlord of the public house, were Blakes; and the parish clerk, the glazier, the tailor, and the keeper of "the shop," where almost every thing was sold, Hickories. Numerous matrimonial alliances were formed among the young people of the two families. As the Blakes were manly, and the Hickories handsome, it happened, rather luckily, that the children of the former were, for the most part, boys, and those of the latter, girls. If a male child were born among the Hickories, he grew up puny in frame and womanly in features; and there was not an individual, among the few females of the Blake family, who did not bear the strongly marked features and robust frame, characteristic of the race from which she sprang. The young men of the house of Hickory were too much like their sisters, to be good–looking fellows; and the damsels of the other name resembled their brothers too closely, to be beautiful women; they were, apparently, stout enough in form, and sufficiently bold in heart, had not the days of chivalry been past, to have been esquires to "mettlesome knights of hie renown;" while the striplings of the other family were more adapted, from their lady–like limbs and gentle looks, to be bower–pages to these high–born dames, for whose honour and amusement, their chivalric lords occasionally broke each other's pates in the tourney.

Notwithstanding these disparities, some strong attraction seemed to exist between the blood of the two families; not only did the "manly Blakes" take unto themselves wives from among the "handsome Hickories,"—this was natural enough,—but the young yeomen of the tribe of Hickory, intermarried with the spinsterhood of the Blakes. Perhaps it was Hobson's choice with the youths,— these or none;—being scarcely another name in the village except those of the "two great houses"—Hickory and Blake; and in those days, but few of its young folks travelled far beyond the landmarks of their native place.

The Blakes and Hickories, at length, grew so numerous, that the village did not offer sufficient resources for their support, and several of them emigrated;—some to the neighbouring towns, but the greater part to the metropolis, where they were soon lost in its mighty tide of population, which is constantly recruited by "supplies from the country," as the river, whose banks it ennobles, is supported by the tributary streams which eternally flow into its huge bed. A great number of the descendants of those females of the Blake family, who had intermarried with Hickories still remained; but it was in vain to seek for the fine Herculean forms, which tradition had assigned to the Blakes, or the surpassing beauty, which, according to old tales, was once possessed by the female Hickories. It is true, that the features of each family were to be seen, scattered among various individuals; but no perfect specimen, in the prime of life, of either race, could be found. Two or three gaunt fellows, the oldest men in the parish, who were issue of the first unions between the two houses, still stalked about, with melancholy countenances, thinking but little of the present, and more often of the past than the future; but as their fathers had been Hickories, and their mothers Blakes, it was said that they did not possess those excellencies of form or feature, which their cousins, who were Blakes by the father's side, and Hickories by the mother's, were reported to have been endowed.

A single individual of the Blake family, in whose veins none of the Hickory blood flowed, remained alive; that individual was a woman, fettered by age and infirmities, to a chair on the kitchen hearth of one of her descendants. Dame Deborah was venerated as a relic of old times, rather than beloved. The beings about her had come into the world when she was aged; and those, to whom she had given life, had passed away before her; leaving their mother to the care of a third generation. To her, those little acts of kindness, which are so endearing in the first stage of human decay through "length of days," were rarely performed, because she was too withered in mind and feeling to appreciate them. She lived among relations, but had no friends. All her wants were scrupulously provided for; but the attentions, which her grand–children and great–grand–children paid her; were acts of duty rather than affection. The days of her glory, even as an old woman were over: she had ceased to become a domestic adviser; the last child she had nursed, for one of her daughters, was now "a stout and stalwart" young fellow, nearly six feet high; and those, to whom she had told tales of other times, when her memory and breath were both equal to the task, were getting old themselves, and beginning to relate the same chronicles, round the kitchen fire, on winter nights; generally without acknowledging, and often forgetting, to whom they were indebted for that legendary lore, the possession of which so exalted them in the opinions of the young.

From the dark cloud, which usually obscured Dame Deborah's mental faculties, a gleam of youthful memory occasionally shot up, which much amazed many of her descendants. One evening, a warm discussion took place in the kitchen where she sat, as to the precise ages of Ralph Hickory and his cousin Harry. After a world of talk, without an atom of conclusion, Dame Deborah placed her hand upon the arm of one of the disputants, and said, in a tremulous but distinct tone: "Susanna Hickory, who was big Anthony Blake's seventh child, and only daughter; and married one of the young Hickories of Hickory Hatch, was brought to bed of a boy on the second day of our Whitsun revel, the same hour that her cousin Polly had twins,—both boys,—but only one of them lived to be christened. I stood godmother to the two babes. Susey's boy was called Ralph, after my first husband, and Polly's after my second goodman, Harry. That was the year when lightning struck the steeple, and Matty Drew, the witch, was drowned. She told the children's fortunes, and said of them,—

'Merry meeting—sorry parting;
Second greeting—bitter smarting;
Third struggle—'

Dame Deborah could not finish Matty Drew's prediction; and this was the seventh time, within as many years, that she had at tempted to do so, but in vain; a fit of coughing or abstraction invariably seizing her on these occasions, before she could articulate the remainder of the line. The debaters stared with wonder on each other at the old dame's unusual fluency; for she had not spoken, except in monosyllables, during many preceding months; and they looked upon it as an omen of Deborah's death, or some great calamity to one of her living descendants. On examining the church books, they found her account to be correct, so far as regarded the baptism of the two boys, and the interment of one of Polly's twins; and some of her neighbours recollected that the church was struck, as Deborah had related, in the same year that Matty Drew was drowned, by a farmer and his two sons, who supposed she had bewitched them and their cattle;

and ducked her, under the idea that, if she were a witch, she could not be drowned; little thinking of the consequences to themselves, if she did not survive the ordeal. Two of them had fled the country; the third was taken and tried. He stated, in his defence, that he had reason to believe predictions Matty was a witch, for her predictions were always verified by events; and that once, when his mother could not succeed in her churning, he and his father twisted a hazel switch, as tight as their strength would permit, about the churn, and behold, at last, in came Matty, shrieking and writhing, as if in agony, and beseeching them to unloose the gad; which, she admitted, was sympathetically torturing her own waist. He called in witnesses to this fact; and, notwithstanding the ingenious argument which his counsel had written out for him, wherein it was stated that "an unlettered clown" might well be forgiven for entertaining the same opinions as some of the kings of England, and one of her most eminent judges, in old days, the young man was convicted and executed, for acting under an impression that those powers existed, for the possession of which, a century before, helpless old women were found guilty, by twelve of their fellow countrymen, and doomed, by a strong–minded judge, to be burned;—more than one of the old creatures having crawled, it is said, when led from the cold dungeon, to warm their chilled limbs by the fire that was kindling to consume them.

Ralph Hickory and Harry Hickory, the objects of Matty Drew's doggrel prophecy, are the heroes of our tale—the Counterpart Cousins;—rather alike in disposition, but bearing no resemblance to each ether in outward appearance. Ralph inherited all the strength and height of the Blakes, without their fine form,, or the handsome features of the Hickories. His shoulders were broad, but round, and his neck did not seem to rise exactly in their centre: his arms were long, muscular, and well shaped; but his legs were crooked, and too brief in proportion to his body. His maternal ancestor's features were rather of the Roman order, and the wags of the village said, that Ralph had a Blake's nose run to seed:—it was thin, sharp, and disagreeable. Every body confessed that he had the Hickories' merry black eyes;—but his mouth gaped, and looked like a caricature of their pouting and slightly parted lips. The Hickories' teeth were brilliant and pearly; the Blakes' quite the contrary:—the lips of the former delicately exhibited their dental treasures; while those of the latter were so close and clenched, that it was difficult to obtain a glance at the awkward squad which they concealed. Ralph unfortunately inherited the bad teeth of the Blakes, and the open lips of the Hickories; as well as the fair hair of the former, and the dark eyes and long black lashes of the latter: so that Ralph was rather a singular looking being;—but precisely, or nearly such a person as the reader must have occasionally met with;—exhibiting an union of some of the beauties, and many of the deformities, of two or three of the tribes of man.

Harry was very different in person, but not a jot more beautiful than Ralph. His body was broader and more robust than that of a Blake, when the family was in a flourishing state; but it was remarkably short, and shapeless as a log. His head seemed to be squeezed into his shoulders by some giant hand, and his light but well-proportioned Hickory legs exhibited a striking contrast to the clumsy hulk of his huge trunk. The butcher said, that Harry would resemble his big block, with a calf's head on its surface, only that it stood on three legs, and Harry possessed but two. His arms were thick, bony and stunted; and his hands of such an immense size, that he was often called "Molepaw" by his competitors in the wrestling ring. Harry had the large blue eyes of the Blake family, and a thick, short, snub nose; which, the good gossips said, could be traced to nobody. There was a striking resemblance in his other features to the by-gone Hickories: his mouth and chin were really handsome; but an unmeaning smile usually played about his lips; and he had a vacant sort of look, that betokened good humour allied to silliness. But when Harry's blood was warmed by an angry word or two and an extra cup of drink, though he did not "look daggers," he frowned furiously, and looked, as well as talked, broomsticks, cudgels, kicks on the shin-bone, and various other "chimeras dire." In such a mood, Harry was dangerous to deal with, and avoided by all those who were peaceably disposed.

In this particular, Ralph was his counterpart. There was not a more kind or sociable being in three counties than Ralph Hickory, when he was sober; but liquor made him quarrelsome and rash; it whetted his appetite to give and receive kicks and bruises; and if he could not rouse any one, by insults and taunting, to wrestle, fight, or play a bout at back-sword, or cudgels with him,—he lashed himself up into a fury, attacked, and either scattered those who were about him like chaff, or got felled by a sturdy thwack of fist or cudgel, and fastened down until reason returned hand-in-hand with shame and remorse. To both of the cousins liquor was pure

Lethe; they never remembered any thing that occurred, from the time of their passing the rubicon of intoxication, until the moment of their waking the next day.

Ralph and Harry considered themselves as relations to each other, on the credit of certain of the gossiping oral genealogists of the village, who proved, in a very roundabout way, to their auditors, but entirely to their own conviction, that Ralph and Harry were, what are called, in the West Country,—second and third cousins. Each of them was the offspring of a match between a male Hickory and a female Blake; and both were bad specimens of the two fine families, whose more gifted descendants, in regard to personal appearance, the issue of those unions which had been formed between "the manly Blakes" and "the handsome Hickories," were the individuals who had quitted the village, impelled by a spirit of adventure, when they felt themselves too crowded in their native place, on account of the increase of its population.

Hickory was now the paramount name in the parish; there was not a single Blake in its little community, except old Dame Deborah, whose boast it had been, when she could babble apace, that she was the last of either of the pure stocks left. She had often stated, in the autumn of her life,—that season when the mind yields its richest fruits of memory,— that the good old Blakes began to lose the ascendant, from the time of the battle of Culloden. It will appear strange, that the downfall of the Pretender's forces in the north, should be associated, in Deborah's mind, with that of her family, whose abiding place was in the west. We will explain this nearly in the old dame's own words: "On the 16th of April, in the forty–six, my brother Gilbert,"—thus her story ran,— "who was then an officer in the Duke of Cumberland's dragoons, which rank he had attained, partly by money, partly by merit, did such service under the great Hawley, against the lads in tartans, that he was promised promotion by the famous Duke, who gave him his pistols, in the field, as an earnest of more favours to come. A few days after, while the dragoons were scouring the country, in quest of prisoners of consequence, it was whispered, by some who envied him, that Gilbert had been won by the honeyed words and rich jewels of a noble northern lady, to let her husband, whom he had taken, escape. This report reached Gilbert's ears; and the next day, while he was mounting his horse, an orderly came with commands for him to attend the Duke with all speed. Gilbert directly drew out his men;

gave some orders of importance, which were afterwards executed, and proved very beneficial to the service, and directed his junior officer to lead the soldiers off to perform it: he then stepped aside, and, with one of the pistols the Duke had given him on the sixteenth, blew out his brains! On the very evening the news arrived of my brother's death by his own hands, a sad disaster happened to the Blakes:—my father was, that afternoon, beating an apprentice, rather too severely, perhaps, in a field where some of his labourers were hacking–in wheat; when one who was among them,—a little fellow who was not much more than five feet high, but remarkable for his good features and fine form,—left his work, and advancing to my tall and powerful father, reproached him, in so insolent a manner, for beating the boy, who was a favourite with the labourer, that the bad blood of the Blakes became immediately roused, and he inflicted a blow or two on the man's shoulders with his stick: the fellow stepped back a few paces, and then running against my father at full speed, drove his head into the pit of the old man's stomach with such violence, that it laid him dead upon the spot. I don't know why, or wherefore, but true it is, that the labourer was acquitted of blame on his trial; and he was the first of the Hickories known in these parts. The same evening, my aunt Elinor, the widow of Frank Cooper, who had sailed round the world with Anson, died away in her chair, without any previous illness. Had my father been killed an hour later, he would have heard of the suicide of his son; and had not my aunt Elinor died before sunset, she would have known, that both her brother and her nephew had gone before her to the grave: but both of them were saved from the bitterness of such news on their dying day. From that time, the Blakes dwindled, and the Hickories rose. They have matched and mated much since; but it is said, perhaps truly, that the Hickories are doomed to root out the Blakes, and then destroy themselves;—they met in the valley of death, and blood will be mixed in their stirrup–cup. My grand son Ralph has now more of the Blakes in him than any other man; and thick Harry, although he has a double dash of us in his veins, is more of a Hickory than any other I know. They are both Hickories in name, but not truly so in nature. Ralph looks upon himself and is looked up to, as the head of the poor remnant of my father's race; and Harry is in the same situation, as a descendant of the labourer, who took his master's life, on that master's own land. They have both a great many of the bad qualities, and but few of the virtues of the two families;—and I, for one, say—God keep them from drinking deep out of the same cup!—for liquor is likely to be their bane."

This sort of language was too frequently repeated, and the witch Matty Drew's prophecy too often alluded to, by old Deborah, in those days when her tongue still talked triumphantly, although her limbs were incapable of motion, not to produce a deep and lasting impression upon her hearers. One half of the village was in a constant state of alarm, after Ralph had returned, a man, from the "up–along" counties, to which he had departed, a boy, in order to learn some improved mode of cultivating land, lest the two cousins should meet and quarrel in their cups. If they were seen in the village, passing a few moments in friendly chat, a scout immediately acquainted the parties most interested with the circumstance; and, in a short time, one of them was drawn off, by a fictitious story, of lambs tumbling into ditches, cows getting their legs entangled in hurdles, or children fallen into fits.

Ralph and Harry both loved the pastimes of their native place; they could wrestle, and play at back–sword, in very laudable style; but Ralph was the better wrestler, and Harry surpassed in the use of the single–stick. Devon being noted for its wrestlers, and Somerset for its single–stick players, the cousins were attracted in different directions, to enjoy that pastime in which each excelled; so that, up to the fortieth year of their lives they were, as it will be remembered, precisely of the same age,— they had never, much to the satisfaction of their friends, met in the ring as rivals. Especial care had always been taken that they did not join the same convivial parties; they often attempted to make merry together, for Ralph and Harry really felt an affection for each other's society, but the women invariably out–manuevred them, and the two cousins were greater strangers to each other, than either of them was to any man else in the village, of his own age and station.

Their forty–first birth–day arrived: Ralph attended a review of the yeomanry–cavalry, in which he was a corporal, and Harry went to market for the purpose of selling some steers. On returning home, they were obliged to cross each other's track. They dwelt at opposite ends of the long, straggling village; which were approached by two different lanes: of these, the letter X will serve as a tolerably good substitute for a ground plan;— the market town being situate at the top of the left, and the common, on which the review was held, on that of the right, limb of the letter; at the lower end of which the village meandered along through meadows and corn–fields; Harry's abode being at the right, and Ralph's at the left end of it. The two lanes were crossed, at the point of intersection, by a third, which, on account of its being two or three yards wider, and a little more frequented than either of them, was dignified with the title of "the high road;" and in this "undeniable situation," as George Robins would say, stood a snug public house, called Sawney's Cross; the front of which commanded a view, across the high road, for some distance up the lanes which led to the market town and common.

Harry was proceeding down one lane, at a speedy, shuffling pace, betwixt a gallop and trot, on a powerful blind galloway; while Ralph approached the line of intersection, from the common, by the other, on a gaunt, half–bred horse, nearly sixteen hands high, a strong galloper, and quite ungovernable when put upon his mettle. The galloway and the tall horse were both "home–ward bound;" and "sniffing the manger from afar," each of them was going along, impatient of check, and at, what jockies would call "a tip–top pace."

Ned Creese, the landlord of Sawney's Cross, stood at his door, and beheld the ominous approach of the two travellers: he was mathematician enough to discover, that equi–distant as they were, from he point where their lines of direction intersected each other in the middle of the main road, and approaching toward such point with equal speed, something unpleasant must needs occur to one of the parties, at the transit. He beckoned, and called out to each of them as loudly as he could: but Harry was short sighted, and could not see his motions; and Ralph was rather hard of hearing, and could not make out what he meant; so that neither of them pulled up; and, as they were concealed from each other by the high hedges of the lanes, neither Harry nor Ralph was aware of the danger that menaced them, until they emerged from the bottom of the lanes. Ralph foresaw the event first, and, with might and main, attempted to pull his horse out of the way: he partly succeeded, but by checking his steed, and making him swerve from the direct line in which he was going, he gave Harry a decided advantage in the ensuing shock. The cousins had just time to ejaculate "Hoy, Ralph!" and "Hilloa, Harry!" when the blind galloway bore his off–shoulder against the tall troop–horse's hind quarters, and just such a catastrophe took place as Creese had anticipated:—Harry was thrown over his galloway's head; and Ralph, with his horse, and the galloway at his heels, were carried—to the brink of a horse–pond by the, road side. Ralph fell in the mud, and the horses went over him into the water; where they lay struggling together for a few moments; they then got up without assistance, and each limped homeward, leaving their owners to come after them as well as they could.

"Hoy, Ralph!" and "Hilloa, Harry!" were the first words the cousins uttered.

"Art hurt, lad?" asked Ralph.— "No," was the reply;— "Art thee?"

"Sound as oak; only a bloody nose, and a hump on the forehead."

"That's right, then; I don't feel much the matter myself; but dowl take thy blind galloway, for all that!"

"He's worth his weight in gold;—didn't 'ee see how he capsized you and your troop horse?"

"You charged me in flank when I was filing off;—if I had met 'ee full butt, Harry, I should ha' sent thee and thy galloway clean into the muck, and gone on without abating pace, or feeling a jerk in my balance."

"What, and not ha' turned round to say 'Hilloa, Harry?"

"Odd! yes, to be sure,—I'd say 'Hilloa, Harry!'—and what will 'ee drink, besides."

"Well,—and what *shall* we?"

"I don't mind;—but let's ha' something, and make merry together for once."

"Wi' all my heart!—Here we be, safe from busy meddlers; and dash me if I don't feel inclined to make a day of it."

"Give me your hand;—this capsize was a bit of luck, weren't it?"

"Aye, to be sure,—brought two good fellows together. What shall we have?—It's cold.—What d'ye say to Hopping John, made Tom Nottle's fashion?—Landlord, mix pint of brandy wi' half a gallon of your best cider, sugared to your own taste; and,—d'ye mind?—pop in about a dozen good roasted apples, hissing hot, to take the chill off."

In a short time, the two cousins were seated by the fire, in a little room behind the bar of the Sawney's Cross, with a smoking bowl of liquor on the table before them, and Ned Creese assisting them to empty it. By degrees, the cousins became elevated, and their chat was enlivened by budding jokes and choice flowers of rustic song. Harry's forehead frequently reminded him, in the midst of his glee, of the adventure in the road; and he recurred to it, for the fifth time, since the sitting, as Ned brought in a second brewage of hot Hopping John:—"I'd lay a wager I know where my blind galloway is, just about now," quoth he; "it's odd to me if he isn't stopping at the Dragon's Head, where he always pulls up, and tempts me to call for a cup of cider and a mouthful of hay."

"Gentlemen," said Creese, "I'll give you a toast—a Devonshire one—and it's this:—A back fall, or a side fall, or any fall but a fall out."

"For my part," continued Ned, after his toast was duly honoured,— "I expected no less than a fight, if you were able to stand, after what I saw would happen;—but I hardly hoped to see both get on your legs, with nothing but one bloody nose between the pair of you."

"I must say, landlord, I fell very comfortably, indeed, considering," said Harry.

"And I came down very much to my own satisfaction," quoth Ralph, "only that I soiled my uniform."

"It struck me," observed Ned Creese, "that you must have gone over head and ears into the pond, which is deeper than it should be in the middle; but I consoled myself;—for, thinks I,— if so be that he should, the *frogs* on his dragoon jacket will save him, if swimming can do it. If you'd both broke your necks I couldn't but giggle to see you. It's my belief 'twould have made a horse laugh; as my sign says, it was truly 'good entertainment for man and beast.'—Don't be hipped because I'm jocular: joking's a malady with many a man, and here stands one of 'em; we can no more help it than an ague fit. But come, folks; here's 'The West Country Orchards!'—and then let's rouse the crickets with the old apple–tree hymn.—I'll begin." So saying, Creese commenced, and, assisted by Ralph and Harry, chaunted forth the following rhymes, in a manner that would have amazed Mozart, although it gladdened the hearts of the rustic guests in the Sawney's Cross kitchen.

1.

The white rose was, aye, a dainty flower,
     And the hawthorn a bonny tree;
A grove of oaks is a rich dame's dower;
     But the barley–straw for me!

2.

From his acorn–cup let the Elfin sip,
And the oak–fruit be munched by swine;
The thrush may have both the haw and hip,
Give me but the jolly vine!

3.

Ale you may brew, from the barley–straw;
Neither ale, nor grape–juice for me;
I care not for acorn, hip, nor haw;—
Give me but the apple–tree!

After they had all three repeated the last verse together, and applauded their performance by sundry exclamations of approval, and thwacks on the table, Ralph observed, "Oddsheart! Cousin, we're getting as we should be; a fig for a fall after this."

"Da capo, say I to it," exclaimed Creese; "da capo, I say to it, heartily: da capo, as it is written in the score–book we sing the psalms by, in the gallery, at church."

"Wasn't frightened a trifle, landlord, when thee saw'st us coming?"

"Is the approach of a good bone likely to alarm a hungry dog?—I knew well enough you'd fall; and if you fell, the fall must bring me grist, in meat or malt:—a 'quest jury, if death had been done; board and lodging, in case of broken limbs; and a brace of guests for an hour, if you were only bruised. I shall be much obliged, when you knock one another down again,, if you'll do it before my door. Success to cross–roads, blind galloways, helter–skelter dragooning, and blink–eyed farmers!—Ha! ha!—You'll excuse me gentlemen; we're all friends; I hope no offence.—What are your commands?"

"There's one thing I'd wish thee to do, landlord," said Ralph; "if any body should enquire for us,—don't say we be here."

"No, truly," added Harry; "an' thou dost, thou'lt lose a couple of good customers, and get thy head broke to boot, perhaps."

"Never fear—never fear!" replied Ned; "a secret's safe with me, as though 'twas whispered in the ear of an ass. Thank heaven, I haven't had a woman in the house these seven years; so all's snug.—

"A forester slept beneath the beech,
Heigh! norum snorum!
His full flask lay within his arm's reach;
Heigh! horum jorum!
A maiden came by with a blooming face,
Heigh! rosy posey!
She ask'd him the way to Berrywell Chase,—
With its wine so old,
And its pasties cold;—
Forester, what has froze ye?

"A long song is out of place over good liquor; so I'll not sing the other eighteen verses of that one; its moral is, that a woman can keep a secret, even when the possession of what she desires depends on it; but that her babbling often proves her salvation. A friar comes in sight, while the forester is wooing, and he packs the maid off, for appearance' sake;—telling her; if she'll meet him there the next day, provided she don't reveal his promise to mortal, that he'll give her 'a gown of the richest green,' besprinkled with dewy pearls, or pearly dew, I forget which: but the maiden was so delighted, that when she got to the Chase, she told the warden's niece, and the warden's niece told the maiden's aunt, and the maiden's aunt locked her up for a week: so she saved her reputation, but lost her present, by babbling.—Gentlemen, you don't drink!"

We must here leave the cousins to the care of Creese—they could not have fallen into better hands for the mood in which they met—and remind our readers, that the horses, after extricating themselves from the pond, proceeded homeward as well as the injuries they had received would permit. Their arrival at the village, spread consternation among its inhabitants: parties went forth, in different directions, to seek Ralph and Harry;—the women predicting that they had met and killed each other, and the men endeavouring to stifle their own apprehensions on the subject. Creese, on being asked if he knew any thing of the matter, replied, that "he had seen the horses, without riders, gallop by his door, down the lanes;" and as no one had witnessed the meeting of the cousins but himself; and they were kept close in the back parlour, no information could be obtained from any one else. Lights were burnt, in almost every house in the village, nearly all night; and toward day–break the last party returned without any tidings of the lost sheep. Old Dame Deborah, confiding in the predictions of Matty Drew, said, as well as she could, "Bad is this—there's worse to come;—it will prove to be but a

"Merry meeting—sorry parting"

We must now return to the cousins. On the morning after their concussion in front of Sawney's Cross, Ralph, with whom we shall begin, awoke at day break, and on taking a hasty survey of his apartment, found, to his surprise, that he was not at home. He recollected very well that he had usually worn, for many years past, corduroy small–clothes; and, when he joined the volunteer yeomanry, white doe–skin pantaloons. "Whose black nether garments can be, then," thought he, "those which I see dangling from yonder peg?"—He leaped out of bed, threw open the lattice, and the first object that attracted his notice was the horse–pond; on the miry edge of which, he remembered having been thrown the day before. This accounted for the colour of his doe–skins. "But, how the dickens," thought he, "got I this tremendous black eye? Where's my front tooth? And who the deuce has been bruising my ear?—I recollect, well enough, seeing Creese, the landlord, bring in a third brewing of Hopping John, and my singing, 'Creeping Jenny,' or part of it, afterwards:—but what's come of Harry?"

While these and similar reflections were passing in Ralph's mind, he proceeded to dress himself, which he found a task of considerable difficulty, for he was stiff and sore in every limb. Impatient to resolve the mystery in which he found himself involved, Ralph, before he was completely attired in his soiled uniform, hobbled down stairs, and found Harry, staring at the landlord, as though Creese had just been telling him some very marvellous story.

"Why, Ralph,—cousin Ralph," said Harry, as Ralph entered the kitchen, "what be this the landlord says?—He vows and protests 'twere you that ha' been tearing my clothes to tatters and rags, and beating my face to a jelly!—I ha'n't a sound inch in my skin!"

"Before I do answer any questions, it be my wish to know of you, landlord," said Ralph, in an angry tone, and taking Creese by the collar; "and what's more, I insist you do tell me, who took the advantage of me last night—who it were that knocked my tooth out, when I were overcome?"

"I've lost a tooth myself,—be dashed if I ha'n't!" exclaimed Harry, whose attention was so distracted by his other injuries, that he had not discovered the important fact before this moment; "I'll swear I had it in my mouth last night," pursued he, grasping Creese, with his huge paw, by the collar; "and I'll be told, why and wherefore you've let me be used like a dog, when I were drunk:—answer!"

"Ay, answer, or I'll shake thy life out!" cried Ralph, looking as if he really meant to "suit the action to the word."

"Gentlemen,—guests," said Creese, apparently not in the least alarmed, but putting himself in a strong attitude, and calmly collaring the cousins; "be mild, and you shall hear all; or one at a time, and I'm for the first fair fall, who shall pay last night's smart, with the best, or both of you,—one down t'other come on but if you'll put your hands in your pockets and be peaceable, I'll employ mine to produce your teeth;—that is, if I can."

The cousins now relinquished their holds, and Ned drew out a drawer of the dresser, and requested they would look into it. "Here," said he, "you will find the fragments of your feast of fisty–cuffs: perhaps, among the bits of lace, linen, broad–cloth, frogs and buttons, which I carefully swept up last night, after I had put you both to bed, you may find your teeth; if not, I know nothing about them:—send for a constable, and search me, if you like."

At this offer, the cousins turned to each other and were going to smile; but immediately they were face to face, they stared in so rueful a manner, that Creese was amazingly amused. It was the first time, since Ralph had come down stairs, that the cousins had closely inspected each other's countenances, which might, with propriety enough, as the landlord said, be called "maps of mischance." "But it's all your own doings," quoth he; "the credit and honour belong to nobody but yourselves;—I must say you're both downright dapsters at disfiguration."

"But how were it, d'ye say, landlord?" asked Ralph.

"Ay, truly, how happened it all, according to your story?"—said Harry.

"Why, gentlemen," replied Creese, "after I found you were going to drink more than I could well hear,—when it was high tide almost in my head, and my frail wits began to rock to and fro, pitching me about, when I moved, like a barge in a hurricane,—I very wisely anchored in the bar, and attended, as well as I could, to my business: a nap or two between whiles, as I tended my customers, and one cool pipe, brought me round, and it was calm sailing with me again.—All this time you were getting louder and louder; at last, the short gentleman, my worthy friend, Mr. Harry, persuaded you, Mr. Ralph, to try a friendly back–fall with him. There wasn't much harm in that;—though, I promise you, I tried to prevent it, but couldn't. So I cleared away the crockery and stood by, as 'twas my duty, to see fair. Harry was, clearly, in my mind, the best wrestler; but, somehow, Ralph got the in–lock, and laid him upon the planchin, flat as a pancake."

"Did I, by jingo?" eagerly exclaimed Ralph.

"No,—it's all his lies;—it couldn't be!" quoth Harry; looking very incredulous and displeased.

"I have said it, and I'll stand to it;"—continued Ned; "and when you got up, as you did, with my help, you went over to Ralph, patted him on the back, and, said you,—' Well done, cousin,—I didn't think it was in thee!' You added, with an oath, it was the best and fairest fall you had seen for years past;—that it nearly drove the breath out of your body; and then you patted him on the back again. After this, you both sat down, talked, sung, and,—by–and–bye,—began to broach something about back–sword."

"Likely enough, an't it, Harry?" said Ralph.

"I don't believe a word o' the story," replied Harry;— "but I'll hear it out."

"I did not ask you to believe it," said Creese; "but there's special evidence on your head, as well as on your cousin's; that you played at it, long and lustily."

"And which won?" enquired Ralph.

"Both of you lost blood, as well as temper, at last," replied Creese; "but, I remember, Harry gave you the first broken head."

"Never!" replied Ralph, "it never lay in his shoes: he may be as good a wrestle; or better; but scores of men, that my cousin Harry have often and often given his head to, never could touch me."

"Well! be that as it may," said the landlord, "he certainly had you last night, Ralph, or I'm out of my senses. Why, I remember it as well as if it was but a minute ago:—you broke open the glass buffet, in which the two sticks my uncle and father won the grand match with—Wilts against Somerset— was stuck up, among the china, with silver mountings, and decorated with green ribbons, cut out like laurel–leaves;—and you said they were the best sticks you ever broke a head with: and when Harry cut your ear; and I cried out 'A bout, a bout!' and put the poker between you, you shook Harry's hand, and said you admired him, for he had done what no man ever had attempted,— namely—hit you under your best guard."

"Ha! ha! ha!" shouted Harry. "Odds buttons! Ralph, but there seems to he some truth in this though, for your ear is cut up, sure enough then, clean as a whistle; it must ha' been done as Creese says."

Ralph put his hand up to his ear; and, like Lord Burleigh, in The Critic, shook his head and said nothing.

"All this," continued the landlord, "was friendly and civil: you then ordered a double quantity of brandy in the brewage—if you don't believe me, look in the bill,—and, in about half an hour, I found you fighting in downright earnest, and in all manner of ways;—kicking, cudgelling, wrestling, pulling, punching, tearing one another to pieces very ungentlemanly, and so forth, and clearly bent on destruction. You had cracked the looking-glass, broke the table, 'shod the liquor, and tore the porringer,' as the man said; or, in other words, shed the cider and brandy, and broke the bowl; all which you'll find I've made correct memorandums of in the bill. Then I called in the blacksmiths, from next door, our ostler, and three waggoners who were drinking outside;—we all pitched into you, and, at last, got you asunder: but not before the mischief you see and feel was done; and to shew what minds you were in, when we pulled you, by main force, apart, each of you carried away his hold, like a couple of bull-dogs:—Harry brought off a piece of Ralph's sleeve and his shoulder-belt, and Ralph the fore-part of Harry's coat, full two-thirds of his waistcoat, and a pattern of his linen. We then contrived to get you to bed—as you'll see in the bill; and—and—"

"Aye,—and here we be," added Ralph; "nice objects for a wife and family to look at!"

"Thou'rt quite a scarecrow, cousin Ralph," said Harry.

"Do get him a glass, and let him look at himself, landlord," said Ralph. "I'm sorry for thee, Harry;—it's my belief 't'ant exactly as the landlord says; but we can't belie the story he has told us, so where's the use of disputing? The question is,—what shall we do? "

"Be dashed if I bean't ashamed to go home," replied Harry; "I sha'n't be able to look my wife in the face."

"Ah! that's touching a sore place, Harry. 'Tisn't my bruises, nor thine, that I care much about—after all; but frightening the women, poor dear souls!—thy Jane and my Grace, Harry—by staying out all night, eh?"

"Don't talk about it,—but let's get some drink."

"Small ale, or leek broth, let it be, then, and we'll start while we be sober and solid. We'll get a couple of carts—you shall go to my wife, and smooth her over, and I'll go to thine; and then, at night, let 'em come and fetch each of us home."

"Well! so be it, Ralph; but sha'n't we have a stirrup–cup?"

"No, not this time.—Your hand, Harry—I like thee, cousin; but it strikes me there's some truth in old women and witches. I wouldn't pass another evening with thee, for half the land from here to Axminster."

A week after the rencounter at Sawney's Cross, each of the cousins was lying at his own home,—a–bed, bandaged, and still suffering from the bruises which they had conferred on each other. They soon, however, recovered: the watchful care of their friends was doubled; neither of them evinced much inclination for the other's company, and a whole year passed away, without any thing remarkable occurring between them.

The birth–day of the cousins was, however, again unlucky.—Harry, perhaps on account of his success in the bout he had with Ralph, at Sawney's Cross, or, it might be, from mere whim, practised back–sword–playing, and became a frequent attendant at the various single–stick matches in the neighbourhood. Some capital pastime having been expected, at a revel, about ten miles up the country, Harry and Ralph, on their forty–second birth–day, totally unaware of each other's intentions, set off to see and join in the sport. The malice or curiosity of some of the parties present, or, perhaps, mere accident, brought the cousins on the stage as opponents. Ralph was going to descend but Harry whispered in his ear, "If we don't have a bout or two, Ralph, they'll jeer us, and say we be old women." Ralph still evinced an inclination to retire; when his cousin said aloud, "Now, Ralph, here's a chance for getting the head you lost to me at Sawney's Cross." "Aye, true,—true," replied Ralph, taking a stick, and preparing for the play. They shook hands; both, as usual, said,—"God save our eyes!"—they threw themselves into attitude; and one minute had scarcely elapsed, before Harry received a blow from Ralph's stick, which totally deprived him of sight, in one eye, for the remainder of his existence.

An inflammation of so violent a nature ensued, that Harry's life was, for some time, considered in danger. One day, when his wife came to Ralph's house, weeping, and exclaiming that little hope was left of her husband's recovery, Dame Deborah, in a low, broken tone, said to her, "The day's not come; it is but—

"Second greeting—bitter smarting."

"Bide a while—there's no fear yet."

Deborah was right: Harry recovered his health and strength, and none ever heard him regret the loss of his eye; about which, he said, poor Ralph "took on" unnecessarily, for it was purely an accident. The forty–third and forty–fourth birth–days had passed; and the minds of the relations of Ralph and Harry grew more composed; although they still continued on the alert, to prevent them getting together over "a cup of drink." It happened that Harry had a heavy crop of oats, in a large field, which were dead–ripe; and bad weather being expected, it was an object of importance with him to get the crop "cut and carried" as quickly as possible. According to the custom of the village, every farmer, who was not in a similar predicament, came, with such servants as he could spare, to assist his neighbour in distress. Ralph was one of the first in the field, and set so fine an example to his companions, that the oats were all down, long before sun–set. The work was severe, the weather sultry, and the hospitable Harry did not grudge his cider during the day. Deep draughts had been quaffed, and Harry could not suffer his guests to depart, without a cup round of his best. As they were about to quit the field, a grey–headed man unfortunately remarked, that they were standing on the spot where, on that day and hour, a great many years before, little Dick Hickory had killed old Reuben Blake. This produced a string of observations from various individuals of the party: the merits and demerits of the action were freely canvassed; the debate grew hot, and more cider was brought from the house. Ralph and Harry, naturally enough, joined in, and, at length, led the discussion. Ralph blamed Dick Hickory, and Harry applied several harsh epithets, in the warmth of the moment, to Reuben Blake. The cheeks of the spectators grew pale, as the cousins abruptly broke from the original argument, to abuse each other: a well–meant interference increased, rather than allayed, their rage; they cast the alarmed mediators aside, flew toward each other, and grappled:— as Ralph was rushing in, Harry crouched, lifted his cousin off the ground, and threw him completely over his head,—never to rise again!

When his sorrowful companions brought home the body of poor Ralph, they found old Deborah repeating, in a low, shrill, and, as they afterwards said, unearthly tone, the rhymes of Matty Drew: but the last words of the third line died away on her lips; and when some of the family ceased, for a moment, to gaze on the livid face of Ralph and turned toward the kitchen–hearth, they saw that Dame Deborah was dead in her chair.

CADDY CUDDLE

ON the second anniversary of their wedding–day, the Honourable Charles Caddy, and Lady Letitia, his high–born and beautiful wife, entertained a large party of guests at Caddy Castle. Until a few months previously to this event, the old building had been left nearly desolate, for a period of eleven or twelve years: a few domestics were its only inhabitants, except old Squire Caddy Caddy, its unfortunate owner, who had lost his wits, and was confined in one of its comfortable turrets, under the care of a couple of stout and wary keepers.

The castle had recently been put in order for the reception of the Honourable Charles Caddy, a distant relation of, but next heir to, the lunatic, who was entrusted with the care of Caddy Caddy's property. He came down to Caddy Castle, with a determination of making himself popular in the neighbourhood; and began by giving invitations to all the gentlemen and ladies of respectability, within a circuit of several miles. A number of his own personal friends, and those of Lady Letitia, had followed them, shortly after their departure from town, to spend the Christmas holidays at Caddy Castle; so that the ancient edifice was by far more gay than it had ever been, even during the time when the once jovial Caddy Caddy was lord paramount in the halls of his ancestors.

Among the guests assembled in honour of the day, was Mr. Caddy Cuddle, a quiet elderly bachelor, of small fortune, related, on his mother's side, to the Caddy family, who had been one of Caddy Caddy's most intimate associates, in former times. By order of the medical gentlemen who attended on Caddy Caddy, Mr. Cuddle, as well as all his old friends, had been denied access to the lunatic, from very proper motives, at the outset of his confinement. Caddy Cuddle's cottage was eleven miles distant; the Castle had lost its chief attraction; and this was the first time he had been near it, for several years.

In his younger days, Caddy Cuddle was of a very active and enterprising spirit; he shared the perils of his father's three last voyages, and would, in all probability, have made as good a seaman as old Herbert Cuddle himself, had it not been for the solicitude of his mother; who, losing her other two children rather suddenly, persuaded young Caddy that a life of ease, with sufficient to satisfy the desires of a moderate person, was preferable by far to the dangers attendant upon a chance after Fortune, on the perilous ocean. Caddy then amused himself by studying the learned languages; and, at length, as some of his simple neighbours said, had got them so completely at his fingers' ends, that it was a pity his parents had not made him a parson.

He was simple, kind, and innocent of evil intentions, as it was possible for a man to be; but it was his misfortune, owing to his ignorance of that most useful of all sciences, a knowledge of the world, to touch the feelings of his host rather smartly, on several occasions, during the discourse that took place, over the bottle, among the guests at the Castle. Cuddle was naturally taciturn; but two or three extra glasses of wine produced their usual effect upon such a temperament, and rendered him too loquacious to be pleasant. The happiest hours of his life, were those which he had passed, above a dozen years before, at Caddy Castle; and he repeatedly alluded to his unhappy friend, poor Caddy Caddy,— the feats they had performed, the jokes they had cracked, the simple frolics they bad enacted, and the songs they had sung together, over their ale and tobacco, in the good old days.

The Honourable Charles Caddy felt particularly annoyed at the fact of his lunatic relation's confinement in the Castle,—which, perhaps rather in bad taste, he had made the scene of festivity,—being thus abruptly revealed to his fashionable visitors; but he was too well-bred to display the least symptom of his feelings. Watching, however, for an opportunity, when he might break in upon Cuddle's narratives, without palpably interrupting him, the Honourable Charles Caddy, adroitly, as he thought, started a subject, which, he imagined, would be at once interesting to his neighbours, and turn two or three of his metropolitan friends from listeners to talkers.

"I have been looking over the common, this morning," said he, "and it occurs to me, that, in a neighbourhood so opulent as ours, races might be established without much difficulty. The common would afford as pretty a two-mile course as any gentleman could desire. If such a thing were set on foot, I should be happy to lend it all the support in my power. I would take leave to offer a cup, to commence with; and I think I could answer for a plate from the county members. Indeed, it surprises me, rather, that the idea has not before occurred to some gentleman in the vicinity."

"Cousin Caddy, it has!" exclaimed Cuddle; "our respected friend and relation, up stairs, gave away a dozen smock-frocks and a bundle of waggon–whips, for seven successive years; and would, doubtless, have done so to this day, had not his misfortune deprived him of the power. The prizes were contested for, regularly, on the second day of the fair,—which then took place on the common,— immediately after the pig with the greasy tail was caught; and the boys had eaten the hot rolls, sopped in treacle; and the women had wrestled for the new gown; and —"

"Women wrestle!" exclaimed one of the Honourable Charles Caddy's friends.

"Mr. Cuddle is quite correct, sir," replied young Tom Horner, who had lately come into possession of a snug estate in the neighbourhood; "I have seen them wrestle, in various other parts of the county, as well as on our common."

"Never heard of such savages since the day I drew breath! Egad!—never, I protest!" said the gentleman who had interrupted Caddy Cuddle.

"Why, it's bad enough, I must admit," said Horner; "but I think I heard you boast that you were a man of Kent, just now, sir; and, as I am told, the women of that county play cricket–matches very frequently. Now, in my opinion, there is not a very great difference between a female match at cricket, on a common, and a feminine bout at wrestling, in a ring. In saying this, I beg to observe that I mean no offence."

"I take none; I protest I see no occasion,—no pretence for my taking umbrage.—I am not prepared to question the fact,"—added the speaker, turning toward his host; "not prepared to question the fact, you observe, after what has dropped from the gentleman; although, with permission, on behalf of the women of Kent, I take leave to declare, that I never heard of their indulging in such an amusement, before the gentleman mentioned it"

"Well, sir," said Caddy Cuddle, who had been very impatient, all this time to blazon the generosity and spirit of his friend, Caddy Caddy; "I was going on to state, that, after the gold–laced hat was grinned for, through a horse–collar; the pig was caught, and so forth,—the expense of all which pastimes Caddy Caddy bore;—the waggon–horse–race was run, for the whips and frocks."

"A waggon–horse–race!" said the gentleman of Kent; "I beg pardon; did I hear you correctly?—Am I to understand you, as having positively said—a waggon–horse–race?"

"Certainly, sir," said Tom Horner; "and capital sport it is: I have been twice to Newmarket, and once to Doncaster; I know a little about racing;

I think it a noble, glorious, exhilarating sport; but, next to the first run I saw for the St. Leger, I never was half so delighted with any thing, in the shape of racing, as when Billy Norman, who now keeps the west gate of Caddy Park here, exactly sixteen years ago, come August, won the whips on the common."

"Indeed!" simpered the gentleman of Kent, gazing at Tom Horner, as though he were a recently imported nondescript.

"Billy, on that occasion, rode most beautifully;" continued Horner; "he carried the day in fine style, coming in, at least seven lengths, behind all his competitors."

"If I may be allowed," observed the gentleman of Kent, "you would say, *before*."

"Not at all, sir; not at all;" exclaimed Caddy Cuddle; "draught horses are not esteemed as valuable in proportion to their speed: in the waggon–horse–race no man is allowed to jockey his own animal; the riders are armed with tremendous long whips; their object is to drive all their companions before them; he that gets in last, wins: and so, sir, they slash away at each other's horses;—then, sir, there's such shouting and bellowing; such kicking, rearing, whinnying, galloping, and scrambling, that it would do a man's heart good to look at it. Poor Caddy Caddy used to turn to me, and say, as well as his laughter would let him,—'What are your Olympic games,—your feats, and fine doings at the tombs of your old Greek heroes, that you prate about, compared with these, cousin Cuddle?'"

The Honourable Charles Caddy smiled, and bit the inner part of his lip with vexation: he now tried to give the conversation another turn, and introduced the chase; thinking that it was a very safe subject, as Caddy Caddy had never kept a pack of hounds. "I feel very much inclined," said he, "anxious as I am to forward the amusement of my neighbours, to run up a kennel, beyond the rookery, at the north end of the park,—where there is very good air, and a fine stream of water,—and invite my friend, Sir Harry Parton, to hunt this country, for a couple of months during the season. One of my fellows says, that there are not only numbers of foxes in the neighbourhood, but what is still better, a few,—a very few,—of those stags, about which we have heard so much. I think I have influence enough with Sir Harry to persuade him; at all events, I'll invite him; and if he should have other existing engagements, I pledge myself,—that is, if such a step would be agreeable,—to hunt the country myself."

"Our respected and unfortunate friend, cousin Caddy," said Cuddle, "had a little pack of dogs—"

"A pack of *dogs*, indeed, they were, Mr. Cuddle," interrupted young Horner; "five or six couple of curs, that lurked about the Castle, gentlemen, which we used sometimes to coax down to the river, and spear or worry an otter; and, now and then, wheedle away to the woods, at midnight, for a badger–hunt, after drinking more ale than we well knew how to carry. I was a boy then, but I could drink ale by the quart."

"Ay, ay!" exclaimed Caddy Cuddle, "those were famous times! 'Tis true, I never went out with you, but I recollect very well how I enjoyed poor Caddy Caddy's animated descriptions of the badger–hunt, when he came back."

"Oh! then you hunted *badgers*, did you?" said the gentleman of Kent to Tom Horner, in a sneering tone, that produced a titter all round the table.

"Yes, sir,—we hunted badgers," replied Tom; "and capital sport it is, too, in default of better."

"I dare say it is," said the gentleman of Kent.

"Allow me to tell you then, sir, that there is really good sport in badger–hunting; it is a fine, irregular sort of pastime, unfettered by the systematic rules of the more aristocratic sports. The stag–hunt and the fox–chase, are so shackled with old ordinances and covert–side statutes, that they remind me of one of the classical dramas of the French: a badger–hunt is of the romantic school;—free as air, wild as mountain breezes;— joyous, exhilarating, uncurbed, and natural as one of our Shakespeare's plays. Barring an otter–hunt, (and what's better still, according to Caddy Cuddle's account, who has been in the North Seas, the spearing of a whale,) there are few sports that suit my capacity of enjoyment, so well as badger–bagging.—Just picture to yourself, that you have sent in a keen terrier, no bigger than a stout fitchet, or thereabouts, to ascertain that the badger is not within; that you have cleverly bagged the hole, and stuck the end of the mouth–line in the fist of a patient, but wary and dexterous clod–hopper; (an old, lame, broken–down, one–eyed gamekeeper, is the best creature on earth for such an office;)—and then, what do you do?— Why, zounds! every body takes his own course, with or without dogs, as it may happen; hunting, yelping, hallooing, and beating every brake for half a mile, or more, round, to get scent of the badger. Imagine the moon, 'sweet huntress of yon azure plain,' is up, and beaming with all her brilliancy; the trees beautifully basking in her splendour; her glance streaming through an aperture in an old oak, caused by the fall of a branch, by lightning, or bluff Boreas, and fringing the mallow–leaf with silver; the nightingale, in the brake, fascinating your ear; the glow–worm delighting your eye:—you stand, for a moment, motionless;—the bat whirrs above your head and the owl, unaccustomed to the sight of man, in such deep solitudes, flaps, fearless, so near as to fan your glowing forehead with his wings:—when suddenly you hear a shout,—a yell,—two or three such exclamations as—'There a' ees!'— 'Thic's he!'—'At 'un, Juno!'— 'Yonder a goath!'—'Hurrah!'— 'Vollow un up!'— 'Yaw awicks!' and 'Oh! my leg!'—You know by this, that 'the game's a foot;'—you fly to the right or left, as the case may be, skimming over furzy brake, like a bird, and wading through tangled briar, as a pike would, through the deeps of a brook, after a trout that is lame of a fin. You reach the scene of action; the badger is before, half a score of tykes around, and the yokels behind you.—'Hulk forward! have at him!' you enthusiastically cry; your spirits are up;—you are buoyant—agile as a roe–buck; —your legs devour space—you—"

"My dear fellow, allow me to conclude," interrupted Caddy Cuddle, "for your prose Pegasus never can carry you through the hunt at this rate. To be brief, then,—according to what I have heard from my never–to–be–sufficiently–lamented friend, Caddy Caddy,—the badger, when found, immediately makes for his earth; if he reach it without being picked tip and taken, he bolts in at the entrance; the bag receives him; its mouth is drawn close by the string; and thus the animal is taken.—But, odds! while I talk of those delights, which were the theme of our discourse in the much–regretted days of Caddy Caddy, I forget that time is on the wing.—I suppose no one is going my way."

"I am," replied Tom Horner, "in about three hours' time."

"Ay, ay! you're younger, friend Horner, than I have been these fifteen years," said Cuddle; "time was, before Caddy Caddy lost his wits, when he and I have sat over midnight together, as merry as crickets; but since his misfortune, I have become a very altered man. '*Primâ nocte domum claude:*'—that has been my motto for years past. Mrs. Watermark, my good housekeeper, is, I feel convinced, already alarmed; and it would not become me, positively to terrify her: besides, I am not on very intimate terms with my horse, which I borrowed from my friend, Anthony Mutch, of Mallow Hill, for this occasion: the roads, too, have been so cut and carved about, by the Commissioners,—doubtless, for very wise purposes,—since poor Caddy Caddy's time, that I had much ado to find my way in the broad day–light; and these spectacles, I must needs say, although I reverence the donor, are not to be depended on, so implicitly as I could wish. Let me see—ay—'tis now twelve years ago, from my last birth–day, since they were presented to me; and, believe me, I've never had the courage to wear them before. I hate changing,—especially of spectacles; I should not have put them on now—confound them!—had it not been for Mrs. Watermark, who protested my others were not fit to be seen in decent society."

"Under the circumstances you have mentioned," said the Honourable Charles Caddy, "I must press you to accept of a bed. Pray, make the Castle your own; you will confer an obligation on me by remaining."

"Cousin Caddy," replied Cuddle, rising from his seat, and approaching his host, whose hand he took between both his own; "I rejoice to find so worthy a successor of poor Caddy Caddy, master of Caddy Castle. It would be most pleasing to me, if it were possible, to remain; and, I do protest, that I positively would, were it not for the feelings of Mrs. Watermark,—a most worthy and valuable woman,—who is now, perhaps, sitting on thorns on my account. But I feel so grateful to you,—so happy in your society, that I will actually quaff another bumper, previously to taking my stirrup–cup; yea, and truly, were honest Jack Cole—old king Cole, as we used to call him, in Caddy Caddy's days,—were Jack here, with his fine bass voice, I would actually proffer a stave or so,— say, for instance, the Dialogue between Time and the Drinkers,—if Tom Horner would chime in, as he used to do when a boy, here, in this very room, with honest Jack, poor Caddy Caddy, and myself, in times past.—Honest Jack! most excellent Jack! rare king Cole! would he were here!"

"I should be sorry, cousin," said the Honourable Charles Caddy, "to have omitted, in my invitation–list, the name of so respectable and staunch a friend of our family, as Mr. Cole, of Colebrook. If I do not mistake, he sits immediately below my friend Wilmot, at the next table; I regret that I have not had an opportunity of making myself more known to him."

"Jack! honest Jack!" exclaimed Cuddle; "old king Cole, here, and I not know it?—Little Jack, that's silent to the grave, except when he thunders in a glee!—Where, cousin? Oddsbird! eh?—Jack, where are you?"

"Here am I, Caddy," replied a diminutive old gentleman, with a remarkably drowsy–looking eye; "I thought you were not going to accost me."

The deep and sonorous tone in which these words were spoken, startled those who sat near old Cole: they gazed at him, and seemed to doubt if the sounds they had heard really emanated from the lungs of so spare and puny a personage. Cuddle crossed his arms on his breast, and exclaimed, "And is it, indeed, my friend Jack Cole?"

"Don't you know me, when I speak even?" growled old Cole, "or d'ye think somebody has borrowed my voice?"

"'Tis Jack, himself!" cried Cuddle; "honest Jack! and I did not see him!—these glasses I cannot help stigmatizing as an egregious nuisance."

"Well, Mr. Cole, what say you, will you join us?" inquired Horner .

"No, sir," replied Cole; "sing by yourself; one ass at a time is bad enough; but three braying together, are insupportable."

"The same man,—the same man as ever;" exclaimed Cuddle, apparently very much pleased;—"begin, Horner;—you know his way;—he can't resist, when his bar comes. He had always these crotchets;—begin, my boy; I will pledge myself that he falls in with the stream of the tune."

Horner and Cuddle now commenced the glee; and, as the latter had predicted, Cole, after closing his eyes, throwing him self back in his chair, and making sundry wry faces, trowled forth the first reply, and afterwards, all the other responses of old Father Time, in the following verses.—

> "Whither away! old Father Time?
> Ah! whither dost thou run
> Low,—low,
> I've a mob to mow;
> My work is never done."

> "Tarry awhile with us, old Time,
> And lay thy scythe aside!"—
> Nay!—nay!
> 'Tis a busy day;
> My work it lieth wide."

> "Tell us, we pray thee, why, old Time,
> Thou look'st so pale and glum?"—
> Fie!—fie!
> I evermore sigh,
> 'Eternity, oh! come!'"

"Art thou, then, tired, old Father Time?
Thy labour dost thou rue?"—
"Long,—long,
Has it been my song,—
'Could I but die like you!'"

"Tell us, then, when, old Father Time,
We may expect thy death!"
"That morn
Eternity's born,
Receives my parting breath."

"And what's eternity, Father Time?
We pray thee, tell us now!"—
"When men
Are dead, it is then
Eternity they know."

"Come, fill up thy glass, old Father Time,
And clog its sands with wine!"—
"No, no;
They would faster flow,
And distil tears of brine!"

Caddy Cuddle, at the conclusion of these verses, took possession of a vacant chair, by the side of old Cole, and soon forgot that there was such a being as Mrs. Watermark in existence. He quaffed bumper after bumper with honest Jack;—an hour passed very pleasantly away in talking of old times;—and Cuddle wondered to find himself slightly intoxicated. He immediately rose, took his leave rather uncourteously, and went out, muttering some thing about "eleven miles," and "Mother Watermark." In a few minutes, he was mounted, and trotting toward the park gate which opened on the high road. "A fine night, Billy Norman;—a fine night, Billy;" said Cuddle, as he rode through, to the old gate-keeper; "pray, Billy, what say you? Don't you think they have cut the roads up cruelly, of late years?—Here's half a crown, Billy.—What with planting, and enclosing, and road-making, I scarcely know the face of the country; it's as puzzling as a labyrinth.— Good night, Billy!"

Cuddle, who was a tolerably bold rider, for a man of his years, now struck his horse rather forcibly, with his heels, and urged him at once into a brisk hand–gallop.

"He hath a spur in his head," said Billy Norman to himself, as Cuddle disappeared down the road; "I hope nought but good may happen him; for he's one of the right sort, if he had it."

The roads were dry and hard, the air serene, and Billy stood listening, for a few minutes, to the sounds of the horse's feet; he soon felt convinced, by the cadences, that Caddy Cuddle was increasing, rather than diminishing, his speed. The heat of the hoofs became, at length, barely audible; it gradually died away; and Norman was going in to light his pipe, when he thought he heard the sounds again. He put his hand behind his ear, held his breath, and, in a few moments, felt satisfied that Caddy Cuddle had taken the wrong turning, and was working back, by a circular route, toward Caddy Castle again. As he approached nearer, Norman began to entertain apprehensions that Cuddle's horse had run away with him, in consequence of the violent pace, at which, it was clear, from the sound of its feet, that the animal was going. Norman stepped off the pathway into the road, and prepared to hail Cuddle, as he passed, and ascertain, if possible, what really was the matter. The horse and his rider came on nearly at full speed, and Norman shouted, with all his might,— "Holloa! hoy! Stop!"

"I carry arms! I carry arms!" cried Cuddle, urging his horse forward with all his might.

"Zauns!" exclaimed Norman, "he takes I for a highwayman!—He must ha' mistook the road, that's certain; the horse can't ha' run away wi' un, or a' 'uldn't kick un so.—Sailor, you be out o' your latitude."

The circle, which Caddy Cuddle had made, was about two miles in circumference: he went precisely in the same direction again, without, in the least, suspecting his error; and having, as he thought, mastered four miles of his road homeward, and given his horse a tolerable breathing, he began to pull up by degrees, as he, for the second time approached the little rustic lodge of Caddy Park, from which he issued at his departure. Norman again hailed him, for he felt tolerably satisfied that Caddy carried no other arms than those with which Nature had endowed him. Caddy now knew the voice, and pulled up:—"Who's there?" said he; "A friend, I think; for I remember your tone.—Who are you, honest man?"

"Heaven help us, Mr. Cuddle!" exclaimed Norman, "Are 'ee mad, sir, or how?"

"Why, nipperkins! Norman, is it you?"

"Ay, truly."

"And how got you here?—I thought nothing had passed me on the road. Where are you going, honest Norman?"

"Going!—I be going no–where," replied the gate–keeper; "I be here, where you left me. Why, doant'ee know, that you ha' been working round and round, just like a horse in a mill?—And after all this helter–skelter work, here you be, just where you were!"

"D—n the spectacles, then!" said Cuddle; "and confound all innovators!—Why couldn't they let the country alone?—I've taken the wrong turning, I suppose?"

"Yeas,—' reckon 't must be summat o' that kind:—there be four to the right, out o' the strait road, across the common; the three first do bring 'ee round this way, t'other takes 'ee home but, odds! Muster Cuddle! do'ee get off!—Here be a girth broke, —and t'other as old as my hat, and half worn through, as 't you must go back; you must, truly, go back to the stables, and put the tackle in order."

Cuddle seemed rather loath to return, but old Norman was inflexible: he led the horse inside the gate, which he safely locked, and put the key in his pocket, and then hobbled along, by the side of Caddy, toward the stables. As he passed the outer door of the house, he whispered to the porter; his fears for Cuddle's safety, if he were suffered to depart again, and begged that the porter would contrive to let his master be made acquainted with the circumstance of Caddy's ride.

The information was immediately conveyed to the dining–room, and half–a–dozen gentlemen, with the Honourable Charles Caddy at their head, immediately proceeded to the stables, where they found Cuddle, perspiring very copiously, and endeavouring to obtain information for his guidance, in his contemplated journey, from those, who were, from the same cause, as incapable of giving, as Cuddle was of following correct directions. The Honourable Charles Caddy, in spite of his good breeding, could not help laughing, when he heard Cuddle's account of the affair; but he very judiciously insisted on Cuddle's remaining at the Castle until morning. Caddy vowed that he would acquiesce only on one condition; which was, that a servant should be immediately dispatched to his cottage, to allay the fears of Mrs. Watermark; and that such servant should be specially enjoined, not to blab a word of his mishap, to the good old gentlewoman. "If he should," said Cuddle, "Mrs. Watermark will be terrified, and we shall have her here before morning, even if she walk all the way."

It was in vain that the Honourable Charles Caddy and his visitors entreated Caddy Cuddle to return to the table; he preferred retiring to rest at once. "You must put up with one of the ancient bed–rooms, cousin Cuddle," said the Honourable Charles Caddy; "but you fear no ghosts, I apprehend?"

"Nipperkins! not I!" replied Cuddle. "If I am to sleep out of my own bed, I care not if you place me in the most alarming room in the Castle. To confess the truth,—but this under the rose, cousin,—I feel a touch of the influence of Bacchus, and '*dulce periculum est,*' you know, when that's the case."

The bed–chamber to which Cuddle was consigned, still retained its tapestry hangings; and the good man quivered, either with cold, or at the solemn appearance of the room, when he entered it. A very prominent figure in the arras actually appeared to move, as Cuddle sat down in a capacious old chair, at the right–hand side of the bed, to undress himself. After gazing earnestly at it, for a moment, with his stockings half drawn off, he corrected himself for indulging in so ridiculous a fancy:—"None of these Pygmalion freaks," said he; "none of your Promethean tricks, Mr. Imagination of mine; and yet, perhaps, I am accusing you wrongfully, and these mischievous glasses have endowed yonder figure with seeming vitality; I hope I may not break them, in a pet, before I get home."

Caddy Cuddle was one of those unfortunate beings who accustom themselves to read in bed; and who; from long habit, can no more compose themselves to sleep, without perusing a few pages, in their night–gear, than some others can without a good supper, or a comfortable potation. Caddy discovered two or three old, worm–eaten books, in a small table drawer, and selected that one which was printed in the largest type, for his perusal, when recumbent. It was a volume of tracts, on geomancy, astrology, and necromancy. Cuddle read it with avidity, and by the time the small piece of candle, with which he had been furnished, was burnt out, he had filled his brain with images of imps and familiars. Finding himself, suddenly, in utter darkness, he laid down the book; and then, turning himself on his back, very soon fell asleep.

No man, perhaps, ever kept a log–book of his dreams; and yet, such an article would certainly be more amusing than many an honest gentleman's diary; for there are persons in the world whose waking adventures are as dull and monotonous as the ticking of a clock, while their biography in bed,—their nightly dreams,—if correctly narrated would, in some cases, he exceedingly droll; and, in others, insupportably pathetic. The happiest people by day–light, often suffer agonies by night; a man who would not harm a worm, with his eyes open, sometimes commits murder, and actually endures all the misery of being taken, tried, convicted, and half executed, in imagination, while he lies snug, snoring, and motionless, beneath a pair of Witney blankets. It is rash to say that any individual is, or, at least, ought to be, happy, until we ascertain how he dreams. A very excellent country 'squire, in the west of England, was once told, by a person of discrimination, that he appeared to be the most comfortable man in existence:—"Your desires are within your means;"—thus the 'squire was addressed;—"your wife is most charming in temper, manners, and person; your affection is mutual; your children are every thing that a parent could wish; your life has been so irreproachable, that you must be as easy in mind as it is possible for a man to be: no one bears you malice; on the contrary, everybody blesses you: your house and your park are delightful; you are most felicitous, even in your servants and cattle; you are naturally—" "True, true, to the letter," impatiently interrupted the 'squire; "but what's all the world to a man who, without why or wherefore, dreams that he's with old Nick every night of his life?"

Caddy Cuddle was not much addicted to dreaming; but, on the night he slept in the ancient room, at Caddy Castle, he felt satisfied, as he afterward said, that in the course of a few hours, his imagination was visited with fantasies enough to fill a volume; although he could not recollect, with any distinctness, even one of them, half an hour after he awoke. The moon was shining full upon the window, and making the chamber almost as light as day, with her radiance, when Caddy opened his eyes, after his first sleep, to satisfy himself, by the view of some familiar object, that he was not among the strange creatures of whom he had been dreaming. Perched upon his nose,—threatening it with whip, as Caddy saw, and galling it with spur, as Caddy felt,—he beheld an imp, whose figure was, at once, more grotesque and horrible, than any of those which had flitted before his mind's eye, during his slumbers!

The creature seemed to be staring at him with terrific impudence, and jockeying his feature, as though it were actually capable of running a race. Caddy's eye–balls were almost thrust out of their sockets with dismay; his nether–jaw dropped, and he groaned deeply, under the influence of the visible nose–night–mare with which he was afflicted. For more than a minute, Caddy was incapable of moving either of his limbs but he summoned up resolution enough, at last, to close his eyes, and make a clutch at the fiend, that rode his nose in the manner above described. With a mingled feeling of surprise, mortification, and joy, he found the nose–night–mare to be his spectacles!—He had gone to sleep without removing them from his nose; and, by tumbling and tossing to and fro, in his dreams, he had displaced, and twisted them, sufficiently, to assume a position and form, that might have alarmed a man of stouter nerves than Caddy Cuddle, on awaking in the middle of a moonlight night, after dreaming of more monsters than the German authors have ever located on Walpurgis Night in the Hartz.

Caddy tried to compose himself to sleep again; but grew restless, feverish, and very uncomfortable: he beat up his pillow, shook his bed, smoothed his sheets, walked several times up and down the room, and then lay down again;—determined, at leas to doze. But Morpheus had taken leave of him; and Caddy, at last, resolved on dressing himself, going down to the kitchen, and, as he had tobacco about him, to smoke a pipe, if he could find one, clean or dirty. He attributed his want of rest to not having indulged in his usual sedative luxury, before going to bed; and very resolutely taxed himself with the commission of an egregious folly, for having drank more than he ought. Anthony Mutch's horse, and the Commissioners of the roads, he very copiously abused, while dressing himself: the spectacles were, however, the grand objects of his indignation; but, bad as they were, he conceived that it was necessary to coax them into shape again, and mount them on his nose, previously to attempting, what he deemed, the perilous descent, from his chamber, which was on the third floor, to the kitchen below. Caddy, however, was too well acquainted with the topography of the house, to incur much danger: moreover, the moon beamed with such brilliancy, through the glass dome that lighted the great circular staircase of Caddy Castle, that a man, much more short–sighted than our hero, might have gone safely from the top to the bottom, without the assistance of glasses.

In a hole in the kitchen chimney, Caddy found two or three short pipes; he congratulated himself on the discovery, and immediately filled one of them from his pouch. The Castle was now as quiet as the grave; and no soul, but Caddy himself, seemed to be stirring. He felt rather surprised to see the stone floor of the kitchen, for above a yard from the chimney, covered with embers of expiring logs, while the hearth itself was "dark as Erebus." Caddy Cuddle, however, did not trouble himself much about this circumstance: he had often seen the kitchen in a similar condition, after a frolic, in Caddy Caddy's time; and very gravely lighting his pipe, he deposited himself on a warm iron tripod,— which had been standing on the hearth, probably, the whole evening, —in preference to a cold oak chair. The kitchen was comfortable, notwithstanding it was dark, (for the embers, as we have already stated, were expiring, and Caddy was without a candle,) and he smoked the pipe so much to his satisfaction, that he determined to enjoy another. Kicking the bits of burning wood together, as he sat, in order to light his tobacco, he, unintentionally, produced a little blaze, which proved rather disastrous to him:—as he stooped to light the pipe, he heard a noise, that attracted his attention; Caddy looked about, and, on the spacious hearth, beheld some thing, that bore a rude similitude to a human figure!

Caddy was rather alarmed; and he uttered an exclamation, which seemed to rouse the object of his fears. It raised itself on its hands, and after staring Caddy frill in the face, as he afterwards stated, began to uncoil itself and, at length, rose, and stood, tolerably terrified, to judge from appearances, gazing at the odd–looking figure which Caddy cut, with his night–cap, spectacles, and pipe, on the large iron tripod. Cuddle now perceived that his companion, although of masculine frame, was arrayed in female habiliments, which were black as the exterior of an old stew–pan. It was Martha Jones, the scullion, a Welsh girl, who, whenever she could, indulged herself with a night's rest, in her clothes, on the warm hearth of Caddy Castle kitchen, instead of a comfortable bed in one of its turrets. On these occasions, she previously swept the embers from the hearth, to the stone floor; as Caddy Cuddle had found them, on entering to smoke his pipe. She was indulged in these and a few other odd vagaries, on account of her excellence as an under–strapper to the cook, who frequently said, that she could, and would, do more work in one day, than a brace of the ordinary run of scullions did in a week. Martha possessed a pair of immense muscular arms, which resembled, in hue, the outer leaf of a frost–bitten red cabbage; her cheeks were of the same colour, when clean; and shone, after a recent ablution, as though they had been smeared with bees'–wax and turpentine, and polished by means of a furniture–brush. Caddy Cuddle, in his subsequent description of Martha, said, that her hair was jetty as a black cart–horse's tail;—her lips pouted like a pair of black puddings; and her eye,—for truth to say, she had but one,—was as fiery and frightful as that of a Cyclops. Martha's features were, however, though large, remarkably well–formed; and more than one ploughman, in the neighbourhood, already sighed to make her a bride.

After Martha had gazed, for more than a minute, at Caddy Cuddle, who ceased to puff and almost to breathe, from the moment the scullion had first begun to move, she burst out into a loud fit of laughter, in which she indulged for some time;—occasionally stirring and raking the embers on the floor together, to create a better blaze, in order that she might enjoy a full view of Caddy Cuddle, who was now quite as ludicrous in her estimation, as she had been terrible in his. Cuddle, at last, waxed wroth; threw his pipe on the floor; thrust one of his hands beneath the breast of his waistcoat; placed the other behind him, under the tail of his coat, which he considerably elevated by the action; and, in this, as he deemed, most imposing attitude, asked how she dared to insult one of her master's guests in that manner.—"Stand aside," continued he, "and let me withdraw to my chamber, woman!"

"Ooman!" cried the scullion, ceasing to laugh in an instant, and putting on rather an alarming frown:—"Ooman!—her name is Martha Jones, and no more a—Yes, her is a ooman, though, tat's true;—but Martha Jones is her name, and her will not be called ooman py nopoty, look you; that is what her will not.— Ooman, inteet! Cot pless her! To live six long years in the kitchen of 'Squire Morgan, and one pesides, at 'Squire Caddy's, with a coot character, and her own aunt a laty, to be called 'ooman,' py a little man in a white night–cap! look you, I sall tie first!"

Caddy Cuddle's experience with the woman–kind, as our excellent friend, Jonathan Oldbuck yelps the fair part of the creation, was very limited: he had read of heroines, in the Latin and Greek authors; spoken to a few demi–savages, when a boy, during his nautical adventures in foreign parts; occasionally chucked a dairy–maid under the chin, when

Bacchi plenus, in the reign of Caddy Caddy, at Caddy Castle; and had a few quarrels with his housekeeper, Mrs. Watermark. He was of opinion, from what he had witnessed, that a little flattery was of sovereign virtue with the sex; and, in order to escape from Martha's clutches, of which he felt in considerable awe, Caddy Cuddle essayed to soothe and allay the fever into which he had thrown the scullion by calling her a woman, with a few compliments. But, like all inexperienced persons, Caddy Cuddle could not hit the golden mean; he over stepped the mark so much, as to make honest Martha imagine that he really admired her. Caddy was not aware to what an extent his flattery was leading him: he plumed himself on his tact and discretion, when Martha's face began to relax into a smile; launched boldly into hyperbole, as soon as she curtsied at his compliments; and, in order to effect a dashing retreat, by a bold *coup–de–main,* attacked the enemy with a brigade of classical metaphors,. The scullion could hold out no longer; she strode over the intervening embers; clutched Cuddle in her colossal grasp; and, in an instant, she was seated on the tripod which he had previously occupied, with the very alarmed little gentleman perched upon her knee.

The nose–night–mare was a trifle, in Cuddle's estimation, compared with what he now endured: he struggled, and roared with all his might;— called Martha Jones, "Circe, Canidia, Scylla, Medea, Harpy, Polyphemus, and Witch of Edmonton," without the least effect: she seemed to consider all these appellatives as endearing epithets, and kissed Caddy, so vehemently, that he thought his heart would break.

And it was not merely the warmth of the scullion's gratitude or affection—whichever it might be—that so discomposed Caddy Cuddle; Martha, in striding across the blazing embers, had ignited her greasy, and, consequently, very combustible apparel; and although she, in her raptures, seemed to be quite unconscious of the circumstance, Caddy Cuddle felt that the incipient flame had begun to singe his stockings. At length, Mistress Martha herself, became, somehow or other, cognizant of the fact; and she instantly threw Caddy Cuddle off her knee, shrieked like an infuriated maniac, snatched up the kitchen poker, and flourished it about Caddy's head, threatening him, by her actions, with immediate annihilation; as though he, good innocent man, had been the cause of the combustion.

Luckily for Caddy and the scullion, their *tête–a–tête* had been so boisterous, as to have alarmed the Castle; and the French cook, with two or three other men–servants, burst into the kitchen at a very critical instant both for Caddy and Miss Jones. A bucket of water, dexterously applied by the coachman, quenched the blazing petticoats, and somewhat allayed the fiery heart of the scullion; who retreated behind a pile of pots and kettles. While Caddy apostrophized the cook, Martha was loud in vituperation; the men–servants were noisy as Bedlamites; and the *cuisinier* himself, a recently imported Frenchman, imprecated, very loudly, in his own language,— consigning Caddy, the scullion, coachman, and his fellow–domestics, with all other the English people, past, present, and to come, in one lot, to the care of King Pluto and his sable adherents. Alarmed at the uproar, the guests at Caddy Castle came in by twos and threes, and, in a few minutes, the kitchen was thronged.

The Honourable Charles Cuddy had scarcely closed his eyes, when the exclamations, from Caddy Cuddle and the scullion, reached his ears; the lovely Lady Letitia having amused herself by giving him a curtain lecture, of some two hours' duration, after they had retired, on his gross and most apparent gallantry to the plainest woman among the visitors at the Castle. He leaped out of bed, on hearing the noise, rather to escape from the dulcet abuse of his beautiful better–half, than from any strong feelings of interest or curiosity; and, as soon as he could make himself fit to be seen, hurried toward the place of declamation. There he found Caddy Cuddle, encircled by twenty or thirty people, (who, although they were his guests, and had dined with him, he positively did not know in their night–caps,) exclaiming, prodigiously, against the scullion, and endeavouring, by dint of vociferation, to prove that he was not at all to blame.

The Honourable Charles Caddy soon cleared the kitchen, when he found that nothing of consequence had occurred: the guests and servants retired; and Caddy Cuddle, after making several apologies and protestations of innocence, whatsoever the scullion might say of him, to his cousin, took up a candle, which somebody had left on the dresser, and marched off to the staircase. The Honourable Charles Caddy, who had detained the cook, now inquired who and what the creature of darkness was behind the saucepans; and while the cook was explaining, and Martha Jones was giving the most excellent account of herself, Caddy Cuddle proceeded toward his bed–chamber. As he passed Lady Letitia's door, he knocked, and whispered, through the key–hole, a long string of apologies, in which he was interrupted by the lady's husband; who, after politely marshalling him to his room, made him a most ceremonious and courtly bow, and wished him a very excellent good night.

Caddy paced two or three times up and down the room, lamenting his misfortunes, and inwardly vowing never to quit his cottage for a castle again. He was so anxious not to disturb the household, that he neither stamped on the floor, nor groaned audibly; but rather "stepped a–tip–toe," from the window to the fire–place, and thence to the window again, scarcely breathing as he moved. Finding but little relief from this state of constraint, he threw himself on the old chair that stood on the right–hand side of the bed, and began to recover a little of his usual good humour. He reviewed the circumstances which had happened during the night; and they now presented themselves in so droll a light to Caddy's mind, that he could not help smiling at his mishaps, and proceeded to unbutton his waistcoat. All at once, the remembrance of the moving tapestry flashed across him, and his eye was instantly fixed on the figure that had alarmed him, previous to his retiring to rest. "Surely," thought he, "it could not have been imagination, for it moveth, even now most palpably!—or my visionary organs are singularly impaired;—or these new spectacles lead me into very unpleasant errors. Would that I had never accepted them!" He removed the suspected offenders from his nose, wiped them carefully with the tail of his coat, and was going to put them on again, when a tall, stout–built person, slipped out from behind the arras, and advanced, with hasty steps, toward him, exclaiming, "Soho! friend Caddy Cuddle, you're come at last!"

"What, in the name of all that's good, art thou?" exclaimed Caddy, feeling surprised that he was not more frightened;—"who art thou?"

"Don't you know me, Caddy?" said the intruder, laying his hand on Cuddles arm; who was very much pleased to feel that his visitor possessed the property of tangibility, and was, therefore, no ghost.—"Don't you know me, Caddy?" repeated the figure, in rather a reproachful tone.

"I dare say I should, sir, if you would permit me to put on my spectacles,—bad as they are," replied Caddy; "and if you'd step back a yard or two, so as to get, as it were, at the proper focus of my sight:—suppose you take a chair."

The tall man retreated some paces, and Caddy put on his spectacles:— "Now, sir," said he, "we shall see:—Where are you?—Oh! I perceive— Why, bless my soul, sir—is it—can it be? Are these glasses really playing me tricks? or have I, in truth, leaped out of the frying–pan into the fire?—You surely can't be my very unfortunate and most respected friend, Caddy Caddy, of Caddy Castle!"

"The same," replied the tall old man, with a sigh:—"Caddy Caddy, sir, of Caddy Castle."

"And how the nipperkins did you break loose?" cried Cuddle, rising from the chair, and advancing two or three steps.

"Where now, where now, sir?" said Caddy Caddy, taking a gentle hold of Cuddle's arm:—"Where now, friend Cuddle?"

"Where?—why, to the door, doubtless!—Am I doomed to do nothing but alarm the castle?"

"Alarm the castle!" exclaimed Caddy Caddy; "are you out of your senses? why, they'd lock me up, man, if you did."

"To be sure they would, and that's precisely what I want them to do.— My dear sir, I beg pardon; I wouldn't give offence I'm sure,—neither to you nor the people of the Castle; but I can't help it.—You must allow me to give the alarm.—I cannot submit to be shut up with a madman."

"So, then, you join in the slander, do you?" said Caddy Caddy; "Cuddle, you hurt me to the soul!"

"Well, well,—my dear friend,—my respected friend,—I am sorry I said so;—it was but in joke."

"Cuddle," replied Caddy, "I was ruined by a joke:—somebody called me a madman, in jest; the rest of the world joined in the cry, though it was a fool who gave tongue; and, at last, they ran me down; proved, to their own satisfaction, that I was out of my wits, for being in a passion with, and turning upon, those who were hunting me. Nothing is more easy than to prove a man mad:—begin, by throwing a slur upon his mental sanity; watch him narrowly; view all he does with a jaundiced eye; rake up a score of facts, which occurred a year apart,—facts that are really frolics, freaks, whims, vagaries, or what you will, of the like nature; place them all together, and the business is done; you make as fine a picture of lunacy as a man would wish to look at. I assure you, Caddy Cuddle, I am no more a lunatic than you are,—take my word for it; so sit down and tune the fiddle."

"Fiddle! what?—where?—which fiddle?"

"Oh! they allow me my fiddle; I should go crazy in earnest without that. I left it behind the arras;—come—"

"Come! come where?"

"Come and fetch it," said Caddy, dragging Cuddle toward the place from which he had issued.

"Nipperkins, cousin!" cried Cuddle, "go and get it yourself."

"No, no," replied the other, with a knowing look; "If I were to do so, you'd slip out, while my back was turned, and raise the Castle. I've had trouble enough to elude their vigilance, during the bustle, to lose my liberty so easily again. By–and–bye, we'll go down stairs together, and break open the cellar;—it's all my own, you know, if right was cock of the walk. I'm for gamocks and junketting, I forewarn you, and we'll have a jolly night of it."

By this time, Caddy had approached the arras, with Cuddle fast in his clutch; he stooped down, and drawing forth an old fiddle and stick, put them into the hands of Cuddle; who, as may readily be imagined, was by no means enamoured of his situation.

"Now," said Caddy, "in the first place, my friend, play Rowley Waters. I have been trying to recollect the two last bars of it for these three years, but I cannot. Do you remember how beautifully my drunken old butler, Barnaby, used to troul it?"

"Ay, those were merry days, cousin," said Cuddle; "poor Barnaby! his passion for ale laid him low, at last."

"And many a time, before."

"What! was it in time of your sanity? I beg pardon—Do you remember, then, our finding him, flat on his back, by the side of an untapped vat of the stoutest beer that ever Caddy Castle could boast?—Methinks I can see him now, with the gimlet in his hand, with which he had made an aperture in the cask, and sucked the blood of barley–corn, to such an abominable extent—the old beast did—that —"

"Don't asperse him, Cuddle," said Caddy; "he put a peg in the hole before he died. He was the best of butlers; if he always drank a skinful, he never wasted a noggin. But now for Rowley Waters —play up, and I'll jig."

"No, no," said Cuddle, laying down the instrument; "I'll do no such thing;—I won't, by Jupiter!—that's resolute."

"Well, then, I'll play, and you shall dance."

"Don't make me swear," said Cuddle; "don't, Caddy Caddy!—What! raise a riot again?—You don't know, perhaps, that I have, already, sinned egregiously;—although, I protest, without the least evil intention. Besides, it would produce that very effect which you wish to—Eh! what was I saying?—Well, I don't mind if I do give you one tune."

"Thank you, kindly, cousin Cuddle," said Caddy, taking up the fiddle; "but you have raised an objection, which I admit to be of great weight. Oh! cousin Cuddle! Did you want to betray me?—I thank you for the hint:—we should, indeed, alarm my enemies. You overreached yourself, and saved me, cousin."

"Well, I scorn a lie," replied Cuddle; "such a thought as you suspect did occur to me; for I protest I am not very comfortable in your company, much as I respect you. Go back to your bed; do, pr'ythee now, be ruled—oblige me, cousin;—for your own sake, go."

"Oh! what a thing self–interest is!" exclaimed Caddy; "'for your own sake, go,' quoth he, when it is solely for his! Cousin Cuddle, I shall not;—that's a plain answer for you."

Caddy now placed a chair immediately opposite to that one on which he had found Cuddle sitting, on his entrance; he forced the alarmed little gentleman into his seat; and, in a few moments, resumed the conversation.

"Cuddle," said he, looking very seriously, "as the world goes, I take you to be an honest man, and my friend. Now, I'll confide something to your ear that will perfectly astonish you. The people about me, don't know a syllable of the matter; I kept it snug from them; if I had not, they would have restricted me to one room, instead of allowing me the liberty and use of three.—Draw your chair close.—About three years' since, I broke loose."

"So I heard," said Cuddle, trembling as he remembered what had been related of Caddy's violence on that occasion. The great staircase of the better part of Caddy Castle, was circular, and surmounted by a magnificent dome, which lighted it completely down to the hall; Caddy had thrown himself over the banisters, and must, inevitably, have been dashed to pieces, had it not been for a scaffolding, which some workmen had erected within the circle of the staircase, for the purpose of repairing some part of the masonry, a few days before. Caddy fell among the people on the temporary platform, and was taken up, apparently, lifeless; but, in the course of a couple of months, his bodily health was restored,—his mental malady remaining nearly in its former state.

"You know," continued Caddy, "of my leap; I gave them the slip, then, cousin, in good earnest. I fell a terrific depth, and did the business at once. I recollect the moment of my near approach to the scaffolding, of the erection of which, I was ignorant; but, as it happened, it did not frustrate my intentions."

"I feel very ailing—very indisposed, indeed," said Cuddle; "pray, cousin Caddy, permit me to—"

"Nonsense!" exclaimed Caddy; "you are as well as ever you were in your life; I am sure of it; so hear me out:—of course, you heard their account of restoring me to health;—but they know nothing of the matter, cousin Cuddle:—when I seemed to them to revive, I felt that I was *disembodied*!"

"Disembodied!" cried Cuddle, staring wildly at Caddy.

"Ay, disembodied, cousin," said Caddy; "and my sole wish, except for liberty, now is, to obtain a disembodied companion, who—"

Cuddle could hear no more. To describe his thoughts or feelings at this moment, would be a task beyond the power of our feeble pen. We shall attempt only, to relate his actions.—He threw himself back in the capacious chair which he had hitherto occupied, but by no means filled; brought his knees on a level with, and as near as he possibly could to, his face; and then, suddenly throwing out his legs, with all the energy he possessed, struck Caddy in the breast with his feet so violently, as, in an instant, to turn him and his chair topsy–turvy on the floor. He exhibited a specimen of that agility for which he had been famed in his younger days, as well in this, as in his subsequent proceedings. Skipping over Caddy and the chair, he flew to the door, and made for the staircase at full speed. It is useless to conceal that Cuddle was dreadfully frightened; he heard Caddy striding after him at a fearful rate; and felt satisfied, by the evidence of his ears, that his dreaded pursuer would very speedily overtake him. People in similar situations adopt plans for escaping, which men, sitting calmly over their coffee, would never dream of. Cuddle knew that he should have no chance in a grapple with Caddy: it was ridiculous to hope for help if he cried out; for, before any one could come to his assistance, Caddy would have sufficient time to disembody his spirit; and his pursuer was evidently an over–match for him in speed. Cuddle was desperate: he suddenly determined on attempting to evade his enemy by a bold and dangerous man. He leaped upon the banisters, which were massive and broad enough for a man to stand upon with ease; caught hold of the rope, by which the dinner bell, above the cupola, was rung by the porter, in the ball below; and threw himself upon it,—in a style which would have done honour to a thorough–bred seaman,— at the moment the tops of Caddy's fingers touched his heels. We cannot wait to describe the consternation into which the ringing of the dinner bell, at that time of the night, threw all the inmates of Caddy Castle;—our hero claims our undivided attention; for his position was most perilous—at least, in Cuddle's own opinion.

Having descended, with moderate haste, for a few yards, he felt, by certain jerks of the rope, that Caddy had followed his example, and was pursuing him down the rope,—with such hair–brained velocity too, as he very speedily ascertained, that he was in greater danger than ever. The rope was swung to and fro, by his own exertions and those of his enemy,—bumping him against the banisters with considerable force; but the blows he thus received were beneath his notice; he thought only of escaping. Finding that Caddy gained upon him, he contrived, as the rope swung toward the side of the staircase, to catch hold of one of the stout iron rails of the banister;—secure in his clutch, he quitted the rope with considerable dexterity, and had the satisfaction, while he dangled, of seeing Caddy slide by him. He now began to roar lustily; but his efforts were needless, for almost every living creature in the house was already on the alert; the watch dogs were barking without, and the lap–dogs within; the ladies were shrieking; the gentlemen calling the servants, and the latter wondering, and running here and there, exceedingly active, but not knowing what to do or what was the matter. By degrees, the male portion of the inhabitants of the Castle became concentrated in the hall: lights were procured; and while the ladies and their attendants peeped over the rails of the great staircase, in their night–caps, to watch the proceedings of the party below, Martha armed with the kitchen poker, volunteered to search every hole and corner in the Castle: but her master forbade her on pain of his displeasure; "For," said he, "I feel satisfied that it is a disgraceful hoax of some scoundrel in the house, who shall certainly be ducked if ever I discover him.—Is any one absent?"

"All the men servants are here, sir," said the coachman; and all the gentlemen, too, I think."

"No, they are not," exclaimed Martha, with a ludicrous grin; "where is my sweetheart, can you tell?—I do not see him."

"Oh! he's fast asleep, good man!" said the Honourable Charles Caddy.

"I wish he were;— I do most sincerely wish he were!" quoth Cuddle, who had released himself, by his own exertions, from his pendent position, and was now hastening down the lowest flight of stairs. "You may stare, my good host;" continued he, "but to sleep in Caddy Castle is perfectly impossible!"

"So I find, to my cost," replied the Honourable Charles Caddy; "and if I can find out the rascal who—"

"Do not waste time in threats," said Cuddle; "but fly—disperse, in quest of my respected, unhappy friend, poor Caddy Caddy, who has been with me this half hour, and would have disembodied me, if I hadn't given him a kick in the stomach, and put my trust in the bell–rope."

At the request of his host, Cuddle gave a hurried detail of what had taken place between himself and Caddy Caddy; while those domestics, who had the immediate care of the lunatic, hastened up to his rooms. they returned just as Cuddle had concluded, and stated that Caddy Caddy was undressed, and fast asleep in his bed;—that they found the doors locked, and every thing about the apartments in the precise state in which they had left them. One of the party said, that he slept in the next room to Caddy Caddy, and was quite certain that he should have been, as usual, roused, had the lunatic but merely moved: and as to the old Squire having been at large, the fellow swore that it was impossible.

It was useless for Cuddle to vow and solemnly declare that Caddy Caddy had been with him, in the face of this evidence: the gentlemen shook their heads; the men grumbled; the ladies on the stair–case tittered; and their maids pronounced Mr. Cuddle's conduct to be altogether shocking.

"It is a very distressing case," said the Honourable Charles Caddy; "and I protest I never was in so awkward a situation before. I feel bound to apologize," continued he, "to every lady and gentleman in the Castle, for the uproar, which my relation, Mr. Caddy Cuddle, has, doubtless, unintentionally, produced. I am bound to add, in justice to myself, that, upon my honour as a gentleman, I had not the most remote idea that either of my guests was a somnambulist."

"Is it possible that you can allude to me?" exclaimed Caddy Cuddle. "Is my veracity impeached? Am I to be a martyr to our poor mad relation's freaks?—Or, possibly, you will tell me that I ought to doubt the evidence of my own senses?"

"I never presume," was the reply, "to dictate to a gentleman on so delicate a point. Perhaps you will allow one of my servants to wait on you during the remainder of the night."

"I'll do no such thing," said Caddy Cuddle: "Let the horse be saddled directly. I'll go home at once, and endeavour to make my peace with Mrs. Watermark, from whom I expect and merit a very severe lecture, for so cruelly cutting up her feelings as to stay out a whole night nearly. Cousin Caddy, good b'ye; ladies and gentlemen, your servant."

Caddy Cuddle immediately departed, vowing, *per Jovem*, as he went, never, after that morning, to bestride Anthony Mutch's horse,—to dine at Caddy Castle, or any where else out of his own house,—or to put on a strange pair of spectacles again.

THE BRAINTREES

IT was the boast of old Samuel Gough, who, during a period of thirty–two years, had been landlord of The Chough and Stump,—a little, old–fashioned house, with carved oaken angels supporting the roof of its porch,—that, notwithstanding the largest road–side farm–house in the village had been licensed and beautified; though tiles had been substituted for its old thatch; a blue sign, with yellow letters, fixed over its entrance; and a finger–post erected at the top of the lane, about the middle of which his own tenement stood, directing travellers to The New Inn,—The Chough and Stump still "bore the bell." "Richard Cockle," he would often say, "being twenty years butler to old 'Squire Borfield, ha' made friends among the gentlefolks. The petty sessions is held in his best parlour, now and then; he hath a' got a pair of post–horses, and tidy tits they be, I must say; his house is made post–office; and excise–office, to the tail o' that—for this and the five nearest parishes; he pays for a wine license, and hath two or three gentlevolks may be, once a month, for an hour or two; but not much oftener, as there be few do travel our cross–country road; and he do call one room in his house a tap:—but for all that, and his powdered head to boot, gi' me The Chough and Stump still."

Gough's boast was not altogether without warranty: his comfortable, old–fashioned kitchen, with its bacon–rack, broad hearth, dingy walls, and rude mantel–slab, enriched with strange hieroglyphical scratches, in which his neighbours traced, or affected to trace, the names of their grandfathers, was endeared to the inhabitants of the village;—there were old feelings, and pleasant associations connected with it. Sam Gough was a jolly host, who regaled himself, among his guests, from morning till night; habitual drinking, for a long time, having rendered him, as Abel Harris, the schoolmaster of the village, said, "invulnerable to intoxication:" he not only could, but often did, sing a good old song, and tell a good old story;—never repeating either the one or the other on the same day; for he was orderly in his entertainment, and had his Monday's songs and his Tuesday's songs, as well as his morning stories and his evening jokes: he never sponged upon a customer, but paid his share of the reckoning to his wife, who officiated as mistress, while he appeared to be only a constant guest. His ale was generally "clear as amber, sweet as milk, and strong as brandy." In the tap of The New Inn, which was the name of the rival house, the company generally consisted of the postilion and ostler of the establishment, a few out–door servants from some of the neighbouring gentlemen's houses, and three or four of the gayest, youthful, village bucks: but the elderly and middle–aged men,—"the substantials," as Abel Harris called them, usually congregated, to smoke their evening pipes, round the oak in front of The Chough and Stump, when the weather would permit, or in the kitchen settle, before a blazing fire of logs and turf, when the rustics sat up three or four hours after sunset.

Schoolmaster Abel, although he was one of the pair of parish constables, patronized The Chough and Stump, and grumbled mightily at being obliged to pay five shillings for a dinner, once a year, at the New Inn, with the churchwardens, and other official persons of the parish; which dinner had been instituted solely for the benefit of Richard Cockle, and much against the inclination of several of those, who were almost compelled, on account of their connexion with his wealthy supporters, to attend it. It was at The Chough and Stump that all the village news was to be heard; and if one of its customers were not found at his post, on the settle, at the usual hour, old Gough concluded, that he was either bad, busy, or gone to the rival tap, to glean gossip about the great families, from the servants, in order to retail it, the next night, to the grateful crew at The Chough and Stump.

One winter's evening, although it was neither a Saturday, a holiday, nor a fast day, the settle was not only completely occupied, but several occasional visitors to the old kitchen were closely packed along a narrow bench that ran across the back wall. Many of the poorer inhabitants of the place were lurking about the porch, and several women, with their check aprons thrown over their red and almost frost–bitten elbows, stood peeping in at the window, and eagerly listening to an old dame, who had placed her ear to a little corner from which the glass had been broken, and occasionally repeated what she heard passing within.

"I do pity the mother o' the lad, troth do I," said a woman about twenty–five years of age; "her hath a got but one zon—no more have I—and truth to speak, I do pity her."

"And well thou may'st, Tabby Mudford," said the old dame; "for constable Abel hath just a' told thy husband, that the boy's taken off in a cart, wi' 'Squire Stapleton's coachman a one side o'un, and constable Tucker o' t'other, hand–cuffed, and leg–fast, to the county gaol."

"Poor Meg Braintree! poor soul!" cried several of the women, shearing this, and one or two of them actually began to sob aloud.

"Poor Meg Braintree, forsooth!" exclaimed a little sharp–nosed female, with a high–cauled cap, and leathern stomacher;—"I don't zay no zuch ztuff—not I," added she, in a shrill, disagreeable voice; "it hath a' come home to her now; and I said would, two–and–twenty years agone come Candlemas, when she scoffed and vlouted poor Phil Govier, and took up wi' Zaul Braintree, a'ter she'd a' most a' promised, as I have heard tell, to in Phil. In my mind, he loved her better, worse luck vor un, poor vellow, than ever this Zaul Braintree did, and took on zo for two or dree year a'ter, that there was some that thought he'd never ha' got over 't."

"Vor shame, Aunt Dally," said Tabby Mudford; "Meg Braintree never done you wrong."

"I don't know that," replied Dolly.

"It be true, I ha' heard mother say, you cocked your cap at Zaul, yourself; as you did to many more, though you never could trap any body to have 'ee, aunt; but I never could believe it."

"The vellow did, once upon a time, look up to me," said Dolly, lifting her chin, and curling her thin and slightly–bearded lip; "but I scorned 'un. I wouldn't ha' had un if his skin were stuffed wi' gold."

"And yet you do blame Meg vor scorning Phil Govier! Vor my part,—I were a child, to be zure,—but by what I do recollect of 'em, I'd rather ha' had Zaul, wi'out a zhoe to 's voot, than Philip Govier, if every hair on the head o' un were strung wi' pearls."

"Don't talk to me, Tab," cried her now incensed aunt, flouncing off; "it don't become thee. I do zay it ha' come home to her;—her zon be zent to the county gaol, vor murdering the man whose heart she a'most broke more than twenty year agone:—get over that if you can. It ha' came home to her, and I'll de by it;—wi' her blue clocked ztockings, and putting up her chit of a daughter to smirk wi' the young 'squire!—I ha'n't a' got patience wi' zuch pride."

The supervisor, who was going his rounds, and intended to sleep that night at The Chough and Stump, now rode up, on his sturdy little grey cob; and before he could alight, some of the loiterers about the porch had, in part, acquainted him with the cause of their being assembled round the inn–door. The old man, however, as he said, could make "neither head nor tail" of what he heard; and hastened, as well as his infirmities would allow, into the kitchen. The landlord rose on his appearance, and conducted the spare and paralytic old man, to the post of honour, in the settle, between his own seat and that of the exciseman,—a cunning–looking, thick–set, fat, or, to use an expressive West Country adjective, podgy, little man, between forty and fifty; with a round, sallow, bloated face, begemmed here and there with groups of pimply excrescences, resembling the warts that are occasionally seen on the cheek that is turned to the sun of a wounded pumpkin. One of the exciseman's eyes glared at his beholder, dull and void of expression, while the other was almost concealed beneath its lids;—a circumstance occasioned by an inveterate habit of winking, all his life, at every tenth word, with the latter; which operation be was totally unable to perform with the former.

"Here hath been a sad to–do, sir," said Gough, addressing the supervisor, as soon as the latter was comfortably seated; "a sad to–do, indeed."

"Ah! so I hear, Gough,—so I hear;—but what is it?—No affray with the excise, I hope."

"No—fear of—that, sir," replied the exciseman, winking, and puffing the smoke front his lips thrice as he spoke; "we've no enemies here.—I'll tell you all—about it—sir, when—I have wetted—my lips." He now raised the jug to his mouth, but before he had finished his draught, little Tailor Mudford, who sat by his side, taking advantage of the moment, placed his right elbow on his knee, and still keeping his pipe between his teeth, leaned forward, and bore away the glory of the announcement from the exciseman, by stating, that Philip Govier, 'Squire Stapleton's gamekeeper, had been killed; and young Robert Braintree committed for trial, as the perpetrator of the crime.

"Robert Braintree! Robert Braintree!" calmly repeated the old man; "Preserve us from evil! Haven't I seen him?"

"To be sure you have, sir," replied Gough; "a tall, straight–limbed chap, between eighteen and twenty, and as fine a young fellow as ever stood in shoe–leather. I shouldn't ha' thought it of him."

"I should," said the exciseman; "a down—looking—"

"Ah! I be zorry vor the lad," said Mudford, again interrupting the exciseman, in the brief interval occupied by a puff and a wink; "nobody could zay harm o' un, except that his vather made un go out a poaching wi' un, and so vorth: but a zung in the choir o' Zindays; and though he never were asked so to do, often joined in, wi' the rest o' th' neighbours, to

reap a little varmer's bit o' wheat, or mow a tradesman's whoats;—he ha'
done zo by me, many's the time, wi'out any thing but thanks, and a bit o'
dinner and a drop o' drink, which he never wanted at home. He'd ha' been
the last I should ha' zuzpected."

"But the evidence," said constable and schoolmaster Abel, "the
circumstantial evidence, doth leave no doubt, either in the mind of me, or
the magistrate, of his guilt."

"You be d—d, Yeabel!" cried a bluff old fellow in a corner; "Who be
you, I should like to know?—Marry come up, then times be come to a
vine pass, I trow, when a pig–vaced bit of a constable, two yards long, and
as thin as a hurdle, do zet hi'zelf up cheek–by–jowl wi' the 'squire!—Who
cares vor thy opinion, dost think?"

"Farmer Salter," responded Abel, with affected humility; "I am
educating your son and heir:—you are a freeholder, and ha' got a vote for
the county—"

"I know that well enough, stupid! and zo had my vather avore me, and
so shall my zon a'ter me.—Poor buoay! you ha' often licked un, Yeabel:—
may be you be right—may be you bean't; but this I do know, tho' I ha'n't
a told un zo, that I do vind, upon casting things over, whenzoever I do gie
you a bit ov a clumzy wipe here, at The Chough and Stump, over night,
Jack's zure and zartin to get breeched in your school–room the next day;
now that be odd, yean't it, Gough?"

"Farmer Salter," pursued Abel, as Gough nodded in acquiescence, and
Salter chuckled at what he had said; "I repeat, you are a freeholder:—
you've a slip of land between the two 'squires' estates, upon which you and
your forefathers ha' grazed a cow, raised a crop of wheat, hay and potatoes,
to last 'ee for the year; and built a small edifice for yourselves, and a sty
for your pigs you do wear a looped hat at all times, and, oil Sundays, a
blue coat, wi' a red collar and cuffs, and crown pieces of the reign of King
Jacobus, for buttons; a flowered and flapped waistcoat; leather breeches,
wi' seven–shilling pieces and silver buckles at the knees; and half a pack
o' cards figured wi' colours in each o' your stockings: you do strut tip to
church, just as a 'squire would, and your father did,—whose finery you
ha' saved for such service,— half a century ago:—but you know nothing
either of law or good breeding for all that, farmer Salter."

The freeholder was about to bristle up indignantly when Abel concluded,
but Zachary Tickel, the hereditary herbalist, or, as he denominated himself,

apothecary of the village, whose nick–name was "Bitter–Aloes,"—and there were few of his neighbours who were not as well known by some equally appropriate baptismal of the laity,—took him by the collar, and endeavoured to tranquilize, while he forcibly held him on his seat:—meantime, the super visor inquired what had induced the constable to suspect Robert Braintree of the murder.

"Why, zir," said Mudford, cutting in, as a coachman would express it, before Abel and the exciseman, (each of whom intended to reply,) while the asthmatic constable was cleansing his throat by two or three hems, and the exciseman was puffing out a magazine of smoke, which, at that moment, he had drawn into his mouth, to be retailed and divided into a dozen or twenty whiffs;—"the vact, zir, is this," said Mudford; "the body were vound, dead and stiff, this morning, in the copse, t'other zide o' the hill;— there was a nail or more of znow on the ground, and vootsteps ov a dog and a man were traced vrom the body to Braintree's cottage:— the dog's vootsteps were, likely enough, the vootsteps ov Ponto, a dog belonging to the Braintrees; a sort ov a cross bred pointer, az strong as a bull, and wi' more sense in his tail–end, as the saying is, than many men ha' got in their whole bodies, head and all."

"The shoe–marks, permit me to observe, said Abel, "were decidedly made by the shoes of Bob Braintree:—I've sworn to't, because I compared 'em; and I apprehended him wi' those identical shoes on his feet."

"Now, d'ye hear, volks?—d'ye hear?" exclaimed farmer Salter; "how Yeabel do belabour us wi' vine dixonary words? 'Apprehended,' and 'identical,' quotha!—Why, I should be azhamed to talk zo–vashion. 'Those identical zhoes!' says he;— 'those!'—Bless us, how vine we be!—'Those,' vorsooth —Why doan't the vool zay 'they there zhoes,' like a man?"

Abel cast a glance of contempt on the freeholder, but did not condescend to reply. A brief silence ensued, which was broken by the herbalist; who observed, after throwing himself back in the settle, "Bad bird, bad egg—that's all I've to zay. I bean't zo compassionate, and all that, as some yolk. How hath Zaul Braintree ha' got his living vor eighteen year past, but by smuggling and poaching, and, may be, worse, vor what I know? Why were he discharged by 'Zquire Ztapleton, but vor doing what he should not do? Didn't poor Phil Govier, that's lying dead, when he were under Zaul, detect and prove to the 'zquire, that instead o' Zaul's doing his duty, as game–keeper, he were killing hares upon the zly, and zending 'em to market? And when Phil got Zaul's place, have they ever met without looking at one another like a couple o' dogs that was longing vor a vight, and yet stood off, as though they were aveard to pitch into one another? What d'ye think Braintree hath instilled into Bob, but hatred and malice against Govier?"

"You may talk and talk, old Bitter–Aloes," said Salter; "but vor my part, though the 'zquire believed Govier's story, and turned away Zaul, in a way enough to nettle a parson, I didn't think it quite as it should be. I ha' zeen things o' Phil, what I won't tell ov, now he's gone, as I didn't while he were alive; but if I had to choose, vor all Phil's quiet tongue and humble looks,—which were all zlyness, in my mind,—gi'e me Zaul, I zay."

"Well," quoth Gough, "I say nothing—why should I? But Bob was a good boy; and though he'd noose a hare, or decoy a vlock o' wild ducks, or stalk a covey, I don't think he'd any harm in him. He'd do what Zaul bid him, to be zure, but I don't think Zaul would ever tell him to commit murder; and if I must speak my mind—I don't agree wi' Abel Harris."

"Abel—I must say,"—muttered the exciseman, "the constable, I mean;—he—he's no conjuror."

"I can't make out," growled Salter, "how he came to be made constable, seeing az he's the most uncapable man in the perish. I ha' seed un run, as if 'twere vor his life, when he, thought nobody were nigh, vrom my gander! — Poor Jack! thou'lt suffer, may be, vor this to–morrow; —but I can't help speaking the truth. Yeabel, doan't thee baste un, or dang me if I doan't drash thee!"

"There is one thing," remarked a spare, but hale–looking man, who sat next the herbalist, "one thing, or, may be, a thing or two, I'll make bold to observe, which is, namely, this:—though Zaul Braintree were never over and above vriendly to I—that be nothing—the man's a man—and I do say, the 'zquire were a bit too hard upon Zaul, to turn un off wi'out more nor an hour's notice, and not gi'e un a good character:—and what vor, I wonder?—Because this here Phil Govier, a demure, down–looking twoad, zaid a' poached a bit! A'ter this, what were Zaul to do? Wi'out a character, he couldn't get a zarvice, and a poor man bean't to starve: zo a' poached, and that in downright earnest;— and it strikes I, no blame to un neither."

"Oh! fie! fie!" exclaimed the supervisor; "you should not preach so, friend; the practice of poaching is highly illegal."

"Highly illegal,—indeed, —John,—that is,—James Cobb," said the exciseman, in his usual manner; "we must not hear— this sort of a—thing; must we,—constable?"

"Why, it bean't treason, master exciseman, he it?" asked a tall old fellow, who stood at the end of the settle.

"Do you hear—that?" said the exciseman, turning to his superior; "do you hear that?—and he an earth—stopper,—and gets his bread by—the game laws."

The supervisor looked aside toward the bottom of the narrow table, and while the ensuing conversation went on, took a deliberate view of the earth—stopper's person, apparel, and accoutrements. He was a squalid—looking figure, with half a week's growth of grey beard on his chin and cheeks; the edge of a red woollen night—cap, which he wore under a weather—beaten dog's—hair hat, was strained across his pale, wrinkled brow; his legs were thin, puny, and bent outward in such a manner, that they seemed to have been moulded on the carcase of a horse.

"Well," quoth the earth—stopper, in reply to the exciseman's observation, shouldering his pick—axe and shovel, and lighting the candle in his lanthorn, as he spoke; "I zuppose a man may move his tongue, if a' be a yearth—stopper,—or else what he the use o't to un?—I were one o' the virst to lay hands on young Braintree, and always ha' ztood vorward on zuch like 'casions; but what o' that? I'd help to take up thee, or thy betters by the zide o' thee there, if thee wert zuzpected and accused; but vor all that, I'd speak up my own mind, and say, I thought thee wert innocent, iv so be as I did think thee so—mind me:—and now you ha' put me up, I'll go vurther, and ask 'ee, what business had Phil Govier a' got in the copse that time o' night?"

"Ay, that's true," observed the landlord; "for it be well known the 'squire's strict orders was, that the keepers shouldn't go out o' nights. 'Let the poachers have a little o' their own way,' I have a heard un say;—'I'd rather lose a few head o' game, than ha' blood shed upon the manor; and meetings by night, betwixt poachers and keepers, often do end worse than either one or t'other a' looked for.'"

"It's true as I be here zitting," said Mudford; "that the gamekeeper,—I mean Phil Govier, of course,—had a' got a hare in one pocket, and a cock pheasant in t'other;—I seed 'em myself."

"Come, come;—no ill o' the dead, pr'ythee, now," quoth the herbalist.

"No ill o' the dead!" cried the man who sat next to him; "I do say yea, iv it be truth; and moorauver, in my mind, it be better to say vorty *lies*, even, of them that be gone, than to tell one that may do harm to them that be living. Them wern't the virst Phil pocketed, by night or by day, vor his own profit, as I do think. 'T'ant clear to I, that a' didn't play voul wi' Zaul, long ago;—I wouldn't lie down upon my back and zwear that a' didn't kill the game what he 'cuzed Zaul o' poaching, and zo got Braintree out of his place, and popped into't hi'zelf."

"This is going too far, landlord," said the supervisor.

"Do 'ee think so, sir?" asked Gough, with a knowing look, accompanied by a shake of the head, which finished in an acquiescent nod to the man who sat next the herbalist.

Mudford asked the constable if Saul had seen his son after the committal of the latter. Abel replied, that an interview had been permitted by the magistrate, just previously to Robert's removal; "which interview," added he, "took place in the presence of myself and colleague."

"And what did 'em say?" eagerly inquired three or four of the persons present.

The constable replied, that it would be highly improper for him to divulge all that took place, even if he were capable of so doing; but there was much that he did not hear, and more that he had forgotten. One part of the brief dialogue he perfectly well remembered:—after having whispered for a short time, the youth said aloud, "But I be innocent, vather; you be zure I be."—"Well, well!" replied Braintree, in a low, but nevertheless, audible tone; "zuppose things should go against thee, wou'lt thee die like a man, Bob?"—"I doan't know, vather,—I be but a boy! I'll try, iv it do come to that; I hope it won't, though; vor I be aveard I can't bear it—I can't, truly, vather." "Zo, thee dost call thyself a buoy, dost?" said Saul; "a vellow here within a head as high as I be, and gone eighteen these zix weeks!" "You always tells me I be but a boy." "Well, and zo I do—thee'rt my boy; but a boy to nobody else. But I zay, Bob, wou'lt thee mind now, and speak up to the lord judge just what I told thee?" "Yeas, doan't be aveard." "Ak! but wou'lt tell't cool and zober–vashion, Bob?" "Never you vear," replied Robert;— "bless 'ee, I shall tell't out to un, just as iv I were telling out zixpenn'orth o' ha'pence." "And Bob—" But here Braintree's voice subsided into a whisper again, and Abel heard no more of that part of the conversation.

The parties in The Chough and Stump kitchen now ceased the regular sort of discussion which had hitherto been supported, and talked in couples. The earth–stopper and Abel Harris, by their looks and gestures, seemed to be maintaining a warm debate; the herbalist crossed over and took a place next the supervisor, which tailor Mudford relinquished in his favour, and sat down by the side of farmer Salter. So many persons speaking together, had not, for some time, been heard in The Chough and Stump; but though his customers made a great noise, as Gough observed to the exciseman, they drank but little. This was, indeed, the case; for the interest created by the subject of their discourse, made them almost forget their cups. Each of the speakers grew louder in his tone, in order to make himself heard and understood, amid the "hubbub," by his listening neighbour; and thus the general noise was increased to such a degree, that the exciseman had already taken up his empty mug to strike the table, and call "order," when, in an instant, every tongue was motionless, and every eye turned toward the door. A man, on the autumnal side of the prime of life, exceeding the middle stature, with rather handsome features, had just entered. He was dressed in a round, grey, frock coat, a deer–skin waistcoat, corduroy small–clothes, and jean gaiters. His frame was athletic, but by no means clumsy; he looked calmly about him, or, perhaps, rather affected to do so; for, as the herbalist afterwards remarked, his lips appeared as if they had just been blanched with boiling water. A very large, stout–built, liver–coloured dog, stood before him, wagging its tail, and looking up in his master's face, as the latter remained, for a mo motionless, and with his eyes seeking for a vacant place on the settle. Every seat had its tenant, and no one moved for the newly–arrived guest, or spoke either to him or to any other person present.

"Why, volks! you do all zeem dazed ov a zudden!" said the man, ironically; and then immediately assuming an angry expression of countenance, he turned to the landlady, who had just entered the kitchen, and, in a sharp, surly tone, called for "a pint o' drink."

"I ha' been trying to squeeze room for thee, Zaul," said the landlord, addressing his new guest; "but I can't."

"Don't trouble thyself, Gough," said farmer Salter, from the opposite side of the settle; "I be vor home, and Braintree can take my corner in a minute."

"Thankye, master Zalter," replied Saul; "but Abel Harris ha' just stepped out, and, may be, won't come back; zo I'll zit down in his place; and iv a' do return, I can but gie't up to un again; and by that time, you can vinish your pipe wi' comfort."

So saying, Braintree took possession of a nook in the settle, which Abel had quitted, in consequence of the landlady having beckoned him out, while Gough was speaking to Saul. Two or three of the guests attempted to strike out new subjects for conversation, but their efforts were ineffectual; and when Dame Gough came in, with Saul's ale, she found her customers, who had lately been so clamorous, silent as statues. Braintree lifted the cup to his lips, but immediately placed it on the table again, without swallowing a spoonful.

"Why, what's the matter, Zaul?" said Gough; "have a mad dog bit 'ee, that you do gasp and heave at the liquor so?"

"There were a bit o' hop got in my mouth," replied Saul; "and your yeale bean't zo good to-night,' I think, as 'twere;—ha'n't it got a strawberry smack?"

"No, no, Zaul; your mouth be out o' taste wi' trouble,—that be it;—there's no fault in the ale. You do want comfort in a closer compass; and if you'll ha' a drop o' Hollands, my wife will give 'ee some and welcome. Though I don't sell spirits, I can't help Dame Gough's keeping a bottle in her bureau;—it stops her tooth-ache."

"You be cruel good, master Gough," replied Saul; "and I do thank 'ee vor't; but I don't like to drink in a public-house, wi'out paying my penny for a landlord's penn'orth."

"Oh! that be folly," said Gough; "but come, gi'e me your pint o' drink, and I'll treat you wi' a glass o' Hollands.—Dame, bring in a thimble-full."

Dame Gough bustled out, and soon returned with a small old-fashioned tea-cup, full of the liquor. Saul took the cup, and so far forgot his manners, as to swallow the spirits it contained, without a word, or even a nod, to Gough, or any of his guests. A dead silence succeeded.

"Sharpish weather vor the young wheats," at length observed Salter.

"Main and sharp!" was the reply of the herbalist; and another pause took place.

"I ha'n't a' zeed Jacob Wall lately;" was the next observation made: it came from the lips of tailor Mudford, but no one honoured it with a reply.

Braintree now began to feel that he was in an unpleasant situation; and guessing on what subject the minds of those about him were brooding, he observed, with a sigh, "A bad job this, o' mine, neighbours!"

"Bad, indeed, Braintree!" replied Gough; "but I hope your son may get over it!"

"Hope, did 'ee zay, landlord? why, d'ye think there be any vear on't, then?"

"Excuse me, friend," observed the supervisor; "I am a stranger to you; but, in my opinion, that is,—speaking candidly,—I'm sorry to say— remember I've no ill–will toward your son—nor, understand me, do I wish to bear on a bruised reed; but it's folly to buoy a man up with false hopes;—the case is, if what I've heard be true, most decisive against the young man."

"And what have 'ee heard, old gentleman?—what have 'ee heard, zir?"

"That, Saul,"—said the exciseman, "that, it is—needless to repeat;—but the shoe–marks,—Saul—"

"Well, and what o' them?" interrupted Braintree; "mightn't my zon ha' gone that way avore Govier were killed? or mightn't he ha' vound un dead, and come whoam straight, intending to tell the news az zoon az he axed I how a' should act?"

"True, Zaul, true," replied Salter, who had not yet departed; "it do zeem ztrange that no vootsteps were vound in the snow 'proaching towards the zpot."

"I can easily account for that, I think," said the supervisor, with a smile of self–complacency: "the snow—"

"But hark to this," cried Saul, again interrupting the old man; "hark to this:—how be we to know, that they what zaid they round the body wer'n't the criminals, eh?"

"Lord bless us and zave us, Zaul!" exclaimed the little tailor, starting up; "Bless us, Zaul! Why, 'twere I, good now, what raised the hue and cry. I were coming vrom varmer Butt's, vive mile off, where I a' been thee days at work, making a coat; I'd a' started avore 'were day, zo as to get to work about Jack Blake's new suit, what he's a going to be married in o' Zinday;— and zharp doings it will be to vinish it as 'tis:—zo I took the path through the copse; because it zaves a mile, you do know; and anan, my little dog, rin into the hazels and back again in a minute, barking as iv he'd a' zeen a ghost. I were a bit vrightened, you may judge, vor I'd

a' got my zilver watch, and half–a–crown, (my dree days' wages,) wi'
ten shillings bezides, what the varmer had paid me vor a pig he bought
o' me last Zinday vortnight, when he comed over to church. Well, and
anan, my little dog, rin into the copse again, and come back growling
worse nor avore. Thirdly and lastly, I patted the back o' un, and away he
rin again, and when he overtook me,—d'ye mind?—by the light 'o the
moon, I zeed there were blood upon the nose o' un!—Wi' that, I and
the dog rin vit to break our necks, 'till we got whoam. Zo then I raised
the hue and cry, and Phil's body were vound but I had no more hand in
the death o' un than you, Zaul. I can handle a reap–hook, or a needle,
wi' one here and there, but I never vired a gun off in my life—wish I
may die if I did!"

"Well, well, Mudford," said Braintree, advancing toward the tailor; "I
didn't know 'twere thee; gi'e us thy hand;—there—we be vriends, bean't
us?"

"I do hope zo, Zaul Braintree," replied the still terrified tailor; "but you
shouldn't—"

"There, do 'ee hold your tongue and zit down," interrupted Saul: "I
were wrong but,—d'ye mind?—Bob be my zon; and if counzel can zave
un, he sha'n't lack; vor I'll zell my zhirt to zee un righted."

Braintree had scarcely reached his seat again, when constable Abel, pale,
almost breathless, looking very important, and bearing his staff of office
in his hand, strode into the kitchen, and immediately laid hands on Saul.
"Braintree, thou'rt my prisoner," said he; "aid and assist, if need be—every
body—but especially you, earth–stopper,—in the King's name."

Saul was paralysed; he stared vacantly at Abel, and before he could
recover his self–possession, the dexterous constable had handcuffed, and
almost completed the task of tying his right wrist to the left arm of the
earth–stopper.

"Thy prisoner, Yeabel!" at length uttered Braintree; "thou bee'st joking,
zure!—Dowl ha' me if I can make out—"

"You'll make it out well enough by–and–by, Saul," interrupted Abel, as
he pursued his task of knitting the earth–stopper fast to Saul; "I ha' been
sent for by the 'squire, and I've got his warrant. Master Cockle, of The
New Inn, churchwarden of the present year, ha' been making inquiries;
and things ha come out, Saul, that do look black against thee."

"What be 'em, Yeabel?—What be 'em, pr'ythee?"

"Why, *imprimis*," replied the constable, pompously, "it is well known, Ponto never followed anybody but thee—nothing could make him do so; and he and Bob never were friends. Surgeon Castle saith, that the shot went horizontally into Govier's forehead; and as he was not above five feet six, the gun that killed him must have been fired from the shoulder of a man as tall as you be:—if Bob had done it, seeing that he's shorter than Phil were, the shot would ha' gone almost upward; but, no, they didn't:—lastly, and most formidably, Saul, as the magistrate saith, the marks in the snow were printed there, by shoes made right–and–left fashion; and the right–foot shoe being marked o' the left–foot side, and the left o' t'other,—it don't seem likely they could ha' been worn by the feet they were made for.—So now you do know what you've a' got to answer, come along quietly."

In a few minutes The Chough and Stump kitchen was utterly deserted even Gough himself followed his customers, who, without exception, accompanied the constable and his prisoner, to Stapleton Hall, the magistrate's residence. After a brief examination, Saul was ushered into an apartment, three stories above the ground floor, called "The Wainscot–room;"—which, on account of its peculiar situation and construction, although it had once been used for better purposes, was then appropriated to the reception of those who happened to be under the ban of the law, previously to their discharge, on finding "good and sufficient main–pernors" for their appearance at the ensuing assizes or sessions, or their removal to the county gaol, according to the nature of the offence. For the honour of the village it is proper to remark, that "The Wainscot–room" was but seldom occupied. It was there Saul had, only an hour before, taken leave of Robert, who was now far on his road to an accused felon's cell. Braintree had just been told by the magistrate that, early on the ensuing morning, he must follow his son; but he suffered a strong rope to he fastened round his waist, by a slip–knot, and tied to an iron bar in the chimney, not only without murmuring or resisting, but actually joking with those who performed the operation. Although Mr. Stapleton considered that it was impossible for the prisoner to escape from his temporary prison, yet for better security, on account of the crime with which Saul was charged, he ordered the constable to keep watch, either in, or at the door of the room, during the night.

Before the earth–stopper quitted "The Wainscot–room" to go on his solitary task, Saul had made him promise to acquaint Martin Stapleton, the 'squire's only son, that he, Braintree, earnestly desired to see the young gentleman, before he went to bed. The old man so well performed his promise, and urged Braintree's request to young Stapleton with such warmth, that in less than an hour Martin entered the room.

"Abel," said he to the constable, as he came in, "you may go down stairs; I'll remain with Braintree while you get some thing for supper."

Abel, "nothing loath," tripped down to the hall, and Martin, who was a fine young man, just verging on manhood, walked up, with a sorrowful countenance and a heart full of grief, toward the man, under whose humble roof he had passed some of his happiest hours. Martin's mother died in giving him birth, and Saul's wife had been his nurse. Although disgraced by 'Squire Stapleton, Saul Braintree had ever bean a favourite companion of young Martin, not only on account of his intimate acquaintance with those sports in which Martin delighted, but because Saul had always testified a fondness for him from his boyhood upward; and, besides these attractions, the poacher's cottage contained a magnet, in the person of his pretty daughter, Peggy, which often drew Martin beneath its roof, when his father thought he was otherwise occupied.

"Well, Master Martin," said Saul, as the young 'squire approached; "here you be at last! I were vool enow to think, I shouldn't ha' been here vive minutes avore you'd ha' come, if it were only to zay 'How are 'ee, Zaul?'— But there, why should I grumble? Hit a deer in the shoulder, and then put the dogs on his scent, and what will the herd do?—Why, vly vrom un, to be zure, and no vools, neither;—but come, vine preaching doant cure corns:—virst and voremost.—will 'ee get me a drop o' brandy, Master Martin?—I be zo low az the grave, az you may guess; get me a thimble–vull, and then we'll talk a bit."

"I have brought my shooting–flask Saul," replied Martin; "there is not much left in it."

"Ah! this be kind!—this be good of 'ee, Master Martin. What, you thought how it would be with me? You knowed me long enow, to be zure that I should want summat to cheer me up, did 'ee? Never mind the cork, Master Martin," continued Saul, as Martin, with a trembling hand, fruitlessly endeavoured to extract the cork; "put it betwixt my teeth; and pull; I'll warrant I do hould vast enow; or knock off the neck o' un against my hand cuffs. What, it bean't your leather vlask, be it? Odd! cut un open wi' a knife.—I be a choaking for it, Master Martin;—I be, truly."

By this time, Martin had pulled out part of the cork, and thrust the remainder of it through the neck. He handed the flask to Saul, who gulped down one half of its contents in a few seconds.

"There is not enough to divide," observed Martin, "you may as well finish it."

"No, thank'ee, Master Martin," replied Braintree, returning the flask; "you'll want a drop for yourself presently."

"I, Saul!"

"Ay! you, Martin!—Look thee, lad,—there be times when the best ov us would be glad ov it. Brandy be a God–send; but we don't use it—that is, zuch as I be, doan't—as we should. There be times, I tell 'ee, when it be needed."

"That's true enough," said Martin, endeavouring to force a smile; "I have often been glad of it, after a three hours' tramp through the stubble and turnips, on a cold day, under a heavy double–barrelled gun, with a belt brimful of shot, and no birds in my pocket."

"That were for thy body, lad; but thou'lt want it, anan, for thy soul. I be gwain to vright—to terrify thee!—Thou'st a tightish heart, and thou'st need ov it now. Mind me, Martin, I bean't romancing. It ha' been smooth roads and no turnpikes wi' thee all thy life; there's a bit o' rough coming, thee doesn't dream of."

"Good God! Braintree! your manner alarms me!—What do you mean?"

"Martin!—I zuppoze thee thinks, I ought to be obliged to thee vor coming to me;—vor bringing a man accused as I be, brandy,—but I bean't. If thee hadst not a' come, I'd ha' brought thee, though a waggon and zix horses were pulling thee t'other vay. There's my hand; I ha' put it to thee through a hole in the window at whoam, a'ter thou'st a' wished me good night, and the door were vast;—I do put it out to thee now through a velon's wristband—wou'st take it?"

"Excuse me, Braintree!—I would do all I could; —I have even gone beyond the line that a sense of propriety dictates: but you must not take such advantage of the familiarity which commenced when I was a child, and has since, through peculiar circumstances, continued;—you must not, I say, presume upon that, to ask me, to shake hands with a man—"

"Accused ov murder! that's what thee means, yean't it?" asked Saul; and his brows were knit, and his lips slightly quivered, as he spoke. Martin stood silent.

"Then I'll tell thee what, lad," pursued Saul, vehemently; "that stomach o' thine shall come down:—I'll *make* thee!"

"Braintree," said the young man seriously, but in considerable agitation; "what do you mean by this?—Are you mad?"

"Noa, noa;—not yet, not yet;—but handy to it.—Not mad!" exclaimed Saul, striking the iron, which bound his wrists, against his head; "but don't trouble about I, lad; look to thy own wits, young chap,"

"Really, Saul, I cannot put up with a continuance of this:—you are not drunk; I know it by your manner. I have never seen you thus before. I pity you; and pray to God, that you may obtain a deliverance, by the verdict of a jury."

"I'll never be tried!" exclaimed Saul in aloud whisper.—"I'll never be tried! Zaul Braintree ha'n't kept his wits brooding all these years, to be caught like a quail, and ha' his neck twisted! No, no; they ha' brought me to the wrong gaol for that; it's like putting a rat in a fishing-net."

"I don't think, Saul, there is any probability of your escaping," said young Stapleton; "and I advise you not to make the attempt."

"Don't talk to I.—Ha'n't I, when you was a buoy, no bigger round than my thigh,—ha'n't I heard you read, when you zat a-top o' my knee, about the mouse gnawing the lion out o' the znare:—ha'n't I?—Ah! you do recollect, do 'ee?"

"I do, I do, too well, Saul," replied Martin, as a tear trickled down his cheek; "and I am sorry—I am grieved—I feel more than you can imagine to see you here. But what has the fable to do with you?"

"Every thing—I shall get out—strength can't do it for me, but—"

"Saul Braintree, I now see what you are driving at," said Martin; "but do not flatter yourself with so vain a hope. You are accused of a crime, of which, I hope—nay, I think—you wilt prove yourself guiltless: but though I am but young, I feel that I ought not, dare not, cannot interfere between you and the laws of your country. My father—"

"Now, doan't 'ee preach; doan't 'ee make a zimpleton o' yourzelf, I tell 'ee:—but, can any body hear us?—be the constable nigh?" eagerly inquired Saul, dropping his voice to a low tone.

"No," said Martin, "you may be sure of that; or I would not have remained, thus long, exposed to the madness or insolence of your remarks;—I know not which to call it."

"Why, thou jackanapes!" said Saul, sneeringly, though his eye, at the same time, glared with an expression of the utmost fury on young Stapleton; "thou young jackanapes! dost thee tell I about insolence?—Thee shalt down on thy knees for this."

"Braintree, good night," said Martin, moving toward the door: "I did not expect this conduct."

"What, thee'rt gwain to leave me, then? Zurely, thee bean't in earnest?" Martin had, by this time, reached the door, and was evidently determined on quitting the room. The prisoner, perceiving his intention, immediately assumed a tone of supplication. "Now, doan't thee go, Master Stapleton," said he; "doan't thee!—do come back—do hear me, if it be but vor a minute. I were wrong, I were, indeed. Doan't thee leave me yet—doan't thee—doan't thee—doan't thee! Come back, Master Martin;—on my knees I do but of thee:—do come back—for Peggy's zake."

Martin withdrew his hand from the door and returned. "Saul," said he, as he approached, "I never felt till now, the truth of what you have often told me, namely,—that if I encouraged an affection for your daughter, I should rue it. I do now, most bitterly. Poor—poor Peggy!"

"Ah! poor girl!—Come nearer, Master Martin—poor Peggy!" "Now, Saul, I'll hear you for one minute only; and this must shall be our last interview—unless—"

"Vor one minute, didst say?" exclaimed Saul triumphantly, clutched the wrist of Martin in his powerful grasp; "thou thalt hear me vor an hour;—thou sha' not quit me, till thou and I do leave this place, hand–in–hand, together. Ah! thou mayst struggle; but thou knowest the old zaying, A Braintree's grip is zafe as a zmith's vice:—if thee wast a horse I'd hold thee."

"Scoundrel! villain!" exclaimed Martin, endeavouring, with his might, to release himself; "let go your hold, or I'll—"

"Ah! do—hit me now, do—now I ha' got the handcuffs on; any child might gi'e Zaul Braintree a zlap o' the face now. Hit me—why doan't 'ee,—wi' your t'other hand? There's no danger o' my drashing 'ee vor't. Hit me—doan't 'ee unclench your vist —here's my head—hit me, Master Martin."

"For heaven's sake, Saul!" exclaimed young Stapleton, "if you ever esteemed me, let me go!—If you do not, I must alarm the house."

"Oh! if you did, Martin!" replied Saul, "you'd ruin us both. I wouldn't have 'ee do so, vor the hope I've a' got of living a week over the next zpring assize. If you did 'larm the house, Martin, you'd drop from a young 'zquire into a poacher's zon, and hang your own vather to boot."

"Hang my father!"

"Ah! doan' 'ee look round the room that vashion:—you be zure there be no one listening?"

"Positive!"

"Then turn your eyes here, lad:—Meg Braintree was more than your nurse.—She's your own mother!—Now I'll let go thy wrist; for I've got a grip at thy heart. There, thee bee'st vree! Why doesn't go?—I doan't hold thee: go, if thee canst."

"Saul, you surely are not in your senses!"

"May be I bean't, for trouble turns a man's brain;—but you be, bean't 'ee? You can't ha' vorgot how often I ha' pushed Bob off my knee to put you upon it. Why did I do so?—'cause thee wert my zon, and he were 'Zquire Ztapleton's.—Haven't I hugged thee up to my breast, until thee'st a' squalled wi' the squeeze, when nobody was by?—I'd a grudge against the 'zquire;—why, thee know'st well enough;—zo I made Meg, who nursed 'ee both, change buoy for buoy. I thought to ha' made a vine vellow o' my zon at the 'zquire's expence, little thinking I should ever want 'un to zave my life. I thought, when you was a man, to ha' comed up to 'ee and zaid, "Zquire, I be your vather,—zo and zo were the case,—make me comvortable, or I'll be a tell-tale.' That were my project; to zay nothing of having a bit of revenge upon the 'zquire!—Lord, Lord! how I ha' chuckled to myzelf thinking on't. Can any man zay I ever used Bob like my own son? Answer me that. D—n un! I always hated un, vor his vather's zake: though the lad's a good lad, and, if he were mine, I should love un;—and I do, zometimes, I dunno' why:—but I ha' drashed un,—and while I were drashing un, I've a'most thought, I were drashing the vather o' un. But I ha' done un a good turn when he didn't know it. I ha' kissed un when he were asleep,—a'most upon the zly, like, even to myzelf. And when he broke his leg, I tended upon un, as you do know; and he's a' loved me zo, ever since, that I ha' scores and scores o' times been sorry for it; for I do hate un because he's the son of his vather:—but what be the matter wi' 'ee? What's amiss? Why d'ye stare and glower zo?"

"Saul Braintree," said Martin, "whether your words are true or not—and what you mention, I have observed—you have made me the most wretched being on earth; for whatever comes to pass, I must still suspect—Margaret, my heart tells me, may be —Oh! that horrid *may*, which is worse than certainty—may be —nay, I cannot pronounce it! Oh! Saul! if I could but believe you—if I could but make up my mind, even to the worst, it would be a comfort."

"Martin Braintree,—for that be your name," said Saul, "didn't I warn 'ee about Peggy? Didn't I—when I saw you were getting vond of her—didn't I try to offend 'ee, zo az to keep 'ee from coming to our cottage? Didn't I insult 'ee? — but you wouldn't take it."

"You did, Saul, grossly insult me; but my love,—perhaps, my accursed love,—made me overlook it. What a gulph of horror is opened before me! Peggy my sister! and you—you my father!—It cannot—it is not so, Saul. Unsay what you have said, and I will save you."

"I won't unsay it; it's out now, and I can't help it. If thou still doubt'st, Martin, go down and ask my wife—ask Meg; if thou still doubt'st, lad,—ask thy own heart—young as thee bee'st —if a vather could let a son be hung for a crime of which thic zon bean't guilty!"

"And is Robert innocent, then?"

"Ay, lad, as thou art."

"But you—surely you—"

"Take a drop of brandy, and I'll tell thee all, buoy: thee'rt my own vlesh and blood, and I'll talk to ther as I would to my own heart. Now, do 'ee take the flask; halve it, and gi'e me the rest; —or take it all, if thee dost veel qualmish.—I be zad enough, but don't stint thyself, Martin."

The youth swallowed a mouthful of the liquor, and returned to Saul, who, after draining the contents, resumed the conversation. "Martin," said he, "Robert, poor lad, is az innocent az a lamb; and I know it."

"And will you—can you, then, permit him to—"

"Hold thy tongue, buoy, and let me speak. Rob is innocent, but he's James Ztapleton's zon; and if I were to take his head out of the halter, and put my own into it, it wouldn't be many miles off self–murder. Rob is innocent; for he never harmed a worm, except I made un do 't; and he can go up to his God without a blush:—I can't—may be, he couldn't, if he came to my years; for there's no one do know what thay happen to the best ov us. I be zure I little thought, a score of years ago, when I were tip–top man here, and had az good a character as any body in the country, and there wer'n't a bad wish against mortal in my heart, that I should ever be tied up here, where I be, accused of any crime vhatzoever—much less murder: but you see I be; and there's no knowing, as I said avore, what any ov us may come to. Bob's zure of peace hereafter; and it be well vor un. I'd be hung willingly, to–morrow, if I were in the like case; but I bean't. Oh! Martin, thy buoy! I ha' much to answer vor. I be brave, people zays, and zo I be; but there bean't a man within a days' ride, so aveard of death as I be; and I'll tell'ee why:—it's because I ha' been such' a viend—zuch a wretch, ov late years.—I wouldn't die vor all the world. I do want time vor repentance! and I must ha' it at any price!—Therefore, Bob must die vor me; and, may be, I does un a good turn; at least, I do think so,— by sending un to his grave avore he hath had temptation to be zinful."

"Your doctrine is most atrocious!" exclaimed Martin. "Oh! why—why was I reserved, for this? From what you say, Saul, hear—"

"That I killed Phil Govier?"

"I hope not."

"Hoping's no good:—he hit I over the head with the butt–end of his gun;—zee, here's the mark;—and when I came to myzelf, he was gwain to do't again; zo I ztepped back three paces, lifted my piece, and blew out his brains—bang!—Ay, Martin, it were your vather did it; and 'Zquire Ztapleton's zon must zuffer vor it. I thought I had managed capitally; but things ha' come out I didn't dream of. Iv I be tried, I may be vound guilty, and that won't do. Bob's zure to zuffer, poor lad!—But I must not be tried."

"But how do you make it appear that Robert is guiltless, when the proofs are so strong against him?"

"Ah! that be my deepness! I hope I zhall be pardoned vor't. I'll tell 'ee just how 'twere. Bob were getting to bed, and he knowed I were gwain through the village, up the hill, toward the copse t'other zide o' the Nine Acres:—I'd a' promised a brace o' pheasants to Long Tom, the mail coachman, the day bevore,— he'd got an order vor 'em,—and in, the copse I were zure o' vinding 'em, but nowhere else: zo Bob zays to I, 'Vather,' zays he, 'I wish you'd take my t'other pair o' zhoes and leave 'em at Dick Blake's, as you do go along, and get he to heel–tap 'em for me.' Zo, I zaid I would; and zure enough, I took 'em; but Dick were a–bed when I come by, and I went on, with the zhoes in my pocket, to the copse. When I got there, I looked about, and Ponto,—you know Ponto—he'll point up—ay, if 'twere a–top of a elm, as well as under his nose in a stubble,—Ponto stood; and just above my head, on the lowest branch of a beech, there were perched a cock pheasant wi' two hens,—one o' each zide o' un—all dree within reach. I hit the cock and one o' the hens down wi' the barrel o' my gun, and just as I were pouching 'em, up come the keeper. Phil and I, as every one knows, hadn't been good vriends vor twenty long years. Zummat occurred betwixt us, and Phil was zoon on the ground under me. I wasn't as cool as I should be over a rasher of bacon—you may guess; but up he got again, and laid the butt–end of his piece over my head. I were stunned for a second, but when I came to, he'd a' got his gun by the muzzle, wi' the butt up over his head, and aiming at me again. If he'd a hit me, I shouldn't ha' been talking to you here now; zo I ztepped back, and to zave my own life, did as I told 'ee. When I zeed un draw up his legs, and then quiver all over just avore a' died, all the blood in my body were turned into cold water. I thought I should ha' shivered to death; and there I stood, staring at Phil, where a' laid, as if I were 'mazed!—Just avore this, it begun to znow, and while I were looking at Phil, it thickened zo, that I were a'most zole–deep in it; zo then I begun to cast a how I should act, to zave myzilf vrom zuspicion. While I were thinking, the znow stopped valling; and, thinks I, they'll vind out who 'twere by the vootmarks; and if there were no vootmarks to zuspect any one else, they'd guess 'twere I, vor vifty reasons: zo I took Bob's zhoes out o' my pocket, put mine in their place, squeezed my veet into the lad's zhoes as well as I could, walked straight whoam, and went to bed without a soul hearing me. I were wicked enough to put Bob's zhoes close under his bed avore I went to my own; but I hope even that will be vorgiven me:—zo Bob were taken up, and most likely will be vound guilty, upon the evidence o' the zhoes. But vor vear of accidents, Martin, you must contrive to let me out; vor I won't be tried, d'ye mind? therefore, you must manage zo as. I may 'scape, lad; and once out, I'll war'nt they doan't catch I again."

Martin Stapleton stood, with his eyes earnestly fixed on Saul, for nearly a minute after the latter had finished his story of the death of Philip Govier; his faculties were benumbed by what he had heard; and he probably would have remained much longer motionless and speechless, had not Saul seized him with both hands, and given him two or three violent shakes. "Come, come," said he, "doan't go to sleep like a horse, standing up!—This bean't a time for dozing!—Odd! if I'd a' got poor Bob here, I should ha' been vree half an hour ago. He'd ha' zet vire to the house, and come and ha' pulled me out o' the vlames, by this time, if he couldn't gi'e me my liberty any other way."

"And yet, *you*, Saul," said Martin reproachfully, "you scruple not to sacrifice him to save yourself"

"What be that to thee?—He'd do as I tell 'ee, because I be his vather—that is, he thinks zo. I ha' done what I did do, because he yean't my zon;—but *thee* bee'st, Martin—*thee* bee'st—and thee knows it;—thy heart tells thee I ha'n't been lying to thee:— thee'rt my zon,—and I do expect that thou'lt do thy duty; thou canst do't, and no harm come to thee. Bob would risk all vor me, though I ha'n't been the best o' vathers to un."

"What would you have me do?" asked Martin, rather petulantly. "How shall I act?—What do you wish of me?"

"Just to let I get t'other zide o' these walls," replied Saul; "I doan't care how;—I leave that to you;—choose your own way; it doan't much matter to I,—doan't 'ee zee?—zo as I gets out. Why, you'd a' married Peggy, if zo he as I'd ha' let 'ee—wouldn't 'ee, now?—in spite ov old Ztapleton, and the whole of your ztiff–backed aunts—wouldn't 'ee, now? answer me that."

"I should—I should:—but mention it no more; you make my blood curdle."

"Well, then," pursued Saul, heedless of the passionate request of Martin; "you see, I'd no vear ov your seducing the girl; and you can't think I should ha' put up a gate against my daughter's being a young 'squire's wife—if that young 'squire weren't what he were."

"Talk to me no more on this subject:—I will—I do believe all you have said; only, I beseech you, don't—don't dwell on this," exclaimed Martin, wiping large drops of "the dew of mental anguish" from his brow.

"Well, well, Martin! cheer up, lad," said Saul, fondling the youth; "cheer up, and I won't:—but, I say, how shall we act?"

"Oh! I know not.—In assisting you to escape I become an accessary to Robert's death;—and if I refuse—"

"You do hang your vather," interrupted Braintree; "an awkward place vor a body to stand in, Martin;—but blood's thicker than water;—I be your vather, and he yean't even one o' your kin. I won't dreaten 'ee wi' blabbing and telling who you be, on my trial."

"I care not, Saul, if you did."

"I know,—I know;—but I doan't dreaten 'ee wi't, doan't 'ee—mind?—Keep znug, and be a 'zquire."

"Indeed, I shall not. I will tell the whole story to–morrow; and if I can save poor Robert—"

"If 't'an't at my expense, do save un, and I'll thank 'ee; but I think it yean't possible. As to your up and telling old Ztapleton who you be, that will be silly ov 'ee;—but it be your business;— I've put 'ee into a good nest, and if you do throw yourself out on't, 't'ean't my fault; my intention were good. Howsomever, Martin, gi'e me dree hours' law; and doan't give tongue, and so get a hue and cry a'ter me, avore I can get clear."

At this moment a loud tapping was heard at the door; Martin started, and exclaimed,—"If that should be my father!"

"Vather, indeed!" said Saul; "you do vorget yourself; you must ha' lost your wits, to be vrighted zo–vashion; you ha'n't a'vastened the door, have 'ee? and your vather, as you do call un, would hardly be polite enough to knock. There yean't much ceremony used wi a prisoner. Why doan't 'ee say, 'come in?'"

Before Martin could utter the words, the door was opened, and a fair, curly–headed youth, who was Martin's immediate attendant and frequent companion, peeped in, and said, in a loud whisper, —"Master Martin! the 'squire is inquiring for you: where will you please to be?—in the fen, setting night–lines for eels, or up at Gorbury, seeing the earths well stopped? The fox–hounds throw off at Budford Copse, to–morrow, you know;—or shall I say you're here, or where?"

"You need not tell any lies about the matter, Sam, thank you," said Martin; "I shall be in the parlour almost directly."

"Very well, sir," replied Sam. "I wish you'd been down in the hall just now, though. Constable Abel has been making a speech about drink being the beginning of every thing bad; and, he says true, Abel must be ripe for mischief, for he got three parts gone before he had done; and he's coming up stairs with the brass top of his long staff downard.—Eh! Why, this can't be he, surely, coming at this rate?"

A series of sounds had struck Sam's ear which resembled those three or four persons running up stairs in a hurry, and then galloping along the passage toward the place where he stood. A moment had scarcely elapsed, from the time he had done speaking, when the door was burst wide open, and Ponto, the prisoner's dog, dashed into the room. He had been howling round the house for a considerable time; and probably watched for an opportunity of stealing in to join his master. He flew toward Saul; gambolled round him; leaped up to his face, and exhibited, by his looks, his low barks, and his actions, the joy he felt at being again in the presence of his master.

As soon as Sam, by the order of Martin, had retired from the door, Saul pointed to the dog, and, without uttering a word, gazed reproachfully at young Stapleton.

"I understand you," said Martin; "but you don't know what I may do yet; therefore, pray, spare me those looks."

"Wou'lt do't, then—wou'lt do't?" eagerly asked Saul: "Ah! I knew thee wouldst. Ponto yean't my zon, and yet—but, odd! there bean't a minute to lose. Abel will be here directly. Ponto, my dog, thou'lt save us a mort o' trouble. Tell 'ee what, Martin,—only cut the rope, and go to bed. Never mind the cuffs;—cut the rope vor me, and I be zafe:—out wi' your pocket-knife,—make haste," continued Saul, in a hurried tone, as Martin searched his pockets with a tremulous hand;—"here, lad, let I veel vor un—here a' is—now cut—cut through: gi'e me dree hours' law, as I told 'ee, and then do as you like.—Why, lad! thee'lt be a month; I'd ha' cut down an oak by this time."

"What have I done?" exclaimed Martin, as he, at length, separated the rope.

"Done! why, done your duty," was Saul's reply; "kneel down there, Martin, and take a vather's blessing vor't;—a vather's blessing, lad, let un be ever zo bad a man, won't do thee hurt." Martin, almost unconsciously, knelt, and the murderer, placing his hand on the young man's head, solemnly and most affectionately blessed him.

When Abel entered, Martin had nearly reached the door; he pushed the constable aside, and rushed out of the room, in a manner that perfectly amazed the old man. "Well!" said he, as he endeavoured to strut, but in fact, staggered in rather a ludicrous manner, toward the prisoner;—"if that's behaviour to a parochial functionary—if any jury will say it is—I'll resign my staff of office. What do you think, Saul?"

"Bad manners, Yeabel;—bad manners, in my mind," replied Braintree; "but he be vexed like;—and I'll tell 'ee why:—I ha' been trying to coax un over to help me out o' the house."

"You ha'n't, surely, Saul!"

"I tell 'ee I have, then—why not? Wouldn't you? answer me that!—but the young dog revuzed; zo then I abuzed un, and a' left me in a pet. But, I zay, Yeabel, you be drunk, or handy to't, bean't 'ee?—You shouldn't do that! It's wrong ov 'ee, Yeabel: every man, in my mind, should do his duty; and you bean't doing yours to get voggy wi' stout October, when you've a–got a prisoner in hand."

"None of your sneering, Saul; I am *compos* and capable," said Abel.

"You bean't, Yeabel! upon my life, you bean't!" replied Saul; "you shouldn't do so—no, truly. Why, now, suppose I were to 'scape."

"Escape!" exclaimed Abel, cocking his hat; "elude my vigilance!—come, that's capital!"

"Why, you'll vall asleep avore half the night be over."

"What! sleep upon my post!—never, Saul,—never."

"You'll prance up and down there all night, I'll war'nt, then, and zo keep me from getting a bit of rest:—you be aveard to lie down, ay, or zit."

"I am afraid of nothing and nobody," replied Abel, indignantly; "and you know it, neighbour. Braintree: but no sneering of yours, will tempt me; I'm up to thee, Saul; so be quiet;—or say your prayers. I'm never so fit to serve my King and country, or the parochial authorities, as when my wits are sharpened by an extra cup or two."

"Or dree, I z'pose?" added Saul.—"Poor zoul! thee wants a little spirit put into thee."

"I want spirit! when did I lack it?" exclaimed Abel.—"Not a man in the parish ever attempts to raise a hand against me."

"No, truly, Yeabel; I'll zay this vor thee, thou'rt such a weak, harmless, old body, that a man would as zoon think of wopping his grandmother as wopping thee."

Abel's wrath was now roused, and he began to speechify and swagger. Saul said no more, but stretched himself upon the mattress which the 'squire had humanely ordered to be placed on the floor, within reach of his tether, holding the rope under him, so that, without turning him over, it was impossible to discover that it had been severed. Just previously to the constable's entrance, Ponto, in obedience to the command of Saul, had retreated beneath a large oak table; the flap of which altogether concealed him from observation; and there lay the well–trained animal, with his head resting on his fore–paws, and his eyes fixed on Saul, perfectly motionless, and watching for further commands.

About an hour after midnight, when all seemed quiet below–stairs, Saul turned on his mattress, and beheld Abel still tottering to and fro, like an invalid grenadier upon guard. He waited for an opportunity, when the constable's back was toward him, to start up, seize Abel by the throat, and lay him flat upon the floor. "Yeabel," said he, in a low tone, "I hope I ha'n't hurt thee much. I be sorry to harm thee at all, old buoy; but needs must. I be gwain off, Yeabel;—I doan't mean to put the county to the expense o' prosecuting me,—zo I be gwain.—Doan't be aveard,— I won't choke thee:—there," added he, relaxing his powerful gripe; "I'll let thee breathe; but if thee speaks—remember, Yeabel,—I be a desperate man,— and I must zilence thee:—one knock o' the head 'ud do't; zo keep thy peace, and do as I tells thee quietly;—I won't have a word, mind me. Take thic thingumbob out o' thy waistcoat pocket, and unvasten these bracelets thou'st put about my wrists. In thy conscience to thy King and country won't let thee do't wi'out being put in bodily vear, I'll trouble thee wi' another grip o' the droat. But, I doant wish any thing o' the sort myzelf, unless needs must.— Ponto, dog!"

Ponto started up and was by his master's side in a moment.

"That infernal dog here too!" ejaculated Abel.

"Ay, zure!—but zilence! It yean't wise vor I to let thee open thy lips: so go to work like a dummy. Make haste, and dost hear, Yeabel? put down the handcuffs quietly. Now doan't tempt me to hurt thee, by making a vool o' thyself. Be ruled, that's a good yellow. I can get off,—doan't 'ee zee?—spite o' the cuffs; but it will be more convenient and agreeable to leave 'em behind." By this time, Abel had set Braintree's arms completely at liberty.

"Now, Yeabel," continued Saul, still kneeling over the constable,—"now, old blade, I'll leave thee wi' Ponto; but doan't thee move or call out, if thee values thy old droat. He'll worry thee like a wolf 'ud a wether, if thee moves or makes as much noise as a mouse: but be quiet—be still, and he'll stand over thee and not harm thee vor hours. Thee knowest the dog; and thee know'st me well enough to be zertain I wouldn't leave thee, vit to make a 'larm, if I wer'n't sure o' the dog. I doan't want to hurt thee, so I leaves thee wi' un: but, mind—he'll hold thy droat a little tighter than I did, if thee wags a hair.—Ponto!" added Saul, turning to the fine animal, who seemed to be listening to what he had said; "mind un, Ponto!—Steady, good dog!— Soho! and steady! but mind un!"

Ge^o. Ck. del. Ba 1846

To use a sporting phrase, Ponto immediately "stood;" he threw himself into an attitude that even Saul, as he departed, pronounced to be beautiful. His eye was keenly fixed upon Abel; the roots of his ears were elevated and brought forward; one of his fore–legs was held up, and curved so that the claws nearly touched his body; his tail no longer curled, but stood out straight on a level with his back; every muscle in his frame seemed, as it were, to be upon the alert; he appeared on the point of making a spring forward; but no statue ever stood more motionless on its pedestal, than Ponto did over the prostrate and terrified constable.

Braintree lost no time after he left the room which had been his temporary prison: he descended cautiously to the ground–floor, and versed as he had been in his boyhood, and for several years after time had written man upon his brow, in the topography of the old Hall, he easily found an outlet, and escaped without creating any alarm.

In a paddock adjoining the pleasure–grounds of the Hall, he caught a horse, which had been turned out on account of a sand–crack; twisted a hazel, from the hedge, into a halter and mouth piece; leaped the fence; and, in less than half an hour, by dint of hard galloping across the country,— clearing every thing as though he was riding a steeple–chase,—Saul reached his own cottage. Meg and her daughter were still up, the wife weeping, and the child praying for Saul's safe deliverance. He beat at the door, and Meg clasped the girl to her breast and exclaimed, "Oh! what now?— what now? They're surely coming for thee, Peggy! They'll leave me to murder myself—childless!"

"Open the door, Meg—my own Meg!" said Saul, without; "'tis I, Meg;—thy poor Zaul."

Braintree was soon by his own hearth, with his wife and daughter weeping and hanging round his neck.

"Well, and how is it, Saul?" inquired Meg, as soon as she could find utterance.

"Art discharged, father?" said Peggy.

"No, child," replied 'Saul; "I be 'scaped! I shouldn't ha' zeen thee, wench, nor thy mother neither, but whoam laid in my road. I be zafe yet till day–light, if Ponto's as true as I've a' zeen un avore now. But I shouldn't zay *if* vor I be zure ov un."

In reply to the inquiries of his wife, Saul briefly related the result of his conversation with Martin, the manner of his escape from old Abel, and his intention to fly the country for ever, if he could. "Not," added he, "that I think they could bring aught whoam to me, upon trial; though I didn't think zo, when I were tied up by a rope to a chimney–bar, in the Hall; but now it ztrikes I, there wouldn't be much danger ov my getting acquitted—and vor why?—It's clear the man were killed by *one*—not *two*. Now, if Bob's vound guilty, I must be turned out innocent; and guilty a' will, be vound, or else I've blundered blessedly."

"Heavens above us, Saul! what d'ye mean?" cried Meg.

Braintree now frankly told his wife the circumstances relative to Robert's shoes; and concluded, with a forced smile, sighing deeply as he spoke,—"And zo, the young un be nicked for no man's–land, wi'out a bit of a doubt;—that be certain, I reckon."

"Oh! Saul!" cried Meg, "Saul Braintree, what hast thee done?—thou hast murdered thy son!"

"Murdered my viddlestick! He's the 'zquire's—Jemmy Ztapleton's buoy; Martin be mine."

"Martin Stapleton, father!" almost shrieked Peggy.

"Ay, wench; and he cut the cord vor me, like a Briton."

"Saul! Saul!" replied Meg, "doan't thee smile; my poor heart be bursting. I never thought I should see this night!"

"Woe's me, mother; I was almost killed wi' trouble before, and now such news as this!" sobbed Peggy, pressing her hands to her eyes.

"What be the matter, missus?—All's right; —doan't be dashed."

"If thou didst kill Govier, Saul," said Meg, "thou bee'st a vather, vor all that; and I do pity thee:—thou hast laid a trap vor thy own son. When thou went'st away a smuggling that time, just after the 'squire had discharged thee, and when we knowed he was looking out for another nurse—"

"Well, what then?" interrupted Saul.

"Why, Saul, thou didst tempt me to change the children. I promised thee I would:—I tried, and I couldn't!—Thee thought'st to deceive 'Squire Stapleton, but I deceived thee, Saul. I couldn't send away my own boy—my virst–born—my darling. If thee wert a mother, thee wouldst vorgive me. Oh! that I had done as thee told me! Saul, Saul, thee hast murdered thy child! Bob's thy own vlesh and blood,—and Martin Stapleton be no kin to thee."

"Oh! mother!" said Peggy, dropping to her knees; "I am almost ashamed to say how I thank you for those words; they have a'most saved my life;—but then, my brother—my poor, poor brother!"

"Bob my own vlesh and blood!" said Saul, turning pale as a dying man while he spoke; "Bob my zon, a'ter all!—Tell'ee he an't! I won't believe thee:—dost hear?"

"As I hope to be vorgiven vor all I've done here below, he is;" replied his wife.

"Meg, Meg!" said Saul, dropping on a bench, and throwing himself back against the wall; "you ha' turned me sick as a dog."

Margaret and her daughter now threw themselves about Braintree's neck again, and began to weep and wail in the most violent and passionate manner: Saul remained motionless only for a few moments. " Gi'e me air," said he, suddenly pushing them aside and leaping up; "I be choking! I'd gi'e the world now, if I had it, that instead o' zhooting Phil, Phil had shot I!—Deceived! bevooled! in thic vashion!—Meg, doan't thee bide near me, or I shall lay hands on thee presently; I do know I shall."

"I don't vear thee, Saul," said Meg; "thee never didst lay a vinger in wrath on me yet. If thee'rt a' minded to kill me, do't!—I wont vly vrom the blow.—My Bobby in gaol, accused of murder, and my husband guilty of doing it!"

"You lie, you vool!" vociferated Saul; "'twere no murder! We vought, hand to hand, vor life or vor death, and I got the best o't. If I hadn't a' killed he, he'd ha' killed I; so how can 'ee make it murder?"

"The lord judge will make it out so, I fear," said Peggy; "won't he, think you, mother?"

"No doubt on't; and Saul knows it," replied Meg. "Oh! Bob, my child—my dear—dear boy!"

"Good night, Meg," interrupted Saul. "I be off;—you do know I can't abide to hear a woman howl."

"But where art gwain, Saul?"

"No matter;—thou'lt hear time enough o' me:—good night!"

"Nay, but what'll thee do?—Peggy, down on thy knees wi' me, girl, and beg him to tell us, what we be to do!—Oh! Saul—bide a bit; I woan't let thee see a tear—look, they be all scorched up.—I won't vex thee, any way, if thou'lt but bide and comfort us."

"Doan't cling to me zo," said Saul, struggling to rid himself of the embraces of his wife and daughter, who clung about his knees;—"it be no use; let go, or I'll hurt 'ee!—There now," continued he, as he freed himself, "once vor all, good night. It won't do vor I to bide here another minute."

Braintree now rushed out of the cottage, leaving his wife and daughter on their knees: each of them clasped the other to her breast, and listened, without a sob, until the receding footsteps of Saul were no longer audible. They then attempted alternately to solace each other; but the comforter of the moment was so violent in her own sorrow as to increase that of her whose grief she tried to allay; and thus the hours passed on with them till dawn. They felt the misery of seeing the sun rise and chase away the morning mists as usual;. the autumnal song–bird,—the robin,—much loved of men, chirruped merrily on their cottage–roof as he did a week before, when they were comparatively happy; and the sleek old cat, brushed his glossy sides against their garments, as if nothing was the matter. There are few persons in existence, whose lot it has been to pass a night of such extreme mental agony, as that was with Margaret Braintree and her daughter; and yet, strange to say, at six o'clock in the morning, Meg was raking together the embers of the turf fire, and piling fresh fuel on the hearth;—the kettle was, soon after, singing merrily above the blaze; and, before the church bells had chimed seven, Meg and her pretty daughter, miserable as they were, with swollen eyes and aching hearts, sat down to that womanly comfort,—a cup,—or as it is still called in the west—a *dish* of tea.

We must now return to the Hall, which, before day–break, became a scene of uproar and alarm. Every body seemed to be in a bustle, but no pursuit was made, or plan of action determined, on. The 'squire had sent for a neighbouring justice of the peace, who was so far stricken in years, that it was necessary for one of his own men, assisted by Stapleton's messenger, to lift him on horse–back, and hold him on the saddle, the whole distance between his own house and the Hall. The old man, although of a remarkably irritable disposition, was scarcely wide awake when he arrived. The 'squire, however, without waiting to inquire whether or no his auditor was in a proper state to receive his communications, began to give a minute history of the capture, brief imprisonment, and escape of Braintree. He had gone as far as Saul's seizing the constable, when old Justice Borfield, for the first time, interrupted him, by inquiring, with warmth, what they all meant by using him as they had done? "Here have I been," added he—"Ay, now, I recollect—Yes—the scoundrels broke into my bed–room;—so I suppose, at least;—dragged me out of bed; and when I awoke, —for, odd! sir, and as I'm a gentleman, all this was hurry–skurry, and passed on like a dream,— but when I awoke, I found myself in my best wig, on the back of a high–trotting horse; and lo, and behold! I saw—for my miscreant of a man had fastened on my spectacles, though, as you see, he forgot my left shoe—I saw one of them on each side, holding me down to the saddle, by my waistband. I struggled and exclaimed; but the villains heeded me not!—Now, sir, what the devil does all this mean? What am I accused of? I insist upon being answered."

"My dear neighbour, my very worthy friend Borfield," said Stapleton, "I need your a presence—your advice in this matter."

"You're very complimentary, indeed!—What! now you've made a blunder, you drag me into your counsels to bear half the blame!—Neighbour Stapleton, I'm a very ill–used man, and I won't put up with it. Talk of the liberty of the subject, and the power of a justice of the peace!—Why, I've been treated like a tetotum! At this rate, a magistrate's an old woman; or worse—worse by this hand! Brute force beats the King's commission! I'm dragged out of my bed at midnight, by lawless ruffians—lifted into a saddle, when I haven't set foot in stirrup these twenty years— and brought here, on the back of a rough–trotting galloway, close prisoner, to sign some documents, I suppose, which wouldn't he legal without the formality of a second magistrate's name. I'll tell you what, James Stapleton, I don't like it.—If I'm an old man, I'm not a machine. Your satellites have brought the horse to the brook, but you can't make him drink. I'll sign nothing; I'll die first:—for I'm hurt and insulted."

The old man now grew exhausted, and Stapleton once more attempted to pacify him. By dint of excuses, and a few flattering compliments on the freshness and vigour of his intellectual powers, and the value of the advice of a man who had so much experience, Stapleton, at length, prevailed upon him to hear the end of his statement, relative to Saul's escape.

"Well, well! then order coffee and dry toast," said Borfield; "for if you need advice, I lack refreshment. Order coffee, and let the toast he cut thin, and baked by a steady hand—by–the–by, let my own miscreant do it,—and then we'll see what can be done."

It appeared that Braintree's escape had been discovered sooner than he expected. The old earth–stopper, on his return from Gorbury, where he had been following his vocation, saw somebody cross a field, at full speed, on a horse which he well knew to be Martin Stapleton's pie–bald hunter. He fancied, too, that the rider bore some resemblance to Braintree.

But whether the man were Braintree or another, it was clear that all was not right. The earth–stopper, therefore, thought proper to put spurs to his poney, and, instead of turning down the next lane toward his own cottage, to push for the main road, and trot up to Stapleton Hall. As he passed the paddock he looked round it; but saw no horse. When he reached the gate–way leading to the house, he raised such a clatter, by ringing the bell and beating against the door, that several of the servants, and Stapleton himself, were soon roused from their beds. Before the earth–stopper was admitted, Stapleton inquired from the window, what had occurred. "I beg your honour's pardon," replied the old man; "reckon I ha' zeed Zaul Braintree,—or iv 'tean't he, 'tis a man like un,—riding athirt tailor Mudford's 'tatee–patch, in Mistletoe–lane, saving your worship's presence, upon a zpringy zwitch–tailed pie–bald, a blood–like weed ov a thing, so var as I could see; but I'll zwear he were a zwitch–tailed pie–bald; and the young 'zquire's yean't in the paddock."

Stapleton threw on his dressing–coat, and hurried up stairs to the room where Saul had been confined. The lamp was still burning; and, by its light, he discovered, at a glance, that the prisoner had effected his escape. Abel's staff lay upon the mattress, and, at a little distance from it, Stapleton beheld the constable on the floor, apparently lifeless. "The villain has murdered him!" thought he; but his fears were instantly dispelled, and his indignation roused, by a sonorous snore, which evidently proceeded from the nostrils of Abel.

Stapleton took up the staff of office, and turned the constable over with it two or three times, before he could wake him. In reply to the questions put to him by the 'squire, Abel gave a tolerably clear account of what had taken place: the last thing he recollected was seeing the eyes of Ponto glaring at him, as he lay on the floor. Search was immediately made for the dog, but without success: he had either effectually concealed himself in some part of the house, or made his escape. Abel begged for a warrant from his worship to apprehend and hang the animal, "He aided and abetted the prisoner," said he, "in getting his liberty; and I am ready to swear, and what is more, with your worship's leave, I do insist upon swearing, that I lay in bodily fear, o' the beast. But Ponto," continued he, "was not the sole and only one that lent the delinquent a helping hand; he hath a friend in court: the rope was cut for him, that's clear; for he never could have done it himself. Your worship, this looks awkward against somebody."

The morning dawned through the eastern window of the library, as Stapleton finished his statement, and old Borfield his second cup of coffee. The latter now suggested that all the persons in the house should be rigidly examined, and the depositions of Abel and the earth–stopper formally prepared. The whole of the household, as well as the two last–mentioned worthies, were then called in; and after a few questions had been put to the domestics in a body, it came out, that somebody had heard Sam say, before he went to bed, that the poachers dog had burst into the Wainscot– room when he (Sam) went up to call the young 'squire down to supper. Sam, upon being questioned, prevaricated and became confused. Perceiving this, Stapleton inquired for Martin. "He ha'n't left his room yet, sir," said Sam; "I'll step and call him."

"No, no!" exclaimed Borfield; "by no means: stay you there, and let the constable go for him."

"I forgot to say," said Abel, "that Master Martin did certainly condescend to be beadle over the prisoner while I took needful refreshment."

"Then you ought to be whipped for suffering him to do so," quoth Borfield. "Mr. Stapleton, this begins to be serious," continued he;— Stapleton turned pale as he proceeded, and now wished he had not sent for his brother magistrate;—"the youth's your son; but it is our duty, in such an investigation as this, to pay no respect to persons.—And so, when you returned," he added, turning to the constable again, "the bird was flown, was he?"

"I will be judged by any man here, if I said so!" replied Abel. "Saul and I had some chat after my return; he was there, and, seemingly, safe enough; but the cord must have been cut by somebody while I was away."

"And who did you find in the room besides Saul?" was the next question put by old Borfield.

"Sam ran against me, as I went up over the stairs, and the young 'squire did the like, more disagreeably, just after I had crossed the threshold."

Borfield shook his head, and said to Sam, "Young man, consider yourself in custody; and, constable, fetch down Master Martin Stapleton;—is strange, amidst all this uproar, he has not made his appearance!"

"Has no one seen him?" inquired Stapleton, in a tone of unusual solemnity: he looked anxiously round the circle, but no reply was made. "Open that window," continued he, pointing to one near him, in the recess of which stood the earth–stopper, who obeyed him, as fast as his stiff joints would permit. A perfect silence reigned through the room for nearly a minute, after Abel had quitted it, in obedience to Borfield's commands, when the old earth–stopper said that he heard a tired horse galloping up the high–road, about a mile distant, and he thought it was the young 'squire's pie–bald. Upon being asked what induced him to think so, he replied, "Why, your honour, Master Martin's horse were lame from a zand–crack in the near vore–voot and the horse I do hear, don't ztrike the ground even; I be zure he's lame;— and az I do think—"

The earth–stopper would have proceeded, but Abel and Martin now entered the room. The young man's dress was in disorder; his hair was matted; his eyes were swollen; and his whole appearance indicated that he had not passed the night asleep in his bed. "I understand," said he, addressing himself to Stapleton and Borfield,— "I understand that—."

"You have but one question to answer, Martin," interrupted Stapleton.

"And answer it or not as you think fit," said Borfield; "recollect, young gentleman, that you are not compelled to implicate yourself:—be careful!"

"The caution, sir," said Stapleton, "is kind and well–meant, but, I am sure, needless. Martin—did you, or did you not, aid Saul Braintree in his escape?"

Martin was silent.

"Don't press him," said Borfield, forgetting to whom he was speaking; "we have quite sufficient, without his own acknowledgment, to warrant us in concluding that he did.—The constable's evidence—"

"Borfield! Borfield!" cried Stapleton, casting on the old man a look of reproach that silenced him; "let him answer for himself. What say you, Martin? Acquit yourself, I insist—I entreat!—Did you cut the rope for Braintree?"

"All that I have to say, sir," replied Martin, firmly,—but his voice faltered, and he burst into tears, and hid his face in his hands as he concluded,—"All that I have to say, sir, is, that the man proved to me he was my own father!"

"Martin, you're mad!" exclaimed Stapleton, starting from his seat.

"Braintree your father!" said Borfield, removing his spectacles, but speaking in a calm and unconcerned tone; "How's this?— Then where's Mr. Stapleton's son?"

"In the county gaol, abiding his trial for murder!" replied the young man.

"Martin, your wits are wandering!" almost shrieked old Stapleton; "What do you mean?"

"It is but too true, sir, I fear.—Meg Braintree changed us when children at her breast."

"No, zhe didn't, Master Martin," said some one at the lower end of the room; "No, zhe didn't; worse luck!

To the amazement of all present, Saul Braintree, who had just entered, now walked up toward the justices, and stood within three paces of the table, behind which their chairs were placed.

Old Stapleton was still on his legs; and, with a vacant and almost idiotic stare, turned from Martin, on whom he had been gazing, to the weather-beaten face of Saul.

"'Tis you ha' done all this mischief, 'zquire," pursued Braintree; "Oh! you used I—but, it doan't matter—Meg, too, to play zuch a trick, and not tell me o't!—Master Martin, zhe didn't do as I tould her; but never, avore this night, did I know I'd been made zuch a vool ov!—Your horse valled lame as a cat wi' me, coming back; but you'll vorgi'e me, I do know, vor bringing 'ee zuch news. I bean't your vather;—there—there, it do zeem, he stands: 'zquire, this be, truly, your zon; mine be in irons; but I'll vree un! i'll vree un!" repeated he, raising his voice suddenly to a high pitch; "he sha'n't bide there long! I be bad enough, vor zure and zartin; but I can't let un die vor I!—Oh! I be beat out and out!—I can't ztand it; zo, justice, take my convession."

Borfield touched the elbow of Stapleton, who was now totally inattentive to the scene before him, and affectionately embracing Martin. "Take the pen, sir," said Borfield; "and, prisoner, reflect a moment on what you are about to do: you are in a state of great excitation; we are willing to hear you; but, I repeat,— be cautious!"

"Cautious!—cautious, d'ye zay?—No, I won't! Caution's been the ruin o' me. Caution doan't zeem to I to be any use in theze parts. I ha' zeed men wi' no more forecast than chilver hogs, do well all their lives, and keep out o' harm's way, vlourishing like trees:—now I ha' been as cautious as a cat, and you do zee what I be come to."

"I cannot write, indeed, Mr. Borfield;—I cannot write a word:—you must excuse me," said Stapleton, throwing down the pen.

"Well, well, then, as we've no clerk, and I have written nothing but my name these seven years," said Borfield, offering the pen to young Stapleton, "suppose, Master Martin, you take down the prisoner's confession."

"Pardon me, sir," said Martin; "*that* I never will do."

"Then we must adjourn the examination for an hour," said Borfield; "let the prisoner be searched, and conveyed to a place of security. I will specially swear in the earth–stopper and my man to assist you, Abel; my man shall remain in the room with you, and the earth–stopper may watch outside the door: be attentive, earth–stopper."

"And above all things," added Abel, "take care that his dog don't get in."

"Doan't'ee be aveard o' he, Yeabel," said Saul, "I ha' killed un, poor blade!—It were the last zhot I shall zhoot. He ha' done much mischief vor I, poor dumb beast, and he might ha' done more vor a worser man;—vor I reckon I beau't zo bad az some be, and that's a comvort.—I knocked up varmer Zalter, and borrowed his double–barrelled gun, to gi'e the dog his dose. Ponto knowed what a gun were, well enough; but he seemed to vancy I were in vun like, when I pointed the muzzle o't to un; vor a' wagged his tail and looked as pleasant up in my vace, that be dashed iv I weren't vorced to shut my eyes avore I could pull the trigger. But, oh! Master Martin, iv you had but heard his one short deep howl, you'd ha' gone 'mazed—that is—iv you were I. Truly, I do think, I should ha' zhot myself iv 'tweren't vor two things:—Virst, I couldn't ha' vreed poor dear Bob, bless un! iv I had; and next, I'd a' given my word and hand to varmer Zalter, I wouldn't harm myself, avore he'd lend me his gun."

Martin now asked his father's permission to offer Saul a little refreshment; the 'squire immediately acceded to his request, and the kind–hearted young gentleman whispered Sam, in Saul's hearing, to get a little brandy from the housekeeper. Braintree, however, much to Martin's surprise, requested that no liquor might be brought for his use. "Master Martin," said he, "it yean't wi' me, as 'twere last night. I be past the help o' brandy, now:—I be done vor. Ponto's gone, and I shall zoon vollow un; he did'nt deserve it,—nor I neither, may be;—but I zhall ha't though, vor all that. But Bob shall be vreed—no offence, justices; but, d'ye hear?—Bob shall be vree! My buoy shan't never zuffer vor I. No, no, that wouldn't be like Zaul Braintree;—eh! Master Martin?—would it, neighbours?—My wife zhan't zay to I again, as she did, poor zoul, last night, 'Zaul, thee hast murdered my zon:'—'tean't pleasant. —Your zarvant, Justice Borfield: you ha' been my ruin, 'zquire Ztapleton; but I doan't bear malice; I do vorgive 'ee wi' all my heart.—Will'ee be so good as to make vriends, sir, and think o' Meg, if aught should happen to me?—will'ee, zir—will'ee—will'ee?"

Saul stretched forth his hand across the table, and Stapleton, apparently without knowing what he did, or, possibly, actuated by a return of those kind feelings which he had entertained for Saul, twenty years before so far forgot his own character and situation and those of the prisoner, that he put forth his hand towards that of Braintree; a short but hearty mutual squeeze ensued, and Braintree immediately left the room, closely followed by Abel Harris, the earth–stopper, and Justice Borfield's man. He had scarcely proceeded a dozen steps from the door, when, as if something of importance had suddenly occurred to him, he turned about, and earnestly inquired for the young 'squire. Martin was soon by his side. "Master Martin," said Saul, "there be one thing I've a' got to say to 'ee—"

"Your wife, I suppose, Braintree—"

"No, no, not zhe; I spoke to 'zquire about she:—besides, Bob will be vree, and won't see poor Meg lack;—pine zhe will— but he can't help that."

"Can I do any thing for you?" inquired Martin.

"Not vor I—not vor I," replied Saul. "I ha' got but a vew words to say to thee, lad, and I'll zpeak 'em vreely. Peggy yean't your zister, now:—when I be gone, iv you can't do her no good, doan't do her no harm, vor my zake, lad; doan't, pr'ythee now!"

"I never will, you may depend, Saul."

"Then God bless thee, and good bye!—Now, Yeabel!"

Saul how followed Abel into the Wainscot–room again, and resumed his handcuffs. Old Borfield, who had been roused to unusual energy, and even displayed a portion of that acuteness, for which he had been famed in the county twenty or thirty years before, sank into a doze. Long before he opened his eyes again, Stapleton had received Saul Braintree's confession; which, coupled with other circumstances, while it convicted Saul, clearly exculpated his son from any participation in the offence. The father and son were tried together; the former was found guilty, and the latter acquitted. Saul, however, evaded the execution of the law: a strong fear of death came over him, after his own conviction; he made a bold attempt to escape, the particulars of which it would be needless to enumerate; suffice it to say, that he was not only unsuccessful, but perished in a most resolute struggle with some of the gaoler's attendants, who intercepted his progress. Another paragraph will finish our tale.

Old Stapleton, who had long been in a declining state, died within a few days after Martin came of age: the young 'Squire shortly after sold off his estates, and, as it was confidently said by some, but disbelieved by others, dwelt happy and contented, as it falls to the lot of most men to be, in a distant part of England, with his old nurse under his roof; Robert Braintree, the tenant of a capital farm, within a morning's ride of his mansion: and pretty Peggy his wife.

THE SHAM FIGHT

"WELL, Jones,—who's gone?—any body?" This was the first question which the excellent hostess of The New Passage Inn put to the waiter, as she descended one morning, rather later than usual, to her breakfast. Jones replied, "Every body's gone, ma'am: two parties, and one single gentleman, went across in the boat, without breakfasting—"

"Without breakfasting, Jones! I hope they've taken no offence."

"Oh! no! I'm pretty sure of that, ma'am:—they went away very comfortable, on rum and milk."

"Rum and milk!"

"Yes, ma'am; glasses round, with biscuits."

"Oh! well! come!—And how did the ladies in number nine go?"

"In the yellow chaise; and the people in the back drawing room, went with Tom Davis, in the green coach; and what with one and another, there isn't a turn–boy but Sam, in the yard:— he's got no chaise, you know, ma'am; and his hand–horse won't be fit to work, the blacksmith says, till Tuesday."

"Oh! well! come!" replied the hostess. "Then we've no company left."

"Oh! yes," said Jones; "one gentleman came over in the boat, this morning, too late for a chaise; and there's a traveller got down from Bristol, on horseback, too late for the boat."

"And where have you put them, Jones?"

"They haven't come in–doors yet, ma'am."

"What are they doing then, Jones?"

"One of them is throwing stones into the water, and the other is looking at him, seemingly, ma'am."

"Pretty amusement!" said the landlady, shaking her head as she peeped through the bar–window, and saw the two gentlemen, at a little distance from the house, amusing themselves as Jones had stated. The active party was a man advanced in years, stout and squat in person, wearing a profusion of powder, and having the appearance of a respectable tradesman. He did not seem to be aware that he was observed, and continued to exert himself very strenuously in throwing pebbles into the water; until the other traveller, who stood within thirty paces of him, burst out into a shout of laughter, which the tradesman no sooner heard, than he, naturally enough, turned about to see from whose lungs it issued, feeling by no means gratified at being made acquainted, in such a manner, with the proximity of a stranger. He slyly dropped two or three pebbles which he had in his hand; hummed the chorus of a song, very much out of tune; and assumed a pompous and important stride, which rendered him exceedingly ridiculous in the eyes of the stranger, who in vain attempted to control himself, and laughed louder than before. The tradesman now resolutely tucked up his sleeves and resumed his exercise. He had thrown two or three dozen pebbles among the little waves, when the stranger, to his surprise, approached, and, in a very handsome manner, begged pardon for the circumstance which had peremptorily obliged him to intrude with an apology. The elderly man protested that he did not understand the gentleman who thus addressed him:—"Sir," said he, "I know not why you should apologise, for you have given me no offence. I do not remember to have heard or seen any thing on your part, at which I could possibly take umbrage. However, if my hand were not dirty, I should be happy to offer it you, as I would to any military man in the kingdom: though you seem to have but lately reached the years of manhood, your weather–beaten face convinces me; sir, that you have seen service. If there's no objection on your part, I should be happy to join you at the breakfast–table. I've smelt powder myself; but I'll warrant, now, you would hardly have been keen enough to detect any symptoms of the soldier about me, if I hadn't let the cat out of the bag."

"Indeed I should not, sir, I must confess," replied the young officer.

"But," continued the other, "allowances ought to be made; dress is every thing, as our lieutenant–colonel used to say. Now, if it were not for that stripe on your trousers, your military cloak, and foraging cap—"

"It's very likely you would not have guessed I was in the service," said the officer.

"Exactly so," replied his companion. "But what say you, sir?—shall we breakfast together?—I'm a respectable man, and well known in most towns in the West of England. I travel in my own line, and do business extensively on commission, in old or damaged hops, especially in Wales, where I'm going the next trip the passage–boat makes."

"I can have no doubt of your respectability, sir," said the officer; "and accept your invitation very cheerfully."

"'Well, come along, then, my boy!" exclaimed the traveller, descending, for a moment, from his dignity of deportment; "and we'll have a dish of chat. Have you been abroad?"

"Yes, sir," replied the young officer; "I had the honour of serving, with my regiment, at Waterloo."

"Bless my soul! I'm very glad, sir—very glad, indeed:—there are two or three points, about which I have long wished to have my mind settled, relative to that business;—but I never yet had the luck of meeting with an eye–witness of the battle. Why, sir,—it's the oddest thing in the world, you'll say;—but at the moment you addressed me, I was thinking of Hougoumont, and the other places whose names you recollect, no doubt, better than I do.—And what do you think put it into my head? Why, I'll tell you:—as I was walking along, the waves, with their bold flow, surmounted by spray, with the sunbeams dancing about them, reminded me of a regiment of cuirassiers advancing to the attack: so, to get a better appetite, in the enthusiasm of the moment I metamorphosed myself into a battery, and began playing away upon them with pebbles.—Child's work, you'll say, and derogatory to the character of a man of dignity."

"I do not exactly agree with you, sir," said the officer; "great men have often indulged in the most childish amusements; we are told of one who caught flies, another who made himself a hobby–horse for his little family, and a third who enjoyed the frolics of a kitten:—on the authority of these, and many similar precedents which I recollect, there seems to be no good reason why a gentleman, who travels in South Wales, on commission in the damaged hop line, should not, in a moment of relaxation, Don–Quixotise on the banks of the Severn, by turning the waves of its rising tide into French cuirassiers, and pelting them with pebbles."

"Sir, I like your manner amazingly!" exclaimed the traveller; "and if you will take any little extra, such as a pork chop or so, with your chocolate—"

The officer interrupted his companion, by stating that he never took pork chops with chocolate; and immediately began talking about the battle of Waterloo, of which, during the walk to the inn, and while breakfast was preparing and demolishing, he gave the traveller a very animated and interesting description. His companion, in return, volunteered a narrative of the most important military event he had ever borne a share in. "I allude," said he, "to the great sham fight, that took place eleven years ago, near a certain ancient and respectable borough, in a neighbouring county, at which I had the honour of being present, with a corps you have, probably, heard of, rather by the honourable and appropriate nick–name of 'The Borough Buffs,' than by the one which appeared on its buttons and orderly–books. There was not, perhaps, a more loyal association in the kingdom: we had not a single French frog on our uniform; which, although I say it, was one of the most elegant specimens of regimentals that has yet been produced. Our lieutenant–colonel was as brave and talented a volunteer–officer as ever wore a sword; and so much satisfaction did he give to his fellow–townsmen, or fellow–soldiers,—it matters not which, for they were both,—that a gold cup was presented to him at a public dinner, the very day before the sham fight took place, in testimony of the gratitude felt by the whole corps to their worthy and respected lieutenant–colonel,—whose name was Nickelcockle. The party consisted of all our own officers, and six or eight guests, who were attached to a division of a marching regiment, with blue facings, that happened to be quartered in the borough. Perhaps you never sat down to a more elegant dinner:— eatables excellent,—every thing that was expensive and out of season; wine of the first price; and the speeches any thing you please but parliamentary. That of our major, Alderman Arkfoot, when he presented the cup, was one of the neatest things I had then heard: but it was rather eclipsed by lieutenant–colonel Nickelcockle's reply; who, to his other gifts, added that of eloquence, in an extraordinary degree.—He was, indeed, an eminent man: ambitious, daring, and talented,—he had, as he frequently boasted, risen from the shop–board to be one of the greatest army–clothiers in the kingdom; and retired, in the prime of life, with a splendid fortune, and one daughter, Miss Arabella Nickelcockle, who is now the wife of a baronet.—But to return to his speech:—'Gentlemen, and brother officers of The Borough Buff Volunteers,' said he, 'this is the proudest moment I ever experienced since I have been a soldier.' At this early period of our lieutenant–colonel's speech, several of the officers belonging to the marching regiment, testified their approbation by crying, 'Hear! hear! bravo! Hear!'—'Gentlemen, and brother officers,' continued the lieutenant–colonel, 'my gratitude is immeasurable, and therefore, inexpressible.'—'Cut the shop, colonel!' whispered the adjutant, who sat on his right hand, and who, it must be confessed, too often prompted the lieutenant–colonel, both at our convivial meetings, and on parade, to be quite agreeable: indeed, the fact was frequently noticed by the corps, and whenever the circumstance was broached, the parties who mentioned it, invariably sneered; which clearly shewed their opinion of the matter. The lieutenant–colonel was too good–natured by half and took the intrusive hints of the adjutant much too easily; at least, in my opinion.—'Gentlemen, and brother officers of The Borough Buffs,' resumed the lieutenant–colonel; 'anxious as I am, at all times, to avail myself of the advice of our worthy and experienced adjutant, I cannot make it fit my own feelings to do so at present: he says,' Cut the shop, Colonel!'—Now, although I have retired, I cannot forget that I owe my present situation to trade and commerce. I rose, by my own merit, to the highest civil posts in the borough; and, brother officers, I also did ditto from the ranks of this corps to be its lieutenant–colonel!' Here the shouts of approbation were nearly deafening: the regular officers at the lower end, seemed, by their 'bravos!' to pay a compliment to the gentlemen–tradesmen, who were about them; and, no doubt, enjoyed the vexation of the crest–fallen adjutant, if one might judge by their laughter. Several glasses were broken; and one of the corporation took off his wig, and flourished it so enthusiastically round his head, that a shower of powder descended on the persons who sat on each side of him, as well as those immediately opposite. As soon as order could be restored, the lieutenant–colonel proceeded with his speech. 'Gentlemen,' said he, 'without any disrespect to our guests, I beg to say, that an armed citizen is the best of soldiers. And why?—Because he has his shop, his goods, his book–debts, et cetera, as well as his King and country to fight for.'—'Bravo!' and 'hear him!'—'I know that some of the wits, as they call themselves,— the opposition party of the borough,—and those who are out of place, I have always remarked, shew their wit much oftener than those who are in;—I say, gentlemen, that some of the outs have been sneering at the cup and its trimmings: they say that the handle of it looks more like a goose than a swan; which is, doubtless, a hit at my profession:—but to the utter confusion of the discontented wise–acres, for once in their lives they are right! I confess, much to the credit of the artificer, that it does look more like a goose than a swan. And why? Because, gentlemen—because it was intended for a goose!—It is, to my knowledge, cut out from an old Roman pattern, which, I presume, was originally made about the time when the bird I mentioned came into notice among the first circles, for having saved Rome, as you all have read in ancient history or elsewhere.' Major Arkfoot, who had manifested considerable,—and, if I may say so,—very unbecoming impatience, during the latter sentence or two, here interrupted the lieutenant–colonel, in a most un officer–like manner, and flatly stated that he was labouring under a mistake:—he, Major Arkfoot, had been honoured with the orders of the committee, to make the cup, and he offered to pawn his entire credit, that the figure was intended for a swan; although, he confessed, there was a slight deficiency in the resemblance 'but that,' said he, 'with the greatest respect I say it, lies at the committee's door: they spoiled the ship for a ha'porth of tar; if they had only given me the other five guineas, which I demanded, the bird's neck would have been at least an inch and a half longer, and so made all the difference.' 'Well, gentlemen, goose or swan,'—pursued the lieutenant–colonel; but before he could utter another word, several members of the committee rose at once, to address the major, who vowed that though its neck was rather abbreviated, it certainly was, to all intents and purposes, a swan; the officers of the marching regiment, at the lower end of the table, vociferated, 'A goose! a goose!' and Alderman Major Arkfoot, finding he had the worst of it, rose again, and roared loud enough to be heard, 'Well, gentlemen, as my dissentient voice does not seem to yield infinite delight to the company, without offence to the lieutenant–colonel, a goose let it be dubbed!' And it was so most unanimously. While the lieutenant–colonel endeavoured, as he said, to pick up the thread of his discourse, which had been interrupted in the manner I have mentioned, I cast my eyes toward the lower end of the table, and, truly, I never remember to have seen any gentlemen more cheerful at table, than the officers with the blue trimmings. The lieutenant–colonel next touched upon the important subject of the great sham fight, on the ensuing day. After describing the general appearance, the advantages and disadvantages of the field, viewing it with a military eye,—he descanted at length, on the importance of the post to which The Borough Buffs were appointed. It was a hill that rose almost perpendicularly from the bank of a swift brook, and was nearly inaccessible at all points except in the rear. 'Brother–officers,' cried the lieutenant–colonel, 'the gallant general who commands us, on this occasion, pronounces the post to be impregnable;— and I feel most grateful to him for the high honour of having entrusted its defence to the gallant corps of Borough Buffs under my command. We form, gentlemen, the right arm—the adjutant says, 'wing'—but I say, the right arm'—'Wing!' interrupted the pertinacious and very unpleasant adjutant. 'Well, the wing,'—thus the lieutenant–colonel went on; 'the gizzard–wing, of what are supposed to be the English forces:—our instructions are, to maintain our post against a regiment of breechless Highlanders; and I doubt not but that success will crown our efforts. Let not our renown be tarnished by the non–attendance of any of the officers or privates of the corps;—let not any man's wife or family, by vain fears, induce him to hang back on this occasion. It is the first time we have ever had an opportunity of distinguishing ourselves; and I pledge my word that there is no more danger than in an ordinary parade. The general, when he inspected us, did me the honour to say, that there was not a corps in the service whose accoutrements were cleaner, or whose coats fitted better. Brother–officers, let us prove that we fit our coats, as well as they fit us;— let us shew those who sneer at us for being tradesmen, that, if we do—as they say—if we do drive bargains upon parade, we can also drive the enemy in the field!' The applause which had been gradually increasing at every interval between the lieutenant–colonel's sentence; here reached its climax; the officers at the lower end of the table very freely joined in it, out of respect to the corps; indeed, the conduct of these gentlemen was exceedingly flattering on this occasion. But to continue:—'Gentlemen,' exclaimed the lieutenant–colonel, 'I know that your feelings match exactly with my own; but, remember, we have a keen enemy to encounter; we must, therefore, be as cool, as collected, and as sharp as needles. We shall be supported by two companies of infantry, who will take up a position, at a little distance on our left, and so connect us with the main line. The companies I allude to are of that glorious and gallant regiment to which our worthy guests with the blue facings belong: they, as well as a troop of yeomanry, which I expect will muster six or eight–and–thirty strong, will be tacked to The Borough Buffs and receive my orders.'—'Compose, with our corps, the division under my command,' muttered the adjutant. But the lieutenant–colonel either did not hear, or would not heed him, and went on with his speech. 'Gentlemen,' said he, 'I have only to repeat my thanks for the honour you have conferred on me;—to beseech the greatest punctuality, neatness, and despatch, to–morrow; and to drink success to the loyal and efficient corps of Borough Buff Volunteers!' The tumultuous cheers with which this toast was received, I will not attempt to describe. The lieutenant–colonel sat down very well satisfied with himself, as well he might, and everything went on amicably for above an hour; when the peace of the party was rather disturbed by a violent quarrel, between Alderman Major Arkfoot and Alderman Lieutenant Squill, one of the committee–men, relative to the goose or the swan,—whichever it might be, on the presentation–cup. Words, at last, rose to such a height, that

Alderman Arkfoot—very indecently referring to connubial affairs, totally without foundation,—for I do not think any man, besides her husband, was better acquainted with the private life and domestic virtues of Mrs. Squill than myself,—most injudiciously, in his heat, called Alderman Squill 'a cuckoldy cur!' Alderman Squill asked, very warmly, 'what he meant by his *double entendre?* And the corps might have been seriously disgraced, by an effusion from that feature whence no military man wishes to shed his blood, when the lieutenant–colonel, with that infinite presence of mind for which he has always been admirable in business, the council–chamber, or the field, rose up, and placing a hand on each belligerent party's mouth, who were sitting, or rather, standing, within his reach, and opposite each other,—called upon one of the officers with the blue facings, for a sentiment or a song. A tall captain, whose face, if I may presume to say so, was too ferocious to be genteel, but who had, I must needs testify, been very prominent in applauding the lieutenant–colonel's speech, immediately complied, and, with his victorious voice, soon vanquished the inimical and unsociable uproar at our end of the table, which ought to have set a pattern to the junior officers in the centre. But a good–natured gentleman's song or saying, often produces an effect very different to what the singer or the sayer intends; and this was the case with the ditty of the captain of the ferocious aspect and colossal voice. His burthen, or chorus, which he meant as a compliment to us, was turned into a sneer, by some who sat near the colonel, and who always felt sore even at a compliment on the corps from any of the regulars. The words of the chorus were, simply, as I shall here specify;—to wit,—as the law says:—

> The Borough Volunteers, my boys,
> Are men both stout and bold;
> And when they meet the enemy,
> They scorn to be controll'd

"For my own part, I felt obliged to the gentleman, and considered the expressions as highly gratifying to every member of the corps; but there were some about me who thought differently. They said, that the word 'stout,' in the second line, was palpably meant satirically, on account of the portliness of the greater part of the officers of The Borough Buffs; and that the two last lines were intended to be offensive, because the singer well knew that our corps, never yet having had the good fortune to be opposed to an enemy, could not possibly have exhibited its valour. There were two riders tacked to this reading of the lines; one of which was, that the words, ' They scorn to be controlled!' amounted to an impeachment on our discipline: the second, I recollect, went further, and broadly stated, that those words implied cowardice; and that, were the corps ever to be brought face to face with an enemy, we, The Borough Buffs, should, in our fears, so scorn, control, as to shew our adversaries a regiment of heels! Alderman Arkfoot observed, that as we were all in regimentals, we ought to feel and act as gentlemen, and call the individual to an account for his obnoxious chorus; which, he doubted not, might be explained away; but for the honour of the corps, he thought it ought to be noticed. The lieutenant–colonel, and several others, were of the same opinion; and it was unanimously agreed, that the officer, with the ferocious aspect and exceedingly stupendous voice, should be hauled over the coals.— The discussion was held in a low tone of voice amongst ourselves, at the head of the table; we had arrived at that point, when men break into knots, and discourse in dozens, so that our debate was unheard and unnoticed by those who were below us. It was agreed that satisfaction should be demanded; and there the matter seemed to rest, or rather; to be dying away, for nobody volunteered to do the needful. At last, when another subject had been started, the adjutant mooted it up again, by saying, that we reminded him of the fable of the mice, who decided on putting a bell round Grimalkin's neck, but no valorous individual would undertake the exploit. —'Gentlemen,' continued he, 'that the officer at the bottom of the table did intend an insult to the corps, I have no doubt;—far be it from me to say we do not merit his sneers;—but that matters not; it behoves us to keep up a character, though we know we do not deserve it. The gentleman must be spoken with. I should do myself the honour of presenting him with my card, but that it would be a high breach of military decorum for me to take precedence, in the business, of the lieutenant–colonel and Major Arkfoot; on either of whom I shall be proud and happy to attend on this most peremptory occasion.' The lieutenant–colonel and Alderman Arkfoot now thought they saw the expressions in rather a different light: they very properly animadverted upon the evil of bickering or quarrelling about trifles;—protest that a joke was a joke;—observed that the gentleman was their guest, and to–morrow was appointed for the sham fight; and, finally, began to joke and jog off, by degrees, to other affairs;—giving such a favourable colour to the matter, as they dropped it, as to excite my admiration and respect. But the bull–dog adjutant still persevered in pinning them to the point; and, in the end, positively drove our reluctant friends into a tacit compliance with his request, to be constituted the second of one of them in the affair. He would not speak to the officer with the ferocious aspect and blue facings on the subject at table, but said he should defer it until the party broke up. He then began to be horribly gay and loquacious. Melancholy reigned among the rest of us, at the upper end of the table, during the residue of our stay, and we wished our worthy lieutenant–colonel and Alderman Arkfoot 'good night!' with aching hearts;—blessing ourselves, individually and silently, as we went home, that we were not field–officers of The Borough Buffs. The adjutant, sure enough, spoke to the officer who had sung the song, that night; but the gentleman would give no satisfaction, and was so fastidious, as to refuse fighting either the lieutenant–colonel, the major, or, as he said, any other mechanical or counter fellow in the corps: but as for the adjutant, (who had served, I must tell you, in a marching regiment, and sold out,) he'd fight him with the greatest pleasure in life, because he was a gentleman. The next morning they met; our adjutant was attended by a one–armed lieutenant of the navy, because the friend of the officer of the ferocious aspect refused, like his principal, to meet any of us on the subject. Thus the adjutant dug a pit for himself; and none of us were more sorry than became us for it, except that it deprived us of his advice in the ham fight; for the wound which he received in the duel with the officer, although by no means dangerous, was sufficient to prevent him from leaving his bed for a week.

"The next morning, half the borough was in arms, and the remainder in an uproar. We mustered, at an early hour, in a large field, adjoining Captain Tucker's tan–pits; and only nine men and one officer did not answer to their names. The officer was Surgeon Tamlen; —he was obliged to remain in attendance on Lieutenant Squill's good lady, who was really of such an affectionate and anxious turn, that her forebodings lest the lieutenant should get hurt had so worked upon her nerves, that he left her with positive symptoms of fever. Nothing, however, could deter him from doing his duty; he felt satisfied that all her wants and wishes would be attended to by Surgeon Tamlen, in his absence, and joined us in very tolerable spirits, considering all things. I forgot to mention that, besides the defaulters, a third of the grenadiers were absent on some secret service, the nature of which we could not divine, notwithstanding the lieutenant–colonel winked

very significantly when we noticed their non–appearance. Several ladies, in
barouches and landaus, with buff favours in their bosoms and bonnets, —the
wives and daughters of the officers and other leading men in the borough,—
saluted us as they dashed along the road which bounded the field, on their
way to the hill. Such a circumstance as a sham fight had not occurred in our
neighbourhood within the memory of man; and every lady was, naturally
enough, anxious to witness the interesting scene, in which her husband
or father was to bear some conspicuous part. Precisely as the clock of the
Borough Hall struck eight, we marched off, with drums beating, colours
flying, and everything agreeable and auspicious. I must give the lieutenant–
colonel the credit to say that, in our preliminary manoeuvres, as well as
during the march, the officers and men were much more comfortable than
if the adjutant had been with us; the latter being a man who was eternally
finding fault, where no other individual in the regiment could perceive any
thing to be amiss. After a distressing march of two hours and a half, along a
dusty road, we reached the rear of the hill. There we halted for about twenty
minutes, and then proceeded to mount the acclivity, all the difficulties of
which we overcame, and on our arrival at its summit, were gratified by a
prospect which fully recompensed us for our toils. The secret service on
which the grenadiers had been sent was now very pleasantly palpable. Our
excellent lieutenant–colonel, whose prudence and attention on all occasions,
no words of mine can sufficiently applaud, had despatched, at day–break,
two artillery–waggons, which he had requested for the purpose from the
general, under convoy of our grenadiers, to the post we were to occupy. The
first waggon contained thirty rounds—not of ball–cartridges—but beef, a
strong detachment of turkies, a squadron of hams, a troop of tongues, and
several battalions of boiled fowls and legs of mutton. The second waggon was
garrisoned by hampers of wine, ale, and liquors; and plates, knives and forks,
bread, cheese, mustard, and all the *et–ceteras* of the table, were billetted in the
various crannies and corners. There was only one drawback on the delight
which the appearance of so many good things produced:—the men; not
having been made acquainted with the lieutenant–colonel's kind intention
of ordering a cold collation out of our surplus funds, for refreshment after
our intended repulse of the Highlanders had each brought his dinner in
his knapsack; or, where no private and individual provision had been made,
messes were arranged, and every man carried his separate quota for the
general good. For instance:—one had charged his knapsack with a beef–

steak pie, another with a ham, a third with a fillet of veal, a fourth with a keg of ale, and so on. Notwithstanding this, we could not help admiring our lieutenant–colonel's foresight, in providing for our wants and comforts. It was certainly to be wished though, that he had not restricted him self to a wink or a nod on the occasion; and this was the chief mistake in judgment which he committed, much to his praise be it spoken, in the course of that arduous and eventful day. The ladies, who had left their landaus and barouches at the foot of the hill, were busy, on our arrival, laying out the refreshments in the most elegant and tasteful manner imaginable:—each dish was garnished by laurel leaves; and in the centre of the cloths, which were laid upon a part of the ground that was levelled and mown for the purpose, we beheld, as we marched along the flank of the collation, a device in confectionary, which excited the warmest approbation of the whole corps—officers as well as men: it consisted of a variety of expressive and appropriate martial ornaments, around which buff ribbons were entwined, supporting a splendid cage of barley–sugar, with a bird cut out of currant–jelly inside it, and a cap of liberty surmounting the whole!—We gave three cheers at the sight, and instantly prepared for action. But the colonel, with evident indignation and his accustomed dignity, reprimanded the corps in general, and two of the privates,—butchers and brothers, by–the–by, who were sharpening knives on their bayonets,—in particular, for this improper and very unsoldier–like ebullition. He pointed to the Highlanders, who were already forming for attack at the foot of the hill; and bade us remember that, in his last general orders, he had specially enjoined every officer and man in the corps to eat a good breakfast before he left home; so that no one had any excuse for being hungry these two hours. The grenadiers were ordered to fix bayonets in front of the collation, and the main body of the corps immediately obeyed the word of command to march. In a few moments we were at the brow of the hill; and there, in the presence of the Highlanders and, indeed, two–thirds of the whole field, the lieutenant–colonel put us through as much of the platoon exercise as he thought fit. Only three muskets were dropped during the drill; and, at its conclusion, the lieutenant–colonel, Major Arkfoot, and the other officers who were picked out for the staff, rode through the ranks, diffusing courage and confidence, with small glasses of brandy, to every man in the corps.

"At length we heard the enemy's right wing opening a tremendous fire far away on our left; the lieutenant–colonel immediately dismounted, for his horse did not exhibit sufficient symptoms of discipline to warrant our commander's retaining his seat; and, at that moment, the Highlanders struck up a popular tune on their bagpipes, to which, on turning our eyes towards the munitions, we observed our fair ladies reeling it away, very elegantly, with the gallant grenadiers. On came the enemy, gaily, as if they were going to a wedding; but, wait a bit, thought we, they will look rather foolish when they come to the bank of the brook,—of which they really did not seem to be aware. We were all ready to break out into one universal shout of laughter tt their surprise, and immediately to gall them with a tremendous volley of blank cartridge; when, to our astonishment, on reaching the bank, they marched into the water, and slap through it, without breaking step, or the time of the tune they played on their bagpipes!—Our lieutenant–colonel, as may very naturally be supposed, was totally unprepared for this; even though they did not wear breeches, he could not have foreseen that they would have marched above their knees in water, at a sham fight:—but he did not lose his presence of mind; he immediately ordered the drums to beat, the fifes to play, the colours to be waved, the whole corps to fire, and every individual, officers and all, to increase the noise of the volley, by a stout and hearty hurrah!—We had scarcely obeyed his orders, when the ladies set up a shriek which shattered every man's nerves in the ranks. We looked over our left shoulders at the sound, and, to our infinite dismay and amazement, beheld a body of Highlanders at our backs, advancing in double quick time, with bayonets fixed, to charge us in rear! The lieutenant–colonel, perceiving the critical posture of affairs, and ever alive to the welfare of the corps, ran round to meet the enemy; and cried, with all his might, 'Halt! remnant of the Highlanders! Halt! remnant of the Highlanders! Halt, I repeat!'—But the savage rogues, who had marched round the hill unperceived by us, while their comrades advanced in front, heeded the lieutenant–colonel as little as if he had been an oyster–wench, and still came on at a dog–trot pace; while the other fellows of the regiment, who had, by this time, nearly reached the brow of the hill, did the like, with loud shouts and fixed bayonets, as though it were a real, instead of a sham fight. At last,—the lieutenant–colonel in the rear, and Major Arkfoot in front, being actually within a few paces of their points—the lieutenant–colonel, out of a most fatherly regard for those under his command, thinking the matter began to be above a joke, and not knowing to what extent the terrific enthusiasm of the Highlanders might carry them, gave at once the word, and a most excellent example to all who chose to follow it, for retreating. Thus, we were compelled, through violence and a fraudulent *ruse–de–guerre*, which we were totally unprepared to expect in a sham fight, to leave our ladies, legs of mutton, turkeys, wine, hams, and other provisions, at the mercy of a rude and breechless enemy! One or two of our fellows, who could not get away, described to us, afterwards, the unseemly glee with which the hungry, half–starved Highlanders, sat down to our rounds of beef, boiled fowls, tongue, and other dainties and drinkables; and how soon these things disappeared before them. But what really irked and annoyed us more than the mishap and loss of our collation, was, that the ladies, for months after, vaunted the gallantry and politeness of the Highland officers, who,—confound them!—it seems, protested against the amusements of the fair ones being interrupted by their appearance; and, after devouring the lieutenant–colonel's cold collation, insisted, with the most marked urbanity, on our wives and daughters continuing their reels to the sound of the bagpipes, substituting themselves for the flying grenadiers. We heard of nothing in the town, for ten months after, but the gallant High and their handsome legs, and a dozen other matters to which husbands and fathers have solid objections to listen. Lieutenant and Alderman Squill had the ill–nature to say, that he felt exceedingly happy that his wife had been taken so very unwell that morning, as to be placed under the care of Surgeon Tamlen; and those villains, the epigram writers, in the poet's corner of our country paper, had the impudence to lampoon us, for leaving, as they said, our Dalilas in the hands of the Philistines. But we bore our taunts with manly fortitude; though, I must say, the fact is not yet forgotten in the borough; and the young ladies grieve, who were not old enough to be on the hill, with their mamas or sisters, when the gallant Highlanders, as they call them, routed The Borough Buffs.

"We retreated in such disorder as circumstances rendered inevitable for above a mile, when our wind failing us, we rallied. The line was no sooner formed than somebody proposed that we should lunch; the motion was carried unanimously, and down the men sat to devour the contents of their knapsacks: the lieutenant–colonel, Major Arkfoot, and the rest of the staff, advanced to the carriages where the ladies had left their provisions, under the laudable pretence of reconnoitring;—for field officers must eat, although they should seem to be above it, as well as privates. We occasionally heaved a sigh for the poor things we had left behind us, and determined to effect a rescue at all hazards; but none of us indulged in such unmilitary sorrow as to blunt the edge of our appetites, and we proceeded to lunch very satisfactorily. But another misfortune, which no human foresight could prevent, occurred to the corps while we were eating. We had very naturally concluded that the Highlanders would have remained content with obtaining possession of the post; or, at any rate, been retained by the attractions of the collation and the ladies; we, therefore, felt quite easy. But, strange to say, the fellows not only devoured our provisions, danced, drank, and sang, while we were retreating, but actually came upon us again before we could fully sacrifice to the cravings of nature. The lieutenant–colonel and the whole of the staff were taken prisoners, and driven off, under an escort of Highlanders, in solemn mockery, in the landaus and barouches, to our ancient borough; and we, who were now without an efficient leader, felt obliged to scamper—we scarcely knew where. We acted as a hive of ants, when their haunt is suddenly invaded by a ruthless brood of juvenile turkeys; each of us snatched up a gun, a knuckle of ham, a knapsack, or a loaf, no matter to whom it belonged, so that each individual was freighted for the general good, and away to go!—We had not proceeded far before we were overtaken, and our progress was arrested by the troops under the orders of the captain of the ferocious aspect, blue facings, and terrific voice. No sooner had he ascertained the situation of our affairs, than he assumed the command, and ordered us to halt, in a tone and manner that nobody felt inclined to disobey. The Highlanders, finding that they were not a match for us in retreating, had, previously, relinquished the pursuit, in favour of a regiment of cavalry, who came down upon us at full speed. The captain of the ferocious aspect seeing this, immediately drew us off into a field,—for we were now in an inclosed country,—and after commanding his own men, the yeomanry, and the centre company of our corps, to fly in the greatest apparent disorder, ordered us to draw up, with a quick–set hedge and a deep and very dirty ditch between us and the enemy. When the cavalry had reached within a few hundred yards of the hedge which protected us, the captain with the huge voice said, in a whisper which was heard from one end of the line to the other:—'The Borough Buff Volunteers will all lie down in the ditch!' This order spread consternation through the corps; but down we were obliged to go—in the filthy, abominable puddle and mire, lying in close order from one end of the ditch to the other, and fouling our regimentals in a manner that made us, collectively and individually, grieve in the most superlative degree. Anon, the cavalry came up,—little dreaming that we were lying in the mire and puddle,—leaped the hedge and ditch, in line, and scampered off after the fugitives. They had scarcely galloped a hundred paces, when the captain with the ferocious aspect ordered us to rise, form on the bank, and pour a volley, which we had kept in reserve, into their rear. The centre company, the regulars, and yeomanry, no sooner heard the report than, in pursuance of orders they had received, they formed and faced about for attack.—We then charged the enemy, in front and in rear at the same moment; and there being no outlet to the field on the right or left, the cavalry were completely placed at a nonplus; and had the business been a *boná fide* engagement their position, as you must–needs admit, would not have been altogether exquisite.—This manoeuvre of the captain with the blue facings and ferocious aspect retrieved the honour of the Borough Buffs; and we returned home with drums beating, colours flying, and great eclat, notwithstanding we had lost our field–officers, our ladies, our provisions, and possession of the impregnable hill."

THE BACHELOR'S DARLING

ON a fine summer's morning, a few years ago, two travellers were observed by the turnpike–woman approaching along the high road, towards Bilberry Gate; both were on foot, and one of them led a very pretty poney, laden with two or three half–filled sacks, and an assortment of new and second–hand saucepans, ladles, and similar wares. As they advanced, the turn pike–woman amused herself, by picking up such crumbs of their discourse, as the distance between her and the interlocutors would permit; and by putting what she thus gleaned together, Dame Hetty discovered that they were strangers to each other;—the tinker's companion having scraped acquaintance with that worthy only a few minutes before, on the ground of their both being, apparently, journeying in the same direction. The tinker, she thought, was about thirty, or two–and–thirty years of age, at the utmost; he was a rough, thick–set fellow, of a middling size, with a loud voice and swaggering deportment. His companion, Dame Hetty set down in her own mind as an Irishman, by his brogue;—he was, most likely, she thought, a beggar or a ballad–singer, or both, by his accoutrements; he had a wooden leg, a patch over his right eye, and the left sleeve of his ragged military jacket seemed to be empty. Hetty conjectured from these appearances that he might be an old soldier; but thought it was more probable that he had lost his limbs and eye by casualties not produced by war; and had assumed regimentals, as a striking costume for a maimed beggar or ballad–singer, although, perhaps, he had never smelt powder since he fired off penny cannons in his urchinhood.

These ideas came into Dame Betty's head, without any solicitation on her part: she cared as little about the travellers as they did about her; but she looked at them and thought about them merely for want of a better subject, while she waited at the gate–side in expectation of the tinker's toll. When the two men and the poney arrived within a few yards of the turnpike, they turned suddenly to the right, and entered a lane which led towards a village a few miles off. The poney's tail had scarcely disappeared, when the dame entered the gate cottage, muttering that this was the fourth time she had been disappointed, early as it was in the day, by folks going down the lane. instead of coming along the high road. "But, odd!" said she; "I mustn't expect every horse that comes in sight will pass the gate, when it's revel–day in the village. If there were a bar, now, put across the

lane, as hath long been talked of, I should ha' caught the tinker's penny:
but though he hath leave, my husband never will do't, that's certain;—a
stupid toad! if 'tweren't for I, he wouldn't have a hole to put his head in;
and much thanks I get! Lord! if I were but a man!"

While Dame Hetty was soliloquizing to the foregoing effect, the tinker
and his companion proceeded at a quiet pace down the lane: the narrow
road had a verdant margin on each side, of considerable breadth; it was
broken into knolls in some parts, and here and there a hawthorn flourished,
or a bramble sheltered a family of tall weeds: the thorns and briars bore
evidence that sheep were occasionally permitted to pasture in the lane;
a horse, with a huge log chained to one of his hind legs, to prevent him
from roaming far, was quietly grazing on one side of the road; and nearly
opposite him, a pig, wearing a collar, as an estoppel to his invading the
fields, by creeping through their hedges, lay dozing on the other, near an
old dung–heap that was nearly covered with "summer's green and flowery
livery."

The travellers had proceeded but a few paces down the lane, when
they observed a thin stream of smoke rising from behind a large bush,
which grew within a little distance of the right–hand hedge, and they
immediately turned their steps across the turf towards it. On approaching
nearer, they discovered a tall, lean man, in a plaid cloak, actively engaged
in raking together the embers of a fire, and placing bits of dry wood
upon a little blaze that shot up from its centre. "Is this a gipsy's old place,
I wonder?" said the Irishman; "and is the pedlar, for so I take him to be,
making it up to cook his breakfast?—God save ye kindly!" continued he,
as he came within hearing of the man in the plaid coat.

"Whither awa', friend?" quoth the pedlar.

"Is it to the revel ye're budging, Sawney?"

"What would ye give to ken, Paddy?—And if I were ganging that gate,
why for no, eh?—Ye seem to be cattle for that market yoursel'; wi' your
bits o' ballads, and them scraps or fragments o' mortality ye've saved fra' the
wars. Ye're some broken–down beggar, I doubt. Sauf us a'! isn't it rare to
see sic trash perk up to a travelling tradesman, and address an honest and
respact able person wi' a plain 'Sawney?'—a mon, though I say it, whose
bill for sax, ay, or aught pounds, in Bristol or Frome—"

"Aisy! aisy, man!" interrupted the other; "aisy, or we'll quarrel, I'm
sure;—and when I quarrel, I fight; and it isn't before breakfast I like

fighting:—everything's good in its season; so we won't fight now. As for your bill, though, I'll make bold to say this,—so I will, any how—as for your bill, I wouldn't give the worst ballad I have, for the best bill you or the likes o' ye ever made:—but don't let's be quarrelling, for all that.—Do you mark, though? if you cast any more dirt upon my person or my goods, I'll indorse that bill of yours, that sticks up betuxt your two eyes, in the place of a nose, with the fist that's left me. I'll engage, if I put my hand to it, it won't add much to its value, if you wished to raise money on it: but aisy, both of us; quarrelling does no good."

"Come, come,—I like thee for that, comrade," said the third traveller; "now that's nature;—so shake hands, both of 'ee, lads."

"Oh! wid all my heart!" said the Irishman; "Darby Doherty isn't the boy to bear malice: but when a big fellow, with all his legs and things o' that kind left, tells me about my fragments, it puts me up—do you see?—puts me up, sir:—though I'm not one for quarrelling, yet I'd like to have a pelt at him; but it's before breakfast.—Why should he notice my legs? It's true then, sure enough, I've only one arm, one leg, one wife and a child;—Just a thing of a sort:—but suppose it's my fancy to be so; why should he throw it out at me?—wid his dirty pack—his case of trumpery there!—May be I like number one; why shouldn't I?—Now if I was given to quarrelling, here's an excuse, isn't there? But I'm not.—How does he know, tinker— for a tinker I take you to be"—

Here the tinker bowed, and again requested Mister Doherty to shake hands with the North Briton. By his endeavours, in a few moments, peace was restored; the Irishman seemed to have forgotten what had passed, but the Scotchman sat rather sullenly by the side of the fire, which blazed away very pleasantly. The important subject of breakfast was soon broached, and Doherty, made a proposal to club the contents of their wallets. The tinker had a loaf of black, dry, barley–bread, and a triangular morsel of cheese, which, Doherty said, was fit food for cannibals, who wore hatchets in their mouths instead of teeth. The pedlar drew forth a tin can, containing a small quantity of meal. The Irish man had nothing eatable, but, as he assured his companions, an appetite that would make up for the deficiency. "I never carry any food outside my skin," said he; "when I've a trifle of money to spare, I invariably invest it in whiskey. I've just nine pen'orth in my bottle here now; or may be more, for it wasn't empty when I made the last purchase; and I'd share it most generously wid ye, if ye'd anything aqual in value to offer me in return:—but you, tinker, have nothing but black bread, and a little yellow bit of granite, you call cheese—"

"Nothing,—that's it," replied the tinker; "except a feed for the poney. He! he! mayhap you'll eat a oat?"

"Oh! go to Otaheite,—where Captain Cook couldn't dress his dinner. Do you take me for Caesar, or any similar savage?—And you, Mr. Pedlar, have nought in your wallet but dry meal, to make cold stirabout, or a roley–poley bolus, worked up wid water, in the hollow of your hand."

"Didna I tell ye so?" said the pedlar; "and a wee bit it is, as ye may see."

"And you've nothing in the wide world else?"

"Nought that ye can eat."

"Then ould Ireland for ever! I'm a made man!—If you've nothing eatable but meal, these red herrings are mine: I just picked them up from the grass where your pack stood, a while ago, when you were dipping into it for the meal–can. They can't be yours, you'll own!"

"I tell ye they are, though," cried the pedlar, advancing towards Doherty; "and what's mair—"

"Aisy, aisy, again, or else we'll quarrel," said Doherty, pushing him gently aside; "I'll abide by what the tinker says."

"He's an intarasted patty," replied the pedlar; "and I'll no constitute him arbitrator."

"Well, well, then,—I'll tell you what we'll do;—don't let's quarrel;—to settle everything amicably, I'll trate you to a herring a–piece.—You won't? Did you ever see the likes of him?— I'm sure we'll quarrel: I'm sure we'll have a fight at last; though I wouldn't for five farthings,—and that's money you'll own;—but Jove himself couldn't stand this."

The ballad–singer speaks fair, in my mind, pedlar," quoth the tinker.

"Hech! now, nane o' your havers! I'm no sic a puir daft body as to be gulled o' my guids, by birds o' your feather; rad harrings dinna swim into a mon's wallet, wi' whistling; you must bait your fingers wi' siller to catch them in these pairts,—and groats dinna grow upon bushes noo–a–days."

"Well, that's true enough," said the tinker; "give him his fishes, and we'll buy one a–piece of him."

"Let's know what he'll take, though, before we part wi' them," said the Irishman; "may be we'd quarrel about the price after."

"Right,—very right," replied the tinker.

"Sirs," quoth the pedlar, "business is bad; the girls dinna pairt with their hair noo, as they used, for a bauble or so,—a mon must hae guid guids for them. I'd be free, and invite ye to share wi' me,—but prudence wouldna tolerate it in ane like me, that has eleven bairns."

"Now that's what I call nature!" exclaimed the tinker with considerable emphasis.

"An arithmetical excuse for being stingy," quoth Doherty; " Eleven children! and I've one at home,—which is a bag at his mother's back,—that would eat as much as any seven of them. I'd another, once, but the blackguard gipsies coaxed her away. from the side of us, when we was singing, 'Rogues around you,' at Weyhill. They did it by ginger–bread, or something like it, I think;—bad luck to them!"

"Ay! ay! just as the pigeon people do decoy other folks' young birds by hemp–seed and salt–cats. Oh! it's natural.— Why, now, there's a chap, whose sweepings I ha' bought lately"—"Whose what?" inquired Doherty.

"The sweepings of his loft," replied the tinker; "he's a pigeon–keeper, and I a collector."

"Oh! a sort of scavenger to the birds?"

"Ay, truly; there's many dove–cotes hereabouts, and collecting be my main business; they do use the sweepings in tanning. I pays a shilling a bushel for 'em if they be clean, and so turns an honest penny.—Tinkering isn't half what it was, since iron crocks have come in so much. To be sure, the maidens do save the broken spoons for me to melt and mould again when I comes round; and there's a cullender or so, now and the; to solder;—but what's that? — I'm a tradesman, as well as the pedlar, and what's more, a mechanic; but if my trade won't support me, why should I support my trade, eh?—Well, what did I do; but take to waddling, as we call it, for wood–ashes to sell to the soap–makers, and pigeon–cleanings for the tanners; and so I contrives, one way and another, to make a pretty good bit of bread."

"Is this a specimen?" said the Irishman, taking up the tinker's bat— "If it is, faith! then, the world's but a middling oven for you."

"Stop!—here!" cried the tinker, as Doherty was about to roll the loaf along the grass "Don't do that;—my poney is the biggest thief as ever I knowed,—that is, for a horse. He'd snap it up in no time."

"Would he?—Then I honour him for his talent; though the less we say about his taste the better. Who taught him them tricks?"

"Why, I did—that is, partly—but somebody stole him from me."

"Musha! then the man who did that, wouldn't scruple to rob a thief of his picklock. Well!"—

"Well, he got into the riders' hands;—them chaps that goes about to fairs, and revels, you know."

"Yes, I know;—and they finished his education; and when you got him aguin he was quite accomplished, without any trouble or expense to yourself Tinker, you're a lucky man! I don't think you and I would ever quarrel upon a point o' conscience."

"No, no;— wouldn't be natural"

"Friends," observed the Scotchman, " we're wasting time; and time to a prudent mon, is siller:—ye're wasting it in idle discourse. The harrings—"

"Oh! dirty butter upon your herrings and every one of them! Would you pick a quarrel with me again?" vociferated Darby. "Tinker, bring me one of your second-hand kettles, or crocks, and let's make soup or something, and go to breakfast. If you'll club your herrings, your meal, and your bread,—why then I'll be my whiskey."

The pedlar acquiesced with the best grace a man, who is compelled to give his consent to a proposition, possibly could: a debate ensued, as to the best mode of cooking the food; it was, at length, decided that the meal should be boiled in a gallon of water, and that the herrings should be broiled, and then put into the pot to give the mess a flavour. "If that won't make it salt enough," said Darby, "a bit of burnt stick will do the business royally. The finest salt in the world is the ash of an ash stick. Now, boys," continued he, "see, here's the whiskey bottle. I'll just hitch it up, by the string that holds it about my neck, to the branch above us here;—so that, when we sit down, we can swing it one to the other, drink, and let go again, without any fear of its being upset. Oh, then! discretion's a jewel any day in the year."

Doherty now began the culinary task, in which he exhibited a considerable degree of dexterity, considering his bodily deficiencies. While his only hand was employed in preparing the herrings for the gridiron, with which the tinker had furnished him, his wooden leg was whirled rapidly round the crock, to mix up the poor ingredients that served as the basis of his broth. An onion, which the tinker found in his coat-pocket, was shred and thrown in, with a few wild herbs, which the pedlar, with his pack safely strapped to his back, condescended to gather from the adjoining hedge–row. A steam, at length, began to rise from the crock, which the parties interested in the contents, found most grateful to their olfactories: the broiled herrings were immersed in the broth; Doherty drove them, vigorously, two or three times round the crock; and matters approached fast to a crisis. The cook exerted himself to his utmost; and, in the enthusiasm of the moment, perhaps rather over–zealously, took his wooden leg out of the broth and thrust it beneath the crock to stir up the embers, when some one, who had approached unperceived by either of the party, gently touched Darby's elbow. He turned half round, and beheld a little girl smiling by his side.

"Will you please to tell me, if I am in the right road to the revel, sir?" said the little girl, in a very winning and innocent tone.

"Is it the road to the revel, darling?" said Darby; " Whys then"—Here Darby stopped short, and his eye wandered over the features and person of the young inquirer. She was apparently about ten years of age; her skin was remarkably fair; and her eyes, as Darby afterwards said, were as blue and beautiful as little violets. She was dressed in a black stuff frock, a tippet of the same material, and a seal–skin cap, with a gold band and tassel, which seemed to have been very recently tarnished by the weather. She wore gloves, but had neither shoe nor stocking; and the sight of her delicate, white, little feet, as she held them up, one after the other, toward the fire to warm them, convinced Darby that she had but very lately been compelled to walk barefooted.

"Oh! sir, you're burning your wooden leg!" said the little girl, while Darby was gazing at her, and wondering who and what she could be; and so absorbed was the worthy ballad–singer in the interesting speculation, that he had, in fact, forgotten to withdraw his leg from beneath the crock, where he had just placed it, as will be recollected, when the little girl touched his elbow. At the moment she advised him of the fact, Darby received a hint or two that corroborated her assertion;—the flame had twined up the stem, and rather warmed his stump, and the fire blazed with such vigour, recruited as it was by the supply, that the broth boiled over. His two companions, who were close at hand, both observed this latter circumstance an instant after the child had spoken; the pedlar cried aloud to Darby to save the broth, and the tinker shouted with glee to see the Irishman sacrificing his trusty support for the common good. Doherty did not lose his presence of mind: he withdrew his leg from the fire, and popped it into the pot;—thus extinguishing the stump, withdraw the additional stimulus to the fire, and breaking down the rebellious head of the herring–broth, by that single and simple act.

The child could not refrain from giggling, miserable as she evidently was, at the scene; and Darby looked alternately at her and his leg, when he withdrew it from the pot again, in so droll a manner, that the little girl burst into a fit of laughter, which the Irishman, very good–naturedly, subdued, or rather, smothered with kisses.

"Well; my pretty little maid!" said he; "and where have you come from, agrah! eh?"

"Oh! a long—long way; it's farther than I thought it was when I began."

"And what do you want at the revel?"

"I mustn't tell you."

"Eh, then! why not, eh?"

"If I was to tell you why I mustn't, you'd know what I wanted at the revel."

"And where's your stockings and shoes? Have you put them in your pocket, as the girls do in Ireland?"

"No, indeed;—I wore them out yesterday."

"And how far have you walked barefoot?"

"Oh! ever so far!"

"And how far's that?"

"I can't tell.—Is this the road to the revel?"

"It is;—but what hurry? Won't you wait and take pot–luck with us?"

"I'm hungry, thank you, sir, but I don't think I could eat any pot–luck,—it smells so odd; I never tasted pot–luck in my life; but I thank you, sir, for all that, you know."

"Now, do you hear that? Do you hear the innocence of her? God send we'd better for you!—though you won't tell us where you come from."

"I shouldn't wonder but she hath been stole away," said the tinker; "stole away, and carried afar, and now hath got liberty, and is seeking home again. That's nature, you know:—a pigeon would do it; a carrier, a horseman, a dragoon, or a middling good tumbler even; and why shouldn't a child?"

"Wha may ye be in mourning for, my wee lassie?" inquired the pedlar. He was proceeding to ask something about her father and mother, when Darby put his hand on the pedlar's mouth, and whispered "Wisht! wisht!

why not now, eh?—Aisy, or we'll quarrel. Don't you know, you old snail, you! that a child in black should never be axed who it's worn for? May be her mother's dead," continued he, raising his voice, and fondling the child as he spoke; "and your goose of a question raised her dead ghost up to the little one's memory. Look there—see that now— if the tears ar'n't running out of her eyes: may be she hasn't a father;—and you—ye spalpeen, to hurt her feelings that way! Oh! fie upon you, sir!"

"Eh, mon! dinna prate; it's your ain sel' that did the business.—Come hither, lassie! lassie, come hither!—Could you eat— that is, ha' ye appetite for—a bit of a harring, daintily broiled? An' ye could stomach it, I hae just ane in my pack, and I'll broil it mysel', and ye shall eat it wi' a bit o' biscuit, I think there may be in the pack too."

The child smiled in the pedlar's face, and, with a nod, signified that she would accept his offer. The pedlar then produced a fine herring from a corner of his pack, and after a diligent search, discovered a piece of biscuit, which he gave the little girl, who curtsied as she took it. these transactions by no means gratified Mr. Doherty: he was in a passion with the pedlar; first, for possessing a fourth herring; and secondly, for alluring their little guest with it from his arms: he also considered the North–Briton's emphatic offer to broil it himself, as a sneer upon his own culinary achievements. Darby was actually at a loss for words to express his feelings, and he had recourse to action: thrusting his hand deep into his bosom, and twisting his hip to meet it, he seemed to be diving into some pouch, that was rarely visited, and difficult of access. In rather more than a minute, his hand re–appeared, with a little odd–shaped bundle of rags in its clutch. With the aid of his teeth, he contrived to take off several pieces of ribbon and linen, and, at length, a small metal snuff–box, in the shape of a high–heeled and sharp–toed shoe, emerged from the mass. He opened it and took out a sixpence. "There," said he, (for he had now recovered his speech,) throwing the coin toward the pedlar, "take the price of your herring and biscuit, and give me the change.—She shan't be beholden to you!—Little one!" continued he, addressing the child, "don't listen to him; don't bite at his bait, nor don't go wid him, darling.— Will I tell you what he is?—He's one o' them people that cuts the long hair off the girls' heads, and gives them gew–gaws for it. He'll take you under a hedge, or, may be, when you're asleep, pull out a big pair of shears and clip off all them pretty locks, which he'd make shillings of again, from the hair–merchants; for I see you've longer hair than most maids of your age; and, faith! it's beautiful and he knows it. He's looking at it as a cat would at a mouse.—He's a bad man, my dear."

"Is he?" said the little girl, apparently half alarmed, but still feeling rather inclined to doubt Darby Doherty's account of the pedlar;—"Is he a bad man?—Then why do you stay with him?"

"I won't—no, not while you'd whistle, after I've ate his herrings;—that is, if you'll come wid me.—Will you?"

"Perhaps," replied the little girl, "he'll say you are a bad man; and then what can I do?"

At this the tinker laughed and muttered something about nature. The pedlar still held the child, and putting his hand under her chin, turned her face upwards, and then looking down upon he; spoke thus:—"My wee woman, I hae eleven bairns, some younger than yoursel', and I wouldna harm sic a puir, wee, defenceless child as thee, for the worth of an ingot of pure gold; it would weigh down my heart on a death–bed, and carry my soul into the sorrowfu' pit. I'm a tradesman, and traffic in hair, as he has just told you, and have a family,—eleven bairns, a wife, myself, a daft brither, my first wife's aged and bed–ridden mither, and a sister's son, as wee and as fatherless as ye seem yoursel';— saxteen mouths to find food for to–day and to–morrow, and every morn that I rise. I travel far and near to get it."

"Just like a good cock–pigeon," interrupted the tinker; "I've known an old bird feed the young squeakers in one nest, and his mate to boot, while she was setting over her eggs in another tightish work!—but there—it's natural."

"And I dinna scruple," continued the pedlar, without noticing the interruption of his companion; "I dinna scruple to do my best, and barter, as well as I can, in order to get bread and 'cheese;—but not with the like o' thee, cherub. I canna' take thee by adoption, for I hae eleven o' my ain.—I'll hold out no temptation o' that sort; but I'll carry thee, on the head o' my pack, safe and clear to the revel, if there's ony there ye hae a wish to see."

"For that matter," cried the tinker, "she can ride a–top of my poney, with the pots and that."

"Oh! don't be bothering!" shouted Doherty; "she shall ride upon my wooden leg, or anywhere about me, for have her I will; to the revel she goes wid me, right or wrong, in spite of man or baist, tinkers, tay–kettles, pedlars, packs, pilfering ponies, and the whole fratarnity of ye.—I've said it, and so it shall be.— How do I know,—answer me this,—ho do I know that she isn't the child I lost long ago, eh?—That was a girl, and isn't this a girl? Now don't be trying to bother my brains with a reply.— Darby Doherty is my name, and I'm to be found any day, here or there, one place or another, if you go the right road.—Pedlar, stop thief! the tinker has stole a herring out of the pot."

"Ay, truly, it's time to fall to," quoth the tinker.

"Wait a moment!" exclaimed the Irishman; "one moment, and we'll all begin amicably. Hear w'hat I've to say:—I've spoken what I thought about my honourable friend the pedlar's scheme on the little one; and why mayn't I indulge in an idea that the worthy tinker, in offering to let his poney carry her, doesn't speculate—bad luck to his black paws, how he's streaked the broth!—doesn't speculate upon the value of the child's ear–rings and little necklace?—for these reasons; I'll let neither of you have her:—now I'm aisy."

"Why, do you mean to throw out hints—" said the tinker, laying his herring on the grass, and advancing with a formidable frown and clenched fists toward Darby; "dost thee mean—"

"Now don't babble; the question's settled," said Darby; "don't prate, or we'll quarrel."

"And I'll be jiggered if we don't,—whether thee likes or not. I'll stand up for my own character;—it's nature:—so ax pardon, or strip."

"Strip! How the devil do you think I'd ever get my tags on again, eh? Ha! ha!"

"Come, come; a joke won't carry it off; it's too heavy. Talk to I about her rings!—I—I—I—Oh! d—n thee! I'll thrash thee!"

The ballad–singer held up his stumps, and hopping back two paces, cried, "What, would you assault one with not a plural offensive or defensive about him?"

"Oh! dang that!—thee'rt right, though;—it's natural. Here, pedlar, help me to tie up my leg and arm, and put thy necker–chief athirt my eye:—fair play's the word."

The little girl now screamed loudly, and beseeched the pedlar to interfere. "Oh! pray, dear Mr. Pedlar, don't let them fight! Oh! he's going to kill the poor man with the little wooden leg!"

"Do ye hear—do ye hear?" exclaimed the pedlar, "how the bit creature—the cause o' your quarrel—"

"Oh!: pray let me go away," sobbed the child; "and then perhaps they'll be friends;—do let me go!"

"Stay, darling," quoth Doherty; "rather than frighten the child, I'll consent to apologise:—the heat of the argument made me singe the whiskers of my friend the tinker's honour;—but if the child wasn't where she is, and we were after breakfast, just now, right or wrong, tinker, we'd quarrel."

"But not fight, it strikes me," muttered the pedlar.

Calm was again restored, and the trio sat down to their breakfast. The tinker's loaf was divided; each man devoured his herring, and the soup was dipped out of the crock, and drank from a little second-hand saucepan, which alternately served each of the party. Darby's bottle, which was suspended from the branch above, before the meal was half concluded, had nearly proved an apple of discord between the tinker and the pedlar. Darby began, by taking a tolerably good sup of the contents; he then swung the bottle to the pedlar, who held it so long to his lips, that the honest tinker became alarmed lest he should not obtain his share. The pedlar did not withdraw the bottle from his mouth; and when he raised it to an angle of nearly forty-five degrees with the horizon, the tinker could no longer sit easy on the turf. He started up, rushed across the crock, which he upset in his transit, seized the pedlar by the throat with one hand, and clutched the bottle with the other.

"Hold hard!" said he; "not a drop more goeth down thy gullet! Quit thy hold o' the bottle, or I'll choke thee!—I will, faith!—it's natural:—thou hast had my bread, let me share in the whiskey."

The residue of the broth made the fire hiss and send forth fumes, the odour of which was truly disgusting. The little girl screamed again, and Darby Doherty was in high hopes that the brawny pedlar would have resented the tinker's attack on his person: but he was disappointed.

"You'll excuse me," said the tinker, bowing as he succeeded in obtaining possession of the bottle. "You'll excuse me, but, truly—"

"Dinna mention it, friend," quoth the pedlar. "I was wrong—I forgot mysel';—it was vara well of ye to look to your ain:—I forgot mysel', and should have taken it down to the ultimate drop; it glides away like a joyful dream. It's Farintosh, I doubt: and vara excellent gude as I've tasted for mony a day."

The child was much amazed to see storm and calm succeed each other so rapidly; she felt alarmed at those whom chance had made her associates and would-be protectors; but appetite mastered fear, and she soon dried her eyes, and ate the remainder of a piece of the herring which the pedlar had broiled for her while his companions were debating, and the biscuit he had discovered in his pack.

After breakfast, the question as to who should take the child to the revel, was again started. Each of the men spoke resolutely; and a third quarrel was already budding, when the little girl stood up between the brawlers, and proposed that, as all three of them were so kind as to wish to take her, and neither of them would let her go with either of the others, she should walk on alone; or, that all of them should go with her together.

An immediate assent was given to this proposal; the motion, as Darby said, was carried by acclamation; and preparations were immediately made for starting. While the pedlar was buckling on his pack, the poney neighed; and the tinker exclaimed, "Who comes hither, I wonder, a–horseback?"

"Faith, no one that I see or hear, a–horseback or a–foot," replied the Irishman.

"Ay, but there do, though, sure as death," said the tinker; "my poney yean't no false prophet. I'll lay pints round, a horse is coming: I won't swear for a man,—mind me;—but a horse I be sure of:—and, look—dang me if 'tean't Parson Hackle!"

"And who's he, then?" inquired the Irishman, as a tall, thin, middle–aged man, in a black coat, with long leathern leggings, reaching from his toes to his hips, and mounted on a fat, ambling, old coach–horse, turned from the high–road, into the lane. "I'll just make my obedience and compliments to him as he goes by."

"Thee'st better not," said the tinker.

"Why not, then?—May be he'd drop me a keenogue and be civil."

"Not he, friend; he's a magistrate, and though a good man in the main, mortally hates beggars."

"Beggars!" exclaimed the Irishman; "sir, I'm a wandering minstrel— one of the tribe of Orpheus of ould; who, as the song says, the stones followed; and who, moreover, could move stocks themselves with his music:—maning, I suppose, that he often got pelted by bad boys, and whistled himself out of the stocks, with no thanks to the beadle.—Musha! that I mightn't, then!"

"Well! I can only tell thee, lad," said the tinker, "Parson Hackle looks as black at a ballad–singer; as his brother, the 'squire, do at a man who happens to be misfortunate wi' a maiden."

"Bad luck to the pair o' them then!"

"So say I," quoth the tinker; "I ha' been in their clutches afore now, and I'll warrant the person you spoke of couldn't ha' bought his liberty wi' an old song, if he got into their wooden gaiters."

"Oh! sir, sir! pray—dear sir!" said the little girl, who had several times in vain attempted to make herself heard, during the preceding dialogue between Darby and the tinker; "did you say the gentleman's name was Hackle?"

"Yea, I did, troth!" replied the tinker; "Parson Hackle."

"Parson Hackle!" repeated the little girl; "where is he going?"

"Down to the revel, I reckon," said the tinker, "like we be; only he goeth a–horseback, and we poor folks a–foot; and he goeth to help to keep the peace, and we, mayhap, to help to break it. I can't answer for myself much more for my friends, after one o'clock."

The tinker was right in his supposition that the reverend gentleman was on his way to the scene of the revel, and necessity compels us to accompany him; leaving the little girl and her three friends, to follow us at their leisure. The Reverend Reginald Hackle rode on at a quicker pace than his steed was accustomed to: Reginald partook, in some degree, of the hereditary impatience of the Hackles; the humour broke out but rarely, for Reginald's life was as seldom ruffled, as the gentle stream which glode along by the garden–hedge of his quiet abode: but he was now on his way to pass a few hours with his brother Archibald, whom he had not seen for a number of years; and the old horse, unused to such exertions as those to which his reverend rider, on this occasion, urged him, smoked like a dumpling recently lifted from a crock, by the time he reached the village.

Hackle Hall, the ancient and odd–looking edifice, toward which Reginald turned his horse's head, on emerging from the lane, was the residence of his elder brother, Sir Waldron; a man noted, as the tinker had stated in other words, for being harsh and unforgiving to those rural rakes, from whom scarcely any village in the kingdom is free. Neither Sir Waldron nor Reginald was married; their younger brother, Archibald, had a wife and a large family. Reginald, in addition to his duties as the pastor of a neighbouring parish, educated six or eight youths of the first families in the county, and Archibald had agreed to place his only boy, Waldron, under Reginald's care, for three or four years, in compliance with the reverend gentleman's affectionate and frequent invitations. He had stolen away from

London, leaving business, as he said, to take care of itself for a few days, and brought young Waldron down with him. Reginald was absent on his arrival, at a considerable distance, relative to certain affairs, the arrangement of which he would have postponed, had he been made acquainted with Archibald's intended visit; but the latter had determined, very suddenly, on the journey. On taking a mental glance at his affairs one morning, while he was discussing a glass of sherry and a sandwich, at Garraway's, he discovered that there was nothing remarkably pressing, in the way of business, for some days forward: the funds were closed; two or three holidays at the public offices occurred in the ensuing week; he had not been out of town, except to fetch his family from a watering–place, for years past; he yearned to see his brothers,—and sent a ticket–porter to book places by the Exeter mail of the same evening. Young Waldron had scarcely time to take leave of his mother and sisters; and as to packing up his clothes, Mrs. Hackle declared such an exploit to be impossible. "Then what the devil is there in these, my love?" said Archibald, pointing to two trunks, a portmanteau, a carpet–bag, a bundle, and a hat–box, which lay before him. Mrs. Hackle replied, that they merely contained a change of linen, *or so*, and a few immediate necessaries for himself and his son. "Then, I suppose," said he, "Waldron may expect the main body of his baggage by the broad–wheeled waggon."

Partings and meetings between relatives are seldom of any interest except to those immediately concerned in them: we shall not, therefore, indulge in a description of what took place at the departure of Archibald and his son from Mrs. and the six Misses Hackle, nor of what Reginald said to Archibald, or Archibald said to Reginald, during the first ten minutes of their interview at Hackle Hall We rather prefer relating the conversation of the three brothers after they had made a tolerable lunch on a cold pigeon–pie and two quarts of very respectable ale.

"Well, brother Archibald," said the reverend gentleman as soon as the tray was removed, "and, pray, what aspect does your native place wear to your eye, since your long absence from it?— But you were so young when you quitted it, for a dismal, smoky, London–merchant's 'counting–house, that I suppose all recollection of it must have escaped your memory."

"That's the positive truth," replied Archibald; "if I had remembered the place and its people; if the least remnant of a sample had cleaved to me, not even the pleasure of seeing you and Waldron, would have induced me to have quitted the metropolis to pay it a visit."

"You amaze me!" exclaimed Reginald; "the hospitality—"

"Oh! I've had enough of hospitality, believe me; and so had Gulliver, in the arms of the Brobdignag monkey, who ran away with him, and poked pounds of nauseous chewed food out of its own jaws into his; people are sometimes offensively, cruelly hospitable. Here, now, for instance, was I taken yesterday, by my brother, for a treat—mark me—to dine with one Jehoshaphat Higgs—"

"Almost the sole remaining specimen," interrupted Sir Waldron, "of the fine, old–English, West–country yeomen;—a race, alas! now nearly extinct. I honour the man: he farms his own land; sends his sons to the plough; his daughters to the spinning–wheel, and his wife to the churn. He keeps up all the good old customs of the country; raises the mistletoe on his beam at Christmas, and dances round the May–pole, with his buxom dame, at seventy as gay at heart, though not as light of limb, as he did at twenty: I repeat, that I honour such men."

"Honour them as much as you please, Waldron," replied Archibald; "honour them, and welcome; but, I beseech you, do not entrap me to honour another of them,—if indeed, there be such another blade as old Jehoshaphat, hereabouts,—with any more visits. First, brother Reginald, conceive the misery, if you can, of dining in a room, falsely designated a parlour, with a sanded floor! My teeth were set on edge every time I moved a foot."

"Ay, but, brother, provided the table be well covered," observed Reginald, "one might, methinks, even put up with a clean, dry, sanded floor."

"Ay, ay, keep him to that, Reginald," said Sir Waldron, "the table was, indeed, well covered. I have not dined so well these three weeks. We had a full course of downright thoroughbred old–English dishes;—Devonshire dainties of the first water; such as that transcendant lyrist, Robert Herrick, himself, when he dwelt in this country, doubtless, occasionally feasted on; compared with which, your modern kickshaws, your town messes, and hashes, and fricassees, and starved turtle, brother Archibald, are as chaff, compared with its own grain.. You shall judge, Reginald: among other things, there was a remarkably fine–flavoured muggot–pie;—a dish, of which, I find, by an old manuscript, in our library, that the talented and virtuous Raleigh, was remarkably fond, and moreover partook, three days previously to his execution."

"In my opinion," said Archibald, "a man who would be fool enough to prefer muggot–pie to—"

"It's fine eating, Archibald," quoth Sir Waldron; "would that you had tasted it! — and Sir Walter was a great man; — fine eating, on the honour of a gentleman."

"What! calves' tripe baked in a pie, fine eating!" said Archibald; "if this be the result of your dwelling in Devonshire—"

"I never was out of it but thrice in my life," said Sir Waldron; "and each time I had cause to repent of my folly.— But, to waive the muggot—had we not, also, parsley–pie?—"

"Made, as its name implies, of the herb that's used for garnish!"

"Squab–pie—"

"A horrible mixture of mutton–chops, apples, onions, and fat bacon!—Most abominable!—the stench was enough to have defeated an army of civilized beings. In fact, the dinner given by Peregrine Pickle's friend, the physician, in imitation of the ancients—"

"The ancients fed well," observed Reginald; "Heliogabalus—"

"Was a nincompoop to Queen Elizabeth's cook," added Sir Waldron, rather warmly; "whose mistress was served with fine natural meat and drink—"

"Such as muggot, squab, and parsley–pies, I suppose," quoth Archibald.

"The appetites of the Romans," continued Sir Waldron, "were, in latter times, depraved; and so is my brother Archibald's. Smollett very justly ridicules the feasts of the ancients, in that passage of Peregrine Pickle, where—"

"Really, brother Waldron," interrupted Reginald, while a slight blush tinged his cheek, "I must entreat of you to pass on to some other subject; you know we never agree on this: if I have a failing—*if* said I?—I meant, that, among my numerous failings, that of being slightly irritable, when the glorious masters of the world are attacked, by one who cannot appreciate them, is, I am sorry to say, very conspicuous."

"Exceedingly so, Reginald," replied Sir Waldron; "and if I have a virtue in the world—I beg pardon—among my numerous virtues, that of standing forth, manfully, for the customs of old England, and defending its literature against any man who presumes to set up the cold, classical, marbly stuff of the Greeks or Romans, in preference, is, certainly, I am proud to say, most paramount."

"*Findarum quisquis studet emulari*, brother Waldron," exclaimed Reginald; but he was cut short, in his intended quotation, by Archibald, who said,

"And if I plume myself on any merit of mine,—except, from my boyhood, always having balanced to a fraction,—it is on that of preferring a good carpet to a sanded floor; a Hoby's boot to a hob–shoe; a tooth by Ruspini, to fill up a gap made by time, to no tooth at all; a Calf by Sheldrake, to make my left match with my right, to an odd pair of legs; a good dinner of fish, flesh, and fowl, at Cuff's, or the Albion, or in my own dining–room, to muggot, parsley, or squab pies, in Devonshire; a glass of claret to poor pinch–throat cider; punch to such filthy messes as buttered ale (hot ale with sugar, butter and rum!) or *meaty–drinky* (ale made thick with flour!); and the company of two or three intelligent men over a bottle or a bowl, to all the famous authors, from Homer downwards, Greek, Roman, and English; not one of whose works I ever found half so useful as the Tables of Interest, Patterson's Roads, or the London Directory."

This speech by no means raised Archibald in the estimation of either of his brothers. Sir Waldron thrust his hands deep into his pockets, and began whistling "Lillibullero." Reginald sighed, and said to the man of business, in rather a doleful tone, But, surely, brother, you have not forgotten your Horace; we were class–fellows together; you cannot be blind to the beauties of those illustrious names—"

"Chaucer, Sidney, Spencer,"—said Sir Waldron.

"Euripides, Sophocles,"—quoth Reginald.

"Ford, Decker, Marlow," thus the baronet proceeded; "Fletcher, Jonson,—"

"Ha, ha!" exclaimed Archibald; "a list of very good people in their day, no doubt;—indeed, they were clever, for I know it;—but there's not one of the names you have mentioned would make a bill five farthings the better in Lombard Street."

"But don't you ever read, brother Archibald?" asked the reverend gentleman, very earnestly.

"Ay," said Sir Waldron; "don't you sometimes take down a book to amuse yourself?"

"Oh! yes; very often," was the reply.

"Greek or Roman?"—"Shakespeare, Donne, Randolph,—or what book, brother Archy?"

"My ledger, or bill–book, brother Waldron," replied Archibald. His two brothers, on hearing this, immediately rose from their chairs, and walked to different ends of the room. "You may talk of interest, and pathos, and so forth," continued Archibald, "as much as you please, but, egad! I find more pathos in that folio of my ledger, where Crumpton, Brothers, and Cross are debited items, to the tune of thousand pounds (speaking roundly), and their assignees credited with a dividend of seven pence–halfpenny in the pound, than ever I did in all the works you have mentioned. The account of Crumpton, Brothers, and Cross is real; invoices and delivery–receipts may be produced to establish all the items: but the tales of your poets are generally altogether, and always in part, fictitious, like the begging letters which the Mendicity people expose. Now, I can't see, for the soul of me, why men in their senses can ever be such asses as to invent and write tales of sorrow; as if there wasn't enough of *bonâ fide* grief in the world already:—or how, to go further, people can read, and suffer themselves to be affected by such woeful stories, when they have troubles enough of their own to cry over; and, moreover, when they know that what they are perusing with aching hearts, is a farrago of lies:—and, egad! The greater the lie, it seems, the greater the merit;—lying, in this way, is called imagination. Why, sir, if any given author of eminence, were to tell half as many falsehoods in person as he does in print, upon my honour and credit, if he wasn't reckoned a fool, he'd certainly get kicked out of every house in the metropolis—least of all those I visit."

"Brother, brother!" exclaimed Sir Waldron, "I cannot listen to this folly."

"Nor I; indeed, I cannot," said Reginald. "But, perhaps, my brother Archy preferreth the authors of modern days, and they delight him to the exclusion of the fine old spirits of past ages."

"Not so—not so, indeed," replied Archibald; "they are all the same to Archibald Hackle. I would rather have a good dinner than the finest feast of reason that ever enthusiast described. I prefer a roasting pig to Bacon; a Colchester oyster to Milton; a cut of the pope's–eye to Pope's Homer; an apple–tart to Crabbe; Birch's real turtle to Ovid's Art of Love; and a roasted potato to Murphy. While others embark in man–of–war, frigate, merchantman, heavy Dutch lugger, hoy, yacht, bum–boat, gondola, canoe, funny, or other craft, for the wide ocean of literature—let me enjoy myself in port. I would, any day, barter a volume of Sheri*dan* for a bottle of Dan sherry;—a second quarto for the first pottle of strawberries, or a book by—"

"Brother Archibald, pr'ythee do not run on at this rate," interrupted Sir Waldron; "you, surely, are not so lost to all intellectual delights as you pretend; you cannot be always employed at your business or your bottle;—to say the least, you must have some time to kill."

"Kill! kill time!—Oh, dear! no," replied Archibald; "you know nothing about the matter. Time travels too fast by half to please me;—I should like to clip the old scoundrel's pinions. The complaints which I have heard, occasionally, of time passing away so slowly, ennui, and what not, are to me miraculous. Time seems to travel at such a deuce of a rate, that there's no keeping pace with him. The days are too short by half, so are the nights; so are the weeks, the months, and the years. I can scarcely get to bed before it's time to get up; and I haven't been up but a little time, apparently, before it's time to go to bed. I can but barely peep at the Gazette, or any matter of similar interest in the papers, and swallow an anchovy–sandwich, and a couple of cups of coffee, when it's time to be at the 'counting–house. By the time I have read the letters and given a few directions, it's time to be in a hundred places;—before I can reach the last of them, it's time to be on 'Change;—I don't speak to half the people there, to whom I have something to say, before it's time to reply to correspondents; and my letters are scarcely written before it's post and dinner time. Farewell business!—but then– there's no time for enjoyment: dinner, wine, coffee, supper, and punch, follow in such rapid succession,—actually treading on each other's heels,—that there's no time to be comfortable at either of them. It's the same in bed;—a man must sleep fast, or time will get the start of him, and business be behind–hand an hour or two, and everything in disorder next morning.—If I accept a bill for a couple of months, it's due before I can well whistle: my warehouse rents are enormous; and, upon my conscience, Lady–day and her three sisters introduce themselves to my notice, at intervals so barely perceptible, that the skirt of one of the old harridans' garments has scarcely disappeared, before in flounces another. It's just as bad with the fire–insurances, and a thousand other things,—little matters as well as great: a man can scarcely pick his teeth before he's hungry again. The seasons are drawn by race–horses; my family has barely settled at home after a trip to Buxton, Brussels, or elsewhere, before summer comes round, and Mrs. H. pines for fresh air and an excursion checque again. I can scarcely recover the drain made on my current capital, by portioning one daughter, before another shoots up from a child to a woman; and Jack

This or Tom T'other's father wants to know if I mean to give her the same as her sister. It's wonderful how a man gets through so much in the short space of life; he must be prepared for everything, when, – egad! there's no time for anything."

"Can this really be the fact?" inquired Reginald, incredulously.

"I give you my word and honour it is."

"But," said Sir Waldron, "you have actually complained to me, this morning, how the past week has 'dragged its slow length along' with you."

"To be sure it has," replied Archibald; "because I'm here—where I've nothing to do—and nothing to eat."

"Nothing to eat, Archibald Hackle!" exclaimed Sir Waldron, drawing himself up with an expression of offended dignity; "Hackle Hall, sir, is almost an open house, even to the wayfarer;—you are one of its sons. I trust I have supported the honour of our a while it has been in my keeping;—if you think otherwise, brother Archibald, and can shew that I have not deported myself as becometh the head of the family, although you are my younger brother, I lie open to your most severe censure."

"My dear fellow," said Archibald, in a familiar manner, that Sir Waldron deemed altogether unsuitable to the circumstances of the moment, "my dear fellow, I don't care a pepper–pod about the honour of our ancestors."

"Not for the honour of our ancestors, brother Archibald!" exclaimed Reginald, raising his eye–brows, and laying considerable emphasis on every word, so as to make himself clearly understood.

"Ay, sir!" said Sir Waldron sternly; "not for the honour of our house, eh?"

"Not a pepper–pod!" replied Archibald, coolly. "I have other things to trouble me:—I care more about the house of Van Bummel and Crootz of Amsterdam honouring its bill except, indeed, that this house is your property, Waldron;—but I suppose, of course, it's insured;—you couldn't be such a fool as not to insure it;—and therefore, perhaps, the sooner it's burned down the better, if it wasn't for the loss to the company; for, to speak the truth, it's one of the ugliest edifices I ever had the honour of beholding. I dare say it was well enough a few centuries back; but it has been so patched, and with so little attention to order, that it looks as bad as a beggar's coat It's a compound of the tastes of every half century for these four hundred years past, and harmonizes remarkably well, brothers, with the range of our ancestors' portraits in the gallery:—there they are, bow–legs and bandy–legs, fat old fellows in flowing wigs, who remind one of porters at a masquerade, and brawny ruffians in armour, whose looks would half hang them, without other evidence, in any court in the kingdom:—Round–heads, cavaliers, churchmen, and knights of the shire;—mitres and helmets, cocked hats and cones; with women to match, for each generation;—tag–rag and bob–tail, pell mell, higgledy–piggledy,— in all styles, costumes, forms and fashions!"

"Those portraits, sir," exclaimed Sir Waldron, "are invaluable— invaluable, sir!"

"They wouldn't fetch a pound a–piece, one with another, by auction," replied Archibald: "the collection is just like the house itself; to which each generation seems to have added its quota, more in accordance with the fashion of the day, than the character of the building. What remains of the original masonry reminds me of an old iron chest; and the affair altogether, with its turrets and chimneys sticking up, of various sizes and fonts, resembles nothing in the world (except its gallery of portraits) but an old cruet–stand, furnished with odd bottles. The squat, round, flat–headed west turret, with the flag–staff without a flag, over hanging one side of it, resembles a tenpenny mustard–pot; the little trumpery dome that stands up at the east, a pepper–castor; the tall chimney, almost in the centre, the neck of a slender vinegar–cruet; the—"

"'Sdeath! brother Reginald," interrupted Sir Waldron; "are we to bear this?"

"No—really, I think Archibald is going to lengths which are not decidedly to his credit," said Reginald.

"I would take leave to tell him," continued Sir Waldron, "if he were not under my roof; and in the honourable house of his ancestors, that the expressions he has used are derogatory to his elder brother's dignity. I have always endeavoured to support the name of Hackle in the county, in its proper rank: I am proud to say, there is not a blot in my escutcheon; I think I may almost vie with my brother Reginald, in moral deportment; I watch myself with the most scrupulous exactitude; I consider the name as a special trust confided to me for life, and I strive to maintain it pure and unsullied for the next possessor: I mortify myself out of respect to the house of which I am—I trust, not unworthily,—the head. Hospitality in Hackle Hall, is not a mere word—"

"No, indeed," said Archibald; "here is plenty to eat and drink, but nothing eatable or drinkable. In matters appertaining to the table, you are a century and a half behind us in town. I can no more live upon your dishes than I could wear my grandfather's breeches, or old Sir Geoffry's greaves for gaiters. You keep up a custom of dining at two o'clock,—and I don't care a farthing for dinner till five, at the very earliest moment. The post of honour in the parlour, at breakfast–time, is occupied by a huge, blear–eyed, irascible, old stag–hound, instead of an agreeable woman; and there she lies, dreaming of following the stag, where she ought to be sitting, all smiles and sweetness, asking a man if he'd take half a cup more. But night is worse than all; it's so awfully silent, that I can't sleep!—In fact, brother Waldron, although you have done all in your power to make me comfortable,—to speak the plain truth,—when the novelty of the thing wore off, when there was nothing more left to laugh at, — in other words, within twenty–four hours after my arrival, I began to sigh for a lunch at the 'counting–house, sent in hot from the Cock in Threadneedle Street, and a draught of London porter, again. I feel as though I was in a strange country; I can't understand two–thirds of what the people say. With the assistance of my man—whom I brought down, not out of ostentation, but because I can't shave myself; and entertain a mortal fear of a country barber,—I have today discovered, that meat, in the dialect of these parts, means bread, butter, and almost everything eatable but meat; and meat they call flesh! — He had a quarrel with a farmer's son, last night, who threatened to 'scat him down upon the planchin;' and shortly afterwards tripped up his heels: so that, thank heaven! if any one, while I remain here, threatens to scat me down upon the planchin, I shall know, that nothing but my legs can save me from being transferred from a perpendicular to a horizontal position. He tells me, too, that you make broth of hot water poured upon chopped leeks and bits of mutton–suet,— and that, in this country, broth is plural;—that they ask you to have a *few*, instead of some; and tempt you to take some, by vowing, that they—that is, the broth—*are* cruel good.—Item, that when the wind blows dust in your eyes, the bumpkins exclaim, 'How the pellam blaeth!' and that, upon one fellow being asked what he meant by 'pellam,' he replied, 'Muck adrouth.' 'And what's muck adrouth?' said the stranger. 'Why, pellam, to be sure,' replied the bumpkin; and this was all that could be elicited from him, in explanation. If I happen to mention anything metropolitan, which, in their sublime stupidity, they either do not comprehend or believe, they say, with roguish and provoking gravity, 'Ahem! quo' Dick Bates!' and then, if I manifest a little display of venial irritability at their ignorance, they tell me, that I'm 'all of a Mick, like Zekiel Hodder's boot!'—Now, who the deuce Dick Bates or Zekiel Hodder may be, I can't learn. I was offered my choice of three apples, yesterday, and the man who held them, instead of asking me which I would have, this, that, or the other, said something like what I am about to attempt:— 'Well, 'zquire, which 'ull 'ee ha',—thic, thac, or thuc?' Some of the old people, positively, banish 'she' and 'I' from their discourse, using 'her' for the former, like the Welsh, and the kingly plural, for the latter; always, nevertheless, substituting the accusative for the nominative case; as, for instance:—your housekeeper, Sir Waldron, speaking of the housemaid, said to me, to–day, 'Us ha' told her, scaures and scaures o' times, to take up hot water to 'ee, at eight o'clock; but her never heeds, not her, then, vor sooth! her thinks so much o' gallivanting wi' the men–volks!—her's no good, bless 'ee! not a ha'p'orth!' That old housekeeper of yours,—by–the–by,—Waldron, is a grievous nuisance to me; she comes and talks to me daily by the hour. I can't endure the woman."

"My servant annoy you, brother Archibald!—I'm sorry you did not mention this before."

"It seems strange to me," said Reginald, "that Archibald did not give her an admonition, when she first grew troublesome, and so get rid of her."

"Get rid of her!" exclaimed Archibald. "Sir, you may as well talk of tying a tin–kettle to the tail of a comet!—the thing's impossible. Last night, she spent full half an hour imploring me to suffer her to close the shutters and pin up the curtains of the east window of my bed–room, to prevent the rays from my candle shooting across the park–path outside; which rays, as she protests, impede our grandfather's ghost very much, in his nightly rambles: it seems, that he frequently walks down that path; but as a Devonshire ghost cannot cross a ray of light from a candle, the good old gentleman is compelled to go round, or kick his heels in the cold until I get into bed. One of your tenants, brother Waldron, told me, with a very grave face, that he has often met our grandfather, in the middle of the night, with old Geoffry his huntsman, and a whole pack of hounds, hunting a stag at full speed; that he has actually opened the gates for the old man and his ghostly pack to pass through, and that, although 'squire, huntsman, dogs, and stag, are without heads, he recognizes, and honours them! Why, the man must be either a natural idiot, or travelling fast toward lunacy; and yet he's accounted a positive Sir Oracle, in these parts. It is said, our ancestor is seen in all forms, by various persons, at different parts of the village: one scoundrel has had the impudence to tell me, that he met him one night in Blackpool–lane, in the form of a woolpack! and that he gave him a cut with his whip, as he rolled at full speed along the road! Now, admitting that ghosts walk or run, how he could know Sir Jonathan, in the shape of a woolpack, is to me, a miracle:—but, so it was—he knew him; he'll swear to it; and may I be posted at Lloyd's, if the villagers don't believe him. But I'd forgive them almost everything if they'd let the church–bells alone, and wouldn't roar choruses: every evening, between six and eight, some of the brawny vagabonds go to practise triple–bob–majors, or grandsire–trebles, in the belfry;—thus agonizing my ears with the most atrocious music that ever was inflicted on suffering man: to mend the matter, I've a natural antipathy to all bells except the waiter's and the postman's. It occurs very unluckily for me, that I should arrive among you in a week of merry–making, ending with a revel; and go where I will, my ears are assailed by excruciating songs, all of which, without exception, have some terrific chorus tacked to the tail of each verse, which the rogues bellow in such a way, that I'm often obliged to take to my heels in mere self–defence. The song which just now seems to be most fashionable in the village, I have heard so often, that, much against my inclination, I know every word of it; I feel it humming in my brain when I awake in the morning, and my watch ticks it when I go to bed at night. I will be judged by any reasonable man, if the eternal affliction of such words and sounds as those which I am about to utter, vociferated by Stentorian lungs, is not enough to drive a decent being, with a nice ear and moderate taste, mad:—you shall hear."

"Pray, don't trouble yourself, brother," said Reginald.

"Nay, but with your leave, I insist upon giving you a specimen: match it for sense, in all Europe, if you can:—

'My vather a' died, but a' didn't know how,
A' left I zix hossees to vollor tha plough;
Wi' my wim, worn, woddle, oh!
Jack, strim, straddle, oh!
Bubble, boys! bubble, boys!
Down by tha brook!"

"Enough, enough, brother," said Reginald:"I lament that you should be so dissatisfied with your visit."

"Not at all, sir; I'm not at all dissatisfied. I'm perfectly satisfied with it: it has cured me of a mania I've had all my life of enjoying rural felicity, and Devonshire, my birth–place, in my old age: I've seen quite enough of it to make me put up with London or Clapham Common, and rest contented.—Besides, I've seen you and Waldron;—God bless you both, my boys;—I shall be glad. if you will run up to town now and then:—I leave my boy to your care, Reginald;—and to–morrow I start."

The two brothers now approached Archibald, and most affectionately entreated him to prolong his stay with them; and Reginald had just extorted a promise from him to go to the vicarage for two or three days, when a servant entered the room, and stated, that Constables Quality and Batter had brought in some prisoners to he examined before his worship. Sir Waldron desired that they might be taken into his study; and said, that he would descend in a few minutes; but before the servant had quitted the room, Archibald begged that they might be brought up, so as to offer him an opportunity of witnessing, what he called, "a bit of bumpkin police," which he had not hitherto taken an opportunity of enjoying. Sir Waldron acquiesced, and ordered the servant to send up the constables, with their prisoners.

"You will neither be amused, interested, nor edified, I suspect," said Sir Waldron, to Archibald, "by the scene that is about to take place; it is, doubtless, some trifling, ridiculous affair: the constables are two of the most arrant blockheads that ever a magistrate was afflicted with:—as to Onesiphorus Quality, one might as well attempt to elicit evidence out of a mallet, as from him: I assure you, my patience and my temper are often put to the test, by his stupid taciturnity."

As the baronet concluded, the huge form, and meek, beardless face of Constable Quality himself appeared at the door–way, ushering in four prisoners, who were closely followed by a man of a middling size, with sharp features, a large mouth, piercing cat's eyes, and limbs which were puny, compared with those of the gigantic, dull–looking Quality. The person we have described as bringing up the rear, was Constable Batter: the prisoners were our old friends, the pedlar, the tinker, Darby Doherty, and the little girl. The pedlar placed his pack very carefully on the ground, the little girl stood up behind it, and the three men ranged themselves in a line, with Quality, on one side, and Batter, on the other, in front of the table at which the brothers were now seated.

"What is the charge made against these people, Quality?" inquired Sir Waldron.

"Well,—then," replied Quality, "for that matter,—your worship,—you must ask Batter."

"I ha' nought to say,—nought in the world," exclaimed Batter; "but they're oddish bodies—I must say that for Quality. He apprehended and I assisted:—not a thing more."

"Your worship," said Quality, with a most piteous countenance;—"your worship knows better:—I never apprehends nobody."

"That's true enough, Constable Quality, I must needs confess," observed Sir Waldron.

"I thank your worship, kindly, for your good word," quoth Quality.

"Oh! do not be such an idiot as to take what I have said as a compliment. The fact is, Quality, you want either heart or wit enough to capture a fly; Batter, luckily for the Hundred, sins a little on the opposite side to you, Onesiphorus: all is fish that comes near his net; for one real offender, he brings at least fifty innocent people before me. To say the truth, I do not believe another brace of such ignorant blockheads have flourished in one parish, since the days of Dogberry and Verges. Batter, I am sure *you* have taken these people:—what have they done? To begin with this good man, who has the appearance of a pedlar;—what do either of you know of him?"

"Why," said Quality, with a shake of the head and an odd sort of frown which he intended to be very significant; "why, your worship, I can't say that I know any good of him."

"You utterly incomparable ninny, do you know any evil of him?"

"For that matter," quoth Quality, to the baronet, "I refer to Batter."

Batter drew up his Chin and replied to this appeal, "I say nothing, your worship; but—a—that is to say—"

"Go to the devil!" cried the enraged magistrate; "this is what I have to go through, daily, brother Reginald."

"Ay, but, brother Waldron—"

"I know, I know!" exclaimed Sir Waldron, interrupting Reginald; "I know what you are going to say; but my patience has been long exhausted with these boobies.—What did you bring the men before me for?" shouted the magistrate in a thundering tone.

"Well, then, your worship," said Quality, no whit moved, "ask Batter."

Batter, with great gravity, declined the honour, and protested against taking precedence of his senior, Onesiphorus Quality; who, he vowed, had bestirred himself as principal in the affair, and laudably exerted himself to the utmost extent of his mental and bodily powers, to bring the delinquents before his worship.

While the worthy constable was making a speech to the fore going effect, Sir Waldron sat tilting his chair on its hind legs, shaking his head up and down with great velocity, beating the devil's tatoo with the fingers of his right–hand on the back of his left, and gazing at his pale and placid brother Reginald with an expression of countenance, which the latter understood as meaning "Now you hear! could Job himself bear this, brother?" That was, in truth, what Sir Waldron intended to convey to Reginald by his looks; and when Batter concluded, he rose from his chair, and with a stride, which might be pronounced emphatic, moved towards the window, turning his back upon the constables and prisoners, apparently determined to leave the settlement of the affair to Reginald himself. The citizen brother had highly enjoyed the whole scene, and while Waldron was walking away, observed to Reginald, that Batter and Quality differed essentially from the police of the metropolis, who, if they had a fault,—and this he professed, with a roguish sneer, to say under correction,—it was the immense crop of evidence which they were generally prepared to yield.

Let it not be imagined, that during the preceding dialogue, Mr. Jeremiah—or as he chose to designate himself by the diminutive,—Darby Doherty remained voluntarily silent. He frequently attempted to address the magistrate; but Quality, who was not only silent himself, but the cause of silence in others, as soon as Darby opened his mouth, covered the aperture with his broad hard palm, and safely barricaded the portals of speech. Darby, with his wooden leg, trod on Quality's corns; and Quality, notwithstanding the anguish he suffered, replied only by a terrific nudge with his staff in Doherty's ribs, which was imperceptible to all present but the receiver. Quality was very generous with his nudges to prisoners who were at all refractory, and attempted to break silence in his worship's presence much to the indignation of Sir Waldron, who often wondered where he could have picked up the word, Quality denominated these nudges, "apothegms."

The Reverend Reginald Hackle now took up the examination, and, with some difficulty, discovered that the prisoners had quarrelled at the fair, sought out the constables, and insisted upon going before a magistrate. "Upon this," quoth Batter, "we took them into custody. The child," added he, "seemed as glad to come as anybody;—so, what to make of it, I, for one, don't know.— Perhaps I've suspicions they've picked up the girl, and are quarrelling between themselves about her clothes, and ornamental valuables;—that, however, I shall keep to myself.—I have searched the prisoners separately. The pedlar's pack contains ribbons of various patterns and lengths; human hair of ditto ditto; silk and imitation handkerchiefs, bits of lace, and cetera, and so forth; a large pair of shears, a pocket–bible much worn, and three red herrings."

"More red herrings!" exclaimed Darby, emancipating him self by a sudden movement from the gripe of Quality, and advancing to a position whence he could look the pedlar full in the face; "three more red herrings! Well, after that I've done, any how!"

"Next," continued Batter, who had now grown rather communicative, "I searched the Irishman."

"And how dared you do so?" exclaimed Sir Waldron, striding from the window with as great energy as he had strode toward it; "how dared you do so, dolt?—Irishman, what are you?"

"I'm an Irishman, your honour!" replied Darby, and Sir Waldron strode to the window with greater emphasis of cadence than he had strode from it, muttering imprecations as he went.

"Have you been in the service?" inquired Reginald; "it has pleased Providence to pour great bodily afflictions on you;—such losses as those of a leg, an arm—"

"'E' then, your honour," interrupted Darby, "afflictions they are, indeed:— my leg lost a good friend in losing me; I cut his corns for him every week, and kept him warm in a good worsted. stocking, and shoes at never less than seven and sixpence the pair, since he came of age: but that's not the question, your worship's reverence and glory; but this is it,—I ask pardon for contradicting,— but don't fear,—I won't quarrel wid your worship's excellence:—Here's three of us: that's me, the tinker, and the man o' the herrings there—the pedlar; we all wants the child, and no blame to us, for she's a beauty;—and having no kith or kin, that we can find out, nor a soul alive to own her—"

"She escheats," interrupted Batter, "as a waif, or an estray, in such cases, to the lord of the manor, Sir Waldron."

"The lord of Bally–no–place, and my nose, too!" said Darby, snapping his fingers at Batter; "do you call her cattle? ye he–cow, ye!—Well, then, your honour's worship," continued Darby, turning, with a smile on his face, towards Reginald, "as we couldn't agree about her, for she came to us together, and we've no great opinion of one another—that is, I haven't of the pedlar or the tinker, may be; and it's not unlikely they think bad of me,—why shouldn't they?—why then, rather than quarrel,—which I'm not one for, though well able, barring my limbs and eye,—we tould the middle and both ends of it to dirty Butter here."

"Batter, prisoner, if you please," quoth the constable of that name.

"Well, to Batter, be it then; but of all the beasts or constables to boot under the moon, he's the most stupid. Well, then, when we couldn't make him understand our story, we insisted on his comprehending us."

"And here they are, Sir Waldron," quoth Quality.

"This is another of your cock–and–bull stories," said the Baronet, returning to his chair. "What have we to do with this? Who is the third party?"

"The tinker, your worship," observed Quality; "I suspect Batter knows him."

"Truly so," said Batter; "he's the father of Nancy Warton's two children; you'll find his name on record; it's written on the bonds;—a confirmed bad one in respect of—"

"Tinker," said Sir Waldron, assuming a most formidable aspect, "I now recollect your face. Moreover, I have heard that you have not yet quitted your evil ways: you had an affair of a similar sort to that which Batter speaks of, last month, at the sessions.—Fie upon you, man! Venial as this sort of sin may appear to you, to me it seems most grave,—nearly unpardonable. Why not take a wife?"

"That's just what I've said to him," observed Doherty; matrimony is the best of money,—it's pure felicity."

"Are you married, fellow?" inquired Sir Waldron, who felt by no means pleased at the Irishman's interruption.

"Is it married, your worship?" replied Darby; "faith! then, I am, every inch of me."

"And where's your wife?"

"Why, then, I left her this morning eleven miles hence."

"What, you've deserted her, eh?"

"Oh! quite the contrary;—I ran away from her,—we agreed to come different roads; for, to tell you the truth, Mistress Doherty has a tongue: but that says nothing; may be your honour's own wife has one too."

"I have no wife, sirrah!"

"Well! God help you, then! that's all I say.—Though we quarrelled last night, I'd be mighty glad to see Mistress Doherty to-day,—so I would: I wonder she hasn't come. I'll tell you how it was, and you'll judge who did wrong.—We got a fi'penny bed at a road-side house; and when such a case occurs, which isn't often, Mistress Doherty is all for getting as much as she can for her money; so, if I'd let her, she'd go to bed at eight o'clock, and lie till twelve or one the next day, or make me and the child do so: but no, I don't like going to bed at night over soon then, so I don't,—but I'll lie a-bed as long as one here and there, the next morning; for then's the time, if one has such a thing, when a bed's pleasant. Well then, Mistress Doherty, having some places to patch in her coat, bid me go to bed before her, so that I might get up early, and tramp to the revel with her,—just as Dobbin and Joan would, but I wouldn't;—never mind why. Says she—says Mistress Doherty, 'Go to bed, Darby, or the child will be perished with cold; go to bed and warm him, Darby, while I put a patch on my coat;' but I wouldn't; so then she got in her tantarums; I was obstinate, and we quarrelled."

"Ay, ay! I understand," said the tinker, who had not spoken before, "she wanted to beat you to nest, as the hen-pigeon doth the cock, when he loiters; it's natural,—yea, nature all over."

"Whenever I quarrel, I fight," pursued Darby; "and whenever I fight with Mrs. Doherty, she licks me; I'd scorn to be beat by any man breathing; I'll crow like a bit of game as I am, though I've lost half my spurs, but I don't scruple to own, that I knock under to my wife:—so we paid what we couldn't well afford for a bed,—quarrelled and fought all night in it, when we might have slept happy and contented under a tree; and the next morning,—that's this morning,—I tould her, when she was dreaming, to come after me to the revel by her own self; and so she will, I'll engage my last arm; for, if we fight, Mistress Doherty doats on me."

"And who is this child?" inquired Archibald.

"Your worship," replied the pedlar; "I hae held my peace till now, and it is time for me to speak. This wee thing cam' to us where we breakfasted; we ken nought about her; she wanted to come to this revel, and we hae brought her together.—She would hae parted with us, but neither of us would suffer her to do so, without letting us know whither she went; a small broil followed, and here we are ye;—we've done nought but what humanity would justify;—tak' the bairn and question her. She's in your hands, and I've done with her—saving a blessing— Gude protect her!"

"Oh! don't think to gallyboozle the justice with your mealy mouth," said Darby; "I've no great opinion of my friend here, your honour; no, nor of Tom Tinker this fellow with the black face, as I had the honour of telling ye before. Now, if I may be allowed to say one word in my defence,—though nobody accuses me, nor can, that's more,—but if I may speak, I'll just say this by way of advice to your worship:—make yourself a Solomon the second; cut off the child's hair, take every ha'p'orth she has, and then see who'll have her: it isn't the tinker, I'll engage; no, nor the pedlar, with his blackguard red herrings."

"I dinna want the bairn," said the pedlar; "I hae eleven o' my ain; but I'd do to anither mon's child, what I'd expact anither mon would do to mine,—that is to say—sauf her fra tinklers and ne'er–do–weels."

"Come, come, pedlar, 'ware that," growled the tinker; "good words or broken heads, says the old saying."

"Hold your tongue, you reprobate!" exclaimed Sir Waldron.

"Silence!" roared Batter in the tinker's ear, while Quality dealt him an apothegm.

"What you want with the child I cannot comprehend," continued Sir Waldron, "why not take one of those poor things, of whom you're the putative putative? that would do you a little credit.—Why wish for this little stranger?"

"Why, your worship"—The tinker was cut short in his reply to the magistrate's question, by Batter shouting silence, and Quality giving him a nudge.

"Blockhead!" exclaimed Sir Waldron to Batter; "am I not to have an answer to my question? let the man speak, and do you behave with common sense, or, by heaven, I'll commit you.— Speak, tinker, how do you account for your wishing to take this child in preference to your own? I must tell you, that it looks strange and suspicious."

"Why," replied the tinker, "I ha'n't no wish in particular about it:—to be sure, I took a fancy to her; she hath such a main pretty little nob, and a pearly sort of an eye, just like my best almond tumbler pigeon at home— and the poney likes her; so its natural, you see, your worship: but then, I don't covet her; only keep her omit of these chaps' clutches, that's all I say; except, mind me, this:—I wouldn't offend your worship for the world; I'd pretty near die first,—but, look'ee, Sir Waldron, if your constable pokes I in the ribs again, as he hath twice, I'll just make so free as to break his neck, here right, if I do die for't;—it's nature you know."

"This language is improper;—we must not hear it," observed Reginald.

"How dare you strike the man?" exclaimed Sir Waldron.

"I merely gave him a hint—"

"Hold your tongue—quit the room—or stop—stay—I consider whether I ought not to order Batter to take you into custody."

The little girl now stepped from behind the pedlar's pack, and advancing close to Sir Waldron, with a smile playing over her features, said to the magistrate, "If you please, sir, may I speak, now every body's done?"

"Certainly, child," replied the baronet; "what have you to say?—what is your name?"

"Agnes, sir."

"Agnes what, child?—what is your other name?" The little girl made no reply, but looked alternately at Sir Waldron and the prisoners, and the tears gushed from her eyes.

"What is the meaning of this?" said the baronet.

"Perhaps, brother,—you know best," observed Reginald;—"but perhaps there is some mystery in this matter, something that lies deeper than you imagine. The child may be intimidated from speaking the truth in the presence of these three good people."

"Do you think so?—Well, then, I'll take her apart into my study," replied Sir Waldron: "come," added he, addressing the child, "come with me, Agnes; do not be frightened."

"Bless you, I am not frightened," said the child; "I'm very glad."

"Ay, ay," quoth Reginald, "it is as I suspected, very clearly; Batter and Quality, look well to these honest fellows."

The prisoners loudly exclaimed against Reginald's suspicions; but Batter, by dint of bawling, and Quality, by the virtue of his apothegms, soon restored order, and Agnes followed Sir Waldron into the adjoining room.

"Now, my dear," said the baronet, taking a chair, and drawing Agnes between his knees, "what have you to say? Why not tell your name before the people in the parlour? Is either of those men related to you?"

"Oh, no! no, indeed! I never saw them before to–day."

"And whose child are you?"

"Yours!" replied Agnes, looking archly up at Sir Waldron, and placing her little hand on his as she spoke.

"Pooh! pooh! child, don't be foolish," replied Sir Waldron, who felt half inclined to be angry, but, at the same time, could not prevent his features from relaxing into a smile; "tell me the truth."

"I have told the truth; indeed and indeed I have."

"How do you mean, child?"

"Why, if you're my papa, you know, I must be your little daughter:— musn't I now?"

"Truly so, child," replied Sir Waldron; "but as I am not your papa—"

"Oh! but you are, though," interrupted Agnes; "my mamma told me so."

Sir Waldron's cheek grew pale; he stared at the child, and remained for a few moments silent,; then, assuming a stern manner, he said to Agnes rather sharply,—"I suspect you to be a designing, bold, bad child; or the tool of wretches; or, at best, remarkably impudent. Do you know who I am?"

"Sir Waldron Hackle;—at least, so I hope," was the child's reply;—"the men said they were going to bring us before Sir Waldron Hackle,—and that's you, isn't it?—If not, I've kept my promise to my poor mamma finely;—but it isn't my fault."

"What mamma? what promise? How you talk, child!—what promise?"

"Not to tell any one who I was, nor to mention my name, until I saw my father."

"And what is your name?" eagerly inquired Sir Waldron.

"Oh! you know what it is well enough—don't you?"

"How the devil should I?" exclaimed the irritated baronet, who for a moment forgot that he was speaking to a child. "How should I?" he repeated, in somewhat a calmer tone.

"Why, you haven't any more little girls, have you?"

"Ridiculous! Tell me your name, instantly!"

"You won't be angry with me, I hope, for asking you first, if you are Sir Waldron Hackle? My mamma so strictly charged me—"

"Well, well! I am—I am," replied the baronet; "I am Sir Waldron Hackle—"

"Ay; but are you the gentleman that broke his arm at Westbury, and—"

"Yes, yes!—Westbury, said you?—What's this flashes across me? it surely cannot be—"

"Indeed, and it is, though!"

"Hannah Russell's child?"

"Yes! my mamma's dead; and I've walked all the way by myself, and now you won't own me," sobbed little Agnes; and her head dropped upon Sir Waldron's hand, which he immediately felt was wetted with her tears.

"Own you!" said Sir Waldron, scarcely knowing what he said. "How can I own you?"

"I'm sure I don't know," replied the little girl, raising her head, and endeavouring to restrain the sobs which almost rendered her unable to articulate; "you must do as you please about that; my mamma sent her dying love—to you,—and she told me to be sure to say that she had done—her duty, and you need not be ashamed of me!"

Sir Waldron made no reply; but he snatched Agnes up, pressed her to his bosom, and kissed her repeatedly: he then put her at arm's length from him, gazed earnestly on her face, and again most affectionately embraced her.

"Kiss me again, papa," were the first words that little Agnes uttered, after Sir Waldron had placed her on her feet; but the baronet was so absorbed in thought, at that moment, that he did not notice what she said. He sat silent and motionless, with the child mutely gazing upon him, for above a minute. He then started up, wrung his hands together, stamped violently on the floor, and walked to the wall of the room, against which he leant his forehead. Starting thence in a moment, he returned to his seat, exclaiming, "Man! man! thou dost truly merit this agony!"

Agnes now approached him, and familiarly, or rather, endearingly, embracing his arm, said, "Are you very ill, papa?—My mamma tied this bit of love–ribbon on the finger where married ladies wear their rings, that I shouldn't forget to tell you she forgave you with her last breath, and died happy!"

"May she be in heaven!" exclaimed Sir Waldron.

"Amen!" responded little Agnes.

"What to do—what to do, I know not," said the baronet, rising from his chair again.

"Won't you own me, papa?—pray do; or I don't know what I shall do, after walking so far and all. I wore out my shoes and stockings—"

"Bless thy poor little feet—what a sight is this!"

"Won't you own me, papa?" repeated Agnes.

"I do—I do, child," replied Sir Waldron, kissing her; "but I must send you away,—how, I cannot tell.—You must not be known to be mine:—my honour, my reputation;—the character I have maintained—S'death! it drives me mad!"

"Mayn't I live with you, then?" said Agnes.

"It is absolutely impossible."

"Oh, dear! Then I suppose I must find out a place where grapes grow in a wood, and build a little house, as Robinson Crusoe and his man Friday did, for I've nobody to help me but you,—and you won't, you say."

"I said no such thing: you shall never want; but here you cannot remain."

"My mamma said I *was* to;—but then, she told me too, that when she was dead and gone, I was to obey you; and you say I must go,—so I don't know what to do:—I'm very hungry."

"Hungry! pull the bell—but stop—hold—my position is most perplexing. To send the child here! It was cruel—but I merit it. I have brought sorrow on myself, by my own villany.—It is miraculous how you could have reached me."

"I walked all the way!" said the child, with a sigh. "My little bones ache so, you can't think.—My mamma, when she knew she was going to die in a day or two, gave me some money, and told me to go to The White Hart, with a little paper of directions she folded it up in, for the coachman; and she said, that he would give me something to eat on the road, and carry me within three miles of your house: but I wasn't to tell him where I was going; and she told me to carry the paper and money to him the day after she was buried. But,—do you know?—the people where we lodged found the paper, and took the money out; and said, I shouldn't go unless I told them who I was going to, and why, and all about it. But I wouldn't, because my mamma charged me to tell nobody. but Sir Waldron;—that's you,—my papa. So then, I said to myself, I'd walk,—for the place where the coach man was to leave me didn't seem very far in my sampler:—but sometime I thought I should never get here. And I brought my sampler with me to find out the way; but it was all wrong, bless you! there's no red line between Somersetshire and Devonshire, like that I worked in the sampler; so I kept on asking my way."

"My dear little cherub!" exclaimed Sir Waldron, "what thou must have endured!—And where did you sleep?"

"Oh! the people was hay–making, and I lay down upon the nice little hay–cocks;—its no night, hardly, now.—I liked it at first; but I'm stung all over with flies, or something—"

"And did you beg for food?"

"Oh! no! I brought all my pretty money, and spent it in gingerbread and apples;—not all,—for I've two Queen Anne shillings, and another bit of money, I don't know what it is, left."

Agnes, in answer to several other questions put to her by Sir Waldron, told him, that she often followed the waggons, and, in a very early part of the journey, saw the names of several places painted on the boot of a coach, before that one where the coach man was directed, by her mother's paper, to set her down; that she learnt them by heart, and inquired for each, successively: she also related the manner of her meeting with the pedlar and his companions, and stated, that a woman had told her, just before she saw them, that there was a revel at the village, to which, she was inquiring the way.

Sir Waldron was still undecided as to what he should do with Agnes, and sat pondering, with the little girl seated on his knee, and warming her feet with one of his hands, when the child suddenly started from him, and exclaimed, "Oh, dear! I quite forgot the letter!"

"Letter! from your mother?"

"Yes; the people of the house didn't find out that, when they took the money that was in the paper of directions away from me. I brought it all the way safe enough in my bosom, until this morning."

"And where is it now?"

"That naughty constable took it from me. He opened it and read it."

"D—t—n!" exclaimed Sir Waldron; "then all is known, and I shall be every booby's jest."

He had scarcely uttered these words, when the door of the room was opened, and The Reverend Reginald Hackle entered, with an open note in his hand. He was followed by the citizen: Reginald looked more grave than usual; but Archibald seemed with difficulty to restrain himself from laughing:—"Waldron," said he, "we have just wormed a letter out of Constable Quality."

The baronet snatched it from Reginald's hand; looked first at the superscription, which bore his name and address, and then hastily perused the contents.

"The blockhead's excuse," continued Archibald, "for not producing this, which I consider, under correction, a document of importance as regards the examination, is, that you cut Batter short in his statement of the particulars of his searching the prisoners."

"And is this rightly addressed to you, brother? Are you indeed the man?" asked Reginald, in a tone of reproach.

"Well, she's a pretty child; a very pretty child, indeed, Waldron," said Archibald, taking the little girl in his arms, "Come, kiss your uncle, my dear: I suppose I may call her yours, Waldron."

"You may:—it's useless to dissimulate;—so preach, brother Reginald; sneer, brother Archy; jest, joke, and do your worst, world;—she is mine,— my dear, darling child!"

Shortly afterwards, Archibald returned to the prisoners, and, addressing Darby Doherty, informed him that he and his two companions might go about their business.

"And the child—" quoth Darby.

"She will remain with Sir Waldron," replied Archibald.

"Thank your honour, kindly, for this, as well as for the cold meat, which, of course, your honour is going to order us to get in the hall," said Doherty. "His worship has acted upon what, I've always been tould, is the true principle of justice; so I can't complain: —he's taken the oyster himself, and," added Darby, bowing alternately to the pedlar and the tinker as he spoke, "sent me packing with the shells."

Sir Waldron soon became so doatingly fond of little Agnes, that, among all his friends, she obtained the appellation of The Bachelor's Darling. As she approached towards womanhood, the beauty of her person, and the sweetness of her disposition, made a strong impression on the heart of Archibald's son; and five years had scarcely elapsed after the completion of his studies under his reverend uncle, when she became his wife.

The three brothers lie, side by side, in the church–yard of their native village; and the citizen's son, and Hannah Russell's child, are now Sir Waldron and Lady Hackle.

THE LOVES OF
HABAKKUK BULLWRINKLE, GENTLEMAN

ABOUT six–and–twenty years ago, a middle–aged North–country attorney, somewhat above five feet eight inches in height, but immeasurably corpulent, with an old–fashioned calf, mottled eyes, and a handsome nose, settled in a large and uncivilized village in the West of England. The manners of the inhabitants were rude and outrageous; their names, customs, frolics, and language, were such as Habakkuk Bullwrinkle had never before been accustomed unto. They cracked many a heart–piercing joke on his portly person; laughed at his ineffectual attempts to compete with the veriest youngsters in the village, at wrestling, or cudgel–playing; rejoiced heartily when he suffered a cracked pate, or an unexpected back–fall; and never employed him in the way of his profession. He could have borne all his misfortunes with decency but the last;—*that* irked him beyond measure; and he did not scruple to upbraid those who deigned to drink out of his cup, with their folly and villainous prejudice, in measuring a man's wit by his skill at gymnastics, and exclusively patronizing a couple of rascally pettifoggers in the vicinity, whose only merit consisted in their hard pates, and dexterity in breaking the skulls of their clients. The villagers waited with patience until Habakkuk's lecture and strong drink were finished, promised to reform, heartily wished him success in his trade, fell to loggerheads on their way home, and the next morning went for redress to the aforesaid pettifoggers, who fleeced them to their hearts' content for several lingering months, and then mutually advised their employers to settle the matter over a goodly feast.

Habakkuk Bullwrinkle inwardly moaned at the luck of his fellow–priests of the syren, but lost none of his flesh. His affairs, at length, grew desperate. He had been skipping over the land, after the fickle jade Fortune, for many a weary year; but the coy creature continually evaded his eager clutch. What was to be done?—His finances were drooping, his spirits jaded, his temper soured, and his appetite for the good things of this world, as keen and clamorous as ever. He had tried every plan his imagination could devise to, win over the rustics, but without effect. He was just about to decamp clandestinely, and in despair, when, all at once, here collected that he was a bachelor! His hopes rose at the thought. "How strange it is!" said he, unconsciously snapping his fingers with delight, "that the idea of marrying one of these charming rosy–skinned lasses, who are continually flitting about me, should never have entered my caput before! The whole village is one immense family,—a batch of uncles, aunts, nephew nieces, cousins, and relations of every intermediate degree, from one to a hundred. If I can but weave myself into this web of consanguinity, my future ease and fortune are certain. They will stand by one of their own kin, let him be ever so distantly related, to the very last. By the laws! it's an excellent project!—I've a warm heart, a winning way, and great choice; so I'll even cast my eye about for a convenient helpmate; eat, drink, and be merry again."

Reader, these were my thoughts, at the latter end of the year 1803; for I am the identical Habakkuk Bullwrinkle above–mentioned. Pursuant to my resolution, I began to wheedle myself into the good graces of the girls. I often met with a very tolerable reception, considering all things, and had many times nearly compassed the object of my hopes, when the demon disappointment, in the semblance of a clod–hopper, 'yclept Andrew Skelpie,—walked in to dash the cup of happiness from my lips. I never attempted to kiss a lass behind a hay–mow, or an old tree, but what this fellow would thrust his ugly phiz between me and the sweet pair of lips I was longing to salute! If ever I made an appointment to meet a farmer's daughter, and prattle away an hour or two with her, unseen by all, Skelpie and she were generally linked lovingly, arm in arm together, on my arrival.

The first time I ever beheld this destroyer of my peace, was at a village revel. I shall never forget the manner in which he rose from the grass on which he had been drowsily lolloping, and looked out through his half–closed eyelids, at the efforts of the back–sword players on the sward. He was called upon to enter the ring with a fellow about his own height, but more fleshy and comely–looking by half,—being precisely what middle–aged good–wives term "a portly figure of a man," and very much to my liking. Skelpie got up from the cool turf, one joint at a time, and made his way into the circle, by one of the most extravagant and ludicrous paces I ever beheld: it was between the ungainly toddle of an ox, and the loose–jointed motion of a drunken, staggering stripling. The portly fellow was a stranger from a neighbouring county, who valued himself on his prowess at single–stick; he had already peeled the bark off a brace of noses, and the grey–headed rustics, who encompassed the scene of action and glory, trembled for the honour of their native village. An immense shout of applause greeted Skelpie's appearance; for, in him, it was well known, the champion of Wedmore himself would find a redoubtable opponent. He surveyed his adversary with a confident and most provoking glance, accompanied with an upturning of the higher lip, and a smack of his horny fingers, that sounded like the crack of a waggoner's whip. He coolly selected a stick, screwed it into his hand–guard, padded his elbows, gave one stentorian 'hem!' and then—I never beheld such a mutation in my life!—his eyes flew open, his lips clenched, every muscle in his body was instantly awakened, every limb was in active and most turbulent motion: he hit at his opponent's head, with a velocity that, to me, seemed supernatural; I heard a continual and most merry peal of blows rattling about the sconce of the portly stranger, but I could scarcely detect a single motion of the stick. The skin was tough—particularly tough; and, for some time, defied Skelpie's sturdy thwacks. At the close of the vigorous bout he looked amazed, muttered a curse on his ineffective weapon, and was just about to begin again, when, observing something suspicious about the closed mouth of his adversary, he put forth his hand, and parted the swollen lips of the stranger, from whose mouth a stream of blood immediately gushed. The comely man afterwards acknowledged, that he had received a cut under his lip at the beginning of the play, but had sedulously sucked in the blood, and swallowed it, hoping to crack Skelpie's pate before it would be discovered. At this fine old English sport he who draws from his adversary's head sufficient blood to stain muslin, is proclaimed the victor. Skelpie afterwards threw half–a–dozen sturdy fellows at wrestling, and bore off the prizes at the village games, as he had frequently done on previous occasions. He was by no means handsome in face, fairly spoken, well–made, or merry;—the simple wenches idolized the dog for his prowess. He was capricious and false, but they seemed to like him the better. Each, in her turn, hoped to fix the rover, excite the envy of her predecessors in his affections, and bear off the palm, where they had ingloriously failed. He took no trouble to gain their love, and they unanimously doated on him. I often longed to see him get a good thrashing, and many times felt strongly impelled to fall on him myself; but a whole flood of fears and forebodings, invariably drowned the few sparks of courage and vigour in my breast, and I laudably forebore.

My love–suits were innumerable; but although they usually began and went on auspiciously, Skelpie never failed to beat me off the field in the end. The dog seemed to be unconscious of the mischief he made, and that irritated my spirit in a tenfold degree. He seemed to bear no malice against me, and many times rendered me an essential piece of service. I shall never forget the night when he clutched me by the cheek, and pulled me out of a flood–swollen brook, when I was at my last gasp, and then abused and threatened to bethwack me for being such a fool, and giving him the trouble of wading chin–deep to save me. My intellect, on this occasion, was befogged with the fumes of stout October, and I knew not where I went.

It would be tedious to narrate the whole of my adventures during the year which I spent in seeking out a wife; I shall content myself with particularizing what befell me in the pursuit of the four last objects of my love. And, first, let me introduce Ruth,—Ruth Grobstock, the daughter of a rough miller, who resided on a hill about a mile to the left of the village. I secretly wooed her about a month, undisturbed by any mortal; I thought I was sure of her, and began to concert measures for obtaining a dignified introduction to her daddy, the miller.

One evening, after having ruminated for many hours on Ruth's attractions, I determined to roam up to the mill, which I had never before visited,—having hitherto carried on my love–suit with Ruth away from her home, at meetings which were too frequent to be altogether accidental. While I loitered about the mill, pondering on the best mode of drawing out Ruth,—for she had no reason to expect me,—the moon suddenly gleamed full upon me, through an opening in the oak tree which stretched its huge boughs over the white cottage in which the miller dwelt; and methought there was something similar to the malicious smile of an arch woman, when intent upon a prank, gleaming on her sparkling face; her unnecessary glances, as she seemed to peep through the tree, for the express purpose of betraying me to observation, threw me into a panic. I had heard of old Grobstock's moods and manners, and I feared him. I felt sure of a kind and endearing reception from Ruth, although I came altogether uninvited and unawares; but I fancied for a moment that I heard her father's flails whistling about my ears, and felt the teeth of his tykes rioting in my fat. My pulse throbbed audibly; and I was on the point of again making my way into the wood that clothed the hill–side, when a

multitude of clouds, which had been gradually hemming in the light of
the moon, suddenly stretched over her face, and relieved my terrors by
screening me from her afflicting glances. I rejoiced, and waxed courageous
and young in heart again. The curtains of the best room in the little cottage
were negligently drawn, and I had the satisfaction, after sundry leaps, of
getting a glimpse of Ruth's little and exquisite foot, as it danced up and
down before the blaze of a chirruping fire, which sparkled on the broad
hearth. A gentle tap at the window set her on her legs in a moment, and
before I could reach the door, she was there with an outstretched hand,
and a air of warm, ripe, ruddy lips, pouting forth to greet me. This was
delicious!—The friendly clouds were still sheltering me from the moon's
eye; Ruth stepped forth, and we stood close at the foot of the old oak, in
the most impervious and delightful darkness imaginable. I was mute with
delight, but my happy hearted, loving little damsel's speech, after a few
moments of silence, gradually began to thaw, and at length, overwhelmed
me with a torrent of words:—"Oh! I am so glad you are come," quoth she;
"if you had not, we should not have had a moment's talk together for the
week. Daddy's gone out; but to–morrow evening, and the next, he means
to stop at home, and get drunk and, although his over–night's promises in
other affairs melt like mists, in the morning sun, and are quite forgotten
by mid–day, yet, when he says he shall get drunk, he always backs it wi' an
oath, and then makes it a matter of conscience religiously to keep his word;
so that, you see, my dear Skelpie—"

I was struck all of a heap!—The purport of her subsequent discourse
palpably proved, that she had mistaken me, in the dark, for the eternal
and never–failing Skelpie. Her lips once more approached mine; I was
foaming with rage and disappointment; my hand had shrunk from her
grasp, as from the touch of an adder, the instant the detested name of
Skelpie escaped from her lips; I had already taken in a mighty draught of
breath, intending to shower a whole volley of curses on her and Skelpie,
together, —when I suddenly experienced a shock, that deprived me of
all sort of sensation in an instant. How long I lay in a death–like state I
cannot conceive; but I remember well enough, that when I awoke from
my lethargy, trance, fit, or whatever it was, I found myself most painfully
compressed in an aperture of the oak tree, through which the children
were wont to enter into its hollow trunk. The moon was out in all her
glory again, and her light fell upon the white brow of Ruth, and the grey

jacket of the lean, and, by me, abhorred Skelpie. Yes, there he was, twining endearingly round the sylph–like form of the false maid, who seemed to feel a pleasure in his embraces, which, to me, appeared altogether unaccountable. It was plain, from their talk, that they did not conceive I was within hearing. I would fain have persuaded myself that I was dreaming, but my endeavours were ineffectual; the rugged edges of the aperture insinuated themselves into my sides, and pained me dreadfully. Did Skelpie strike me? thought I; and does he imagine that I rolled down the declivity, from the force of the blow, and am now weltering in the ditch at its foot?—Truly, it was a most tremendous assault; and his conclusion of the effect, judging from the force of the cause, would be far from unreasonable. My case was forlorn in the extreme: my head, and one of my arms, were in the trunk of the tree; I was fixed in a most uneasy, slanting position; and my feet were so placed on the outside, that the moon threatened every minute to reveal them. I would have given the world to be even floundering in the mire of the ditch, or anywhere else, out of the reach of Skelpie's fist. I was almost suffocated, and did not dare to breathe louder than a listening roe: a sigh or groan would in some degree have eased my pangs; but the sight of Skelpie, prevented me from indulging in the consolation of the most wretched.

At length, a loud halloo announced the approach of old Grobstock. Skelpie instantly intimated his intention of decamping, but the vile maid desired him to clamber up the oak, and hide amongst its branches, until her daddy went to bed. Here was a terrific request!—"I won't go into the hollow," quoth he; "'cause the zuzpicious ould jakes do always pry into there, avore a' do goa to bed." I took the cuff of my coat between my teeth, and resolutely prepared for the worst; —but Skelpie ascended the other side of the tree. He had scarcely broken off the prolonged salute of the kissing Ruth, when old Roger Grobstock, drunk, and growling, staggered up to the door. "Eh! what, lassie—wench! out and abroad at this time of night!" cried he, as Ruth tripped up towards him. "Ahey! what, vlaunting and trapesing about the whoam–stead wi' some vellow, I'll warrant! Odd! I'll verret un out; only hide a bit, I'll be about un. I be downcast vor want of a frolic to–night; so, icod! lass, I'll duck the lad avore I goes to bed, just vor a bit of a joke like,—all in good vellowship,—but, icod! I'll duck un, if he's a friend; and if he is a stranger,—dost hear, wench?—I'll drash un wi' the flail, just like a whate–sheaf."

Every word of his speech was equal to a blow: I struggled to get free with all my might; I had succeeded so far as to raise myself upright, when the miller, who had entered the house at the conclusion of his threat, re–appeared at the door with a flaming brand from the hearth in one hand, and a tremendous dung–fork in the other. He staggered directly close up to the tree; but the sight of my out–jutting stomach, and alarmed visage, made him retreat a few paces. He thrust out the burning stick so near my face, that it scorched my cheek; and after surveying my disconsolate and rueful deportment for a minute or more, he grounded his weapon, and accosted me in these words: "Why, thee bee'st a purty vellur, beesen't?— And where did'st come vrom—and who bee'st? Art thee a thief, or—but, noa, it can't be,—thee bee'st never come to court our Ruth, bee'st?— speak, twoad, or I'll vork tha!"

There was Ruth, looking over her father's shoulder, evidently alarmed at my appearance; Skelpie's heels were dangling over my head; the pronged fork was close to my waistcoat; I stared in the face of the old man, unable to utter a word, but sweating like a baited bull, and plainly expressing my fears by my woebegone and pallid countenance. I expected some dire punishment for my silence; but old Grobstock, after surveying me for a minute, to my great surprise, burst into a loud laugh, seized my trembling hand, and, with one vigorous effort, pulled me out of my imprisonment. After dragging me, helpless as I was, into the house, and placing me in a chair by the fire–side, he thrust a mug of cider and brandy into my hand, chuckling out, "Why, zooks! chap, how vrighted thee looks!—drink!" Here was a change!

By degrees I summoned up courage: the miller made me drink stoutly of his good liquor; and, more than once, seized the dung–fork, and placing himself in a threatening attitude, thrust the points of it closer to my breast, in order to make me look frightened again, and amuse him. I was twenty times on the point of revealing the whole affair, but a single look of Ruth's eloquent eye froze the words on my lips.

After an hour's laughter, interrupted only by gaspings for breath, and frequent applications to the jug, my old host gave me a broad hint to depart; and after civilly opening the door, and wishing me a hearty good night, gave me a most grievous kick, that sent me galloping down the hill, and betook himself to laughing as heartily as before. I never courted young Ruth of the mill again.

My next love was the pale, down–looking, modest Ally Budd, the niece of that boisterous old harridan, Hester Caddlefurrow; whose name was a hushing–word to the crying urchins for many miles around; they feared her more than Raw–head–and–bloody–bones, the wide–mouthed Bogle, or even the great Bullyboo himself. The lads of the village generally preferred the more hale and ruddy wenches in the vicinity; Ally was not roystering enough for them; she had no capacity to feel and enjoy their rude merriment, or rough frolics; and few suitors doffed the cap of courtship at old Hetty Caddlefurrow's threshold. But Ally was, indeed, a beauty. Her youthful companions and neighbours saw nothing extraordinary in her calm, dove–like eye; but to me, it looked like the surface of a smooth lake, in the still moonlight, with a delicious heaven of love smiling in its blue depths. I met her several times, at a distance from her home, and made her acquainted with my growing passion; but she always chilled my ardour by a ceremonious reference to her austere and masculine aunt. I laid these evasive receptions of my proffered affection to the credit of her modesty, and loved her the better for them. I used to hover about on the tops of the hills which overlooked her abode, watching for the moment when my young dove would glide forth from the thatched cot, that nestled among the trees beneath me, with a feverish anxiety that I never felt on any other occasion in my life. She neither seemed to shun or court my company; but came forth, smiling, and fearless of evil, like the white star of the evening, in the soft summer's gloaming. The presence of other women, with whom I have been in love, has usually thrown me into a turbulent fever; but Ally Budd's pale, beautiful face, soft eyes, and gentle voice, had a calm and soothing influence on my spirit Her words fell like oil, even on the stormy tide of her aunt's rough passions; whose ire she could quell at will, and oftentimes saved the offending clowns in the old woman's employ from an elaborate cuffing. In this exercise, Hester was said to excel any man in the parish: she had a violent predilection for thwacking, or, to use her own expression, lecturing, her domestics for every trivial offence; and nothing but the high wages which she gave, induced the rustic labourers to remain in her service. I was one evening sauntering round the summit of the hill which looked down upon Hester's house, occasionally stealing a glance from the pathway into the wood towards the rich glories of the declining sun, when a rude hand clutched me by the collar behind, and, in a moment, pulled me backwards into an immense wheelbarrow. The gigantic villain who had performed this daring feat, directly placed himself between the handles of the vehicle, and vigorously trundled it down the hill. I was seated, or rather, self–wedged in the barrow, with my legs painfully dangling over the rim, on each side of the wheel: the velocity, with which we descended the steep and rugged declivity, deprived me of all power; the fellow panted and laughed, pushing on with increased vigour, until we came in sight of the wide–gaping door of old Hester's kitchen. His fellow–labourers, who were seated at the porch, immediately rose at the sight of our novel equipage.—Confound the rascal! he was a most experienced ploughman, and deemed this a fair opportunity of shewing his great rectilinear skill, and obtaining the applause of his fellows, by driving me at full speed through the door–way of the house. It stood exactly at the foot of the steepest part of the hill; and, from the tremendous rate at which we travelled, the downfall of the whole edifice seemed inevitable! My senses, which had partially taken leave of me in the course of the descent, returned just as we arrived within a few yards of our destination; I uttered one shriek, desperately closed my eyes, and gave myself up for a buried man.

The next moment I found my body, safe and unhurt, on the hearth of Dame Caddlefurrow's kitchen. There was the dame, seated in her bee–hive chair, staring with surprise, impatience, and anger, at my worship in the barrow. As soon as the clown recovered his lost breath, he proceeded to an explanation of the cause of his introducing such an unsightly and unknown personage as me to her goodly presence. "I ha' zeed the chap," quoth he, elevating the handles of his wheelbarrow to the top of his shoulders, so as to afford the dame a full view of my person; "I ha' zeed the chap scaures and scaures o' times, skulking about the hill, always and vor ever just about night–vail, when I do goa a–voddering the beasts; so, thinks I, thic jockey bean't loitering about here so often wi' any good plan in his noddle: moorauver, I ha' seed un, coming athirt the yields ov a night, just avore harvest, treading down whole sheaves o' wheat at a voot–vall:—that nettled I more nor all; so I looked out vor un to–night, slipped un into the dung–barry, walked un down the hill side, and drove 'un through the ould porch straight as a vurrow so here a' is, and let un gi'e a 'count ov hi'self."

"Ay, let un give an account of himself," said the sturdy dame; "Who bee'st, 'oosbert?"—To say that I was at the point of dissolution, were needless. I began to mutter a few incoherent sentences, when one of the fellows at the door cried out, "He's Habby Bullwrinkle, the devil's–bird, down in the village." "A lawyer!" shouted Mistress Caddlefurrow, in a tone that doomed me, in perspective, to all the horrors of the horse–pond;— "Why, thou bloated raven! thou—" "Zober—sober, mother," whispered a voice behind me; and a hand, at the same time, quietly put the enraged widow back towards her bee–hive; "bide a bit; only bide a bit; hearken to reason." I extricated myself from the barrow, and looked up to see who my protecting angel could possibly be; it was no other than Skelpie. "This gentleman's my vreind," continued he, looking drolly towards me; "he and I be main vond o' one another; I seldom goes to chat wi' a lass, but what he is near at hand; so—d'ye maind?—he often come wi' I to the top of the hill, and bided there, while I just stepped down to court little Ally vor an hur or so; that's all:—I left un there to–night. I axed the mopus to come in, but he's modest, main modest, vor a chap of his years." So saying, he resumed his seat, and tendered me the cider mug amid a spare pipe in such a friendly and unsuspicious manner, that told me all was right in a moment. The clowns retired, and the old dame looked on me as kindly as her features would permit, under the impression that I was the chosen friend of her niece's intended husband; for such, I soon discovered, Skelpie was by her considered!—As soon as the storm in my veins had somewhat abated, I looked around for the mild goddess of my idolatry, the lady–like, modest, soft, silver–eyed Ally Budd. She was drooping in a dark corner, with a cheek apron thrown over her folded arms, and snoring audibly!

I could not bear to think of the heartless creature for a year after; of course I never hovered over the abode of Dame Caddlefurrow again. Skelpie soon deserted the cold lass for another love; and, after being obliged to dance in her stocking–vamps, according to the custom of the country, at the marriages of her two younger sisters, Ally was wedded to an unlucky miser,— the most miserable character under the sun. But to resume:— after lighting my pipe, I sat for some minutes absorbed in reflections on my late adventure. I did not like Skelpie a whit the better for having shielded me from the wrath of the boisterous widow; a blow from his hand would have been much more acceptable than a favour: I imagined that he was rioting on the idea of having vexed me, by his act of apparent good–nature and kindness; and I construed his silence very much in favour of this vagary of my heated imagination. Presently I heard a noise behind old mother Caddlefurrow's chair, which resembled the faint and irregular chuckling of a woman's half–stifled laugh; and, anon, a tuft of hair, dark as the raven's wing, topped by a pheasant's plume, gleamed over the head of the chair; a white brow, and a pair of laughing black eyes, brim full of tears, followed; and in a few minutes, Kate Skelpie, the wicked, mischievous sister of my deliverer, tumbled out of the recess, which the dame's chair had effectually shaded. She was a round, dumpy lass, full of tricks as a frolicsome colt, with an impertinent cocked nose, and a pair of lips, that were continually in waggish and most alluring motion. I had seen her before at a farmer's merry–making, when she picked me out for a partner, and, not withstanding my obesity, obliged me to dance down six–and–thirty couple of giggling girls, and roaring men;—keeping up, all the time, as grave a face as ever sat on the shoulders of an undertaker. I pitched and leaped about like a gambolling rhinoceros, to the infinite diversion of the company, and my own solitary grief and dismay. Kate and I were the only persons in the room who looked at all solid. I felt an inkling of affection for the lass, even then,—why, I know not; and the continual crossings I received from Skelpie, determined me to make love under his own roof, where I should, most probably, be sure of peace and quietness in my trysting; as Skelpie usually past the love time of the nights, about at the abodes of the different village toasts. Here was a glorious opportunity of improving my acquaintance with the twinkling–eyed Kate! She was not such a poetical–looking creature as the snoring Ally Budd, nor so tall and comely as the false daughter of Grobstock; nevertheless, Kate Skelpie was a jocund, pretty, and captivating young lass. I courted her, and prospered.

She had no meddling parents to interfere with us; and Skelpie was, of course, absent from home five nights in the week. Many were the pranks which the dear jade played me; but I did not care;—they kept my flame alive, and her occasional kind looks and unsolicited salutes convinced me that I held a place in her heart. In the meantime, however, I carried on the war in another quarter. I had two nights in the week to spare, and these I spent at a farm–house about a mile from the village, with a slender young maiden, named Amaranth Saffern.

One Saturday evening, Skelpie overtook me as I was journeying towards Amaranth's dwelling. He accosted me civilly; and having some serious notions about his sister, I did not scruple to enter into conversation with him. He had not crossed me for above a month; and Kate had informed me, the night before, "that she should have a good bit of gold, if the old

chap at the Lands' End would but take it into his head just to die a bit:"
these were good reasons for my civility, and we discoursed on the most
fashionable village topics with great urbanity and mild ness. At length,
however, we arrived at Amaranth's door; and then, for the first time, the
truth flashed upon each of our minds. We were both evidently bent on a
love–visit to the fair Saffern. Skelpie looked rather hurt, methought, and
could not help heaving a short sigh. However, we both went in, and found
Amaranth alone. It was market–day; and her crippled grand father, with
whom she dwelt, as we both well knew, was gone to, and in all probability
would remain at, the next market–town until a late hour, according to
his usual custom; otherwise, we should almost as soon have ventured into
a tiger's den, to despoil the animal of a whelp, as pay a love–visit to the
old man's grand–daughter. The miller was a lamb, compared with dame
Caddlefurrow; and that lady a dove in deportment, to old Jagger Saffern.
But more of him anon.

Amaranth, it was plain, favoured me rather than Skelpie. Without vanity
be it spoken, I was, at that time, barring my obesity, which rendered me
somewhat unsightly in the eyes of the lean, rather a personable man, and
not quite forty. I was by no means particularly solicitous to gain the young
Saffern's affections, yet she clung to me in preference to Skelpie, who did
all in his power to please her. He was evidently in love, and for the first
time in his life, felt the pangs of jealousy in his heart. I was his successful
rival!—I, even I, Habakkuk Bullwrinkle, the devil's bird, whom he had so
long despised, had succeeded in warping the affections of his Amaranth!—
He bit his lip, loured and smiled by fits, and, in vain endeavoured to
conceal the state of his heart. Amaranth seemed to rejoice in his torments;
she had always been tolerably liberal in her tokens of affection, but, on this
occasion, she almost exceeded the bounds of probability. I did not much
like it at last; for I began to think she was making a fool of me. We went
on in this way for above an hour, when the old cripple's poney suddenly
clattered into the court–yard. Skelpie started on his legs in evident alarm.
There was no way of escape, but through a back door into a little yard,
which was surrounded by a villainous high wall, so smooth, and well–built
too, as to defy even Skelpie's clambering capabilities.

We had not been a moment outside the door, before the cripple entered
the house. Skelpie was endeavouring with all his might to get over the wall:
he clung like a cat to the bare bricks; but, before he had well reached half–

way up, his foot slipped, and down he came. I was standing disconsolately underneath him; he fell so suddenly, that I had not time to get out of the way, and Skelpie's ponderous and hard skull struck me full in the pit of my stomach, and sent me staggering against the back door, which naturally gave way with the shock, and I was precipitated, on the broad of my back, in the very middle of the floor. Luckily, I came in contact with the table on which the candle stood, and extinguished the light in my fall. The embers were dying on the hearth, and Skelpie had hauled me by the legs, back into the yard, before the cripple (who waited to reach his loaded blunderbuss before he looked round) could catch more than a vague glimpse of my form and features. The door swung inward, and Skelpie easily held it fast enough to prevent the cripple from pulling it open;—at the same time carefully screening his body behind the wall of the house, from the cripple's bullets, which we expected to hear rattling through the door every moment. He growled like an incensed bear, and muttered curses by wholesale on poor Amaranth, whom we heard whining most piteously. At length; he seemed to take a sudden resolution, chuckled audibly, and proceeded to barricade the door with all the furniture in the room. Here was an end to all our hopes of enfranchisement and safety. But, oh! dear me! What were my feelings, when I heard the cripple hobbling up stairs, and trying to open a little window which commanded the yard! We were in a sad situation; our only choice of avoiding the lynx eyes of Jagger was by getting into two water–butts, which stood in the yard. The windows of the house looked into every corner, so that we could not possibly hope to conceal ourselves behind them: In we went together, but my ill luck still attended me; Skelpie crouched comfortably in the belly of a dry butt, but the one, into which I floundered, was half full of water. The chilling liquid rose to within a foot and a half of the brim, the moment I got in, so that it was impossible for me to crouch, being actually standing on tip–toe, neck high in water! It was a bleak night, but my fever saved my life.

The cripple's blunderbuss, of unprecedented calibre, was thrust out of the window, before I could well moderate my quick breathing. He looked into every corner of the yard, but, happily, did not perceive my miserable sconce, which was floating in the water–butt, immediately beneath him. He descended in a few minutes, and removed the furniture from the door, searched all round the yard, and, at length, discovering the marks of Skelpie's shoes in the wall, concluded that we had escaped, and went grumbling to bed: It was a long time before I would suffer Skelpie to help me out of my hiding–place: he effected the job with infinite difficulty, and led me, dripping like a watering–pot, through the house.

About a week after this adventure, I discovered that Kate and Amaranth, who were once bosom friends, had quarrelled about me, and were now as spiteful to each other as possible. They met, one evening, at old Hetty Caddlefurrow's, and, on comparing notes, found that I was playing a double game. Ally Budd was present, but she said nothing. After lavishing the usual abusive epithets on me, they began to look coldly upon each other: from cool looks, they proceeded to vituperative insinuations; and, before they parted, naturally came to an open rupture. Occasionally, I suffered a little from their pouting and touting; but, in the main, I was happy enough between them. Each tried all her arts to win me from her rival; they sometimes met, grew great friends, vowed they would both turn their backs upon me for ever, kissed, cried, quarrelled again, and grew more rancorous to each other, and loving to me, than before. Skelpie became an altered man. Amaranth flouted him, abused his sister to his face, and caressed me in his presence;—although, I believe, the hussy, if she knew her own heart, loved the fellow all the time. Skelpie dressed smartly, discontinued his visits to all other girls, neglected his games, and even his daily occupations, to court Amaranth. He won the heart of the old cripple Saffern; but the lass still turned a deaf ear to his vows:—she was trying to vex Kate Skelpie. I was completely happy; I felt—but wherefore should I dwell on this love contest?—Skelpie is looking over my shoulder, and does not seem to relish the protracted detail. Suffice it to say then, that the banns of marriage were at length published, between Habakkuk Bullwrinkle, gentleman, and Kate Skelpie, spinster;— that we were united in due season;—and that Skelpie, a short time afterward; obtained the hand of Amaranth. The angry passions of the girls soon subsided, and they loved each other better than ever. Skelpie became my bosom friend; I prospered in business; and the two families have lived together for above twenty years, in concord and happiness. The roses have faded in Amaranth's cheek, and the fire of Kate's eye is somewhat quenched; but the relation of my own mishaps, Skelpie's adventures, and our strange courtships, never fails to draw back the youthful smiles of hilarity in both their matronly faces. Heaven bless them!

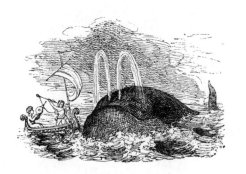

SECOND COURSE:

THE NEIGHBOURS
OF AN OLD IRISH BOY

THE NEIGHBOURS OF AN OLD IRISH BOY

INTRODUCTION

A ONE–ARMED naval Lieutenant, on half–pay, who was distantly related to my mother's family, had the good fortune to he presented, in his declining years, with a little cottage and a small portion of land situate in a village on the coast of Ireland, by one of his wealthy nephews, to whom it was unexpectedly devised by a maiden grand–aunt, who had never seen him above once in his life. I accompanied the lieutenant, from Waterford, for no other reason than because I had nothing, either better or worse, to do, when he went to take possession of his nephew's gift; and to pay a visit, after a separation of some years, to his old shipmate—the friend of his youth, and the companion of his manhood—Jimmy Fitzgerald,—better known by the appellation of the Old Irish Boy, who dwelt in a mud cabin on the skirts of the village: the history of whose neighbours is given in the ensuing pages, as nearly as possible in the same terms as he narrated it to my worthy relative, the one–armed lieutenant, and myself, in the course of the two or three first evenings which we passed in his company.

JIMMY FITZGERALD

JIMMY FITZGERALD and the old Lieutenant had both entered the navy in equally humble situations, at an early age: the friends of the latter, eventually, procured his advancement; but Fitzgerald, whose relations were poor, never had the luck to be rated on any ship's books in a higher station than that of an able seaman. The difference of rank had not the effect of diminishing the respect and affection which the lieutenant and Fitzgerald bore towards each other: in their manhood they were upon as familiar terms, so far as naval etiquette would permit, as when in their boyhood they had been equals. The lieutenant had saved his friend's life, at the risk of his own, in the Mediterranean; and, to judge from appearances, he was, if possible, more partial to Jimmy Fitzgerald than the Old Irish Boy was to him. The preserver frequently is found to display more affection towards the preserved, than the preserved either exhibits or feels towards his preserver.

No two men could be much more unlike each other than the lieutenant and Jimmy Fitzgerald. The former had received a tolerable education before he went to sea; he had taken every opportunity to improve himself while in the service; from the period of his retiring, he had read much on general subjects; and he was, at the time of his taking possession of his nephew's cottage, a very well informed man. Jimmy Fitzgerald, on the contrary, scarcely knew how to read when he left his native village; he had picked up but a slight smattering of such knowledge as is to be obtained from books, in his progress through life; but he possessed a finer mind and greater powers of observation than his friend; and the Old Irish Boy was, perhaps, superior to the better educated lieutenant, in mental riches, discrimination, and eloquence, when they again met, after an interval of many years' separation, under the roof of the former. Jimmy Fitzgerald's style rose with his subject; and he occasionally found himself at such an elevation, that it was a mystery how he had been able to attain it. The lieutenant was always level in his discourse: he neither descended so low, nor rose so high as his friend; nor did he, like Fitzgerald, ever presume to discuss any but common–place subjects. Jimmy occasionally indulged in such daring flights, that he toppled down headlong from an altitude which he was unable to support; a disgrace to which the more sober and matter–of–fact lieutenant never subjected himself. The one sedulously avoided the utterance of anything new; the other, if it had been in his power, would rarely have said anything that was old. The lieutenant was circumspect, and the Old Boy ambitious: the former was stiff, constrained, and rather stately in his language; the latter free, careless, and Hibernically vernacular. Jimmy Fitzgerald was poor, almost dependant on the exertions of a niece and her two sons for support, and so afflicted in his nether extremities, that he could not move from his chair without assistance; but he was always merry, and rarely complained. The Lieutenant possessed a competency, he enjoyed a most robust state of health, his legs, and the arm which the enemies of his country had left him, were still in full vigour; but he frequently repined at his poverty, occasional slight attacks of head–ache, and at being compelled to do the work of two hands with one.

Notwithstanding the difference in their temperaments, the two friends had rarely disagreed; and Orestes and Pylades, or Damon and Pythias, could not have exhibited more affection to–wards each other, after a long separation, than Jimmy Fitzgerald and the lieutenant did, when the latter entered the Old Irish Boy's cabin. My relation had, to use his own expression, been roaming about, here and there and everywhere, for a number of years; and so little positive inclination did he feel for passing the remainder of his life in one place, that he would, probably, have declined his nephew's well–meant offer, had not Jimmy Fitzgerald's cabin been within ten minutes' walk of the cottage, and the sea been visible from two of its four front windows. The village was principally occupied by fishermen; but there were two or three respectable families resident in the neighbourhood: to these the old lieutenant had letters of introduction; so that he felt satisfied, on entering upon his tolerably neat, but humble abode, that he should not be at a loss for society, even if it were possible for him ever to grow tired of that of his friend Fitzgerald.

After a great number of mutual inquiries had been answered, and many expressions of reciprocal friendship had been uttered, Jimmy Fitzgerald drew forth a little tub of pothien from beneath the bed, with his crutch,—which was of no other use to him but to perform this and similar offices,—and protested by several saints, whose names have escaped my memory, that we should have a jovial night of it. "Many's the pitcher of good drink," he exclaimed, "the Lieutenant and I have helped one another to empty: though, I'll say this for him, he'd always thirty–one points and a half more love for sobriety than ever Jimmy Fitzgerald could boast; and at that same time, when he'd make mouths at a third can, and draw back from a fourth, as he would from a dog that was going to snap at him, I drank, and drank,—more shame to me for it,—as though I'd declared war against spirits, and wished to exterminate them,—rum, in particular,—from the face of the earth. I think I'm a better man than I was long ago: no thanks to me, for that, though, perhaps; for I'm out of the way of temptation; and if I'd the pay of an admiral, I couldn't enjoy myself as I did long ago. It's wrong of us to brag of our virtue, when we've no appetite left in us for sin:—that's a saying I stole from the priest, because it plazed me. You'll like Father Killala, mightily, Lieutenant, when you come to know him; as you soon will, won't you? And noticing him reminds me of telling you, that while you're here, I'll engage you'll never get reproached for being a Protestant."

"Toleration, Jimmy—"

"Is it toleration?" exclaimed Fitzgerald, interrupting the lieutenant; "why then, in toleration, Father Killala's flock are all lambkins. I'll add to that,—because, I know you'll like to hear it—we're as quiet as mice in these parts: we've no fighting, nor fairs, nor wren–feasts; and as few ghosts or goblins, Banshees, Lepreghauns, or white women on horseback, as you'd wish: for we don't give such cattle much encouragement. Don't that plaze you, Lieutenant?"

"It does,—it does; and I have no doubt but that I shall pass my days peacefully and pleasantly in your village, my good old friend. Jimmy Fitzgerald and I," continued the Lieutenant, addressing me with unusual animation, "have fought and bled side by side; we were confined together, for four years, in a French prison, from which we escaped in company.; we had but one to bacco–box between us, for fifteen months; and we accidentally fell in love with the same woman. Jimmy acted most magnanimously on that occasion: as soon as he discovered that I was his rival, he instantly resigned his pretensions in my favour."

"And you were quite as polite to me, Lieutenant," said Jimmy, "and I don't forget it to you to this day. You insisted, you know, as strongly as I did: so that as each was resolute in not cutting out his friend, the darling delight of our hearts got neither of us; and she's now living,—an ould maid, as I'm tould,—near upon a mile and a half this side of Thurles."

"Is it possible?" exclaimed the Lieutenant.

"It's as true as you're born, if Corney Carolan is to be believed on his oath. I wouldn't take his word; but when a man swears to what he says, it's not dacent to discredit him, is it?"

"Certainly not," replied the lieutenant. "And so Peggy is living within a mile and a half of Thurles, is she?—unmarried, too, you say?"

"She is; and I don't think I'd be doing my duty if I didn't tell you I'll just take this present opportunity of saying, too, that as you think of settling, and as you're still well–looking, and I'm broke down out–and–out, so that she wouldn't look upon me,—I'd sacrifice nothing,—that is, I wouldn't intirely brake my heart if you wint and married her."

"James Fitzgerald," said the Lieutenant, "you are still the noble fellow you were thirty years ago. You have forestalled me on this occasion: I assure you that I was just working my self up to say to you what you have said to me. You are still a bachelor, Jimmy, and, as far as I am concerned, Miss Margaret M'Carthy is quite at your service."

"Thank you kindly, and good luck to you for this and all that's past," said Jimmy; "but, to spake my mind, — I never cared much about Peg."

"Nor I, upon my honour!" exclaimed the Lieutenant.

"I was glad of an excuse to be rid of her," quoth Fitzgerald.

"Precisely my own case, I protest," said the Lieutenant.

"And I never cared one half so little for her, as I do just now."

"We coincide on this point to a tittle."

"Then what becomes of our mutual devotion, lieutenant? It was all moonshine, you see."

"Not exactly," replied the lieutenant; "man can look back on past occurrences, and see circumstances in their true light—"

"Better thin he can when they're under his nose?" interrupted Fitzgerald. "Is it that you mane?"

"It is: passion and prejudice, as philosophy teaches us—"

"Hould your tongue, Lieutenant," said Fitzgerald "for I think I can find a shorter way for us out of the bog, than your jack–o'–lantern philosophy will light us to. The truth is, we were young and foolish that time; we thought we loved the young woman, and we didn't: so there's an end of Peg. My blessings be on her for all that, though! She never did me harm; and one of us, may be, was wrong in not marrying her."

"She told me to my face,—truth is a jewel, Jimmy Fitzgerald," said the Lieutenant, "she told me, calmly and resolutely, when I informed her that you were as deeply in love with her as myself, that we had mistaken innocent flirting for affection; and that, were a formal proposal made to her, she should indignantly reject it; 'for,' said she, 'I would not have either of you, if one was a Rear Admiral, and the other a Major of Marines.' That was her precise expression."

"Oh! Time, Time!" exclaimed Jimmy; "what a fine ould fellow you are, to be sure! How you open our eyes, and bring things to light! If it wasn't for you, Truth might often go hide her head."

"I think," said the Lieutenant, rather gaily, "that if I wanted a wife, I might probably find one who would suit me better than Peggy, among your neighbours, friend Fitzgerald. And, by–the–by, as I am coming to live among them, I should be glad if you would afford me a little insight to their various characters, circumstances, and histories. I am well aware of your capability to do so:—when I found you on board the Janus, after we had parted company for more than seven years, you did me incalculable benefit, by giving me a descriptive portrait of every soul in the ship; from the cook's boy up to the captain. Will you oblige me?"

"I will, in that or anything else that's in the power o' me," replied the Old Boy. "If I devoted one half o' my life to you, since I was twenty, I'd still be your debtor for the other half: for didn't you save the whole of it at the risk of your own?— You did, then; and I'll never—"

"Psha, psha, Fitzgerald! you know what strong objections I have to your dwelling on that topic."

"Go along with you, and don't be prating so, sir," said Jimmy; "I won't put up with your taking the liberty of doing a fine thing for me, and then bidding me not spake of it. My bits of gratitude, now and then, goes for the interest; but I'll never be able to pay off the debt. Still, though the one is out of my power to do, I'd not be aisy in my own mind if I neglected the other that *isn't*: so that, after all, may be, when we think we're doing great things, by acting as we should to others, we're just egged on to it, by the fear of not being on good terms with ourselves. You've often tould me, Lieutenant, I should be your Corporal Trim,—the man you and I read about, long ago, in Jack Flanagan's bit of a book, aboard the Bellerophon: and I would be so, but my legs took to their heels and deserted me, you know; and so I couldn't, could I? Did you ever get hould of a book, since I saw you, with the middle and both ends of that story in it?—If you did, as we'd only the middle and a bit o' the beginning in Jack Flanagan's greasy library, I'd be glad if you'd tell it me."

"I will, with pleasure, Fitzgerald, when—"

"When I've described my neighbours to you, is it? Well, then, I'll do that, I think, before we part, if the whiskey houlds out, and it don't get much the better of us. But it sha'n't, shall it?—for we'll put ourselves upon short allowance, and drink as we ought, to the renewal of our acquaintance, when I'm done. I'll tell you, before I begin, that you couldn't pick out any nine in the whole barony, knows half so much about the people that's in it, as myself; though I'm fast moored here, like a Trinity–house buoy on a sand–bank: but though I see little, I hear much; and as I can't go to any body, why, every body comes to me."

"I am grieved to the heart, Jimmy Fitzgerald," said the lieutenant, "to behold you so fettered by your infirmities; confined, if I may use the expression, like a pig in a coop—"

"Liberty, Lieutenant," interrupted the Old Irish Boy, "is only comparative at the best; and none of us gets our fill of it. Going about from one place to another isn't freedom, as I think you'll own: so why need I cry out? If it was, nobody, as I said, while ago, has as much as he wishes of it. I'd be delighted to be able to go get mass once a week, and to crawl a quarter of a mile now and then; but my infirmities prevent me: so I don't have my wish. But I'm only like the rest o' the world; and, therefore, I ought to be contented; though, I'll own, I'm not so, exactly. One man sighs to have a jaunt into the country, sometimes,— but his wife won't let him leave the town he lives in; another thinks, he'd be happy if he could p'rambulate about in foreign parts,—but his pocket keeps him at home; even that mighty conqueror, Alexander the Great, if there's truth in the song that's made about him, found the globe itself too little for his desires; and you know, well enough, that little Snookenhausen used to be telling us at Malta, of an ould philosopher, in ancient times, who fell out with his own bread and butter, like a big baby as he was, because he couldn't have another world for a play–ground, so as he might play trap–ball with this. There's none of us but strains the cable by which we're moored, as tight as we well can; and many's the man tries, all his life, to cut it, and sheer off into the main; but he can't. If you tie up a horse in a field, he'll not care half so much about the rich grass that's under his nose, as he will for a few dry blades, which his rope won't let him reach; and he'll be trying for them, when he might be filling his belly with better. If I am, as you say, shut up here like a pig in a coop,—and it's true enough,—I've the comfort of knowing, that he, who thinks himself free, and brags about his liberty, has a ring in his nose, and, may be, two or three other incumbrances, which prevent him, although he's adrift, from enjoying his freedom, or doing as he likes, much more than I can.—But now for my neighbours"

THE NATIVE AND THE ODD FISH

MICK MAGUIRE is a native of these parts, and he's out and out the oddest fish among my neighbours, as I think, and as you'll think too, may be, by—and—by, when I tell you more about him.—Didn't it ever occur to you, that a man may be ruined by a bit of good luck as well as by bad?—I'm sure it must.—I had an uncle at Tralee, who was left seventy pounds by his wife's gossip; and he welcomed the gift so warmly, and caroused so heartily to the honour of the giver, that he never ceased drinking and losing his time,—though he was a dacent man, and did business as he ought before,—until the seventy pounds, and a little to the tail of it, had slipped through his fingers. But that wasn't the end of it: for he got such bad habits as he never could shake off again; so he lived a few years a sot, and died a beggar: all which wouldn't have happened but for the seventy pounds his wife's gossip gave him.—I knew a young woman, whose name I won't mention, for the sake of her family, who lost herself entirely through a love of fine clothes, which she had never cared more about, than just a little, as all women do,—and no blame to them, —before her brother, who sailed for three years in the same ship with me, brought her home a little bag of silks and things above her station, which, when she'd worn them, made her despise her plain, honest, ould duds: but them that was about her couldn't give her better; so she grew sick of home, and did that she was sore at heart for when she came to a death—bed.—Ah! then's the time, if we never did before, when we know right from wrong; — then's the time, when the brain balances things and gives true weight to all our misdeeds;—then's the time, when a man, who could never before recollect what he did that day se'nnight, remembers all the evil he has done in his days, and all the good he might have done, but wouldn't. A dying man's memory, if he has been a bad one, is one of the most perfect and terrible things in the world;—go see one yourself, and you'll own it. We may be 'cute enough to hide what we do from the world all our lives, but we can't do so from ourselves when death puts out his big bony paw to give us a grim welcome to his dark dominions. We may be 'cute enough to shut our own eyes to what we've done, when we're strong and able, and the world's going merrily round with us; and we may be fools enough to think that our sins are blotted out when we have forgotten them;—for I've found that men are just like the ostriches

I've seen myself, in Africa, which, when they're hunted, poke their pates into a dark place, leaving their bodies entirely exposed, and fancy no one can see them if they can't see themselves:—but when we know that the last sands in our glass are running, and the dead sea is glimmering before us, we can't poke our heads into a corner,—don't you see?—or tie a stone to the neck of each of our iniquities, and drown it;—or look another way, and think of to–morrow's dinner, when they're coming to meet us;—or silence their small but very terrible voices, by whistling the burthen of an old song: for,—do you mark?—they won't be served so: they will be seen; they will speak; and, faith! it's hear them we must, whether we will or no. We may have fancied them dead and gone, years ago; but their ghosts start up and surround our death–beds, and clamour so, that we can't but listen to them: and what's most awful, they make a man his own judge; and no earthly judge is so impartial as a man is of himself, when his people are just wishing him good–b'ye for ever. For when we get on the brink of life and death, and know that it's ten to one we'll be dead by the morning, and it's just midnight already;—when we think that in a few hours our ears will be deaf, and our eyes blind, and we can't wag a finger, and our cold white corpse will be stretched out on a board,— motionless, helpless, good for nothing, and lumber more than anything else;—when we know, that, much as we thought of ourselves, the sun will rise, and the birds sing, and the flowers look beautiful, and the ox be yoked to the plough, and the chimneys smoke, and the pot be boiled, and the world go on without us, as well as if we'd never been in it;—then's the time, I say, we get our vanity cut up by the roots, and feel what atoms we've been in it:—and then's the time too, that the soul,—just before pluming her wings, and having half shaken off the dross of humanity,—becomes strong as the body gets weak, and won't be bamboozled, but calls up all our sins past, and places them steadfastly before our eyes; and if we've done wrong—that is, much of it,—a big black bird stretches out her great wings and flutters, brooding like a weight of cold lead, on our hearts; and conscience, though we've contrived to keep her down all our lives, then starts up, taking advantage of our helplessness, and reigns in full power.— but what's all this to Mick Maguire? you'll say.—Faith! then, not much: I began with an idea of getting to him in a few words, but was led astray, by noticing the death of the young woman I mentioned as being ruined by the gift of a brother, who meant it for her good. And you'll think it odd, may be, that the likes o' me casts over things so sariously: but I do, and there's nothing plazes me more than so doing, when I'm left alone here by myself, for hours, and hours together, while all that's near and dear to me is out upon the waves, the mighty roar of which, as they break upon the rocks about me, I hear night and day; and the sound o' them, and solitude, begets sarious thoughts; and so they should, in one that's gone sixty. There's never a day but I think o' death, so that I'm sure I'll be able to meet him firmly when he knocks at the gates of life for me, and bids me come, If I could go about, I'd not have such oceans of odd, out o' the way thoughts, consarning various things; but here I am, fettered by my infirmities to an ould chair, and I've nothing to do half my time, but think. Don't imagine, though, that I'm laid up in a harbour of peace, or that the other half of my time is calm and pleasant: it's no such thing; the woes and the wickedness of the world—good luck to it though, for all that—reaches me here in this corner, though it's harm me they can't much. I'm like an ould buoy, fast moored to an anchor on a bad coast, over which the waves dashes and splashes all day long, but they can neither move it nor damage it. But what's all this to Mick Maguire? you'll say, again. Faith! then, little or nothing: but now I've done, and we'll get on.

Mick, like my uncle at Tralee, has been ruined by a gift. He was once a hard–working man, and did well; until young Pierce Veogh, just after he came into possession of the house that's called "The Beg," on the hill yonder,—which he did at his father's death,—gave Mick an ould gun once, for something I forget; and that gun has been the ruin of him. He works one day in the week to buy powder and shot; and half starves himself, and goes in rags the other six, prowling about the rocks, and firing at sea–gulls and so forth, but seldom shooting one.

Mick's an oddity, as I tould you before; and why *so*? you'll say. Why, then, not for his face, for he's good–looking; nor for his figure, for he's straight and well built; nor for his jokes, for he never makes one; nor for any one thing in the world but his always telling the plain naked truth; good or bad, no matter if it harms him, he don't mind, but always spakes the thing that is, and won't tell even a white lie for himself, much more for anyone else:—and if that's not an oddity, I don't know what is. There's so much lying going on in the world, that if a man just lives in a corner, and sees only three people in the year, he must he now and then; or, somehow, things won't be as they should be; he won't do like them that's about him, and can't get on: why, I don't know; but so it is. Mick was never known to tell a story in his whole life; but he has sworn to so many out o' the way things, that he's often been suspected to be a big liar: for I need scarce say to you, that nothing can look more like a he sometimes than the plain truth. But whatever Mick says, always at last and in the long run turns out to be fact: so that we don't know what to think of the story he has of the fairy he saw on the rocks long ago. It seems as much like a he as anything ever I heard; but if it is one, it's the first Mick tould; and if so, troth then, it's a thumper. And why shouldn't it?—A good man, when he does wrong, commits a big sin; while you and I only does dozens of little ones: and them that sticks by the truth in general, if they happens to tell a lie, faith! then, it's a wonderful big one;—and, may be, so is Mick's story;—but you'll judge for yourself, when you hear it. But don't forget the honesty of Mick's tongue; and bear in mind too, that we shouldn't disbelieve anything simply because it's out of the way to us, and we never saw the likes of it ourselves; for there's so many strange things in the world, that one don't know what to disbelieve; and of all the wonderful things I ever heard of, there's none seems to me so very wonderful as this, namely:—I exist, and I know it. Now for Mick's story:—

"One day," says he, "as I was out shooting on the black rocks, I clambered up to a place where I never was before; and I don't think man had set foot upon it till then: it was higher than you'd think, looking up from the sea, which washed the foot of it; for the great crag itself, which none of us can climb,—I mane that one where the eagle's nist is,—seemed to be below it. Well, thinks I, when I got to the top, I'll have a good pelt at the birds from this, I'm sure: but no, I couldn't; for though they were flying round and round it, divil a one would come within gun-shot, but kipt going about, and going about, until the head o' me wint round wid looking at them, and I began to feel sick, for I'd come out before breakfast, not intinding to stay long; but some how, I wint further and further, and, at last, the sun was going down, and me there, where I tould you I was, a-top of the big crag. 'Michael,' says I to meeself, 'it's time for you to be going too, for the birds won't come near you; and you're hungry, boy, —so you are, Mick; you can't deny that.' And it's true thin I couldn't; for I never was hungrier in my life, than I was that time, and sorrow the thing in my pocket softer than a flint. Well, thin I began to go down; but before I'd got twenty steps, what do you think I saw there, upon the bare rock, where nobody seemed to have been before me, near upon half a day's journey higher than the sea,—what, I say, do you think I saw, lying before me there?—You wouldn't guess in a year. Why thin it was an oysther!—I started, as though a ghost had come across me:—and why wouldn't I?—for I'd no right to expect to see such a thing as an oysther there, you know, had I?—Thinks I, after awhile, 'Here's a fine mouthful for you, Mick, if it's only fresh; but, may be, it's been here these thousand years.—Eh, thin, Mick! but you're lucky, so you are, if it should be ateable.'

"Sitting down on the rock, I put out my hand to get a hould of it, whin what does it do, but lifts up its shell of its ownself!— and there was something inside it, just like an oysther, you'd think; but whin you looked closer, what was it thin, but a small dwarf of a man, wid a beard, and a little broad belly, and two short, fat, little darlings of legs, and his both hands in his breeches pockets; quite at home, and as aisy as you or I'd be in our arm chair, if we had one.

"'I'm glad to see you, Mick,' says he; 'it's long I've been expecting you.'

"Now, there's many that would have run away, and broke their necks down the rock, at hearing the crature call them by their names, and say this; but I'm one that never feared Banshee Lepreghaun, or any one of the little people, good, bad, or indifferent;—why should I?—So I pulled off my hat, and making a leg to him,—' Sir,' says I, 'if I'd known as much, I'd have come before.'

"'Thank you kindly, Mick Maguire,' says he. 'No thanks to me thin, at all at all,' thinks I, 'if you knew what I know:' for I was determined to devour him, if he was ateable. 'And it's by my own name you call me, sir,' says I, 'is it?'

"'To be sure it is,' says he; 'you wouldn't have me call you out of your name,—would you?'—And thin he fell laughing, as though his little face would have tumbled to pieces: and, faith! of all the faces I ever set eyes on, I never saw the likes of his for a roguish look.—'You wouldn't have me call you out of your name, would you, Mick?' says he again.

"'Why, thin, no I wouldn't, and that's truth,' says I; 'but what's your own name? I'd like to know, so I would,' says I.

"'I dare say you would,' says he.

"'And after that,' says I, 'I'd he glad if you'd tell me a small trifle about yourself, and how you live in your little house there, whin you shut down the roof of it; and thin—'

"'Bad manners to you Mick,' says he; 'don't he prying into a person's domestic arrangements.'—Them were his words. 'Mind your own business,' says he; 'and ax me no questions about meeself; for, may be, I won't answer them.'

"'But, sir,' says I, thinking to get all I could out of him, be fore I ate him.; 'sir,' says I, 'it isn't every day one sees betuxt a pair of oysther–shells—'

"'Oh! Mick!' says he, 'there's more out o' the way things than meeself, in the sea.'

"'I shouldn't wonder, sir,' says I.

"'There is, Mick,' says he; 'take my word for it.'

"'I'm sure of it, sir,' says I; 'and yet people says there's no mermaids even: now meeself saw one once, and she'd a fish's tail, and big fins below; and above she was as like a man, as one brogue is like another. Now, sir, I'd like to know your opinion.'

"'Mick,' says he; 'was it in the bay yourself saw the mermaid?'

"Faith! and it was,' says I.

"'Just four years ago,' says he, 'Mick?'

"'Just,' says I; 'come St. Breedien's day; for it was the very week Jimmy Gorman was drowned, so it was: his wife married Tin Carroll, tin months after his wake,—for we waked Jimmy, though he wasn't at home, and drank long life to our absent friend, in the pitcher o' pothien he left in the cupboard,— so we did:—and she has now three children, by Tim; and Maurien, the little one, is two months ould, barring a week, or thereaway; and three nines is twinty–siven, and tin is tin more,—that's thirty–siven, and three months betuxt and betune each o' the children, makes nine more, that's forty–six: thin there's Maurien, she's two months ould, as I said; so that, taking them together, there's forty–eight months, one up or one down, and that many months is four years:—so that, by the rules of multiplication and population, Jimmy's dead four years—don't you see?'

"'Arrah! don't be preaching,' says he; 'sure, meeself knew Jimmy well.'

"'Ah! and is it yourself?' says I; 'and was he on visiting terms wid ye?'

"'I knew him better than ever you did in your life, Mick,' says he.

"'Not a bit of it,' says I; 'did you ever spend your money wid him, like meeself, at the sheeheen–house?—or at the pattarn there above, with the penny–whiff woman? Did you ever once trate him to a glass o' whiskey, sir?' says I;—'not yourself, in starch.'

"'Mick' says he, 'Jimmy and I lay in one bed for seven months.'

"'In one bed!'

"'Yes.'

"'In a bed of oysthers, may be!'

"'It was,' says he.

"'Oh! thin, well and good, sir,' says I; 'but 'what has Jimmy to do with the mermaid?'

"'Mick,' says he, 'the mermaid yourself saw below in the bay was him.'

"'Is it Jim?—And now I recollect—what's as true as that my daddy Jack's a corpse,—the mermaid, sure enough, had a carrotty pole, and two whiskers, and a big jacket, to say nothing of the bradien, though they wouldn't believe me,—so they wouldn't; but betuxt ourselves, sir, by this pipe in my fist, she was dacently clothed as meeself, barring the breeches. Oh! thin, divil a saw saw I of breeches about her; and her legs,—sure, and wasn't her legs a fish? and didn't meeself say so?'

"'Very well, Mick,' says he; 'I'll explain it to you:—a big blackguard of a shark, that was on a travelling tour, happened to be going that way when Jim's boat was upset, and gobbled him up just as he got into the water: but, lo and behould! whin he'd got Jim's legs down his throat, and came to his bradien and big belly; divil a swallow could the shark swallow him:— and there Jim stuck so fast, that if the shark had taken fifty emetics before–hand, he couldn't have cast him up.—With that, Jim, finding his situation unpleasant, began to kick; and the shark, with that, tickled Jim's ribs with his teeth; but he couldn't bite clane through his big coat,—and the more Jim kicked, the more the shark tickled him; and up they wint, and down they wint; and my belief is, that Jim would have bate him, but the fish got suffocated, and sunk, just as Jim was gitting a pull at the whiskey–bottle, which he carried in his side pouch; and down they wint together, so sudden, that Jim, taken up as he was with the taste of the crature, didn't know he was drowned till they were both at the bottom.'

"'Was Jimmy and the shark, the mermaid meeself saw thin?' says I.

"'They was, Mick.'

"'Thin bad luck to the pair o' them,' says I, 'for two impostors!—And how did your honour know this?'

"'Wasn't I in the shark's belly all the time?' says he.— 'Didn't he gobble me up with a salmon, that tried to take refuge in the place where meeself and a few friends laid tin days before? —A lobsther lived in Jim's pocket for a month; and he and all his family used to go out three days a week to pull Jim's nose, for fishing up two of their cousins once,—so they did.—I'd thank ye for a pinch of snuff.'

"'And welcome, sir,' says I, houlding over the snisheen; 'meeself likes to hear news of my friends, sir,' says I; 'would your honour plaze to take a shaugh o' the doothien too?' And politeness, you know, made me offer him the pipe.

"'Mick,' says he; 'is it meeself or the likes o' me, that smoke?—I never took a goll o' the peepa in all my life: over and above that, Mick, I'd feel mightily obliged to you, if you'd blow your smoke higher, or be just ginteel and agreeable enough to sit the other side o' me: if you don't, you're a dirty blackguard, and bad luck to you, sir,' says he; 'for I've no chimney to my house.' With that, I just knocked out the backy from the pipe, and tould him, I didn't mind meeself, and I'd put away smoking at once.

"'Mick,' says he, 'you'd nothing but ashes in your doothien; so the divil's thanks to you!'

"Sir,' says I, not noticing what he said, 'that's a mighty nate little house you have of your own; I'd like to know who built it.'

"'Faith! thin I did meeself, Mick,' says he; 'but I'd like your big finger the better, if it was outside my door.'

"'Sir,' says I, 'if I'd such a nate little cabin, I'd marry Molly Malony at once. Doesn't your honour ever think of getting a wife?—or, may be, you're a widower?'

"'Mick,' says he, 'oysthers don't marry.'

"'Ye live mighty like a hermit, in your cell there,' says I.

"'Mighty like,' says he.

"'I suppose, you have your beads too, and you count them,' says I.

"'I suppose I don't,' says he; 'for I've but one.'

"'Troth, and that's a thumper thin,' says I, peeping into his little parlour: and there, sure enough, was a pearl big enough to be the making of me, and all the seed and breed of me, past, present, and to come, hanging by a bit of sea–weed round his neck

"'Do you know what, Mick?' says he; I'm sick o' the world, Mick; and I'm half inclined to give you lave to ate me.'

"'Sir,' says I, taking off my hat, 'I'm much obliged to you for nothing at all. It's meeself manes to ate your honour, with or without lave,—so I do.'

"'Is it yourself, Mick?'

"'Faith! and it is thin,—though I say it; for I'm hungry: —and, after that, I mane to take the big pearl, I see there about your neck.'

"'Mick, you're a reprobate!—Sure, you would'nt be so un genteel, as to ate a gentleman against his own inclination, would you?'

"'Meeself would thin, and think it no sin, in case the gentleman was a plump little oysther, like your honour.'

"Then, Mick, I wish you good evening!'

"'Qh, joy!' says I, seeing how he was going to shut himself in; 'it's of no use, sir, to do so:—I've a knife in my pocket, and it's not burglary in this country to break into the house of an oysther.'

"'Mick,' says he; 'an oyster's house is his castle.'

"'Castle!' says I; 'is it a castle?—two shells, with a little face in the middle o' them, a castle?—Thin what's my cabin below but a palace?'

"'A pig's palace, it is, Mick,' says he.

"'Musha! bad luck thin,' says I, 'to every bit of you—'

"'Ah! Mick,' says he, interrupting me, 'if I was half your size, I'd bate you blue, so I would.—You're a dirty cur, and so was your father before you.'

"'Say that again,' says I; 'say my father was a cur, sir, again, and I'd be obliged to you:—just say it now, and see how soon. I'll break every bone in your skin.'

"'Bone!' says he; 'sorrow the bit of bone is in me at all!' says he.—'Do you know anything of anatomy, Mick?'

"'An atomy!—that's a thing smaller than a mite, isn't it?'

"'Arrah! no, man: don't you know what nerves and muscles manes?'

"'Nerves meeself knows little about; but is it muscles? Och! thin, didn't I get a bag–full below on the beach, this day se'nnight? Tell me, sir, if you plaze,—is a muscle any relation to your honour?'

"'Ah! Mick,' says he; 'would you insult me?—sure we trace our pedigree up to the days of King Fergus; and the muscles wasn't known for whole ages after: they're fishes of yesterday,— mushrooms o' the ocean:—d—n the one o'thim knows whether or no he ever had a great–grandmother!— Mick, this is a bad up start world we live in.'

"'It is,' says I; 'people thinks o' nobody but just their ownselves; and doesn't mind what inconvaniency they puts their fellow–cratures to, so as they ar'n't harried thimselves.'

"'True,' says he, 'Mick: — did you ever rade o' the Romans?'

"'I'm a Roman meeself, sir.'

"'Phugh!' says he; 'it's of rulligion ye're spaking! I mane the ould Romans,—Romulus and Rebus,—Brutus and Brian Boru,—that sacrificed themselves for the good of their country:—thim's the examples we ought to follow, Mick! We should help our fellow–cratures too, in necessity, if it lies in our power; and not stand, shilly–shally, thinking and turning it over whether it will be to our advantage or not.'

"'Sir,' says I, 'your honour spakes my own sintiments; and sure never could a finer time come for practising what you preach, than now.—Luck up, your honour,—luck up, and see meeself, a poor fellow–crature, in distress for a mouthful;—I'm a part o' my country, and you're an Irishman born, I'll be sworn.'

"'Mick,' says he; 'that's a different sort of a thing, intirely.'

"'Not at all,' says I; 'it's a case in point?'

"'Well, Mick,' says he; 'thin I will, —I will sacrifice meeself.'

"'And no thanks to you, sir,' says I; 'you know you'd be sacrificed by me, whether you sacrificed yourself or no. Ah, ah!'

"'Ha, ha!' says he; 'that's true; and it's the way o' the world, Mick.'

"'And may be, sir,' says I, 'thim Romans yourself spoke about—'

"'Blarney and humbug, Mick!—blarney and humbug!—they did just what Shawn O' Shaugnessy did, while ago,—jump over board to show his bravery, when he knew the ship was sinking.—But don't be in a hurry, Mick,' says he, seeing me licking my lips, and getting nearer him; 'although, Mick, I have no wish to live; for an oysther's life is a sad one, Mick.'

"'Ah! sir,' says I, 'and so is Mick Maguire's.'

"'I've every wish in the world to travel into all foreign parts.'

"'And so have I, sir.'

"'But a snail's better off than I am.—Can't he take a trip, with his house on his back, and look about him whin he likes?'

"'That's just my own case,' says I; 'there's John Carroll, the pedlar, takes his pack on his shoulther, and travels from Clonmell to Carrick,—from Carrick to Stradbally, and all over the rest of the world, two or three times a week.'

"'Oh! musha! Mick,' says he, 'don't grumble; you're not half so bad off as I am:—it's tied by the back, I am, to the floor of my house, and I can't stir a foot.'

"'It isn't much money yourself spinds in brogues and stockings, thin,' says I.—'Ah! thim brogues ates a man out of house and home, intirely!—Does your honour know one Darby Walsh, a brogue–maker?'

"'No, I don't.'

"'Then, mark this, sir,' says I; 'if ever you shake the fist of him, you'll have a rogue in your gripe.'

"'I knew one Jack Walsh,' says he, 'at Calcutta?'

"'And was your honour ever at Calcutta?' says I.

"'I was once, Mick,' says he: 'I wint out in a porpus, who very politely gave me an inside place for nothing: but, arrah! Mick, I was obliged to work my way home.'

"'Did you know one Tiddy Maguire, in the East Indies?' says I.

"'No; but I heard talk of him.'

"'He was a brother of mine, sir; and though I've axed every body that ever come from thim parts, if they knew one Tiddy Maguire, in the East Indies, divil a ha'p'orth o' news could ever I get about him before!—Will I tell your honour a story about Tiddy?—Sure, I will thin:—Tiddy was a boy that used to be given to walking in his sleep;—he'd go miles about, and bring home people's little pigs and poultry; and be all the while innocent of theft—quite intirely,—so he said, any how. Well! to make a long story short, one night Tiddy was awoke by a great knock on the head, abroad there in Morty Flynn's back yard, with a sucker from the ould sow's side, in his hand;—how it came there, Tiddy never could give any satisfactory account. Whin he got home,—'Arrah! Tid,' says I, 'what happened you, man?—and who's been braking the face of you?' And sure enough, the blood was streaming through his hair like a brook among underwood. 'Morty Flynn,' says he, 'struck me while ago.' 'Arrah! man, and had you nothing in your hand to defind yourself wid?' says I 'Troth! and I had thin,' says he; 'but what's a sucking–pig in a man's fist to a dung–shovel?'

"'But, sir,' says I to the oysther, 'it's high time we should be better acquainted:—by your lave, sir,' says I, taking out my skean dubh, and a fine knife it was;—' by your lave, sir—'

"'Luck up, luck up, Mick!' says he.

"Meeself lucked up, as he bid me, and the curse of Cromwell on the crow that was flying over my head just thin;—the bird was bastely enough to dirt the face o' me;—down it fell, just thin as I lucked up, exactly betuxt my two eyes. I was in a terrible rage, you may guess; but hark to what a fool

I was:—instid of getting my gun, and shooting the blackguard, what did meeself do, in the heat of the moment, but pick up the oysther, and away wid it at him, thinking to knock a hole in his black coat!

"'Caw!' says he, sailing off; 'caw–aw!' grinning at me.

"'Caw–aw!' says the oysther, says he to me too, from a ledge o' the rock below me, where he fell; 'caw–aw, Mick!—more sinse and bad luck to ye, Mick!'

"'Ah! sir,' says I, putting a good face on the matter, and thinking whether or no I could get at him;—'ah! sir,' says I, 'did you think I'd be bad enough to devour you?'

"'Faith! you would, Mick,' says he.

"'Wasn't I polite?'

"'Mighty; and may you break your neck going home, Mick! Your brother Tiddy was transported in the East Indies; your father wouldn't fight for his faction; your aunt had a child, that was sent to the foundling, at Dublin; your cousin Jim is a tithe–proctor:—you're a bad set, egg and bird:—your sister's husband is a swaddler; and your own father's mother–in–law's first cousin hung a priest, Mick: moreover—'

"'Hould your tongue, you villain!' says I, levelling my gun at him. 'Hould your tongue, or I'll blow you to atoms!'

"'Who cares for you?' says he. 'Didn't you steal the shot your gun is loaded wid?—Answer me that.'

"'I will,' says I, pulling the trigger, and knocking his house from the ledge, plump into the sea.

"'I've done for you now, ould gentleman, I think,' says I.

"'No, you haven Mick,' says he, peeping out of his shell, as he was falling; 'you've, done just what I wanted. A grate big bird carried me up where you found me; he couldn't open me though, and left me there where I was; and instid of having done for me, you've sint me home, Mick,' says he, 'to my own bed, you blackguard; for which I'm mighty obliged,—and bad luck to you, Mick!' says he, as he sunk in the sea:—and from that day to this, meeself never set eyes on the little man in the oysther–shells,— though it's often I drame about him, and of what he said to me above on the crag there."

TIMBERLEG TOE–TRAP

AS I mentioned Pierce Veogh, 'while ago, when I was telling you of Mick Maguire—'twas he gave Mick the gun—himself it was then—and as I may mention him again two or three times, or may be oftener, before I've done telling you of my Neighbours, I'll just let you know a little who and what Pierce was. At three–and–twenty, he came into fine fortune; his father died then; he'd neither chick nor child but Pierce, and a fine boy he was, but too wild from his cradle to come to much good, 'twas thought. The father was a miserly curmudgeon in many things, and wouldn't live among us much; but kept Pierce here, with a private tutor and a few people, as long as Pierce would let him: but when the boy grew big, he'd no mind to be staying at home all his days,—and no blame to him,—so he wint off; and the father came back then, and lived at The Beg,—so we call his place,—till he died.

Many's the tale they tell of ould James Veogh;—how he'd give a feast fit for a prince, once now and then, just to make the great folks in Dublin have an idea of his wealth, and –what not, and then whip the cat for a year after, to make up for it. No man was prouder; and it's thought he was wrong in cooping up Pierce at home all his young days;—but that's no matter for my meddling. And it's said, his heart grudged the expense of maintaining Pierce abroad in the world, like the rest of the young sirs; and his pride wouldn't let his only son and heir be looked down upon: so to save both money and pride at once, Pierce was a caged bird until he grew up;—then he flew off, and a wild flight he had too.

It's said by his servants, that the father—and this is one of the million stories we have about him—once entertained the great lords and ladies at his house, in Dublin, with a fine masquerade, which cost him a mint of money,—no doubt it did;—and there was himself, in the disguise of the goddess they call Ceres, whose name you have heard before—though I hadn't when they first tould me the joke;—and while his guests were drinking down wine worth its weight in gold,—and it was all galore and glory with them,—Jimmy was seen skulking about, gathering up the scraps, out o' the way o' the strange servants, in a thing he carried, they call something that manes in English, a horn of plenty. That wasn't a bad joke of him, it's said, by them that knows. But there's no doubt, though he'd stoop to pick up a farthing, while Pierce would sooner be skimming guineas over a pond, ould Jim Veogh did more real good than Pierce did at first; for he payed all he owed,—though not a penny more, while Pierce often wouldn't — no, not when he could; and he didn't harry the poor tenants for rent,—which couldn't be said of Pierce,—but gave them time, though he made them pay up at last. And the ould man never did harm to any one in the way of pranks,—not when he was a boy even; and there's more than me recollects his sending Luke Sweeny a cow, when the one he had died.—To be sure, the cow he sent wasn't worth much; but he gave Luke a long day to pay for her, and took lawful interest only on the price,—which was three pounds ten shillings,—until it was paid. And paid it was, to the day: for Luke was as honest a man as ever broke bread, and wouldn't harm a mouse, unless he caught the crature nibbling his loaf,—and then, what harm?—My blessing on Luke!—it's many's the piggin of milk we got from him, in the bad times, when he'd a right to hould his head higher than he can now,—worse luck!—I could tell you a story of Luke, too; but as you're longing, I dare say, to know about Timberleg, I won't baulk you, by giving you dry bread when you're longing for sweetmeats. Luke's isn't a bad story though, for all that; and I'll tell it you, by–and–by, when I've none better left.

Pierce, as I said, wint off, nobody knows where but himself; and being a wild bird, came into bad hands, and got plucked; so that, when the father died—and there's some people don't scruple to say, Pierce, by his conduct, lent him a spur on the road to the grave—when he died, I repate, all the ready money was ate up by paying off post–obits, which Pierce had been giving at the maddest rate ever was known. The day before be heard that his ould dad was just dying, Pierce was in much distress, and so foolish to boot, that he gave some blackguard a bond for five hundred pounds, payable a month after his father's death, for nothing in the world but a good dinner and oceans of wine, for himself and a friend, every day for a week. That's what they call giving a post–obit; and a bad thing it is, as Pierce found.—He just reached home in time to get the father's forgiveness; and when it came to the last, a fine sorrowful parting they made, it's said, as one could wish to see;—for both o' them seemed sorry for the course they'd taken in life, and came to a resolution, if they'd their time to go over again, they'd not act as they had acted: but that could do no good. The father died the same evening; and, by that day month, Pierce was pestered to pay up his post–obits.

There wasn't so much money in hand left by Mr. James Veogh, as Pierce expected; and many of the poor tenants suffered; for he pinched them close, and did what he could to get clear o' the world. But all wouldn't do; and at last the bailiffs were after him night and day. It's said, that then it was Pierce Veogh learned to sleep with his eyes open;—a thing he does to this day, though there's no call for it.

The man that Pierce most feared in the world was one Mick Forester,— a bailiff, who lived in the nearest town to The Beg, on any side. Mick was a fine tall fellow,—six feet, if not more; and few could match him. He'd a nickname, like most of us, and was called "Timberleg;" why, I need not tell you:—but supposing you don't guess—it was, because his left leg was a wooden one. The other, as most wooden–legged men's are, was as stout a bit of material as you'll see anywhere, and Mick was proud of it,—as well he might. Though he'd scarce a word to throw to a dog, he was as 'cute as a fox, as well as being strong as a lion; and it was few escaped him. Spaking of animals, Mick had a dog, that always wint with him, and Mick called him Benjie. Benjie was black as coal; but you wouldn't notice him, for he was neither ugly enough to make any one fall into fits at the sight of him, nor good–looking enough for you to admire him:—he wasn't big or little, good–tempered or cross;—but middling every way. Benjie, though, was of great use to his master: and we accounted a man to be clever if he could outwit Mick and his dog. But outwitted they certainly were, now and then, though: and before I go further, I'll tell you how Mick was served by a surgeon by the name of Anderson, that set up in the next street to Mick's;—and it's many's the time Mick nabbed him, though you wouldn't think it, to see how great a man Surgeon Anderson is at this time. You must know that Mick had a wife, and a fine family, too; and one night a son of his—I think it was Jack, that's now married to Thady Purcell's widow—got taken ill with something sudden and dangerous: so Mick buckled on his leg and threw something over him, and wint and knocked at Surgeon Anderson's door. This was in the middle of the night: so when the surgeon put his head out of window and heard who it was, be wouldn't come down, thinking it was a make–believe of Mick's to nab him again. Mick couldn't blame him; for it's true Mick had often played tricks to get a sight o' the surgeon, when he wanted to take him; for he was almost a match for Mick himself, and not aisily had. So Mick stumped off to another surgeon, but he was out to a man five miles away; and to a third, but he was sick himself; and no one in the wide world could Mick get in the town, to come and see his son, that was a'most dying at home. Back he wint to Surgeon Anderson's again,—so he did;—and after he'd bate the door with his leg a little, the surgeon popped out his head, and says he, "Who's that below there?"

"It's me," says Mick, mighty civil; "it's me, sir, again."

"Oho!—And what story have you now, Mick?"

"The same I had 'while ago, sir:—my son's sick—"

"Divil's cure to him, Mick!—for he's not bad at all, and it's only a trick of yours to delude me."

"Upon my honour and conscience, sir, it isn't," says Mick; "I couldn't get a doctor any where, for I've tried, or I wouldn't trouble you. It's my belief, Jack will die if you don't come at once."

"Go away," says Surgeon Anderson; "go away, Mick; get put of that entirely!—Wasn't I sent for last winter, to a gentleman at the Roebuck; who had broken his leg?—and wasn't it yourself there, and the dirty bit of stick you stand upon tied up with a piece of rope?—and didn't you capture me that time, you blackguard?"

"I did, I did: I'm sorry for that; but pray—"

"And didn't you get a boy to bring me out o' my bed once, to a woman he said was at death's door?—and didn't I go, Mick?"

"You did, you did?'

"Ah! you facetious rogue! I know you're laughing at me now if I could see you:—and who should I meet, at the corner of the street, but your own sweet self, waiting for me?—And didn't you show me a woman lying asleep and drunk at the door of little Paddy Death, that keeps the whiskey shop, in Patrick street?—and, says you, with a grin, 'There's the woman at Death's door!'—didn't you, Mick?"

"I know I did; but as I'm a living soul, sir—"

"Go away, Mick;—go home and read the story of the boy and the wolf; and if harm happens your son, as it did him, it's your own doings, Mick! so good night! for I'm not to be had,— don't you see?"

With that he shut the window, and wouldn't come; but, as luck would have it, when Timberleg got home, Jack was better, and didn't want physic till morning. It's often Mick threatened Surgeon Anderson, but he never had the luck to get him again; for when the surgeon heard that Mick's story was true, and was told of his threats, some say he strove hand and foot to keep out of Mick's clutches for fear, and so got on in the world;—dating his rise from the night Jack Forester wanted physic, and he wouldn't get up to give it him.

But we mustn't forget Pierce Veogh,—though 'tisn't he is my hero exactly, but Timberleg;—still I can't go on without him, no more than the man in the book could play on the organ but for the boy that blowed the bellows. Well, Pierce, as I tould you, had the 'bailiffs about for him;—and as Timberleg seemed to have taken up his abode by The Beg,—which was Pierce's place, you'll recollect,—why, Pierce thought he couldn't do better than sneak off, if he could, to the town Mick came from, and stay there for a day or two: for Pierce was trying his utmost to raise money, and hoped to receive letters, post after post, to tell him things were settled; and a day's delay was worth everything to him;—to say nothing of the horror he felt, in common with most of us, to being shut up between four walls.—Not that a prison, when you're used to it, is the worst place in the world perhaps; for I know a man that hated the name of it, and after he got into one at last, he liked it so well, that when he could, he wouldn't come out of it, but turned turnkey, and kept his post behind the gate, with the key in his hand, doing nothing but opening and shutting the door, and never stirring out of the place, which had grown a world to him, till death came one day, and removed him to closer confinement within six boards, nailed together,—and that manes a coffin.—Now, a coffin's a thing, allow me to remark, that we all hate the sight of; and yet there's not one in ten thousand of us but hopes to come to it at last;—for who'd like to be buried any way but in a box?—And that's a feeling that's laughable to one who looks two inches below the surface of things; for what is it, but a fear of letting the cold clay come to us for a few years?—And come it will, you know, at last whether a man's buried in a large sheet of paper, a big hollow stone, or a lead coffin. And what matters time to the dead?—Or where's the difference, let me ask, between two minutes and twenty thousand years, to them that's under the turf?—Do what we will, the blackguard worms ates us all up at last; and they that takes pains to preserve theft bodies, don't do well, as I think: for, while all that remains of me, after being buried in a dacent and ordinary way, some time hence, becomes a part of the big earth, and can't be distinguished from what it's mixed up with,— the visible and touchable nose of a pickled emperor, a thousand years after he's dead, gets pulled by some puppy that opens his grave, and don't happen to approve of what he did when alive: or, what's worse, the bones of the arm that awed multitudes, gets cut into drunken men's dominos; or the boys and girls of a tenth generation plays with them for sugar–plums, in the shape of two a–penny tetotums, and so forth. Therefore, let me, when I die, have no armour about me; let the worms come, and good luck to them, say I;—the sooner they walk away with .every inch of me, the better.

But we'll never get through at this rate; and such grave discourse as I've led myself into, turns the edge of one's appetite for fun,—doesn't it?—But, *na bocklish*,—forget what I've said, and listen to what Pierce Veogh did. Like the goose that took refuge near the fox's den, when the fox himself was watching for her near her nest, Pierce got away one night, and wint off to the town: there he remained in great safety for some days, as Timberleg didn't know he'd escaped, and so wouldn't raise the legal siege of The Beg House,—why should he?

No letters came; and, at last, Pierce determined to get away altogether, and cut the country for a time, if he could: so one morning, at day–break, he left the little lodgings he had hired for the sake of being private, and was walking off, the nearest way out of town, when just as he came within five feet of a corner, what should he see but Mick Forester's dog,—the dog I described to you, that was always a few feet before, or oftener a yard or so behind, Mick himself.—"Oho!" says Pierce, turning back and taking to his heels; for well enough he knew the dog:—it's himself that did then;—for often he saw him, bating round The Beg, and Mick not far behind him. "Oho!" says he; and "Bow–wow!" says the dog; and "My grief!" says Timberleg, who just then came round the corner, and saw the young legs of Pierce carrying him off five miles an hour faster than Mick could run. Mick wasn't fool enough to go after Pierce;—no, no,—not he, then! He turned on his heel, and walked back the way he came,—giving the game up for lost, out–and–out; and he struck his dog Benjie two or three times, with his leg, for not keeping to his heel.

Now what did Pierce do, think you?—Why, he ran as if he'd everything fearful behind him, and fancied he heard the stump of Mick's wooden leg keeping time with the gallop of his own pulse. Running seemed to be safety to him, no matter which way he ran; for "if Timberleg and Benjie's behind me, it matters not what's before me, so that the way's clear," thinks he;—or rather, he didn't think at all, but wint on, and you'll hear how it ended.

By—and—by, Pierce came to a corner again, with one leg before and the other behind him, as if he'd little Powsett's seven—leagued boots on; or, to spake within compass, the foot that was forward the whole length of his leg more advanced than his body. Now here's the point of my story:— Forester was much nearer Pierce than Pierce expected; to spake out at once, he was close to the corner, only the other side of it; and, as one may say, in a right direction to cross his course. Well, just as Pierce had put his foot that was forward to the ground, about four inches beyond the corner, Mick Forester, quite unconscious of his good luck, was, at that instant, going to put his timber—toe on the flags in a transverse direction. Down it came, pat upon Pierce's foot; the whole weight of Mick's body followed directly after; and the next moment, Pierce found himself within an inch and a half of Mick's nose, staring his enemy full in the face, who looked quite as wonder—struck, but not half so grievous, as himself; for the end of Mick's leg covered a couple of Pierce's worst corns.

This wasn't the first time in the world a man ran into the lion's mouth. Mick put out his paw upon Pierce, and from that day, people called him "Timberleg Toe—Trap."

Pierce lay in Mick's custody for above a month; he then got out by scraping together all he could, and flew off to England for safety: but it was just out of the frying—pan into the fire with him; for,—though a man's good deeds have wings of lead, or just none at all, and travel like the tortoise,—such things as make against him, go at the rate of twelve knots an hour, to every point of the compass at once; or, at least, to all the points be wouldn't have them go, if he could help it; and by this rule, the news of Pierce's being taken for debt by Timberleg, got to England, before he reached it himself; and he wasn't well landed and recovered from his sea—sickness, when one of his creditors had a bailiff to give him a grip by the shoulder. As soon as a man gets clawed, long bills generally come pouring in upon him from all quarters:—it was just this way with Pierce; and his prospects in perspective were almost as unpleasant as his enemies could wish. We'll leave him now though, if you please; and I'll tell you what more happened him by—and—by, and how it all ended; if you don't fall asleep, and by your snoring, give me a hint that it isn't quite so entertaining you find me, as may be I think you ought. But, we'll see.

BAT BOROO

IF you're passing at early morning, above there, beyond The Claugh, you may see Bat, with his back leaning against Mick Maguire's door,—'tis there where he lodges,—smoking his pipe, and looking out under his eye–brows at you, as fierce as a grenadier at a Frenchman. There's nothing warlike about Bat but braggadocio, and a cut across his chin,—barring that he's wasted and worn, you'd think; for his broad shoulders seem to have been better covered with flesh one day than they now are. When he condescends to spake to any of us, Bat talks of the wars, as though he'd been in them; and says he has wounds besides that one on his chin, but they're under his clothes; and then he gives a bit of a cough, and says he's asthmatic, and might catch harm if he stripped himself to shew them. So that nobody has seen Bat's wounds but himself; but no doubt he has many of them: though, to be sure, that on his chin looks as though it was done by the blunt razor of a barber, rather than a grenadier's baggonet, or a dragoon's sabre. However, all's one for that.

Bat's too high and mighty to be much liked by the people about; and a boy says he peeped in at a hole in the cabin one day, and saw something on Bat's back, that looked as if the military cat had been scratching it. But doesn't the boy play the rogue now and then?—Faith! he does; and, may be, Bat is belied by him. How the blade lives, nobody knows; nor why he came here to this place, which is at the very back of God's speed, we can't say. May be, he's a pensioner:—why not?—And, may be too, as some think, he's a native of these parts, and one of the sons of that same ould Dick Boroo, who lived in a cabin on the very same spot where Mick Maguire's now stands. Dick wint to the dogs, long ago, and he and the whole seed and breed of him run the country; and nobody has seen a ha'p'orth of them since; except this is one o' them, come here after the wars, to bluster away, where he used to be beaten; and die one day where he first drew breath.

Bat won't own he's a Boroo; but we all call him that name in the face of him; and when he goes off,—what will they write on the stone by his grave, if he gets one, think you?—Why, then, "Here lies Bat Boroo, who died of doing nothing."

And, faith! it's nothing he does, but walk about like a half–sir as he is,—smoking his pipe the whole blessed morning, for the sake, he says, of getting himself an appetite for dinner. But he needn't take the trouble; for it's just as needless, in my mind, as whistling to the sea, when the tide's coming in; and come it will, like Bat's appetite, whether you whistle or no, devouring almost everything in its way. Without a word of a lie, Bat's the biggest eater in all the barony, and the biggest brag, —that is, he was,—to the tail o' that. But, poor fellow! he don't know his infirmity; and thinks his appetite a sign of weakness, instead of sound health: it's the only living thing he takes on about. "There's nothing, Jimmy Fitzgerald," says he, to me, one day; "there's nothing, in the universal world, I can keep on my stomach,—bad luck to the bit!—for if I ate half a rack of mutton, with peeathees and milk, or a pound of pig's face, or eight or ten red herrings, for my breakfast,—hungry I am, in an hour or two again, as though nothing had happened to me that day in the way of provision."—What think you of that for digestion?

There's three things Bat thinks about, and that's all:—first, his belly;—secondly, making believe he's not to be frightened, by man or beast, nor even the good people that lives in the moats, and frolics away all night on the heath, and goes to bed in the butter–cups and daisies—it's a wonder to some they've played no tricks with him yet;—and lastly, that he has much better blood in his body than the people about him.

Now I'll tell you what happened Bat. 'While ago,—three or four years back,—we'd a cunning woman came here,—and it's but little she got,—how would she, when there was little to give?— it was going to a goat's house to look for wool: and plenty of bad luck she prophesied, for nobody had enough to pay for better. Some of it come true enough; and if she spoke truth, there's more mischief behind. She said to me, I'd have my roof down; but it's safe yet, for I trusted in Providence, and put a new beam across it the week after she wint. At last, when she'd tould a power of ill–tidings to many, and no one would go near her for fear, and she'd stood by the abbey–wall for a long hour, waiting for customers, with the people,—men, women, and children making a circle about her, who should come up but Misther Bat Boroo, just after taking a good dinner with Paddy Doolan?— "What's the murther here?" says he. So they up and tould him, that nobody dared to have their fates from the cunning–woman.

This was a windfall for Bat,—a glorious occasion for making much of himself. Up he marched to the woman, as though he was going to attack an entrenchment, and crossing her ould yellow hand with the copper,—

the best his pocket could afford,—he desired she'd say what would happen him. "Speak bouldly," says he, "for Bat Muggleburgh isn't the man that's to be frightened by a bulrush."

"Man," says she, looking up to him, "you've been a soldier."

"What then?" says he.

"Here's a line in your hand,"—says she, "a line which tells me, that before another year has gone over your head, you'll be more frightened by a bulrush than ever you was by a baggonet; —and that's saying much."

Bat bullied her, but bit his lip for vexation; and, by–and–by, you'll hear how he got on, and what came of the cunning–woman's foreboding. But wait a little, for I'm before my story, and must go back.—You heard me say, Bat called himself by the name of Bat Muggleburgh, awhile ago; and so he did: for, as I tould you, he denied the name of Boroo, because he said he'd no call to it; and that Muggleburgh was what he'd a right to,—and he'd own to it, and nothing else. Now, all this may be true enough; Bat's name may be Muggleburgh, and he Dick Boroo's son for all that:—for did any one ever know, or take the trouble to inquire, what was ould Dick's rale name—if he had one—besides Dick?—Boroo was a nick–name he got for some saying or prank, that was past by and forgotten entirely in my time, though the name still stuck to him. He wasn't an Irishman; but where he came from,—except he was a bit of a Dutch smuggler or something in his young days,—myself neither knows nor cares.

It's often he brags, — Bat does, — of the brave coat of arms that belongs to him, if he had his rights; and what great men the Muggleburghs was in times gone by. But that's no matter at all: —there's a regular descendant of the honourable kings of Meath sells butter at Cashel, and is as big a rogue as one here and there. I myself came from a fine family by my mother's side; but what's all the famous blood of her ancestors now? One of the grandfathers of the worm you trod on o' Monday, had some of the best of it; and for my own part, I don't value that of great Bryan himself a rush and a half: but my mother didn't think so, poor thing,—rest her soul!

Well, by this time, you must be pretty well acquainted with Bat, — and, may be, tired of him; but wait till you hear what happened him.—Many months, but not a year, after Bat had his fortune tould in the manner I mentioned, we'd a poor scholar—a stripling of sixteen or so—with us here, for two, or it might be, three days, at the most. Good luck follow him! He was a lad we all loved, high and low,—and it's not very high the best of us is, sure enough,—for the boy behaved beautifully, though he'd a spice of the wag in him.—And why not?—wasn't he young?— and isn't young days the best of days with us? And if we ar'n't merry then, when will we, I'd like to know?

Bat didn't like the poor scholar, and used to abuse him, because he convinced us all he knew more of the geography of foreign parts than Bat, who had been among them, as he said. And the night before the lad left us, Bat threatened to baste him, for smiling while he was preaching about the Muggleburgh arms, and bewailing the state of his digestive organs: and he would too, if it was not for this crutch of mine, and Mick Maguire's gun, and the piper of Drogheda's wooden leg, and one or two other impediments;—not to mention a feeling of goodness that came over him then in the poor scholar's favour;—for if Bat's a bully and a cormorant, he hasn't a bad heart, when all comes to all:—but the poor scholar didn't forget it to him.

The next morning, those who were up, and passed by Bat's door before he was awake, saw as fine a coat of arms figured out with chalk upon it, as the best of the Muggleburghs, in the height of their glory,—if ever they had any,—could well wish to look upon. And could any one thing suit Bat better?—Faith! then, nothing in the wide world. In the middle, was a dish instead of a shield, with a fat goose—Bat's favourite food—quartered upon it; and each side of the dish, what do you think there was, but a knife and fork for supporters; and, to crown all, perched upon the top was a swallow, for a crest! Then, at the foot, there was a table–cloth finely festooned, and words written upon it, by way of motto, which ran thus: —"BOROO *edax rerum.*" I remember them very well: first, there was BOROO; then came the name of my lady's steward, Misther Dax, with a little *e* before it; —then, after a blank, followed a *re*; and it ended, like a slave–driver's dinner, with ruin—BOROO *edax rerum* —signifying, as the worthy coadjutor informed us, that Bat, like ould father Time, who takes a tower for his lunch, and a city for his supper, was a devourer of all things. The hand that can thaw could make its master understood, where the tongue that spakes seven languages couldn't do a ha'p'orth; or so thinks Jimmy Fitzgerald,— that's me. Now, though we couldn't make out the motto, all of us down to the boys themselves knew what the figures of the goose, and the swallow, and so forth, stood for; and great was the shouting:—but Bat had a glass in his head, and didn't wake.

By–and–by, down he came with the pipe in his mouth; and, suspecting nothing at all, shut the door after him, and leaned his back against it as usual. When his backy was smoked, he threw away his pipe with an air, and strutted off through the place; and, behold! there was the chalk from the door on him, and he, not knowing it, bearing his arms on his own coat. Will I tell you how many boys and girls he had at his tail in ten minutes?— I couldn't, without reckoning every living soul of them, within half–a–mile of this, or I would. For a long time, Bat didn't know what it was all about, and looked before and both sides of him to find out where the fun was, but he couldn't. "Look behind you!" says somebody. Bat looked, and there was the boys and girls laughing, and that was all: so he wint on again.

This couldn't last long though. After awhile Bat found out what made the boys follow him, as the little birds do the cuckoo; and then his rage wasn't little:—describe it I won't, for I can't; but I'll tell you what he did: — he suspected the scholar had played him that trick,—which was the truth,—and he found out which road he took; and you'll be sorry to hear he soon came within sight of his satchel.

Whether the boy heard Bat blowing and blustering I don't know, but he luckily glanced behind him, and. seeing Bat and his big stick, did what any one in his place would, if he could,—put a hedge between him and his enemy. Bat followed him, vowing vengeance in the shape of a great basting, from one field to another; until, in the end,—he didn't know how,—he found he'd lost the boy, and discovered the prudence of taking to his heels himself; for there he was, in the midst of a meadow, and a fine, fierce–looking bull making up to him at a fast trot. Seeing this, Bat began to make calculations, and perfectly satisfied himself that before he could reach the hedge he came over, the bull would dome up with him, and, in all probability, attack his rear. Bat couldn't very well like this: there wasn't much time for pros and cons with him; so he threw his stick at the beast, and away he wint, at a great rate toward a gate he saw in the nearest corner of the field. Though the bull wasn't far behind him, he contrived to reach and climb up the gate–post without being harmed;— but, musha!—what did he see, think you, when he got there?— If ever man was in a dilemma, it was Bat. The gate led into the yard before young Pierce Veogh's kennel, and just below Bat, was a brace of as promising dogs for a bull–bait as you'd like to see, trying all they could to get a snap at Bat's leg, that was banging their side of the gate–post. The dogs looked,

and really were, more furious than usual,—which was needless;—for it
happened to be just at the time when Pierce was away in the safe custody
of Timberleg the bailiff, and they weren't fed in his absence quite so
regularly as they'd wish. Bat knew this; and, thinks he, they'd make but
little bones of a man of my weight, if they had me;—so that it wouldn't
have been wise in him to have ventured into the yard. The gate wint close
up to the garden–wall. But there was three impediments to Bat's going
that way:—first, the gate was well spiked; next, if he didn't mind that,
one of the dogs could reach him aisily from the top of their kennel as he
passed; thirdly and lastly, if he defied the spikes, and escaped with a bit or
two, and got to the garden–wall, there was a board, with "steel–traps" and
so forth, staring in the face of him. And what other way had he of getting
off?—Divil a one but two. One was, by dropping into the meadow
again;—and that he might do well enough, but for the bull, who was
bellowing below to get a rush at him;—the other, I think, was jumping
off the post into the stream, upon he edge of which it was planted. The
water wasn't wide, but was deep, and Bat couldn't swim: and there he was,
depend upon it, in as nice a dilemma as man had need be.—If you don't
credit what I say, draw a map of his position as he sat on the post with
the beasts on both sides, the spikes behind, and the water before him, and
then tell me what you think.

Bat bellowed, and so did the bull, and the noises wint for one, and the
dogs barked, but nobody came. By–and–by Bat saw a figure walking along
the opposite bank, and who should it be but the ould cunning–woman!

"Is that yourself, Bat?" says she.

"I think it is;—worse luck!" says he.

"That post of yours isn't the pleasantest post in the world I think," says
she.

"I think not," says he.

"Didn't I tell you, Bat—"

"Bad luck to every bit of you!" says he, interrupting her; "bad luck to
you and your *bull–rushes* too, and all them that plays upon words! I know
well enough of what you're going to remind me."

"Bat," says she, "it isn't a year since I—"

"Ah! now go away," says he; "go away, now you've had your ends, and
make up for the mischief, by calling some one to tie up the dogs,—or
drive away the bull,—or bring a boat,—why can't you?"

The ould woman sat down, and smoked her pipe, and she and Bat had a little more confab this way across the stream; but, at last and in long run, he persuaded her to come to us here, and tell us how matters stood with Bat, and to beg us to help him off: not,—do you mind?—as I think, out of any humanity to the man, but to shew us how truly she'd foretould what was to happen him. I don't like her, so I'll say no good of her,—but this, namely, — she gave a poor boy who was upon the shaughran, without father or mother, house or home to his head, a penny and a blessing, when it's my belief, she'd little more to give. I say that,—for I'd like to give even a certain elderly gentle whose name I won't mention, his due,—much more a poor ould cunning–woman, that's weak flesh and blood, after all's said and done (though not a bit too good), like one's ownself.

Down came the woman, but she found few at home besides Mick Maguire, for a'most every mother's son that could move, had gone away to get Bat off his predicament before. Mick wouldn't go at all; for, he said, sure he was the bull bore a grudge against him, because he threw stones at his head, and bullied him once.

"Ah! but," says somebody, "may be, he wouldn't notice you, Mick."

"May be, he would though," says Mick; "so it's go I won't."

"But sure we'll all be wid you, Mick."

"That matters not," says he; "for the bull might be ripping up ould grievances, and select meeself, out of all of ye, to butt and abuse."

"But couldn't you bring your gun, man?"

"I could then, but I won't," says Mick; "for I'm inclined to suspect it wasn't to shoot his bull, that Misther Pierce Veogh gave it me."

You wonder how they came to know where Bat was,—won't you!— 'Twas the poor scholar then, that ducked down in a ditch, froth the bull on one side, and Bat on the other; and after that, saw how Bat got on with the bull, and came to tell us. So some of them wint to Pierce Veogh's people, and got the dogs called off, and down came Bat amongst them, swearing that if he'd his big stick,—which, he said, he'd dropped he didn't know how,— he'd baste the bull any day.

THE WITCH'S SWITCH

THERE'S nobody dies, but somebody's glad of it; few people, as I think, but have one person standing between them and what they look upon as comfort or happiness, or something or other they desire, but don't want, for all that, may be. Duck Davie was with me yesterday, foaming away like the sea against a rock it can't master;—and what for, think you? Why, then, only because his wife looks so well and won't die to plaze him. It's my belief he'd be glad to be rid of her, though she half keeps him, and is loved far and near. She does all the little good she can, in the way of nursing the sick, and so forth; and she saved Duck Davie's own life three times, by her knowledge of herbs, and the million–and–one ailments of our poor mortal bodies.

But Duck don't like her;—I'd be spaking what wasn't the truth if I said that he did: and why should I tell a lie on Duck Davie? —I won't on him, or any man if I know it. When he married her she was not young,—that is, full thirty,—but trim and good–looking, which is more than could be said of himself any day of his life; for he has a big nob on his face for a nose, and a mouth so wide that it would be fearful to look at, if he laughed: but Davie is either too discreet or too ill–tempered, morning, noon, and night, to be jovial. He drinks, but don't ever get merry over his cups: and yet his little grey eyes twinkles, and he puckers the wrinkles in great folds about them, and you hear an odd noise in his throat sometimes, when he's tould of a trick, that's malicious and droll, being played off by the boys on any of the ould women he knows. His knee–bands is always loose, and his big coat hitched over his shoulders; he wears red sleeves to his waist coat, with ragged edges that reach to his finger–knuckles; and shoes—not brogues—but shoes, down at heel. He never takes his ould grey hat off his bald head but to pull on his night–cap. He's round–shouldered and short, but stout and strong for his age, which is on the grave side of sixty; and the fronts of his knees is turned in, and they jostle one another; and his feet are broad and flat, with the heels far out and in front, instead of being behind; and this—poor man!—makes him waddle oddly: he's none the worse for that though. After this pedigree of his appearance, most likely you'd know Duck if you met him.

I forgot a thing or two in him that's remarkable:—he turns his head to and fro eternally, as if he were looking for some one, whether he's alone or in company; and even when his eyes twinkles, as I tould you, or if they're sparkling with passion, there's something in them all the while that reminds you of a dog's look when he knows he has done wrong and to be whipped.

Davie was tolerably fond of his wife for many long years after he'd married her; but though she does little or nothing to vex him, that I know of, Duck don't like her, now she's got ould;—any one with half an eye could see that, if Davie didn't own it himself, which he does. It's the way o' the world, you'll say: a man that's passed the prime of life forgets his own wrinkles, though those of his wife, that's about the same age as himself, are day after day staring him in the face;—he sees her years, but if he can walk about, and eat, and get his health two months out of the twelve, he won't let himself fancy he feels his own. That's not altogether the case with Davie; it may be so in part, but not entirely; at least, so thinks them that knows his story.

From the time he first knew the use of a button, it's said Duck Davie had a deep–rooted grudge against ould women; they have always been at war with him, and he with them. Duck lost his daddy before he saw the light; and his mother died when he was weaned, or awhile after. She had an ould aunt, who took the boy under her wing, and did what she could for him, in her way: but, by all accounts, her temper was such that a cat couldn't live with her; and if little Duck Davie's heart was kind as that of a lamb by nature, there's no doubt she ruined it; if it was bad before, she couldn't do otherwise than make it worse. A more terrible Turk in petticoats, and on a small scale, never walked; but after awhile she got little good of Duck. She seemed to live for no other purpose than to vex and thwart and make the poor little fellow miserable. There was no soul but the boy, to take off the scum and bitterness of her temper; and, by–and–by, Duck began to think of nothing but how to pay off the long score he felt he owed her. He should have put up with any thing, you may say, and been grateful for her protecting him, and ate his crust, though it was sopped in vinegar, with thanks and meekness: may be, he ought; I won't argue it one way or another, but simply tell you, he didn't.

The few acquaintance Duck's grand–aunt had, was folks of her own age as well as sex, and having a spice of her own temper: to them she tould all Duck's delinquencies, and they joined her in abusing him; and, what was worse, often helped her to belabour him. Little Davie hadn't a disposition to be reclaimed from his bad ways by a broomstick; may be, kindness might have done better, but it never was tried on him: so on he wint, from bad to worse, and, by the time he was twelve years ould, hated every woman he met who'd a grey head and wrinkled face. He looked upon them as his natural enemies, and did all he could to vex and perplex them.

By–and–by, Duck was put out to a tailor; and he'd done with his grand–aunt, and all other ould women, for ever, as he hoped. But, no;—when he got to his master's house, which he never entered till he was bound, little Duck discovered that his mistress was as crooked with age, and almost as crooked in temper as his grand–aunt. When her first husband died, she just did what many a widow, with a good house and trade left her, has done before and since,—married her foreman. He was a stout, brawny blade, having nothing but his needle to depend upon, but good–looking, and not above thirty.

In the second year of Duck's apprenticeship, a mighty remarkable event happened him; and I'll tell you what it was presently, if you'll wait. He behaved himself, and liked the place, and his fellow–'prentices, and his master too, for many months. Ould Alice, his mistress, was no sourer with him than with the others, all this time: but at last she began to single him out—just as he'd feared she would—as a natural prey to one of her age and sex. She used him, by degrees, worse and worse, until Duck convinced himself he was bound in justice to them feelings he had of his own, to turn upon her, when he could slyly, and annoy her as often as an opportunity for doing so, without danger, occurred. At length, ould Alice smarted under his malicious tricks to such a degree that she grew a fury almost; and the worse she behaved to him, the worse he behaved to her:—for Duck was always obstinate. He'd bad luck though, to meet with such a match for his grand–aunt as ould Alice; hadn't he?—Now for the event I promised to tell you about.

One day, Duck was sent on an errand by his mistress, but instead of getting back quick, as she wished him, though he knew she was just standing on thorns till he got home to tell her what was said to her message, what does he do but turn away out of the road into a field, to pick thistles to put in her bed, the next time he might think fit to be offended.—In one corner of the field was a big hollow tree,—an oak, I believe, but it don't matter, and under it lay an ould woman: her brown skinny arms were half covered with a ragged cloak, and her face was partly hid by a few straggling grey locks of hair, which had escaped from under her bonnet. Instinct made Duck approach, and when he got near the tree, a puff of wind blew up the grey hair, and Duck saw that her eyes were closed. Her snoring satisfied him that she wasn't dead, while it convinced him that she was fast asleep; and his fingers itched to give her a touch of his tormenting talents.

A stick, stuck upright in the ground, close by the ould woman's side, attracted Duck Date's notice, when he got behind the, tree: "What's this?" thinks he, examining it, and feeling little afraid or so, at the looks of it;— and you wouldn't wonder, if you saw it yourself; for they say it was an odd, outlandish staff, made of wood that never grew in a Christian land, thick, twisted, tall as a middling man, and with as ugly a face carved on it as ever you saw in a dream after taking a tough supper—no night mare's could be worse. Bat Boroo's big stick, the mention of which made me think of the story I'm now telling you, was just a bit of a baby's twig, compared with the ugly cudgel Duck Davie saw that day sticking up in the field.

Duck, as I said, was a little dashed at first, but he soon got heart, and, says he to himself, "It is but her stick she's stuck up there, like a centinel, to scare away the boys from teazing her while she sleeps; but I'll just teach her that I'm not to be come over so aisily."

Upon this, with a long barley–straw, from behind the tree where he was, Duck began to tickle and teaze the ould woman's nose, that was almost as rough and as prickly as the ear of the straw.—Did you ever get your nose tickled that way while you were asleep?—If you didn't, take my word for it, and upon my honour and conscience, it's far from pleasant; and so the ould woman found it. She scratched her nose with her long blue nails, muttered a curse upon the flies, and snored again.—Duck was in his glory; he tickled as before, and the ould woman opened her eyes, but he shrunk behind the tree, and didn't breathe: so she dropped off once more. The third time he touched her she awoke at once, and from what she said, and her preparing to get up, Duck knew she was sure of being teazed by something bigger than a fly: so, for fear of anything unpleasant, he moved off, and ran away across the field, chuckling in his own mind at the fine fun he'd had.

When he got within a step or two of the gate, Duck heard a sound with which he was very well acquainted—I mane that of a stick descending with force upon his back; and within much less than a quarter of a second, he felt such a blow across his shoulders as he didn't get for many's the long day. He looked be hind, thinking to see the ould woman, who he now thought was a witch, close at his heels; but no—it was only her stick!— There it stood, staring him full in the face, though its owner was yet but a little distance from the tree, and hobbling towards him, in such a weak way, that Duck felt sure she couldn't have had strength to throw it. Don't think that, while he observed this, Duck wasn't wriggling his shoulders to and fro, and bellowing lustily with the pain of the thwack. It wasn't a little that would make him cry; but roar he did, this while, as loud as ever he roared in his life.

Not knowing what to make of this that had happened him, while the stick stood where it did, he was afraid to turn his back to it again; and there he was, still wriggling and roaring, when the ould woman came up. The state she found Duck in seemed to give her great satisfaction: she took the point of the stick out of the ground, and clasping it round the middle to support herself; gnashed her toothless gums up in Duck's face, and, for his malicious tricks to her that day,—waking her when she was weary, as he did,—promised him a taste of her switch when ever he worried an ould woman again. With this she tottered off, and Duck sneaked home, blubbering as he went, expecting to be saluted with a blow of either the ladle or the sleeve–board, for delaying: but he was disappointed, for he got both;—one from ould Alice, and the other from her husband.

All that happened Duck Davie I can't tell you;—it must only be a bit here and there, and with that I hope you'll content yourself; or may be you don't like him, and the less you hear of hi the better plazed you'll be.—May be, though, you're like me I don't like the man much, but his story don't displaze me; so I'll go to the next thing I recollect hearing of him.—I mustn't pass on though without mentioning how surprised Duck was not to find any mark of the blow he got in the field: he expected his back was well wealed, and so he might; — but it wasn't, "Here's the bump on my head," says he to himself, "from the ladle, and here's the mark of the edge of the sleeve–board; but where's that of the switch, as the ould woman called it?—Now I'm sure she's a witch, or else why wouldn't her blow mark me, as well as them that I got from my master and mistress?"

After this, Duck was as quiet as ould Alice would let him be for a month or more; but then he began again, and you'll hear how it war:— his mistress was well to do in the world, and had her house filled with what's useful; and to tell the truth of her, though stingy in some things, a good housewife—so she was. Duck had a power of fellow–'prentices, for his master did half the work of the town he lived in; and the boys was destructive, as boys will be,—won't they?—Alice was proud of her plates; but they broke them away about this time, at such a rate, by accident and what not, that she was determined to put a stop to it: so what does she do but give orders that no one should use a sound plate, but ate off the broken ones! And when she found one of the boys doing wrong this way, he got a crack on the head with the ladle for his disobadience. One day, Duck wouldn't give himself the pains to look for a broken plate; it was a mischievous moment with him, and ould Alice had just before threatened him for something; so he took down a whole plate from the dresser, and qualified it for his use, by breaking a piece off its edge. The moment he did it, Duck felt a very disagreeable sensation in his shoulders. You'll guess the witch kept her word, and that it was the switch touched him. Faith! then, you're right; there stood the weapon, with its evil–looking head, at Duck's back, though no sign of the old crature herself could he see. And what does the switch do, after Duck had stared at it a little, but make him a polite reverence, face about, jump head foremost out of the window that was open, and hop off down the garden walk, like a man would who had but one leg and that a wooden one.

After Duck had done bellowing, and the pain of the blow was gone off, he felt his back, but it was as smooth as the innumerable drubbings he'd got from one and another had left it. He then asked everybody if they'd seen a stick, with a big black head, hop into the window or go down the garden: but he only got laughed at; and when he tould a pair of his fellow–'prentices in confidence what had happened him, and why it was, they jeered him, and tried to persuade him he was telling her, or going mad: but he wouldn't believe them, for, he had seen the switch with his own eyes, and felt the blow with his own back. The two 'prentices, however, reported the trick to the rest; and from that day, in imitation of Duck Davie, when they couldn't or wouldn't find a broken plate, they knocked a piece out of a sound one. Duck saw them do this often and often, but the switch didn't strike them; and he began to feel sorry that ever he'd tickled the rough nose of an ould witch with a straw.

Time wint on, and ould Alice at last found out the trick of the broken crockery, and who it was put the 'prentices up to it; so poor Duck was in a worse pickle than ever, but didn't dare to indulge himself in mischief against his mistress, for fear of the switch. At last, however, he could bear her behaviour no longer, and resolved to terrify her out of three or four years of her natural life happen what would after it. What brought him to this was a practice of her's, in the cold mornings of winter, which was now come on, of punishing him for the misdeeds of his companions. You'll hear how she managed it. An hour before day–break, without much disturbing her husband, who didn't get up for long after, she'd take a pole that stood by her bed–side, and strike the beam that wint across the ceiling with it, to wake up the boys that slept in a big room above. Sometimes they wouldn't wake; and then she'd go up to them herself, and feeling about in the dark, get hould of the nose that lay nearest the door; that nose she knew well enough was Duck Davie's; and when she had it in her horny fingers, she'd pull it till Duck roared with the pain loud enough to wake himself and all his fellow–'prentices. This way she got two or three of her ends at once:—she vented her spite on Duck, punished one of the delinquents, and awoke the rest. Duck didn't like it; and after he'd been served so twice, vowed revenge, in his own mind, if she did it again. Well, the very next morning, while Duck was dreaming of tickling the witch's nose, up came his ould mistress, and performed as before upon his. Let Duck be as bad as he would, this wasn't well of her, at any rate; and if he did play her a trick after that, I won't say she didn't more than half deserve it. One of the 'prentices said that he'd been awake, with a whitlow on his thumb, for an hour before, and he'd swear the mistress hadn't knocked at all that morning: so it was a piece of spite on her part, that day at least, to punish Duck; and if he wasn't determined before, he certainly became so on hearing this, and wint to work at once on a plan he had laid down for the occasion.

Alice, you'll recollect, had been a widow: her first husband's picture, larger, if anything, than life,—as little men's pictures usually are,—was hung up in the parlour while he was alive; but after Alice got married again, and a year or two bad gone by, somehow it found its way into a lumber room, at the top of the house. Duck discovered it in his rambles; and with it, in the same room, three or four suits which the ould tailor had left off in his life–time, a cocked hat he wore on high days and holidays, and a smooth cane he carried on Sundays. These were all fine materials, and Duck didn't fail to make use of them. He cleaned and patched up a suit of the clothes, brushed the hat, scoured the cane, made an effigy of straw, and dressed it up mighty nate and all that,—for Duck, though obstinate and dull at. his trade, was 'cute and ingenious in all sorts of mischief–making. When he'd got so far, he cut the face out of the picture, washed it with something till it looked as good as new, fixed it into the neck of the figure, with the hat on its brow, and a white cravat under its chin. He then fastened the cane, by manes of an ould glove, to the cuff of the right sleeve; and while the master was out one night, brought it down stairs, propped it up against the parlour door, and then giving a knock, got away in the dark. When the on woman opened the door, the figure bent forward, with the hat on its head and the cane in its hand, just as though it would enter, and looking for all the world like life itself!

Ould Alice shrieked, but Duck had taken care no one should come to her, for he'd locked and barred the entrance from that part of the house were the 'prentices and servants were, to the passage which led to the parlour. But Alice wasn't the only one who made a great noise in the house that night. The moment she first cried out, at seeing what she thought was the ghost of the late tailor, her husband, and all the while she lay screaming in the parlour, Duck Davie was keeping time with her in the passage, by shouting under the blows of the switch, which belaboured him this time, so unmercifully, that he took up the figure, and got away with it out of the house.

Duck Davie never darkened the tailor's door again: he travelled all night on foot, resolving to find some place, if he could, where there was no ould women to torment or tempt him, or where the witch's switch couldn't reach his shoulders. He got harbour and work elsewhere, and wint on for a few years tolerably well, considering all things; hut he found to his cost that there was ould women everywhere, and it wasn't aisy to get away from the switch he dreaded. Elderly persons of the fair sex were occasionally vexatious to him; and his disposition now and then broke out, so as to summon the switch to his shoulders.

At last, Duck Davie became a man,—as boys will, you know, in years, at least, if not in discretion; and he made up his mind to try if be couldn't rid himself of the switch that haunted him. We'll see how he succeeded.

It happened one morning, after he had been brooding over his misfortunes all night, that he drank a little more than was wholesome on a fasting stomach, and did something, almost without knowing it, that produced a slight bruise on his shoulders from the switch. He turned round upon it at once, and resolved to see if he couldn't master it. He began to belabour it, before it had time to make its bow and hop off, as though it was flesh and blood like himself; but only broke his own knuckles against its hard head. He then tried to capture it, but the switch bent and writhed in his grasp like an eel, got clear out of his hands, and then, hopping back a little, gave Duck Davie a blow in the stomach with its head, as he was advancing to make another attack, that laid him flat on the ground. It then made its bow to him where he lay, and hopped off.

Instead of disheartening, this interview irritated obstinate Davie; and the next day, he brought the switch to him again, by purposely tripping up an ould woman's heels who hadn't done him a ha'p'orth of evil. There was a holy well, which ran into a broad stream near the place where this happened, and before the switch had given him a second blow, which he knew he deserved, Duck had gripped it tight to his breast and carried it to the bank. he cast it into the stream, hoping of course to see it sink; but it swam back like a fish,—landed,—finished the drubbing it owed Duck, and hopped away without giving him a chance of getting hould of it again!

It was full five years before Duck Davie had another affray with the switch, which in all that time never failed fearlessly to visit him as often as he offended. It was on All Souls' eve when he had his next fight with it. He did that which brought it for the purpose, and resolutely grappled it with both hands, just under the chin, as soon as it appeared. Some say that it bate Duck while he held it; and others, that it turned and twisted about his body, almost breaking his bones, like them snakes we hear of in foreign parts would: but for all this, Duck got it into the big fire that was before him, and kept it there, with poker and tongs, bating its head down as often as it jumped out of the blaze to grin at him, until it was quite consumed. And we're tould, that it didn't crackle like wood does while burning, but the noise it made was like that of two unearthly voices,—one laughing bitterly, and the other shrieking and groaning as of a crature in agony.

Now whether Duck Davie got rid of the switch this way or not I can't well tell you, for he won't let us know. There's different stories about it. Some say, the witch came to him that time, and begged hard for her stick; but he swore, by the holy iron with which he was banging it, he wouldn't listen to her; and that he never saw switch or witch after. But there's others say they know this, namely—that Duck Davie saw the ould woman long after, sleeping under the tree, with the stick standing whole and entire, where it was when he first set eyes on it.

Duck Davie came to settle in these parts about ten years ago. His wife is one of this place: but she left it in her young days, and Duck met with and married her when she was housekeeper to an apothecary, and he a journeyman tailor in Limerick, where he lived long with her, and came here, one morning, when he was grey, in the wake of Timberleg Toe–Trap the bailiff, for whom he'd been doing many's the dirty job, in making seizures and dogging debtors, and so forth. This was after he'd been refused work by all the master tailors everywhere he could go, because his eyes was got too weak for fine stitches: so he was obliged to do something for himself, and nothing better being offered him, he turned follower to Mick; and when an execution was issued by Pierce Veogh's creditors, which happened about three months after his quitting this country, Timberleg, who made the seizure, left Duck Davie and another of his men, as his proxies, in possession of The Beg. But before he'd been in it a week, Duck had a quarrel with his master, Timberleg, and another was put in his place. So then his wife's brother, Paddy Doolan, who is one of my neighbours, persuaded him to quit the bailiff entirely, and to set up for himself here among us, as we didn't want finer work than he was able to do without straining his ould eyes. Duck took his brother–in–law's advice, and has been with us from that day to this.

He has just as great a dislike to ould women as ever he had; that's why he don't trate his wife as he should do, as many think; and some say, when he gets in a passion,—as he will often, and rave and tear like a madman,—that the stick with the night mare's head has been bating him for abusing his wife. Duck Davie has a good quality or two, but take him head and heels, I, for one, don't much like him. You'll say, may be, why do I employ him, then?—And I'll answer you,—because there isn't another tailor within ten miles of us: and moreover, if I was Paddy Doolan, and had the use of my limbs, when he abused his wife without a cause, as he did yesterday, and often before, I'd give him as fine a basting as he got from the witch's switch that day when he looked over his shoulder, and saw it standing behind him in the field.

THE WEED WITNESS

AS the world goes, there's few places but have had somebody to blacken their good name, by robbery or murder, or crime of one sort or another; and there's few that hav'n't now, nor hadn't before now, but will one day or other, there's no doubt of it:—for as sure as the poppy grows in the corn–field, so will bad passions spring up in the hearts of some of us; and them that's the best in their young days, often turn out the worst when they're ould: so that, as somebody says, it's foolish to be spaking much in praise of a man's goodness of heart, and so forth, until the green grass grows over him, and he can't belie us by braking out into badness. It's a fine shew of potato–plants, that has but a single curly–leaved one among them; and we've rason to pride ourselves, that never within our own memory, or that of the ouldest people the ouldest of us now alive knew when we were little ones,—was there more than one man convicted (I don't say taken up on suspicion—I'd be wrong if I did) of killing, or burning, or shooting, or joining with White–Boys or Break–o'–day–Boys, or the likes o' that, for three miles every way from the door o' my house. To be sure, there's but few people in that space; but they're enough in number to have had black sheep among 'em. If you're uncharitable, you'll say, "So they have; but the rogues have had the luck riot to be found out." May be, you're right; there's many, to tell the truth, I wouldn't swear for. Much to our glory, however, the one that was found out, didn't draw the first breath o' life–here; but came from far away up the country, after he'd done that which brought him to a bad end.

Johnny O'Rourke, as it's said, had a dacent woman for his mother; but, for his own part, Johnny was a downright bad one, —egg and bird. He got into such company when he grew up, as couldn't well improve his morals; and, by–and–by, he'd brought his ould mother—she was a widow—at once to death's door, and the brink of beggary, by his bad goings–on.

One night, after he'd been away for more than a week, Johnny came home, with the mud of three baronies lying in clots and layers on his stockings, white as a corpse, and looking every way as though he'd travelled far and fast, on no pleasant errand.

"It's well you're come," says somebody to him from behind, as he put his hand on the door.

"Why so?" says Johnny; and though he knew by the voice it was one of the neighbours that spoke to him, his heart knocked against his ribs, and then seemed to be climbing up to his throat; for something whispered him, all wasn't well: indeed, he hadn't much reason to expect it.— "Why so," says he, "Biddy?—Isn't the ould woman as she should be?"

"Did you lave her as she should be, or didn't you?"

"Poorly, Biddy, and you know it; for you was wid her whin I wint away. But tell me, now, upon your soul, is she worse?"

"My grief! it's herself that is, then!—You've broke her heart, out and out, God help you!"

"Don't say that, Biddy! or I'll go get a knife and kill meeself. Tell her, I'm here, and that I can't come in 'till she forgives me for all's said and done:—and bring me something to comfort me, for I hav'n't heart to look in the face of her."

"Is it comfort for yourself, you're talking of?—and your mother wailing and howling night and day, as she has been, for the sight of her llanuv!—What has she done to have such a one as yourself, Johnny, no one can tell. Down on your knees, and crawl that way up to her, there where she lies on her death–bed; and don't be thinking of sending me as a go–between; or, may be, your mother may die before you get her blessing."

"Oh! Biddy, Biddy! you're destroying me—root and branch! Sure, she can't be so had as that!"

"Come in and see," says Biddy, taking his cold hand in her's, and leading him at once right into the house, and up to the bed side of his mother, and shewing her to him, propped up as she was, and raving with the little speech that was left her, for her darling, and her llanuv, and her white–headed boy, and the life of her heart, and all the dear names she could call that bad son, who had brought sorrow and misery upon her. And they say it was awful to hear the shriek of joy that came from her, and how she leaped out of the women's arms that was houlding her, when somebody put aside the long grey hair, which in her grief she'd pulled over her face, and shewed her Johnny himself standing by the bed–side, the image of woe and remorse. There wasn't a hair's breadth of his face that she didn't kiss; and though a little before, when he stood like a statue, looking at her as he did, Johnny was too much choking with grief to be able to utter a word, yet, when he'd mingled the scalding drops that burst from his eyes, with the cold tears on his mother's cheek, he found himself restored; and drawing back from her embrace, he had courage enough to look up at her: but he couldn't bear the sight for a moment, and hid his face on her breast again, exclaiming,— "Oh! mother, mother! and is it this way I find you? Why didn't I die before I saw this night?"

"Cheer up, my darling!" said the ould woman, "for I'll now braathe mee last in peace, that you're here to close mee eyes.—Oh! that hand, Johnny!— put that hand close to mee heart!—it's often I felt it there before now,— long, long ago, Johnny, whin it was young and innocent, and I'd no comfort on earth—widow as I was—but the sight of mee baby laughing up in mee eyes;— though the look of you then even brought the tears into them, you were so like him that was taken from me before you were born."

"I've been a bad son to you, mother," said Johnny; "it's now I feel it."

"Take your mother's blessing and forgiveness, my child; and mee last prayer will be, that you'll get as free pardon here and hereafter for all things, as your poor ould dying mother now gives you."

"Oh! you're not dying, mother;—you can't be dying!" cried Johnny, in the greatest agony; "such a thought as that of your dying never crossed mee brain, —and I can't bear it; — Sure, mother, I'm 'home, and I'll watch you, and be wid you night and day:—there's hope for us yet. Isn't there hope, mother? Don't you feel life come into you at the sight of. me, and mee tears and repentance for what I've done?"

"No Johnny," said the ould woman; "I'm sure I'll not see the morning. The sight of you does me good; but I'd live longer iv you hadn't come:— now I've nothing to wait for, as I know my last look will be fixed on the child I bore, and who's the only one that's kith, kin, or kind to me, on the face of the earth. But, oh! mee child!—don't do as you have done!"

"Why spake of it, mother?—be quiet about the past, for it troubles me—so it does."

"I've had bad dreams of you, Johnny. Neighbours, iv you'd let me be alone awhile wid me child, I'd thank you."

The women retired slowly from the room, and closed the door behind them. "What have you been dreaming, mother?" eagerly inquired Johnny, as soon as they had departed.

"There was a river of blood, Johnny, wid yourself struggling for life in it; and me in a boat, widout rudder or oar, not able to save you: and then—"

"Don't go on, mother! it's worse than throwing water on me!—I'm shaking from head to foot."

"You didn't mind dreams once, Johnny;—and you used to laugh at me when I'd be telling you warnings I had that way, about you."

"I wasn't so bad then, may be, mother, as I'm now: bud you'll live long yet, and help me to pray meeself out of all of it; and I'll mind what you say, and go to work for you honestly, instead of feeding you wid what I got in sorrow and sin, if I escape this once, I'll make a vow never to sleep out of mee own little bed there again. Oh! that I never had!—bud it's too late to make that wish."

"Don't despair, darling! for he that's above us is good: and iv you're penitent, and do as your father's son should, my dear, in spite of that other bad dream I had, the grass will grow on your grave, as it does on his."

"Oh! mercy! and did'nt the grass grow over me, mother? And did you see mee grave in your dreams?"

"A thousand times, Johnny, since you were gone:—the little hillock itself was barren and bare, and all round it, as far as the eye could reach, there was nothing bud wild turnips growing."

"Mother! you're mad to tell me so! You couldn't have dreamed that—you couldn't have seen the prushaugh vooe—"

"I see it now, my dear boy, as I did in mee dreams, waving its yellow flowers backwards and forwards, summer and winter, as iv they were to last for ever and ever."

"Oh! mother, mother! spake no more o'them! Iv I thought it wouldn't be the death of you, I'd aize mee mind."

"Pray God, you've murdered nobody!"

"I have, mother!—I have!—Iv you didn't spake o' the prushaugh vooe, I wouldn't have tould you; bud there'd be no salvation for me, iv you died and did'nt forgive me for it:—for though you forgave me for every thing besides, you couldn't forgive me for what you didn't know about. I'd die iv I didn't confess to somebody;—and who's there in the wide world I could open mee soul to bud yourself, mother?"

"Oh! my grief, Johnny! and is it come to this?—Bud are you sure you're not pursued?—(spake low, for they're at the door, and it won't shut close)—are you sure, my dear?"

"I don't know, mother; I think I'm not: bud I'm afraid, as well I may, from what he said to me, and that same thing you dreamed about, I'll be found out and hung, worse luck! who knows?—though I never meant to harm him, as you'll hear, mother, at the last day,—the day o' judgment, whin there's no keeping a secret."

"Who was your victim, Johnny? And where was it you were tempted to risk your soul?"

"It was the Hearthmoneyman I killed!—I'd been watching for him, different ways, day and to rob him of his collection; but he'd always somebody wid him, or there was people coming; or whin there wasn't, I hadn't the heart, until this blessed morning."

"In the broad day?"

"It was;—miles away where you never have been. Bud he was too much for me, mother; and if it wasn't for the bit of ould baggonet I carried in mee sherkeen, without ever intinding to use it, he'd have taken me off to the police: for he got away mee stick from me, and I couldn't manage him; no, nor keep him off, nor get away from him even, till I took out the baggonet."

"Did no one see you?—Was there nobody near?—Are you sure, now?"

"I am:—bud, oh! mother! what do you think he said to me? There was wild turnips growing by the road side, and as he fell among them, says he,—'You think no o sees you; bud while there's a single root of this prushaugh vooe growing in Ireland, I'll not went a witness that you murdered me!' Then he dragged up a handful of it, and threw it in the face o' me, as he fell back for ever."

"My dream! my dream!" cried the ould woman; "Curse his collection! Curse the money that tempted mee child into this sin!"

"I took none of his money!—not a keenogue! How could I touch it after what I tould you?—But what'll I do, mother?"

"Fly, my dear! Go hide yourself far, far away! Go, and my blessing be on you!—Go, for you'll be suspected and pursued!—Go at once, for I'll not be able to spake much more!—Go, while I've mee sight to see you depart!—Go, while I've sinse left to hear the last o' your footsteps, out away through the garden! Mee eyes is getting dim, and the breath's going from me."

"Oh! mother! how can I tear meeself from you?"

"Obey me on mee death–bed, if you never did before. I'd linger long in agonies iv you didn't; and, may be, die shrieking, just as they came to take you up!—Go off, my darling boy, and I'll expire in peace, wid the hope of your escaping. Soul and body I'll try to hould together until morning; and then, iv I don't hear of your being taken,—as bad news travels fast,—I'll think you're safe, and die happy."

Well, at last Johnny promised his mother he'd try all he could to get away to some place where he couldn't be known; and after taking her blessing, and an eternal lave of her,—a sorrowful one it was, they say,—he wint out at the back door of the cabin, and made off as fast as he well could. After skulking about in different parts for many months, at last he came to this place, got a wife, and did as well as here and there one;—nobody suspecting him of being worse than his neighbours,—for eighteen or twenty long years. His wife, who was a cousin of mine, loved him all that while; and said, though he was dull and gloomy at times, and didn't get his sleep for bad dreams he had,—which she thought made him cross,—take him altogether, he was as good a husband as woman could wish.

Well, as I said 'while ago, Johnny O'Rourke lived among us here, for eighteen or twenty years,—under the name of Michael Walsh though, I must tell you,—then you'll hear what happened him. He wint out to fetch a bit of a walk one day, after being bad a week or two, so that he couldn't well work; but he hadn't been over the threshould a quarter of an hour, when he came running back the most lamentable–looking object that ever darkened a door. Every hair on his head seemed to have a life of its own; his eye–balls were fixed as those of one just killed with fright; his mouth was half open; his jaw seemingly motionless; his lips white as a sheet; and around them both was a blue circle, as though he'd been painted to imitate death. Down he dropped upon the floor as soon as he got in; and all his wife and the neighbours could do, didn't restore him to his right senses for hours. At last, he began to call for the priest;—I remember it as well as if it happened but yesterday;—and here it was where they found Father Killala, who was telling me the middle and both ends of the cant at The Beg: for all Pierce Veogh's furniture and things were sould under the hammer that day, and the Monday before, for a mere nothing, or next kin to it. And when Father Killala got to the sick man, he said, that though we'd so long called him Mick Walsh, his raal name was Johnny O'Rourke; and that he'd seen a sight that day, which drove him to do what he'd long been thinking of; namely,—confessing that he was the murderer of Big Dick Blaney, the Hearthmoneyman, who was found, with an ould baggonet in his breast, among the prushaugh vooe by the road side, away up the country, twenty years before. "And," says he, "I can't live wid the load on mee heart;— whether I he abroad or at home I'm always tossing about in a bed of prushaugh vooe, wid the baggonet glimmering like a flash of lightning over mee head: so you'll deliver me up at once, that I may suffer by man for raising mee hand against man, and God help me to go through it!"

And, no doubt, the sight he saw was enough to make him do as he did. A week after he tould his wife his whole history; and how, when he wint out that day when he came home and called for the priest, after walking a little way along the road, thinking of no harm in the world, but with his heart weighed down as usual for the deed he'd done long ago, he was suddenly startled, by hearing somebody singing what he thought was a keentaghaun; and what should he see, on turning his eyes to the bit of wild broken ground by the road–side, but the face of his ould mother! And what was she doing, think you, but tearing up the wild turnip–plants, which were growing on the spot where she stood, as though her life depended on their destruction!— He thought she'd been in her grave years and years before; but there she was, miserably ould, and withered away to skin and bone: but though altered by time, he saw, at the first look, it was his mother. She wint on with her work, not noticing her son, and singing in a low, wild, heart–breaking tone—

> "Still the prushaugh vooe grows!
> For the winds are his foes,
> And scatter the seed,
> Of the fearful weed,
> O'er mountain and moor;
> While weary and sore,
> I travel, up–rooting
> Each bright green shooting:—
> But the winds are his foes,
> And the prushaugh still grows!
> Oh! mee llanuv! mee llanuv!"

And says she, "Mee task will never be ended; for mee tears water the seeds, while I pull up the ould plants that bore them. Oh! Johnny! where are you, my son?—Come to your mother and help he; my darling!"

So then he staggered up to her, but she didn't know him!— the mother didn't know the son she doated on,—but cursed him, and called him "Dick Blaney," and "Hearthmoneyman!"—All this it was that drove Johnny O'Rourke to run home, like one out of his senses, and make his confession.

It's said, that he tried, at the bar, with tears and lamentation, which wasn't expected of him, to save his life; or, at any rate, to get a long day given him:—promising how good he'd be, if he was let live, and pleading the years he'd passed in repentance. But you'd guess, if I did'nt tell you, that such blarney, from one who'd done as he had, would have no weight. So he suffered; and that, too, penitently, as I'm tould by them that saw him at the last. His wife spent all she could scrape together,—as he bid her with his last words a'most,—in search of his mother; but the ould woman never was found, as far as I know, from that day to this; and, may be, the poor soul is still wandering about, tearing up the prushaugh vooe, and singing her melancholy song.

ME AND MY GHOST-SHIP

ABOUT a month after the *cant* at The Beg of all the goods that was in it,—the particulars of which Father Killala was telling me, as you heard while ago, when he was sent for by Johnny O'Rourke,—the large creditors that had claims on the land, and the house itself, made up their minds to follow the examples them by the small fry, who had paid themselves out o' the sale o' the furniture, and things o' that kind,—the goods and chattels I mane;—and news came that the whole domain would soon be publicly put up, and sould to the best bidder. Such tidings as this couldn't but grieve me,—I'll say that much for myself; for I didn't know into what hands the fine ould place might fall. And what would it matter to me, a poor ould cripple as I am, living here in a cabin,—you'll ask,—who had it, since I'd no call to it? —Why, then, I'll tell you; and if you laugh at me for loving The Beg, so be it, and you're welcome. It's in the small room, to the left, as you go up the back staircase, just above what's called the Oratory, and over-right the chamber where there's a portrait of William the Third, the long Orangeman, one side o' the chimney, and a picture of poor Jimmy Stuart, the king, on the other—it's there where I drew my first breath; and it's there, too, on the same day and hour, my mother drew her last. My father lived with the Veoghs, and so did his father before him; and, it's said, we once was owners of The Beg ourselves, and should be so still, if right ruled the roast. There's a pedigree of our forefathers drawn out upon parchment, in the form of a tree, stuck up against one o' the walls, by which it seems we were fine fellows long ago:—but that doesn't matter a ha'p'orth to me now; for I'd rather find a guinea without an owner, than have it proved that my grandfather was king of ten countries, and I could lay claim to the title as his heir, if it was nothing but the bare name I got by it. Not but what if I was a fine fellow myself I must own, I'd rather have fine fellows than vagabonds for my forefathers; but as I'm but a fisherman, or next kin to it, I'd as soon have fishermen as King Ferguses for my ancestors;—and rather, too, may be: for while, in the one case, the honour of those I sprung from might make me strive to be great and honourable myself; that same honour, in the other, might make me draw comparisons, and be discontented with my own lot, and so neglect doing what I might, and go to the dogs, —don't you see?

The night I heard of The Beg's being sould, I was sitting alone here in my cabin, brooding over the bad news, when whose voice should I hear, outside my door, but that of Corney Carolan, the wooden–legged piper and rhymester of Drogheda?—You'll know more of Corney, if you'll just listen to the story I'll tell you, by–and–by, about Luke Sweeney; that is—Fogarty, I should say; for the piper's cousin—that's Luke himself—don't like to be called by his own name, which, to spake the truth, is Sweeney, and nothing else: however, I'll tell you a trifle about the piper now, and especially what happened him the night I sat mum–chance here, making myself sick, at what, if I was wiser, may be; I'd know shouldn't concern me. Corney was bound 'prentice to a brogue–maker, in his native place—which is Drogheda; but, as he tells us, he was too much the lad o' wax to stick to his last, and left a good home, to seek his fortune on the wide ocean. But there's many of us have done as bad: so we shouldn't cry out upon Corney, you know;—should we, now?—The sea is the sole and only thing in the world that an English, Irish, Scotch, or Welch boy, ever feels truly and deeply in love with. The lad that's one day or other to have his name mentioned with Nelson and Collingwood,—or to be the hero of the forecastle, if he comes of poor parents,—may be fond of a toy, or a sugar–plum, or his little cousin Kitty, or thousands of things besides, before he tumbles into his teens; but—mark what I say, if you plaze—the sea alone is the darling he doats on; and no man alive ever fell into a more consuming passion for a beautiful young woman, than many a boy has for the fine ould ocean. It's the hereditary love such numbers of us have, when young, for the beautiful billows, that makes us masters of the main. In other countries, as I've heard, neither whips nor words will persuade lads to take to the sea; in these, stone walls themselves will but barely keep them from it: and bad luck to him, I say, that ever, by word or deed, does a ha'p'orth to blight our national fondness for the waters, which keeps our country afloat.—Hurrah!

The rhymester of Drogheda has made a song of what happened him at sea; — and a mighty queer song it is, as you'll hear, for I think I can give you a sample. After Corney has noticed all he saw and suffered, for four or five years, aboard a man–o'–war, he says,—or rather sings,—

"We met the French one day,
Near what the Nile they call,
And axed them would they play
A friendly game of ball?—

> Isn't it grape they shoot?
> Away my leg they blew;
> And the two—pound note to boot,
> I'd hid inside my shoe."

After that, Corney retired upon a wooden leg and a pension; and, turning his sword into an awl, he transmogrified the corner of an ould stable into a new cobbler's stall. "And you'd think I'd do well," says he, in his song; "for," he continues,

> "Of customers soon I got—
> Ould friends they were—a score;
> But wouldn't I go to pot
> Without as many more?
> Musha! bad luck for me!—
> Attend to this, I beg,—
> They all had been to sea,
> And each o' them lost a leg!"

Going on at that rate wouldn't suit Corney at all: he found the wolf was getting everyday nearer his door; so, at last, I thought he'd try what sort of a trade begging was. It wasn't long before he'd the model of a ship, built and rigged by himself, fastened to his skull—cap; and for many's the year he carried it about to and fro; here and there and everywhere, until he and his pipes—and, by all accounts, he's one o' the finest hands at them you ever heard—were as well known as the bridge of Waterford. For the first time in my life,—the night he looked in upon me, when I was bothering myself about The Beg's being sould,—I saw Corney without his ship.

"Arrah! Corney," says I, "who've you struck your flag to?"

"To the captain of the Dutch merchantman," says he.

"Well, but how happened it, Corney?" says I.

"Why, then," says he, "I tell you:—About an hour ago, upon my arrival at my cousin Fogarty's, after being away since Sunday se'nnight, I heard the whole story about the Dutch vessel being blown ashore, and took a half—a—pint, or so, of the fine hollands my cousin had got from her captain. After that, I was tould how he'd given every soul in the place from one to three quarts of it, for the kindness that had been shewn him, in getting his ship off without damage. And, says Luke Fogarty, —roaring like a bull in my ear,— 'He's just bid us good b'ye; for his vessel's under weigh again, and himself going on board as soon as he gets to the beach.' Very well, thinks I; wooden–legged as I am, I'll see if I can't overtake the Dutchman, and coax him out of a keg, or a bottle at least: for, to tell the truth, hollands is delicious; and I never tasted a sup of any thing drinkable so fine as the hollands the Dutch captain left at Luke Fogarty's. Away I wint; and, in less time than you'd dance down a lame woman at a jig–house, as the night was bright as day itself, I hove up within sight of the Dutchman.

"Making all the sail I could, I soon ran down his hull; but the moment I hailed him, and he took a view of me, he walked away like a race–horse. I followed, as fast as I well could, and a jolly chace we had of it. I'll tell you beforehand that I came up with him at last: and, from one of his boat's crew, who spoke English, I found out what he thought of me, while I was crowding all I could upon his track. He'd often laughed at the stories that was told him of the phantom ship off the Cape; but no sooner had he set eyes on the little model I wore on my head, than he thought he saw the thing itself: and he looked upon it as a special punishment upon him for being an unbeliever, to have the ship not only sent after him there from her own seas, but for her to follow him ashore, and make the air her ocean! The slender cordage rattled with the sea–breeze,—blowing as it was, and the little sails flapped about the spars, as he tacked to get away from me, and I tacked to overtake him; and, no doubt he thought they made more noise than a seventy–four in a gale o' wind. And the fears that were upon him, likely enough, magnified my little boat into a large craft. But what do you think he thought, when I struck up a tune upon my pipes?— music to which he,—poor ignorant soul! until then was a stranger! He cast a hasty glance over his left shoulder at the sound; and, the moon then gleaming full upon me, he caught a glimpse of my face; which, as he said, he took at once to be that of the big ugly fiend o' the storm. I hailed him, but he wouldn't answer me; I swore in Irish, and he began to pray in Dutch: and, at last, when he found he couldn't get away from me, he fell down upon his knees, and began to attack a bottle he had in his pocket, as though no one loved hollands but himself. In a few seconds he was under my fore–foot; and, of course, I clutched the bottle out of his hand: but if you'd seen the look he gave at me and my ghost–ship, while I was drinking, you'd never forget it while you lived. I've no call to find fault with him, though;

for, as soon as he found out I was flesh and blood, he used me well, and gave me the two trifles of hollands I have, slung at each side of me here, and more than, a trifle of money, to boot, for my ship which, to tell no lies, I was going to hang up for ever tomorrow; for she was getting too much for me, or I was getting too ould for her, I don't know which. Besides, I'm now able to do well enough without her,—thanks to my pipes,——and the trifles of songs I've made myself and stole from better men. It wasn't without a groan or two though, that I saw the Dutchman, when he'd bought her, tie a stone to my poor ship's waist, and drown her as spitefully as though she'd been a cur that had bit him."

THE NEST EGG

WELL, who should buy The Beg, do you think, but a fine lady from Dublin, who had never seen it, and, it's said, sould off all she had, to make up the money for it?—And who should the lady be, but that same young Pierce Veogh was once in love with, but who wouldn't have him, because of his wild doings, and wint and married another?—And this other was dead, and the lady was a widow, and bought The Beg, as we thought when we knew the story, because of Pierce; who was then, nobody knew where.

Down she came, in a few weeks, to take possession; and it's soon she was loved by every soul within three miles of the place. Them that was Pierce Veogh's favourites, she did good to for his sake; and them that he never noticed, she helped for her own: so that there was few but blessed her. She gave Mick Maguire a new gun, when he'd burst the one he had from Pierce, by over loading it, and broke his own arm to boot; and she did something for me, too, as you'll hear, by–and–by, though Pierce and myself never was over and above friendly, because I didn't like his goings–on; and what's more,—for I'll confess my frailty,—in all his spending he never spent a penny upon me.

If I was one of a nation that had to choose a queen by her looks, I'd just pick out the lady who bought The Beg; for I never saw any thing in the wide world so fine and so gracious, and so every thing that's good, and above the general run of women,— and I never saw one in the world that I couldn't kiss,—as herself. She hadn't been at The Beg much more than a week, when one morning she sailed into my place here; her movements was more like those of a fine vessel on a smooth tide, than those of one like us that treads upon the earth; and her eyes was of the colour of the sky on a clear night, and a fine star seemed to be twinkling in the middle of each of them; and, says she,— "God bless all here!"—just as a dillosk–girl might, in going into the cabin of a neighbour. I'll never forget her, or the sight of her beautiful small fingers, when she pulled off her glove,—set off, as they were, by a black ring about one of them; and though I'm a poor man, and an ould man, I was in love with her, and she knew it:—*that* I'd uphould against the finest man that ever stood upon two legs, if I could even stand upon one myself,—but I can't.

She came to do good; and after much talking, says she to Aggie, my niece,—"You're a widow, I hear: is it long you've been so?"

"Three years and a half, my lady," says Aggie, who's well spoken enough to hould a confab with any one; though you wouldn't think it, if you heard her aboard the boat.

"And have you any children?" says the lady, in a tone o' kindness, that would make the most bashful as bould as could well be becoming.

"I've two, my lady, as fine boys as ever the sun shone upon; though I say it, you wouldn't match them in a day's walk. The marrow isn't well in their bones yet; but there's nothing, at sea or ashore, they're afraid of, barring one thing,—and that's facing so fine a lady as yourself; they couldn't do that, so they slunk out the back way when they caught sight o' your ladyship coming: I hope that won't be an offence, though."

"By no means," said the lady; "and how was it you lost your husband?— But I ought not to remind you of your misfortune."

"Blessings on your sweet face, my lady," says Aggie; "it does me good to hear poor Larry spoken of, or asked kindly about: it's few that does it."

"Ah!" says I; "the thoughts o' the living drives away that is, partly drives away—the memory o' the dead. Poor Larry ran into the sea, and drowned himself one night, in a fit o' madness brought on by a wound in his head long before, and more whiskey than usual, which he'd been drinking that day. He was the finest swimmer on this coast, and nearly took two or three to the bottom that wasn't bad ones, who wint in to save him. He sunk himself by main force."

And after that, when the lady asked which way it was he got wounded, I tould her how he'd been a sailor in his young days; "And when he was a boy," says I, "there never, by all accounts, was one better loved, by little or big, than himself. He sailed many's the voyage with one Oriel, who was captain and half owner of the brig Betsy,—one of the best sea–boats ever was seen: she'd make two voyages and back, while them that waited for convoy couldn't fetch one. And it's many's the times not be bothering you with sea terms, which your ladyship won't comprehend.—it's often then she bate off such enemies as she was able for, and left those in the lurch she couldn't expect to drub. But, at last and in long run, she met with her match, and more than it every way, in a pirate, manned with a crew of all nations, but sailing under Algerine colours, if I don't mistake. they'd as pretty a little battle for, may be, half a glass or more, yard arm and yard–arm,—that's cheek–by–jowl, you know, my lady, as one could wish to behould: but, by–and–by, Oriel found he was getting the worst of it;

and says he to Larry,—that's my niece's husband that was,—'Larry,' says he, 'you've always obeyed my orders like a good boy.' 'I'll do so still, sir,' says Larry, 'while there's life left in me.' 'Well, then, Larry,' says Oriel, 'they're making ready for boarding us, I think; and as we can't get away, I'll tell you what you'll do:—go down to the powder-room, and when we've fought as long as we're able, and killed what we can above here on deck,—that is, when you think they're all aboard of us a'most, and we can't do much more harm to them,—do you just blow up the brig, like a good boy, and I'll be obliged to you.' 'I will, sir,' says Larry; 'but my mistress—' 'Oh! you blockhead!' cried Oriel; 'don't you see, it's for her sake entirely, that I'm making this sacrifice? Do you think I could die happy with the thought of her falling, in the pride of her youth and beauty, into the hands of these villains?' 'Oh! master!' says poor Larry, poking a tear out of his eye with the top of his clumsy finger, 'why did you bring her with you?' 'Hould your tongue,' says Oriel, 'and don't mind what don't concern you: I took her twice before, and less harm happened me than ever; for she seemed to be like a charm against peril to my poor brig. Now go away down, Larry, and don't blubber that way, or, may be, you'll wet the priming in your pistol; and should you miss fire, and not blow us up as I bid you, if the enemy don't throw you overboard, my ghost shall haunt you all the days of your life: but be a good boy, and do your duty like a man, and we'll all go to heaven, I hope, in company.' Well, down wint Larry, after giving one last pelt with his pistol at the pirates, and loading it again for the confidential service he was trusted with; and away strode big Oriel, determined to kill as many as he could, before dying him self. Soon after, the deck of the Betsy was trod on by the best part of the enemy's crew, and Oriel's people was obliged to retreat, before the superior force that was opposed to them, bit by bit, until they got huddled together about the forecastle; and from that they clambered, and jumped, and tumbled higgledy-piggledy, they hardly knew how,—and Oriel, almost in spite of himself, with them,— over the lee-bow, clane into the enemy's ship that lay close alongside. Before above two or three could follow them, the Betsy gave a lurch, and the vessels parted. Them that was left aboard the pirate couldn't make much head against Oriel's men; but he didn't help them a ha'p'orth;—and when somebody came up to him, where he stood thumping his head with the handle of his cutlass, and congratulated him upon the good turn things were taking, and said they might now use the pirates' own heavy metal against its owners,—he cried out with an oath, that his wife was still aboard the Betsy, and he'd bid Larry to fire into the powder room! At that moment, he caught a glimpse of Larry's carrotty head, poking out of a port–hole, or somewhere, and looking like one amazed, at seeing his shipmates seemingly making them selves masters of the pirate, while he knew, from what he heard going on above, that the enemy was masters of the Betsy. What to do, he didn't know; and felt woful and confounded as ever boy did in the world before. At last, he saw Oriel, who shouted to him as loud as he could; but the noise was too great for Larry to hear a syllable of what he said; and then, Oriel, half frantic, made such violent motions with the pistol he'd snatched out of the man's hand who'd spoken to him, pointing it at Larry, and threatening to shoot him, and I can't tell what, that the poor boy, knowing his mistress was still aboard, thought the captain was in a rage with him for not blowing up the brig before, and made signs, which couldn't well be misunderstood, that he'd go do it directly. At this, Oriel shrieked with passion; and, before Larry could get away, fired the pistol he had at the boy's head;—there being no other way to prevent him from doing what Oriel then thought wouldn't be wise. The ball only grazed Larry's skull, but it took the senses out of him; and there he lay like one dead. It was the wound he got that way which made him lose his right wits, when he drank much, as he did the day he drowned himself, much to my grief! For, oh! Larry, my boy, it's well I loved you! —and so did your wife, and all that knew you!—Your ladyship looks as if you'd like to be tould what happened the captain's wife, and how it ended.—Why, then, the pirates, though in the worst ship, got the better of Larry's shipmates: Oriel was mortally wounded, in a desperate attempt to retake the Betsy; but he had the satisfaction of falling on his own deck, and knowing that his wife had died from a chance shot, a few moments before. The pirates themselves were attacked by a frigate, before they could repair the damage done to their vessel, and Larry was found in the prize, at death's door: but I needn't tell you be got over it, or how would he marry Aggie, and be the father of Paudrigg and Jimmy?—Fine fellows they'll make one day or other, I'll engage for them! Though they're but boys even now, they lent Aggie a good hand at working the boat, from the time poor Larry, their father, was lost to us."

"And do *you* go fishing?—*you* only and your young sons?" said the lady, with tears in her eyes, to my niece.

"I do, my lady," says Aggie; "sign's on me!—what would become of us all else?"

"Faith! then, my lady," says I, "she buckled on Larry's bradien the week after he died, and has missed as few tides as any one, from that day to this,—she and the boys, that is."

"Poor woman!" says my lady, putting something that was right welcome into Aggie's hand; "this trifle may assist you, if you'll accept of it."

"Long life to ye, my lady!" says Aggie, making the best curtsy she could; "I was thinking to ask your ladyship's favour in the way of taking a fish at a fair price from us, time about with Rob Racket; but, upon second thought, Rob has a fry of gorlochs by his new wife, and he's getting weakly, and past going out in a tough rise; while I'm strong and able; Paudrigg and Jimmy are both growing lusty too,—grace and good luck be with 'em!—so, my lady, I'll say nothing about the fish, but make bould to take the money, and lay it by for a rainy day."

"I fear you think of but little more than the present," says my lady; "you should be provident, and save a little in the good season; then you'd be able to look forward to the time of sickness with more comfort."

"Ah! my lady, we have no time to be sick," says Aggie; "ailing or hearty the net must be spread, and nine out of ten of the fishermen die the night after weathering a stiff breeze:—it's rare for any of us to lose above one tide between life and death! —And as to being provident, my lady, half the year we have enough to do, with all our tugging and striving, to make both ends meet;—it's hand–to–mouth work with us."

"But then, at other times, Agnes,—in your harvest, as I may say,—you might save something."

"It's aisy talking, my lady," says Aggie; "and many's the vow we make in the hard season, to scrape a penny or so together the next good time: but when it comes,—my grief!—doesn't half of it slip away before one can look about?—And then it's too late to begin: so it's put off—the hoarding and squeezing time is—till another year. Besides, when it's all plenty galore with us, who thinks of starvation?—It's hard, too,—so it is,—to brake up the day's joy by robbing it of a few keenogues for the morrow. We'd rather be merry—many of us would—one while, and sad another, than divide equally, and so go on, in the same dull way, from year's end to year's end, neither hungry nor full, joyful nor sad, —but just dacent, and half one thing half another. Moreover, when we have the money, away it goes at once;—we make merry, and put to sea again. The citizen may well think of to–morrow, and save,—for he goes to his bed, and, without a chance, tomorrow will be to him another to–day: but the fisherman goes into the waves, and God knows, when his kin wish him 'Good–night!' whether he'll ever hear their 'Good–morrow!' It's so trying to begin, too:—the hen won't lay in an empty nest, nor is it aisy to put a penny by where there was no penny before. And if we do, where's the good of our throwing aside a groat to–day, a mag to–morrow, and a shilling the next?—At the week's end it's just so little, we despise it; and just so much, that it tempts us to have a spree:—drunkenness follows; and so, after pinching from Monday to Friday, we spind the money, and lose the Saturday's trip into the bargain—so we do. One piece o' good gould in our by–corner would make us add more to it: one shilling to forty, makes forty–one,—a great sum;—but one shilling to forty–pence, makes four–and–four–pence;— just enough for doing harm. 'Tis but a shilling either way, you may say; but there's a difference in the two that one feels and knows, but can't spake about or explain.—I wouldn't wonder but myself saves upon your ladyship's gracious gift: any how, we'll never have to put the platter outside the door at a death, nor want a dacent wedding when the boys marry, while we keep it whole itself."

And it's whole we've kept it then, and added more to it, and bought many's the thing to comfort us, which we never should have had, may be, if it wasn't for the nest–egg we got that way from my lady—blessings be on her!—So here's a fine proof, that proverbs ar'n't always to be depended upon. They say three things, which may be true sometimes, but not always:—the first is, that "Fortune is blind:"—now we'd good luck come to us; and it's true we deserved it,—that is, Aggie did, if I didn't;—and what's more, we wanted it. "Aisy got, aisy gone;"—that's another proverb we've given the he to; for what we've laid out we spent discreetly, and on no occasion without many's the pro and con whether we'd do so or no.—Lastly it's said, "An eel won't slip through our fingers faster than the guinea that's given us;"— but I'd knock that on the head any day, by shewing what we got from my lady the first day she set foot in my cabin,—and that's long ago. So that I, and, may be, a good many more, can say, "Fortune isn't always blind;—aisy got, may be held fast;—and all eels are not slippery."

All eels are not slain.

UNDER THE THUMB

DUCK DAVIE'S wife's brother, Paddy Doolan, lives among his pigs, poultry, and potatos, over–right Mick's place,—the man that saw the little Fairy in the oyster–shells. Paddy gets his bread by rearing turkies and geese, and similar commodities, and buying bits o' pigs about here and there, where he can, and selling them at the market in the next town,— may be, once a month or so;—and many's the penny Pat has turned one way or another, any how. Well,—Pat has a wife,—and not a bad one, he ought to think, if he looks about him and sees what other men's are, and draws comparisons. She's not very big; but she has a black eye, and bustles about; and though she wears a whiskey–bottle, she keeps Pat from doing himself harm from much drinking: and if she does have a drop between whiles, more than does her good exactly, why, she keeps up appearances, by always making wry faces whenever she takes a sup of comfort afore her neighbours. She has a limp in her gait, but cooks a cobbler's nob dilicately; and her temper's not bad, though not much better than just middling like the peathees, as we say: still, there's few in the barony with less holes, and holes sooner mended too, in her sherkeen, than Mistress Doolan; and, as wives go, as I said, there's worse than Pat's. She's forty–nine years of age, come Candlemas; but does not keep the house so clane as she might: —but then, to be sure, there's the pigs—

Now for Pat:—he's bow–legged,—which comes, as his wife, who admires him, says, from his riding so much to and fro across the panniers on his garron to market and back: but some think he was so from a boy,—still that doesn't matter;—his legs are quite good enough for every–day work, and nature wouldn't be wise to give holiday limbs to a higgler—would she now? Pat's forefathers must have been from beyond–sea parts, I think; or how would he have such a pale face, and large dull black eyes, without one feature, barring the cocked nose, of us raal ould Irish? If he was a fisherman, may be, he'd get a colour; but, as it is, though he never knows a day's sickness, he's as pale as a white night and his big eye looks like a piece of sea–coal in milk, or a town chimney–sweep in a snow–storm.

Pat seems so innocent, that many suspect him to be a rogue,— a little sly, or that way inclined;—but Pat says no, and so does Mistress Doolan, and that's something. People tell how much some men and their wives are alike,—faith! so much, as often to be taken for brother and sister; and its true of Dick Reardon who buys Pat's poultry wholesale and sells them out retail, that he and his good woman are as like one another, as a couple of ducks. But that's not the case with Pat and his deary, for they don't match, and you'd wonder what made them mate.

Seventeen or eighteen years ago,—I can't say precisely to a year, but I'll swear to the day,—it was a Tuesday; by token, that it happened the day after Luna mon moch,—the good woman's Monday,—Pat's wife was looking out for him coming home from market; and as he rode down the hill, she saw one of the panniers on the poney weighed down as if it had a load, and the other up in the air. Pat, I must tell you, was the first who brought panthers into this part of the country; the likes o' them was never seen here before, and few with any but himself since.

"What ails you, Pat?" said the wife, as soon as Pat came within reach of her voice; it's a little voice when you're near, but it goes a good way for all that:—"what ails you?" says she; "couldn't you sell your turkies?"

"May be, I couldn't; what then?" says he.

"Then why not load the garron partly o' both sides?"

"May be, I couldn't," says Pat again.

"And why couldn't you?"

"Mistress Doolan, would you like to he struck in a heap?"

"Is it by you, Pat?—what news, then?—any how why not spake it out?"

"Don't bother me now; isn't it to The Beg I'm going?"

"Wid a load you picked up on the road, Pat, is it?"

"Aha!" says he, "can't I keep a thing from you?"

"What is it, Pat?" said she; and he'd now just met the wife; for, finding the conversation grow interesting, she had left the door, and walked away up the hill to meet him, quickening her pace at each question. "What is it, Pat?" says she, trying to peep into the pannier; but Pat wouldn't let her.

"Sally," says he,—for that's her name;—"would you think it, that there's mighty bad people about?"

"Why not?" says she; "there's bad people all over the world."

"But not had enough to put their babies on big stones by the road-side, and lave them there by thimselves wid a bit of a switch stuck, up, and a shred of a souldier's red jacket on the top of it, the way people might notice thim;—there's not such people as that all over the world I hope,—is there, Sally?"

"Murther, man! is it a child you've picked up, then?"

"Look at that!" says Pat, taking a baby out of the place, and houlding it up to the full view of his' wife; "look at that, and tell me if it isn't enough like a child for a man to swear by, Mistress Doolan!"

"Won't you let me see it closer, Pat?" said Mistress D. And as she took the child out of Pat's clumsy paw, where he sat on the poney, the little crature smiled up in her face, and half stole the very heart of her, before she had once hugged it to her side. It was the most beautiful baby, they say, that was seen for many's the day; and Paddy Doolan's wife took it into the cabin, sat down by the fire, warmed it on her lap, and fed it with new milk, while Pat remained on his panniers, waiting for her to come out again.

"Is it all day you're going to be staying there, Paddy?" says she at last; "ar'n't you coming in?"

"Ar'n't I waiting for the gorloch, to take up to The Beg? I won't be sint back wid it, I'll engage."

"Ah! Pat, why trouble yourself?—Couldn't we keep it ourselves?— Good luck would follow us,—and we've no child of our own, Pat."

Well, where's the use of making a long story of it?—the wife persuaded Pat with much ado, and a dale of begging and beseeching, to let her keep the little crature herself; but he insisted upon first taking it off to the lady who bought The Beg.

"I'll take the little thing up to her at once," says Pat; "and may be, we'll get something for our charity." And sure enough so they did, for my–lady kissed the little crature betuxt the two eyes, and gave Pat a trifle in hand, and promised to allow him so much a week, for keeping the child, until she grew—did I tell you she was a girl?—until she grew up intirely. And a fine young woman she's grown, and all the boys about are dying for her;— as, to say nothing of her good–looking face, Pat has promised her a fortune of fifteen pounds; and I don't know but it might be a match with her and my niece's son Paudrigg, wasn't it for one thing;—she won't have him.

Now, after this, though Paddy Doolan did well by the little one, and had the allowance, and over and above it often, from my lady, things didn't go right with him. He wint on swimmingly for two or three years or so; but from that time, Pat's appearance grew poorer, and the wife's bit of finery wasn't brought home so often, when Pat wint to market. And where he used to crack a joke with a friend, living by the road–side, as he came along, he'd sigh, and say uncivil things of this world, and make wry faces.

You'll think Pat was right, for a good deed ought not to go unrewarded; and you'll like to know how it was. I'll tell you that in a few words,—more or less;—it's foolish to promise.

At the place where Pat carried his property to market, there was a half–rogue of a fellow, Morris by name,—something in Pat's way of business; but he also bought and sould badgers, and foxes, and poisoned rats for people; and wouldn't mind, may be, tying up a dog that followed him home, and lying by till a reward was given out for the brute. What I mane to say is this,—Larry hadn't the very best of characters. One day, after coming from somewhere, where he'd been, it so fell out, that Larry passed by Pat Doolan's cabin, and who should be playing in front of it, but the child Pat picked up that time two years, or thereabouts.

"Whose child have you there?" says he to Mrs. Doolan, who was plucking a duck or a goose at the door.

"Why do you ask, sir?" says she.

"May be, I know the mother of it," says he.

When they got inside the cabin,—for Mistress Doolan was a woman, and hearing what she did, of course, invited him in, to know the middle and both ends of the matter,—she began questioning him: but he was too deep for her, and got the whole pedigree and history of Pat's finding the baby, and the lady's giving him money to keep it dacent, and what else I don't know. Says Larry, when she'd done, "I know the child as if I'd never lost sight of it. The features are oulder than when I last saw it, but not changed: and here's the four little round spots on its temple, like shot–marks, or the picks of a domino. Her mother lodged in a back room of mine, and ran away one day, no small trifle in arrear with me, and I never set eyes on her or the child since, before to–day. So much for the mother;—and"—continued he, in the same breath, turning to Pat Doolan, who just then walked into the cabin,—"may I be moon–struck," says he, pointing to Pat, "but here comes the father!"

What to do, any way; Pat didn't know. You'll agree with me, perhaps, he'd a right to look astonished. There was Mistress Doolan, who had lifted her eye–brows up under her hair with the surprise, standing as mute and as motionless as Pat himself, whose tongue stuck to the roof of his mouth nearly; while the child was innocently giggling below, and trying to undo Pat's gaiters. After a while, Mistress Doolan found her speech. "Is this you, Pat?" says she, quite quietly, for she was too thunderstruck to be in a passion.

"Faith! and why not, Mistress Doolan?" says he, "worse luck!"—for it was true, and he couldn't deny it. And Larry Morris went on to tell the wife, that the child's mother said she was married, and made an excuse for her husband coming to see her now and then only; and who should the husband be, but Pat? Moreover, since she had walked off, the way I tould you, Larry had never seen Pat; and, sure enough, Mistress Doolan remembered that Pat convinced her, about that time, it would be well for him to carry his poultry to another market; and he did so.

Doolan put as good a face as he could upon all this. Larry said he was sorry to be a maker of mischief; but the rogue took advantage of it, for he drew Pat aside, and, from what passed privately between them, Pat carried his poultry afterwards to the town where Larry lived.

From that day, poor Paddy Doolan pined;—wouldn't any one in such a way?—Larry stood between Pat and the market, making Pat sell all his poultry to him at an under-price, and then going to the great buyers that sould them again to the consumers; so making a profit beyond Christian credence out of Pat. And what would you have I do? Wasn't he afraid of Larry's telling upon him? And if he haggled to get any way near a fair price, didn't Larry tell him—"Paddy, boy, ar'n't you under my thumb?" He did: and Doolan was as much afraid of the disgrace of being exposed, as the loss of my lady's allowance. So he struggled and struggled, and every day got worse in the world; and bitterly did he suffer and repent for what he had done. His wife didn't quarrel with the child this while, but loved and nourished it as if it was her own; so did Pat—and he had a right, you'll say:—but I wouldn't swear to that; for who knows but Pat himself might have been cheated, as well as he cheated Sally his wife?

Now I'm coming near the end of my story—no bad news that, you'll say:—Pat was tortured for a long time by Larry, "like a toad under the harrow," as the story goes, till he could scarcely scrape enough together to get on with from week's end to week's end. At last and in the long run, what does Larry do, — like others like him, who, trying to make the most of their villany, ruin all outright,—what does he do, but insist upon Pat's paying him half the allowance he got from my lady, to hould his peace?— Doolan knocked him down with a goose he had in his hand at the time; jumped on his garron; and if you want to know the rate he came home at, ask the people by the road-side. Grogy, his little garron, wondered whether Ireland was sinking, or what was the matter,—and no blame to him.

When Doolan got home, he tould the wife how he had ruined himself by knocking down Larry. "You've done well," says she, "and it was high time you did."—Didn't you ever remark, that when a man gets at his wits' end, and don't know which way to turn, how well a woman will carry him through? I'm sure you have; and seen the courage of the poor creatures too, when men are cowed, and can't look the danger that threatens them full in the face. "You shall be under the thumb no longer, Pat," says she: —"you've done that by me I don't like, but it's forgiven, if not forgot; and let the worst come to the worst, we'll be as well as we are:—so, come with me at once."

"Where'll I go?" says Doolan, staring at her, and drawing back, for he half suspected what she intinded. But Sally was resolute; she took the child in her hand, and half persuaded, half dragged Pat away, up to my lady at The Beg. Doolan went down on his knees, while his wife tould her ladyship the whole story; and when it was done, Pat got such a lecture as he never had before; no—not even from his wife after Larry's first visit.

"Look at the fruits," said my lady; "look at the consequences, Patrick Doolan, of your misdoings:—didn't you know that sin is always followed by sorrow?—that deceit can never long plaster up iniquity? You have richly merited your sufferings, Pat. I shall, of course, stop the allowance, and take away the child from you. When I find you are so far deserving, you shall have my projection, and the little girl again; till then, I withdraw both."

Terribly downcast was Pat, to be sure, as you may guess;— but he was no longer under the thumb. Besides, he'd a hope left, of getting into grace again by good conduct;—so to work he went like a Trojan. Larry came down as hard as he could after Pat, determined to ruin him or make him knock under again: but when he got to the village, Pat was back from The Beg, and had tould all his neighbours what he'd been doing; so that they hadn't much the laugh of him; and as Pat wasn't disliked, the boys and girls made such a mudlark of Larry, nobody could tell the colour of his coat.

Pat began to prosper, and, by-and-by, got on well enough: in a year or two after, the little girl walked into his cabin one day, with a goulden guinea in her hand, and has lived under Pat's roof ever since. Among us, she is, as I tould you, much admired for her beauty,—to say nothing of her being an heiress.

People generally trate a fable as the boys do a dog sometimes, —tie a moral tay-kittle to its tail; and so would I, if my story was a fable: but it's

neither a story nor a fable, but the downright truth, and if I made a moral
to it, you'd suspect 'twas a fable; as the boys suspect the dog, if they meet
him with a kittle in his train, to be a suspicious and a stray dog,—don't
you see?—and so despise and pelt him. However, for all that, there can't
be much harm in just mentioning that a man will do well to take warning
by Paddy Doolan, and do nothing in the wide world that may bring him
under the thumb.

OUR TOMMY

WE'D often be frightened out of our lives a'most, did we know, while we were about them, what mighty events, to ourselves or somebody else, would spring from some of our every–day doings. But it's right we shouldn't. If it wasn't so, Paddy Doolan might be breaking his heart, for the sow that's going to be choaked next Monday, by a bone he'll throw into her trough to–night. There's none of our actions, big or little, in my mind, goes off, without leaving a family: something I did three days,—or, may be, three years ago, was the grandmother of something I'm doing, or that may befall me, to–day. Peg Dwyer's husband threw his can at the head of a cow, that wouldn't give out her milk as she ought, and one of her horns made a hole in its side. That happened him on a Wednesday;— very well;—he wetted his floor, through carrying water in the can with the hole in it, on Thursday; it froze in the night; and early on Friday he got such a bruise, through slipping up on the floor, which he'd wetted by carrying water in the can that he'd thrown on the horn of the cow, because she wouldn't give milk, that it laid him up for a month, and killed him outright in the long run. A boy quarrels with his home and quits it, because he fancies he don't get as much buttermilk to his peeathees, or peeathees to his buttermilk, as some of his brothers; he walks off with himself to the next town; and, a year after, to the next to that, may be: by– and–by he gets taken by the tar, as birds are by birdlime; and, after being aboard ship awhile, casts anchor in foreign parts. Before he can whistle, he's pushed another move further: and something or other continues to poke him from place to place, and from post to pillar, till he reaches the wild Indians at last, and marries Hullamullaloo, the king's youngest daughter, or gets roasted and devoured— just as it may happen—by that lady and her iligant maids of honour. And, supposing he'd a good memory, and could look back, while he stood tied to the stake, or about to be tied to Hullamullaloo at the altar; as the case might be, he'd find each of the moves he made through life was owing, one way or another, to something as simple as his quarrelling, when a boy with his peeathees and butermilk, at his mother's mud cabin here at home in ould Ireland.

Poor Tommy Maloe got his liking for martial music, through thumping a drum, which he'd stolen from young Veogh, when they were both little boys, and didn't know right from wrong; or if they did, wouldn't make a shew of what they knew, by doing as they ought. Though Pierce's parents were rich, and Tommy's were poor, Tommy was Pierce's playmate: they spent most of their time together, and were always at war, and frequently fighting. Tommy was the sole and only boy far or near, that would dare stand up before Master Pierce, when he clenched his little fist; and there was few that Tommy would demean himself to thump or play tricks with but Pierce.

Tommy, as I said, stole a drum from little Pierce, or may be carried it off as booty after a fray; and it was from the delight he got by bating it with the drumstick of an ould goose, that years after, he bartered a new hat for a bad fife;—from which time, for six months and more, morning, noon, and night, the fife was at Tommy's lips, and he trying to coax marches out of it, but couldn't. At last he threw it away in a pet; and took to trapesing after Mick Maguire when he'd be going out to fire at, and sometimes shoot, the water–birds. Tommy, who was now grown a man a'most, never felt happier than when Mick would allow him to carry the gun; and one day, while Mick's back was turned, something or other tempted him to fire it off. By chance, I suppose, he shot a little bird—a tern, or a petrel it was—and from that time, Tommy talked of nothing but shouldering a musket, and getting a pelt at a Frenchman. He walked thirty miles over mountains and bogs, without' a shoe to his foot, (for his father had hid them that he mightn't go,) to see a review of two companies of the North Cork, and three dozen of beggarly volunteers.

Our Tommy—for that's the name he is best known by—from his father's always calling him so—though it was only to himself, a poor doating ould widower, he belonged;—our Tommy, I say, at last determined to enlist. He wouldn't be satisfied, he said, until, as every one ought, he'd killed at least two or three of the enemies of his king and country. His father begged of him not to go for a souldier and leave him alone, when he could get good bread at home: but, though Tommy in other things was as dutiful as most sons, he wouldn't mind his father in this. At one time, however, it was thought he would forget the Frenchmen, and behave himself; for he fell in love with one of the prettiest little girls in these parts, and offered to give up all thoughts of campaigning, and killing his share of the foreigners, if she'd have him. But the little girl gave him a downright denial; and a week after that he got picked up by a recruiting–party at a fair.

Tommy was all on fire to go abroad; and it wasn't long before he got his wish granted of being sent on foreign service. You'll think of the little drum, and the goose's leg, and the bad fife, and Mick Maguire's gun, and the review of the North Cork with the volunteers, and feel sad, for a moment, may be, when I tell you, that the very first Frenchman he saw, run his baggonet right through poor Tommy, in a skirmish, before he could even pull his trigger, and killed him on the spot.

When I say that Tommy was killed on the spot, I mane that he never stirred from the place where he fell; though he lived long enough to see the enemy driven back; and then,—as we heard from a disabled dragoon, who passed through this place on his way home a year after,—poor Tommy Maloe, though he'd been disappointed so sorely,—like a good boy as he was in the main,—departed this life with a smiling eye and a prayer on his lips. And I trust I may do no worse;— I must confess, I'd rather die on a bad bed, than on the finest field of battle,—for I'm not heroic; and in my own mud cabin, than a grand hospital, for I'm not ambitious. And yet I don't know, upon giving the thing a thought;—dying is dying all the world over, and it don't matter much where we do it. I was going to say too, that I'd prefer a natural death in ould age, to the honour of being cut off by a dragoon's sabre in my prime: but there's a riddle about death no one can solve; and it isn't often we see even the ould people go off and melt away like a mist. We may prate and preach as much as we plaze about hard deaths and aisy deaths;—the horror and agony of going off one way, compared with another:—but there isn't a living soul on the face of the earth knows any thing about dying at last. Drowning is spoken of as being the least disagreeable by some; others prefer a bullet; one says one thing, and another says another; even hanging isn't without advocates:—but *I* say, there's no knowing which is best, and which is worst; and we never *shall* know, that's certain, until some of us is dead, and gets brought to life again;—and that you know never can be: for it's nothing but blarney an honest man tells you about the feelings of death, who has been relieved from suffocation by a lancet; or, to go further, it's foolish to listen to what one that has been some time under water, and gets picked up, and restored, as they call it,—to hear such a one tell what little or what much he suffered, with an idea of your gathering enough from his story to know what death by drowning is. If you do that, it's mighty mistaken you are; and I'll tell you why:—them people that gets restored that way or any other, no matter how, know but little about the thing, not much more than myself or you:—and why don't they?—*because they never have died.* You never met with a man in your life, that had died, out and out. You couldn't; for them that dies completely never breathes mortal breath again. My father— rest his soul!—thought as I do; and he'd say, when the fire of existence is once extinguished, it's gone for ever and ever. When death has entirely done his work, the body is clay; then the spirit departs, and nothing human can ever bring it back. A man may lie motionless, breathless, and, what's more, senseless, at the bottom of a well, for an hour, or, may be more,—who can tell?—and yet not die. In that case, by clever means and much work, the dying embers of life may be brought to a flame again; but once fairly dead, we're dead for ever. And so, I say, that the man who gets taken out of the water and recovers, can't say that he was dead. It's true, he has gone to the door; but has he passed over the threshold?—answer me that! If he had, he wouldn't have come back to us again, I'll engage! Don't you see, that we can't take a pair of compasses or a piece of tape, and measure exactly where life ends and death begins? And how do we know, when we take leave of a friend, because he don't move and there's none o' the dew of life on the glass we put to his lips, —that he's dead? — Tossing the arms, or gnashing the teeth, shews pain, hut there may be greater agony without it; for if we're violent, it shews we're strong; and it's suffer we may, much worse perhaps, when we're so weak that we can't wag a finger. Well, then,—and this is what I've been coming to all through my rigmarole, but I couldn't before,—how do we know that,—after the breath goes, and the limbs lose their power, and all is still,—the dying man, without breathing or moving, or his heart beating, don't feel the true grapple of death—the parting of soul and body? — Therefore, I say, as nobody ever came back, as I think, in body,—I don't spake of ghosts,—from the clutch of our enemy, we don't know anything much about him; and it's well we don't:—God be praised! all things in this world is ordered for the best!

It's little or nothing that's left me to add to my story:—poor Tommy Maloe's father, when he heard of the death of his son, got quite childish at once, and unable to help himself any way: so that he'd have had little to look to, but his poor neighbours, if my lady hadn't put him down on her little list of pensioners, and paid Peg Dwyer to mind the poor soul, and make him as comfortable, considering all things, as he well could be. You may still see ould Darby—that's his name—strolling about, from house to house, as he did on the morning after the disabled dragoon brought us news of his son's death, and telling every one who'll listen to him, how his beautiful boy was struck through and through by a baggonet, like a souldier's loaf,—or a tommy, as it's called in the army,—when he wint to fight the French, in foreign parts.

THE DENTIST

MALACHI ROE is known, for twenty miles round his house, as a cow–doctor, and a rat–catcher, and a man of tip–top talent in two or three dozen useful arts and sciences,—as he himself calls tooth–drawing, and dog–cropping, and all the things he's famous for. He has the finest terriers and traps in the whole country; and if there isn't a fox to be found by the subscription pack, that Squire Lawless, and the rest of them has, nine miles off, at the brook of Ballyfaddin, they've only to send a dog–boy to Malachi, before sun–set, and he'll have one in a bag, ready to turn out before them, by the morning. He's very sparing of talk, and when he spakes, it's in short bits; and–he'll look all the while as if he'd a right to be paid for his words: and it's well paid he is for them too, sure enough, by them that can do it. There isn't a hair's–breadth of a horse, from the crown down to the coronet, or below that again, to the head of the nail in his shoe, but Malachi knows: he's as much at home in the inside of a cow as that of his own cabin, and can tell where any thing is, as well in one as the other,—just as if he'd put it there himself. But Malachi prides himself most on his skill in tooth–drawing; and if you ask him what he is, he'll tell you—a dentist.

It's full, thirty years ago, since Malachi came to settle among us. You hadn't then to send for him if he was wanted, for he seemed to scent sickness like a raven; and if your cow was taken ill, the next news you heard was, that Malachi's horn was blowing on the hill; and, in ten minutes more, he stood at your door, with a drench if you wished it.

Malachi now keeps closer to his nest: still he's to be had, if you'll pay him his bill. He's looked upon as an oracle in most things, by every body except Ileen, his wife, who thinks one of her opinions worth two of his, any day; and though Malachi Roe is a wise man, I won't say but Ileen is right. If you knew him, you'd as soon think of saying black was white, as contradicting the dentist: but Ileen don't care a bawbee for him, and often tells him right up to his face that he's wrong. Malachi wishes she'd bide at home; but she'd rather be busy on the beach, having an eye to the girls and women she employs to gather the dillosk: and, though feared, her goodness of heart secures her the love of every one of her neighbours—high and low. By all accounts, she must be the exact temper of her grandmother and namesake Ileen, the Meal–woman; who, though left a widow, at eighteen, with a child looking up to her for support, never got married again; but kept herself dacent, and brought up her little one, without a ha'p'orth of help from man, woman, or child. She put on the manners and resolution of a man, with her weeds;— the mills which her husband had occupied she kept going; and managed so well, that she got more and more grist by degrees, till at last, the name of Ileen the Meal–woman, was known all over the country.

Her child—it was a boy—grew up, got married, and did well, until about the time of his turning the awkward corner of fifty; then it was that his wife, who was three or four years younger than himself,—as wives should be, you know,—fell sick, and died away suddenly. No man could well grieve much more for the loss of his wife, than ould Ileen the Meal–woman's son did for his: he wouldn't allow her to be carried away up the country, and buried among her own kin, but insisted that she should be laid in his father's grave; so that, one day or other, his own remains might be placed by her side.

If you reckon the age of his son, and remember how soon after his marriage he died, you'll find that Ileen the Meal–woman's husband, at the time his daughter–in–law departed this life, must have been buried hard upon half a century. When the grave was opened, his coffin crumbled beneath the pickaxe;—some of his dry bones were carelessly shovelled up by the digger, and there they lay among the earth, which so long had covered him. Ileen knew nothing of this: she had heard of the death of her son's wife, and made all the haste she could away from a distant part, where she was buying wheat, or selling meal, I don't know which, so as to be at the funeral. When she got near home, two or three people tould her that her husband's grave had been opened, to receive the body of her daughter–in–law; but she wouldn't believe them: for all that though, she quickened her horse's pace, and made direct for the spot. The memory of her husband was still fresh within her, long as she'd lost him,—for her heart had never known a second affection. She didn't remember and so see him, in her waking dreams, a poor, broken–down, grey–headed ould man, tottering gradually under a load of infirmities, to death's door, with his tamper soured by time and pain, and his affections froze up by age: but whenever his form came across her mind,—and it's often she looked back to the two short years of happiness, she'd passed with him,—he started up to her thoughts in all the pride of his manhood,—handsome, high–spirited, and affectionate, as he was a week before she parted from him for ever.

The people were just going to lower the coffin of the Meal–woman's daughter–in–law into the earth, when Ileen reached the outer circle of them that came to the funeral. Without spaking a word, she made a lane for herself through the crowd, and at that awful moment, she suddenly appeared, speechless with fury, at the head of the grave. Her son shrunk from her terrible glance; and every one within view of her, stood without motion, gaping in fear and wonder at the tall, gaunt figure of Ileen, and the features of her, distorted as they were by the grief—the rage—the horror—the agony she felt,—and wondered what was going to be the matter. After some little time, during which not a word was spoke, and nobody scarcely dared breathe, Ileen began to tremble from head to foot; big tears gushed out of her eyes; and says she:—"Is that you I see there, Patrick?—Are you my son?—And is this your father's grave?"

"Mother," says Patrick, "what, in the name of the holy Saints, ails you? Don't you see it's me? And ar'n't you sure it's my poor father's last home?—Where else would I bury my wife?"

"Your wife!—And was it to bury your wife, that you broke open my husband's grave?"

"Of course it is, mother;—what harm?—Go on, friends."

"Stand back!" cried Ileen, in a loud and determined tone, placing herself betuxt the coffin and the brink of the grave;—"I'd like to see the man who dare pollute the dust of my husband, with that of a strange woman! I am the wife of him whose grave is here—of him, and of none but him: I lay in his bosom when he was alive—and do you think, any of you, I'll stand by, while there's a drop of blood left in my veins, to see another be put in my place now that he's dead? Have I lived for fifty long years with the hope of one day being united in death to the joy of my life, to have another laid by his side at last? Who broke this holy earth?—What accursed wretch was it?—Where is he?—Shew him to me—that I may grip him by the throat?"

"Mother, mother!" said Patrick, "for the sake of him you spake of, be not so violent! If I've done wrong—"

"*If* you've done wrong?—Thank God, Patrick, it wasn't your own hand did this!"

"Well! I'm sorry now that any hand did it: but it's too late to waste time in words: and I *must* have the remains of my wife respected."

"Wretched—unnatural child!—what respect have you shown to those of my husband—my husband, and your father, Patrick? —Oh! this earth which covered him," continued Ileen, stooping to pick up a handful of the mould she stood upon,—and at that moment, for the first time, she saw the bones!—She shrieked out at the sight, and no tongue could describe the look of agony which she cast at her son.

Patrick, however, who'd more love for the wife he'd lived thirty years with, than the father he couldn't remember, much as he was grieved at the sorrow and anger of his mother, resolved that the corpse shouldn't be treated with a shew of insult: so says he to those about him, "Come, let us make an end of this; I will set you an example."

The words were scarcely out of his mouth, when Ileen snatched up one of her husband's hones, and gave her son so violent a blow with it on his head, that he staggered and fell nearly senseless into the grave.

His friends got Patrick out again as quick as they could: but before he recovered, Ileen had carefully gathered up the bones, folded them in a kerchief, which she tore off her bosom, dropped them into the grave, and proceeded to throw in the earth again with her hands. No one attempted to hinder her—but it was only when she had made the ground level, and cast herself, moaning, upon it, that the people persuaded her son to let them carry his wife's coffin away, and bury it elsewhere.

Just such a one as Ileen the Meal–woman, in temper and heart, is her grand–daughter Ileen, the second wife of Malachi Roe: he'd a son by his first; but has had no children by Ileen. If Malachi's boy was a fool all his young days,—and he's not so now he's grown up—it wasn't Ileen's fault; for she behaved like a mother to him, and tried all she could to make him know a duck from a drawbridge, but in vain. At last, when he was about eighteen, Malachi got him a place in my lady's stables, under the grooms and coachmen she'd just had down with fine horses and new liveries from Dublin— *why*, nobody could guess, except that she was going to give up being a widow.

The first day Malachi's boy got into the stables, the grooms and postillions persuaded him they were much finer dentists than his father; and, to convince him, they tied a piece of whipcord round one of his teeth, and fastened the other end of it to a stall–post: then one of them came and threatened the end of his nose with the prong of a pitchfork, so that the stripling drew back his head with a jerk, and out came the tooth. This, and two or three other of the usual jokes that boys gets played in a stable, put young Malachi on his mettle; so that, after awhile, his father, and even ould Ileen herself, began to glory in him;—thanks to the dentist whose only instrument was the prong of a pitchfork.

THE MUSHROOM

ABOUT six o'clock, or, may be, a quarter less, on a wet summer's evening, all of a sudden the sun peeped out from behind a cloud,—as Corney Carolan said,—looking half ashamed to shew his face, after his bad behaviour all day,—and just cast a glance across the bog, to see who was that so merry and musical in Luke Fogarty's car, bating the garron that dragged it along, with his wooden leg in lieu of a whip. Who was it, then, but the piper of Drogheda, Corney Carolan himself, coming from a wedding, away somewhere in the hills, where he'd been drinking whiskey galore, and playing his pipes, night and morning, for the biggest half of a week! Luke Fogarty had sent his son Rory with the car that morning, to bring home the piper, dead or alive; for it was whispered by many, that great things would be doing in a day or two at our place here; who by, or why for, nobody well knew; but there was to be drinking and dancing:—and what would drinking or dancing be without himself?—I mane Corney the piper.

The sun drew in his horns again,—if you'd believe Carolan,— as soon as he saw it was his ould friend the piper; but he shone quite long enough for Corney to discover that the big mile–stone, put up at the edge of the bog, by mad Henniker, years ago, to judge by the shadow it cast across the road, wasn't anything like its ordinary shape. Corney couldn't make out at all what it meant, or why it was; but, as the car got nearer the mile–stone, the piper perceived that it carried an umbrella.

"Well, to be sure, it's rainy enough, so it is," says Corney; "but mile–stones, I thought, was made to stand wind and weather. Is that any one's umbrella there on Henniker's mile–stone?—Bekase if it's nobody's, why, then, I'll go get it."

The umbrella began to move, and presently Corney discovered that a gentleman and his dog was beneath it. There they sat, shivering, dirty, and making themselves as little as possible, on the top of the stone; and barely able, the one to keep his tail, and the other the skirts of his coat, and the lower part of his legs, out of the water; which, after it rained unusually hard,—as it did that day,—got together in a pool round the stone, and some times rose over it entirely.

"Come out o' that," said Corney to the gentleman; "come away at once, sir; and don't be sitting that way on Henniker's folly all night! May be you're Henniker himself, though,—and then, no wonder."

The gentleman replied, as well as his shivering would let him, that Corney was mistaken

"Then why stay there, sir?" says Corney, "when we've room on the car for you, and the garron impatient to be going!"

"Look at the water," said the gentleman; "how am I to wade through it?"

"Is it wade?—Faith! then, you'll have to swim soon! But take your choice, sir:—I won't persuade you one way or another."

"Where *am* I?" says the gentleman.

"'Where *are* you!—Why, then, look at the side of the stone, and you'll see, cut in legible letters, 'NINE MILES FROM ANYWHERE:' and no mile–stone in the world ever spoke truer. Was it to gratify impertinent curiosity, do you think, that Henniker put up the stone?—Not himself, then!—Mad as he was, he knew that it would be quite enough to make any man move on to be tould he was nine miles from anywhere!—What more did you want? Would you have him keep a horse ready saddled, waiting 'till you'd come?"

"My mare has thrown me and ran away," said the gentleman; "and I merely got on the stone, so, that I might shelter myself and my dog, from head to foot, until some one came by, or the rain ceased."

"Ceased!" exclaimed Corney, bursting into a laugh; "if you waited for that, sir, you'd stay till the crows removed you as a nuisance to the frogs in the slush there behind. Does it ever cease?—Divil a bit, then, for three miles round, morning, noon, or night,—summer or winter,—but keeps pelting and pattering away, at all times and in all seasons, as it has for hundreds of years, and will for ever and ever;—except once in a twelve–month, sometimes, and that's the fifteenth day of the month of July, when St. Swithin is too busy raining down upon the other parts of the world, to mind this which is his watery worship's home. It's fine weather here, if, with three coats on your back, you don't get wet to the skin in forty minutes. I wouldn't insult the Saint, by carrying an umbrella, for Damer's estate! Bad luck and ill chance is the best I'd expect, and so may you; for it's raining now just worse than ever I knew it but once. Had you no idea, then, where you were, sir?"

"I had," says the gentleman; "but I wasn't sure. I never came by this road to The Beg before; and I asked the boy that's with you where I was, when I met him hereabouts, full two hours ago; but he grinned in my face."

"Is it yourself that bate him, bekase he couldn't understand English?"

"I certainly did lay my whip over his shoulders," says the gentleman; "and the young villain then began to pelt me and my mare with stones, so that the animal feared to approach near enough to permit of my beating him again; and at last she got unmanageable, ran away, and threw me off,— that is, I mean— threw me off, and ran away."

"Rory was right, then, and so I said while ago, when he tould me part of the story; for you'd no business to bate him,— had you, now?—But what makes you wait, sir? If you don't come at once, why, then, good night!—For it's not agreeable to be houlding a conversation such weather as this, with one on a mile–stone under a big umbrella.—Is it coming you are?"

The gentleman talked of borrowing a boat, or backing the car into the pool: but Corney said he couldn't get the one, and wouldn't do the other; and, moreover, that the umbrella must be sacrificed to St. Swithin, for he wasn't reprobate enough to ride in its company. After many more words, the gentleman got down from the mile–stone, with his dog under his arm, and walked through the water like a cat through a puddle. At first he insisted on being allowed his umbrella; but Corney was resolute; and away it wint, at last, scudding over the bog,—frightening up thousands of birds, which flew screaming after it,—until it suddenly sunk in what's called "The Saint's Piggin." The gentleman wasn't well seated on the car, before Corney thrust a bottle of whiskey into his hand, and threatened him with a quantity of discipline from his wooden leg, if he didn't take a good pull at it.

"It's merry we'll be, as whiskey and good stories can make us," said the piper: "I don't care a bawbee for St. Swithin, while I've a cork, or even a thumb left, to keep him out of my bottle. But I'll not be disrespectful to the Saint, though, any way;—why should I?—He does me no more harm than my betters; and if I offended him, mightn't he follow me, far and near, and rain on me wherever I went? May be, you never heard how he served the little nation that lived here long ago:—how should you, that didn't know where you were, and you sitting on Henniker's folly? Why, then, I'll tell you:—Once upon a time—long ago it was, in the days of our forefathers— this place was peopled by Mathawns, and one King Ounshough reigned over them, and he and his subjects were all believers in blarney. Well, who should come to the king one day, but a man that said, if he got the weight of what he could ate during nine days, in gold, and had his own people to wait on him, he'd make all the spiders grow so big, that the ladies might wear their webs by the way of veils; and after that, may be, for more gold, he'd carry his invention to such a pitch, that the insects should weave fishing–nets, strong enough to catch whales themselves,—to say nothing of salmon and smaller fish.—Well, while he was at work, along comes another, who sould them a secret for planting trees in such a way, that they'd grow of themselves into ships: and, says he, 'for a trifle, I'll teach you how to sow hemp and flax, in little pots, on their branches, so that they may shoot up into ready–made sails and rigging; and all by philosophy, without a morsel of magic.'—Wasn't this more than men could wish? The boobies bit at the bait,—high and low; and thinks they to themselves, 'what fine fellows we'll be, to catch whales and conquer the world by philosophy!'—While the trees were growing, and the spiders were spinning, there comes another man, and says he, 'Don't you know me, any of you?'—And some suspected they did; and others was almost sure he was related to them by their mother's side; but nobody owned him. So then, says he, 'I'll tell you who I am: that moon yonder, that lights you, is my property; you've had the use of it for years, but I've been too generous. I'm grown poor, and can't be liberal any longer:—you sha'n't have the light of my moon gratis; so pay five hundred a year, or I'll put it out: and then what'll you do?'—Well, what they'd do, sure enough, they didn't know; but before they'd done debating upon it, up comes a smart little man—a foreigner—who advised them to pay what was asked for the present, and if they'd subscribe for him, he'd get up an opposition moon, that should shine better, and be full all the year round, for half the expense of the ould one. Wasn't that too good an offer to be rejected?—It was; and the Mathawns bit at that too. But this wasn't all:—before the new moon was made, or the trees grown into ships, or spiders' webs big enough for veils, the people was persuaded by a traveller to let him build them an umbrella, that should be large enough to keep the rain off every inch of the country; and it was to be so contrived that they could let it down by machinery, if the land wanted water, and put it up when they'd just as much wet as they liked. Now this was so great an insult to St. Swithin, that he began raining at once, and before they could put up their umbrella, dispersed the whole people;—making the country a bog, as you see it; and never ceasing to pelt away with his little pellets of water, from that day to this. But though they were scattered, the boobies wasn't destroyed. You may find some of their descendants in every corner of the world, who are as staunch believers in blarney, as ever their forefathers were in the days of ould Ounshough the king.—Isn't that a fine story for you, now, such a murdering wet evening as this?''

"Bathershin, man!" says the gentleman, with a sneer of contempt; "call it a lie, and give me the bottle, for I'm cold after it."

"Don't you believe it, then?"

"How could I," says the gentleman, "when it's lies, and you know it?"

"Then sorrow the sup out of my bottle you get, sir, and sorrow the step goes the garron, until you believe it. Arrah! Rory,—pturr–r!"

"Pturr–r!" roared Rory, at the top of his voice, and stock–still stood the horse, as in duty bound.

"Is it quite mad you are, you dirty blackguard?" says the gentleman.

"Blackguard your betters!" says Corney: "Musha! then, if the likes o' you was rolled in the bog, what harm?—You couldn't be worse than you were; for it's dirt itself you are!—I'll say that for you, since you put me up."

"Ar'n't you an impertinent ould scoundrel?"

"No doubt I am; but the garron don't stir one of his four pegs till you believe what I tould you, while ago, for all that. I won't ride with a man if there's such a difference of opinion betuxt us."

"Don't you see the rain how it pours?"

"Do you think I'm blind?—or that I can't feel the water running in channels down the wet back o' me?—But I'd weather the rain like a duck, in a good cause; and it's promoting concord I am, betuxt myself and one that's ungrateful and don't mind me, at this moment."

The piper was obstinate; and after awhile, the gentleman was obliged to say he did'nt think the story a lie. It was then, only, that he got a sup of the whiskey; and Corney gave the garron a hint with his wooden leg, to be going.

"Now," says Corney, "as we've made friends,—and I don't think I ever had an enemy but one, a whole day,—I'll entertain you with some of my music: but, before I begin, I'll just remind you, that I said while ago, there was boobies everywhere,—didn't I?—I did, that's true enough, and Rory's one o' them. May be you've been tould of one o' the Fogarty family, who ties a lanthorn to the horse's head, so that the crature may find out his grass in the dark?—This is the boy that does it:—as though the Will–o'–Wisps, and Jack–Lanterns of the bog, wouldn't do what was wanted o' them in that way, for a horse! —Do you believe that now, or don't you?"

"Is it a fool you take me for?" says the gentleman. "Yea or nay, just as you plaize. Arrah! Rory,—pturr–r!" "Pturr–r!" says Rory again; and the garron stopped so suddenly, that the piper himself was like to have been pitched over his head.

"Go on, and good luck to you!" cried the gentleman; "go on, and there's nothing you'll say but what I'll believe; for it's killed with the cold I am entirely!"

"Oh, fie! and the whiskey here at your elbow!"

The piper lifted his leg, and away wint the garron again. After much more talk, and two or three stoppages, Carolan at last says to the gentleman, "Now I'd like to know, sir,—may be you won't tell me, though;—but why shouldn't you?—"

"Ask me no impertinent questions, and behave yourself in every respect, or you'll wish you hadn't a tongue in your head this journey, when you come to know one,—as perhaps you may."

"Perhaps I won't, though;—for I've no great opinion of you. Perhaps, I won't know yow to plaize you. But you'll own I'm right in not riding another step with one that won't tell me which way he'd be going."

"Don't stop the horse again, and you shall know it least where I'm bound to:—indeed, I tould you long ago, it was to The Beg."

"Is it The Beg?—and so you did, now I remember. May be you're a new butler?—No?—A bailiff, then?—Yet why should you? There's nobody there now that's in debt. And if you ar'n't either the one or the other, what can you be?—But it's bad manners in me to be bothering my brains with guessing who you are, when I don't care about knowing. You won't go to The Beg though, anyhow, to–night;—it's a long three miles from where we stop;—a bad road and up–hill entirely, too."

"Can I get a bed, think you?"

"Why, then, Luke Fogarty's is the state cabin o' the whole place, and he'd give up his own bed any day to a stranger, though he hasn't the best of characters; and Ramilies, his pig—"

"His what?"

"Ramilies, his pig; — they say she's a witch: she farrows nineteen, four or five times a year; and she has tushes like ram's horns, only they're straight. She goes miles away by the sea–side, and walks into the water, like a Christian, to nuzzle up crabs among the rocks. It's often I've seen her scrunching them: they nips her—trust them for that—with their claws; but I'm inclined to believe, the pinches she gets out her tongue serves by way of a fillip or sauce to the feast, by the same rule that donkeys like thistles that's prickly, and we ourselves mustard with pork. If I'd a house to pull down to–morrow, I wouldn't wish a better workman than Ramilies, if she hadn't her dinner, and there was fish inside, and the doors barred. They say, she drinks whiskey when she can get it:—but what need have you to be afraid? Won't I be there with you?—Sure I will.—Ramilies has no ear for music, and one blow of my bagpipes drives her. As to Luke,—why, if Luke shouldn't behave himself, it won't be the first time I've poked my wooden leg in the face of him, and broke his ugly deaf head, with the big hollow bull's–horn he has for an ear–pipe, into the bargain. Corney Carolan is well able for him, or any one else, if he's only awake."

"I'm afraid your friend's cabin won't afford much accommodation for a gentleman."

"Why, then," says Corney, "I'll just give you a bit of a bird's–eye view of it, and you'll judge for yourself. As you go in, there's a remarkably fine dunghill, on each side of the door, built up as straight as two walls,— only a little loose at the top,—so that they forms a sort of artificial porch, or portico, to the house; and, at the other side o' the window, there's another wall o' dung, that reaches chuck up to the gable. When you go in, if you look to the right, there's a place where Luke sits and makes brogues when he's in the humour for it; and you'll see a pair of channel–pumps, hanging by wooden pegs in the wall, which he made when he worked in Waterford; and among the tools, —I mane, the awl, and strap, and stone,—no doubt but there's the broken crockery he had his dinner in, this day six months, when he'd a fit o' work on him, and wouldn't, for a moment, quit the brogues he was then making, and which ar'n't finished yet, nor never will: for the next time he sits down to work, he'll begin another pair, and lave off again, when he's just done three quarters of each of them. Though he's the finest workman, they say, within seven baronies, Luke and his family are the best customers to Jack Sheelan the shoemaker, in the whole place: for Luke has other ways o' getting money than with his hammer and awl,—it's himself that has, then! He's come of a fine family too,—though I say it, that's his cousin,—for he's a Sweeney by birth, and has a right to be called so: he *was,* long ago, and would be now, if he hadn't quarrelled with his father's family, and sworn, out of spite, never to wear their name again as long as be breathed: so he took to his mother's—she was a Fogarty;— and you couldn't offend him more any way in the world than you would if you upset his whiskey, singed his nose while he was asleep, or called him Luke Sweeney."

"He's a room above stairs, I hope," says the gentleman.

"He *had*; and the floor of it went three parts across the kitchen; and when you got up, you could look over a board and see your peathees boiling below for breakfast:—and you might, to this day, if the rain hadn't soaked through the ould thatch and rotted the timber, so that it fell down with nineteen of us, one night at a dance, years and years ago."

"Then I'll be compelled to sleep with nothing above me but the bare thatch!"

"That, and the cobwebs:—and you'll see how the big spiders will run down their little ropes, and dangle over the table, when I'm playing Garry–hone–a–gloria!—But there's no harm in the cratures; nor much in ould Ramilies herself, if she hasn't been drinking. I've known her get so drunk, on beer–grounds they gave her at The Beg, that it took seven men and a boy to bring her home, with Luke Fogarty's sister going before, pinching one o' the little pigs, so as to make him squeal out, by the way of wheedling her on quietly."

"Right glad am I that I've my dog to watch me:—but, of course, they'll keep her out if I ask it," says the gentleman.

"They will, if she'll let them; but her word isn't worth a bad song, if you could get her to give it;—and you couldn't, could you?—But, *na bocklish!* hav'n't you your dog!—I'll promise to persuade Fogarty to give you up his own little black oak bedstead, that stands beside the chimney: and then who knows but you'll get the canvass bed stuffed with louchaun—that's the chaff that comes from the oats when they're winnowed—and three rugs to cover you! But what's better than all, though we shouldn't be there till midnight,—and, faith! then, we won't at this rate,—there'll be an iligant supper, and all the gorlochs— except Susey, the eldest—put to bed. What'll we have, you'd like to know, eh?—Well, then, I'd tell you, if I could, but I can't. May be, if Luke's had luck lately, we'll get a bonnov,— that's a little pig, you know;—and if not, there'll be a cobbler's nob, and a dish of caulcannon:—at any rate, we're sure of hot ghindogues and praupeen, or stirabout, or shloucaun,—that's the sea–weed,—the dillosk, you know, that the girls gather, boiled down to a nicety, and which, as they say, is what Saint Ambrose lived upon, and the same thing you rade of in books, by the name of ambrosia. Rory tells me they'd a breast of mutton,— he don't precisely remember what day, but it was lately,—and we'll get that made up into beggar's–dish, with onions, and a bit of tripe, may be, if it's not eat, and Ramilies hasn't stolen it. That pig's a witch, as I tould you before; but sure you needn't mind her with your dog, need you?—If it comes to the worst, we're certain of peathees, trundled out

hot from the crock in the middle of the big table, with a clane hoop on it
to keep them from rolling off: and what's finer than peathees when they're
smoking, and grinning at you through their red jackets? With them and milk
(I'll engage for him, Luke will be able to give you your choice, sour milk
or new) and two or three piggins o' pothien,—we'll be gay as drovers, and
sleep sound wherever we fall. But I'm houlding out all these fine things to
you, only to shew you what good luck you'll miss, if you don't tell me who
you are, and what is it you'd be doing at The Beg; for it wouldn't be well of
me to bring home any one, without knowing head nor hair of him, to my
cousin Fogarty's,—would it, now?"

"It isn't at all necessary that I should satisfy your curiosity," says the
gentleman.

"Maybe, not; but I think so:—so we'd better settle the point before we
go further. Arrah! Rory,—Pturr–r!"

"Pturr–r!" says Rory; "pturr–r, pturr–r!" says he; but the garron was
now too near home to pturr for the brightest man that ever stood in shoe;
and instead of stopping, he put his best leg forward, and carried the car
clane up to Luke Fogarty's door, some minutes sooner than he would have
done, may be, if nobody had said "Pturr–r!" to him at all.

"Kead mille faltha!" cried Luke, as soon as he saw the piper; "long
looked for, come at last!—But who's this with you, Corney?"

"Faith! I don't know, then," says Carolan, who wasn't at all plaized
with the garron, that he didn't stop when Rory bid him; "I don't know a
ha'p'orth about him," says he, with his mouth close to the big end o' the
crooked bull's–horn, that Fogarty held to his ear; "I found him, after losing
his horse, sitting up upon Henniker's mile–stone; and it raining harder than
usual:—so I took him on the car; but he wouldn't tell me who he was.
He's high and mighty enough to be a king; and, may be, if the top of the
dirt was taken off his clothes, we'd find him dressed like a gentleman?"

"Arrah! Corney! now I look at him again, and that he's wiped his face, I
think I know him. welcome, sir," says Luke to the stranger, who couldn't but
hear what the piper had said, yet took no notice of it; "you're welcome, sir, to
a poor man's place, and the best I've got, this bad night:—but don't I know
you somewhere?—Then, if I did, what harm?"—continued Luke, seeing
how the man drew himself up, and, putting on his airs, didn't condescend to
answer what was said to him; "If I did know you, what harm?—and, faith!
then, I do, Corney!" says he, turning to the piper; "sure you heard of one

Andie Hogan, that got a mint o' money a'most, by selling little bonnets he made o' the paper they puts on the walls of fine houses, to the women and girls at pattarns and fairs, far and near;—didn't you, Corney?"

"I did," says Corney, with his mouth at the bull's-horn, "and how he advertised the fine fortune he'd give his lame daughter; and how, while he was making a great match for her, one Purcell, a bit of a tailor, away there at Dungarvan, ran off with her. Sure I've a story as long as from here till to-morrow, and two or three songs about them. Didn't ould Hogan make it up with Purcell, and lave him all he had? And didn't the tailor turn upstart when he'd got the money,—and wouldn't look on his own relations, but cocked his nose at them, and every body that used to know him, as though they were dirt?"

"Well then, Corney," says Luke; "and if you never saw him before, you can get a look at him now, for this is himself."

"Oh! pullaloo! murther and horse-beans!" shouted Corney; "and is it with Purcell I've been riding?—No offence, sir,—and I beg pardon for being bould in the bog there;—but are you now, without a word of a lie,—are you the Mushroom?"

"I hope I'm not brought here to be insulted," says the gentleman.

"Well! but are you Mr. Purcell—or are you not? Is it you that's own cousin to that Thady Purcell, whose widow is married to Jack Forrester— ould Timberleg Toe-trap's club-footed son? Are you the Dungarvan tailor that snapped up Andie Hogan's lame daughter, or is Luke a liar?—Answer me that now, and there'll be an end of our talk."

"I shall not remain here another minute," says Purcell; for it was indeed himself—and Luke Fogarty had seen him at The Beg, dunning young Veogh, for money Pierce owed him, long before:—"I shall try if I can't get civility, at least, under another roof;" says he.

"Sure, I'm not uncivil," says Corney; "or, if I was, I didn't intind it."

"Then have done, fellow !"

"Is it 'fellow'?—Well! calling me names don't break my bones, or I'd give you a poke with my toe, so I would; and there's not much harm in 'fellow:' —I've been called more than that, without taking the trouble to put myself in a passion,—and why should I with you? Any how, I'll make up my mind to this:—you're one o' the wonders, ar'n't you?—I'm sure of it:— for you wouldn't so quietly hear yourself accused of being Andie Hogan's son-in- law, if it wasn't a true bill. Well, to be sure, I've had grate luck, one way and another:—I saw Lord Nelson, and the Giant's Causeway, and the Saltees, and Kilkenny coal, and the horse with two heads, and Mick Maguire's relation, that swore against the priest, and now I see the Mushroom!—what more could I wish?"

"By this time Luke had got out his best pair of yarn stockings, and the channel pumps, he made when he was a journeyman in Waterford, and the newest clothes he had, and insisted upon Purcell's laying aside his own for them: but the Mushroom, instead of minding him, whistled his dog, and seemed to be going. Corney, however, put his leg across the door, and Luke himself got a hold of Purcell by the coat, and swore he'd not let him budge a foot:—"Sure," says he, "you wouldn't think of insulting me so in my own house! I couldn't let a dog go from under my roof such a night as this. If you lived but a stone's throw away, I'd be wrong if I'd let you stir: though they say you were the first that arrested Pierce Veogh, it matters but little to me. May be I like him; may be I don't: but if I'd give you a crack on the head for so doing—I won't say I would though, why should I?—but in case I would if I met you abroad in company, yet in my own house, coming into it as you do, I could not but make you welcome, you know. There's my own bed in the corner for you; and after supper I'll give you as much whiskey as you can carry into it from the place where you'll sit."

Luke Fogarty now gently pushed the Mushroom back to a log o' wood that stood for a chair by the hearth, and began to unbutton his coat. But Purcell wouldn't demean himself so much as to have the likes o' Luke for a valet, and put on the stockings and pumps, which was all he'd accept, without any assistance.

I won't tell you what was served up for supper, by Luke's sister, who was his housekeeper,—the wife being dead,—in the state cabin that night, for I didn't hear; and if I did, I forgot: neither, for the same good rason, will I say what songs the piper sung, or what tunes he played on his pipes, or how many piggins of whiskey was drained: but I know this—that Luke Fogarty reeled in his way to the police where he was going to sleep; and that he left Corney, with the pipes by his side, snoring away on the bare floor, with nothing upon him but what he could stand upright in, except a bit of a rug, that Rory, by way of a joke, had thrown on his wooden leg, to keep the end of it warm.

As soon as Luke was gone, the Mushroom got into the bed that Corney had described to him, and bad as the accommodation was for one of his way of living, he soon fell fast asleep. Though he said nothing about what business brought him to The Beg that night, it was known, afterwards, that he was called there by letter, to receive whatever Pierce Veogh might then be in debt to him. And I must tell you, he wasn't among the creditors that had security on the land, or the house, or what was in it; but only on Pierce himself, who'd often been worried by him, and never could get clane out of his debt; for if he paid him to–day, Purcell would have something else due against him in a month. And to tell the truth, Pierce had so borrowed of Purcell—at short dates, and long dates, on bills and on bonds, and annuities, and I don't know what else,—that if you'd give Pierce the world he never could tell how the reckoning stood. It's been said by many too, that Purcell bought up many of Pierce's debts that was lying out against him, for a mere song; and contrived to keep him in constant fear, and afraid to shew his face near the place of his birth, if he wished it. And why. so, you'll think? Why then, some people suspect, that Purcell had a mind to make up to the lady that bought The Beg, when it was sold by Pierce's creditors; and wished to keep him away from her; as he well knew, they'd once been in love, and now that she was a widow, he couldn't but fear that they might think of ould times, and renew the connexion. And it's true for him, Purcell might well think himself a match, as far as wealth went, for that lady, or any other: his wife died two years after he run off with her, and he'd so twisted and turned the money her dad gave him, and, though a rank rogue, had such lack that he was ten times richer than Andie Hogan could ever expect to have seen his lame daughter's husband: but neither father nor daughter lived to see him in them days, when he held his head highest.

Did you ever in your life awake and find a slip–knot tied round your great toe, and somebody pulling away for the bare life at the other end o' the cord, and you not able to see who your enemy was?—If you didn't you've missed what's a million times worse than the night–mare,—or a pair of cramps knitting the muscles into knots under each of your knees. If you didn't ever get that trick played on you, it won't be possible for you to imagine, or conceive, or picture to yourself, how matters stood with the Mushroom, when dawn broke on him, there where he lay, on the little louchaun bed, in Luke Fogarty's state cabin. It can't but occur to you though, that he'd no right to consider himself quite in paradise, when I tell you that he was awoke and dragged almost out over the foot of the bed, by an invisible something which operated upon his toe. He had felt two or three twitches before, but he wouldn't believe that any thing much was the matter, and thought he'd go to sleep again, and forget it. But the pull I spoke of wasn't to be bamboozled away so aisily: he couldn't but notice it—for he'd never felt any one thing in the world half so unpleasant before. And this wasn't all;—at the same time that he found himself maltreated in the toe, his ears were serenaded with a din so horrible, that he couldn't but think there was goblins about him! The first thing he did, was to throw the clothes from his face,—the pull having buried the head of him beneath them,—and then, naturally enough as you'll say, he looked down to the foot of the bed. It was just light enough for him to see what was the matter. He'd tied his dog Pompey, as he thought, to his wrist, by a bit of cord, so that the least motion of the animal might alarm him: but, lo and behold! the cord was now strangling his toe in a running-knot, and the poodle half hanging himself, by pulling away with all his might at the other end of it! There was the dog in a right line with the foot of the bed,—the eyes of him nearly starting out of his head,—yelping as well as the cord would let him, and looking, as though it was his own opinion he hadn't three minutes to live!

The first thing Mr. Purcell thought of doing, was to coax the animal to come nearer, and by that means aise him; for his leg was pulled out so straight, that though he tried hard to get a clutch at the string, he couldn't. "Pompey! Pompey!" says he, "come here, you rogue!—Murder! —Whew! Whew! Poor fellow, then!—Bad luck to the dog!—What! Pompey, then!—Murder!"

All this time Pompey wasn't idle: he'd got his master lower in the bed, and, the Mushroom found all at once, something bristly scrubbing his foot. It was then for the first time, he perceived what was making, part of the strange noise he heard,—and what it was too, that Pompey was strangling himself to get away from. Corney Carolan lay on the floor betuxt asleep and awake,— neither quite drunk, nor altogether sober,—blowing his bagpipes as though he'd burst them, but without producing such an effect as he'd predicted they would; for athwart midships, between the foot of the bed and Pompey, stood Ramilies the pig, bristling up the, long hairs on her back, curling her tail nearly into a knot, gnashing her tusks, frothing way at the mouth, like a beer barrel that's in work at the hung-hole, and telling Pompey, as plainly as she well could, that she felt very indignant at his presence, but nevertheless quite willing and able to devour him. She had poked through a fresh–mended gap in the wall, to get at a basket of crabs, which Luke bought the night before; and there was the nineteen little ones, that she'd farrowed that day month, squeaking in chorus to her own grunt; and what with Pompey's yelping, and the piper's playing, and Purcell's exclamations, and the shouting and shrieking of Luke Fogarty's sister and seven children, who soon came mulling, just as they were, from their beds, and the noise of the cocks and hens, and the pinches the little pigs got from the claws of the big crabs that Ramilies had upset out of the basket, and which was now crawling about the floor, they ran over the bed, and under the bed, and raced about the place, just as if they were out o' their wits.

All this noise couldn't go for nothing: the whole place was in arms;— Mick Maguire fired off his gun through a hole in the thatch, and Bat Boroo, flourishing his big stick, took Mick under his command; for he thought the French was landed, at the least, —and no blame to him.

When the neighbours broke in Luke Fogarty's door, they found things going on nearly as I described just now. Corney was still blowing the pipes, and the Mushroom roaring, and young Rory Fogarty dancing about in great glee, with the black crock the peathees was boiled in on his head; and the little pigs racing about, and the cocks and hens cackling, and Ramilies preaching to Pompey. Luke Fogarty himself crawled from a corner where he'd been snoring, and putting the bull's–horn to his ear, before he could get his eyes open, says he, "Don't I hear a noise?" But a moment after, when he peeped through his sore lids, and saw what was going on, he grinned with glee; and putting the horn to his mouth, blew something so much like a charge on it, that Bat Boroo, who that moment came up to the door, faced about, and retreated in good order, but quick time, laying all the glory and danger to Mick who didn't run for two rasons:—first, because he didn't notice Bat making away with himself; and next, because he knew nothing about the nature of a charge. So in he marched among the rest of the neighbours, with his gun, as usual, full cocked in his hand.

"Shoot! shoot!" says the Mushroom, as soon as he caught a glimpse of Mick;—and "Shoot! shoot!" says the neighbours; "why not shoot at once, Mick!"

"Aisy! aisy! all of ye," cried Mick; "aisy, and don't bother me! 'Shoot! shoot!' says you; but who'll I shoot?—Is it ould Ramilies or the dog?"

"The dog! the dog!" says the neighbours.

"No!—the pig! the pig!" says Purcell.

"See that, now!" cried Mick: "Wasn't I unlucky all my life? If I'd a double–barrelled gun, I'd oblige both parties at once, and then there'd be no quarrelling: but I haven't. "

Just then, ould Malachi Roe made his appearance in his red night–cap, and having the handle of an ould hunting whip, with a brass hook and hammer at the end of it, by way of a weapon, in his hand: he wasn't a moment inside the door when, without saying a word, he pushed Rory Fogarty, who was laughing most furiously, plump against Ramilies, and taking a knife out of his pocket, cut the cord by which Pompey was tied to the toe of his master.

Malachi had news too of Mr. Purcell's mare; and while the people still stood loitering about Luke Fogarty's door, and Corney was telling the Mushroom, that all his bad luck was owing to his carrying an umbrella on the bog of Saint Swithin, the mare was brought up by somebody—I forget who it was—that had caught her. You'd think, perhaps, that Purcell's pride might be brought down a little by what had befallen him: but no,—he strutted out of the cabin without condescending to say *be, baw*, or a civil word to any one; and rode off to The Beg—mushroom as he was—with his nose in the air, as though the ground wasn't good enough for him to look on.

THE DILLOSK GIRL

I'M a bad hand at describing a beauty, but I'll try my best to give you an idea how Norah Cavanagh looked when she was twenty. The nose is a part of a woman's face that few people spake of in reckoning over her charms; but, in my mind, it's worthy of notice, as well as the eyes. Norah's nose was neither long nor short; too thick, nor otherwise; turned up nor down;—but just delicate, fine, and growing straight from her brow, in a way that it was beautiful to behold, but next akin to impossible to describe. There wasn't much colour in her cheek, but the lips made up for it: you may talk of cherries for a twelvemonth,—but there never was cherries so temptingly red as the lips of young Norah; and when she opened them, you saw two rows of teeth,—not so white as the inside of an oysther, but of a colour you loved better; for they was just exactly as a healthy and handsome young woman's should be;—and they sparkled and seemed to laugh, every one of them, when their owner did. Her eyes wasn't blue nor black; no, nor grey; nor hazel; but a mixture of all, and not a– bit the less beautiful. When you gazed into them, they was like a picture; for there seemed to be a little view of some place in each of them. But this wasn't noticed at a distance; and it's few knew of it, but those who had dandled Norah when a child; for she kept the boys off when she grew up, and, if anything, was thought to value herself a little too much, considering she'd nothing. Norah's hair wasn't so white as to make her look silly:—it had a dash of light auburn upon the ends of the curls; and when the sun shone upon them, they had a gloss that dazzled the eyes of all the boys about. Was I but younger that time, I think I'd have been in love with little Norah myself;—and won her, perhaps, away from them all:—who knows?—

Norah was as nate in her dress as she well could be,—with the little she got for the dillosk she gathered: and on a Sunday—faith! then, who but she!—She'd her stockings and shoes, and a clane cap, as well as the best to be seen at Mass. Miss Honor, and James Dingle's other two sisters,—next to the great lady at The Beg,—are the finest folks in these parts; for their aunt's a great farmer, by the two from this: and they would often be saying,—them curls, that came out in clusters under her cap, didn't become a Dillosk–girl; and tould her she'd have more friends, if she'd comb them back, smooth and sleek away behind her ears: but Norah said, she couldn't; for curl they would, whether she wished them or no. This wasn't believed by the young ladies; they couldn't credit that a Dillosk–girl's hair would curl up in that way, without as much time being spent about it, as there was upon their own long, black, horse–tail locks; and they said,—Norah Cavanagh had better be at her devotions (though they themselves wasn't Catholics) than to be wasting time twisting up her tresses to allure the young men at Mass. And after that, when Norah wint, for a day or two now and then, to help their aunt's maids at a busy time, and they got convinced, by living under the same roof with her, and watching her closely, that Nature was Norah's frizeur, theytould her, she ought to cut off her locks if she'd wish to look dacent and get respected. But though Norah wasn't obstinate in anything else, she was in this; and wouldn't do as they bid her. You'll say she ought, perhaps: but, faith! there's many things we ought to do, though we don't do them; and there's many a beggar–man's daughter wouldn't barter her hair for a silk bonnet:—if you doubt what I say, try two or three, and you'll see.

Norah was little, but nate and well–made:—hasn't it ever struck you, that Nature often finishes off the little folks better than the big ones?— Whether it has or no matters but little; for if there never was another that was at once little and nate, Norah herself was and even those that disliked her never denied it;—and she had her enemies, and not a few, I promise you. The girls hated her, for stealing away the boys' hearts from them all; and the boys, after a bit, wouldn't give her a good word, because she'd refused them.

"Now you'll think, after this, Norah got married to some great lord;—but she hadn't the luck. The fairest bird in the air gets caught for its plumage; while the owl, and birds like him, go through the world with little danger; and just so, beauty, that always adorns, too often destroys, them that has it:—but that you've heard before, no doubt, in them same or other words, and a great deal more, to the back of it, which I could spake, if I liked, but I won't. It will answer every purpose, I hope, if I say plainly, that it got whispered Norah had met with a misfortune. I won't tell you how the girls giggled at this; that's needless;—nor who it was that pretended to pity her, and tried to worm out of her who'd been the destruction of her,—but they couldn't:—that would be making a story that's too long already, longer than it is, wouldn't it?—so I won't. You'll be satisfied, and, may be, a little vexed, to know that, after a time, when Norah wint out to gather the dillosk, there was a baby at her back.

It was a little thing,—very little,—not much bigger than a fairy; but quite strong and healthy, and as handsome as a mother need wish. It was a little picture of Norah, but not like any one else that ever was seen in these parts: so nobody could tell, by a feature or look, who had a call to it; and no power or persuasion could make Norah say whose it was. Mistress Doolan, that time, it was thought, used to follow Paddy, her husband, slily, when he wint out sometimes after dusk for anything, to see would he be going the way to little Norah's cabin; for it's said of her, she had some little suspicion,—or fear, may be,—that Pat might have been backsliding, and playing the same sort of trick that, at last and in the long run, brought him under the thumb. But she was disappointed intirely: for Pat never had the misfortune to turn the way she feared he would,—no, not even by chance.

Norah got paler and much thinner, and her lips lost their colour, and her eyes sunk; but she was just as tidy as before, and held up her head bouldly, in spite of the sneers of her neighbours; so that the few half-friends she had left was obliged to confess she was a bit too barefaced. But, musha! then, was it a soul in the barony—that is, boy or man—that dared leer at her, or try to be upon terms with her that wasn't respectful?—Her nature was changed; and when she repulsed them that made up to her, it wasn't with scorn as before, but downright rage: indeed, at last, though she was mild with such as behaved themselves, a man might as well think of kissing a tigress as Norah.

Big Jack Dax,—he that's my lady's steward at The Beg,— had a nephew, one Misther Millet, a small bit of a man, mighty puny and spruce, with a white face, and pimples on his chin, but no beard; you'd think a breath would blow him away; and about the time I'm spaking of, he came over from Liverpool, —where he was something of a clerk,—on a visit here to his uncle, for a couple of months,—to get his health, as you'd think if you looked at him;—but, as *he* said, to enjoy "the rude romantic beauties of the coast:" — them were his words. He wrote verses, and picked up bits of shells and sea-weed, and amused himself in ways sensible people wouldn't dream of. Some of us thought he was so-so in his senses; but his uncle said it was no such thing,—he was only a genius. Above all things in this world, what should small Misther Millet do, but attack little Norah, after meeting her two or three times, while he was poking about with a long stick, for shells, on the beach where she got her dillosk! He had heard of her misfortune, but didn't know of her deportment to them that attempted to bill and coo with her: so, one day, he struck up to her, quite confident of himself, and began to be familiar. But he got such a rebuff from the little Dillosk–woman, that he gave up shell–gathering, and took to digging for things in the hills, which, he said, was carried away there at the time of the great deluge; and just that day se'nnight after his talking to Norah, Misther Millet didn't come home to dinner,—no, nor supper; and all night they saw no sight of him, —though they sat up in hopes of his coming; and, at last, big Jack Dax gave up his nephew as lost,—no one knew where. It happened rather unluckily for Misther Millet to mislay himself just then, for there was great goings–on at The Beg —you'll hear, by–and–by, what they were about.

It was Norah herself that poor Tommy Maloe offered to marry; and from that, and his doing her a good turn, and saying a kind word for her when he could, some of us thought it was he seduced her. But though he was a fine fellow, and well to do, she wouldn't listen to him. With that, we changed opinions again, and couldn't determine among ourselves, or in our own minds even, how to settle the question. And what bothered us more than all was, that though Norah said downright "nay" to his offers, it's often she begged him to take Bat Boroo's advice, and not go for a souldier: however, he wouldn't heed her. And when news came of his being killed abroad, Norah wint and wept with his poor father, and did all she could to comfort the childless ould crature in his sorrow.

Now we'll go on:—As I tould you, no one could guess who Norah had been ruined by,—and we'd given it up, thinking time would tell us. She never missed passing my door at the turn of the tide, to go gathering the dillosk; and was always the last home,—working, as she did, till the flow again, and going back, step by step, before the rising waters, until they drove her clear off the shore. If industry's a virtue, Norah had it in perfection; and she didn't want, nor ever took bawbee that wasn't earned, from any man,—and that too, honestly.

Away to the west, about a mile below my cabin, there's a ridge of rocks, which runs far out into the sea: that was Norah's favourite spot; for the dillosk was plenty there, and few frequented it. At low water, the very end of it stood high and dry; and I may say the same too, when the waters was half up, during the neap tides; for it rose above the rest of the ridge, and when the floods came, it was barely covered about two foot, or two foot and a half. We call it O'Connor's land–mark:—why, I don't know; but so it was called before I was born, or my father before me,— at least, so he said; and if I, that's his son, wouldn't credit him, who would?

One morning, — it was the day after big Jack Dax lost his small nephew, as I tould you,—Norah wint away to the ridge, as usual, and laid down her child on the rock, with its face looking up to the heavens, and laughing at the clouds, as they sailed along in all sorts of forms. This she did daily while gathering the dillosk, for the baby loved to have the clouds for its play things. It wasn't a fine lady's child, you know, or it couldn't sleep there upon O'Connor's land–mark, among the sea–weeds and so forth, without taking harm; but the place was natural to it: and Norah left Paddy Doolan's daughter to watch it, and look to it, and bring it to her if it woke and wanted anything; and then she began working. After a time, she had well nigh picked up as much as she could carry,—though she wasn't lucky that day, for the weed lay wide, and she was long gathering it, and some sad thoughts she had that morning didn't help to hurry her. At last, she turned back to get the baby and go home; and that moment she heard a shriek from Paddy Doolan's daughter, who had wandered away from the baby, picking the little fish out of the pools in the rock. It didn't seem more than a minute to Norah since she looked round, and saw the girl by her child; and she had heard her singing, up to the time when the shriek came; but more than a minute it must have been,—but it's true, little more would be enough; for between Paddy Doolan's daughter, and, of course, between Norah herself; who was more ashore, and O'Connor's land–mark, where the baby was sleeping, the sea had rose, and flowed over a dent, or steep descent, in the ridge, from the lowest part of which the rock rose up again quite abruptly, till it ended in the peak at the end. You know how fast the tide comes up sometimes just after the ebb, especially when the wind's with it; and you'll not be surprised to hear that, though poor Norah, distracted as she was, nearly flew over the ridge, yet as she was a full stone's throw off, or more, a couple of big waves had got in; and if it was fordable when Paddy Doolan's daughter shrieked, it wasn't so by the time Norah got to the water's edge.

Now it's fit I should tell you, that the shriek Paddy Doolan's daughter gave, when she saw the water betuxt herself and the baby, wasn't a sound, if you heard it, you'd whistle at; it wasn't the scream of a young miss at seeing a cockroach:—it gave tidings of death, and spread dismay all over the ridge, and even beyond it, among the Dillosk that was there. Few of them but had children playing about, or picking up little bits of burthens of the weed,—them that was big enough,—near the ridge, and every one ran to the place whence the sound came. Three or four was much nearer than Norah, and cutting across to the place almost as quickly as herself,—none of them knowing but harm had happened their own,—they got to the brink of the water before her. When they saw whose baby it was on the ridge, they set up a wail, which, if possible, increased poor Norah's speed down the ridge. they felt as mothers,—all of them did,—and knowing well enough, by their own hearts, what the mother of the baby would do, they made ready to stop Norah as she came: —for swim, the knew she couldn't,—it was too late for wading, and if she bate through the incoming waves, the water was so deep in the middle, that drown she must. So they all threw their arms about her, and held her for a second; but the baby 'woke then, and its cry came to her ear. That gave her such sudden strength, that she broke away from them, and burst into the water. Just then, as luck would have it, an unbroken wave was rolling in; Norah met it in its full strength, and was dashed to the shore again; but it would have carried her back with it, hadn't ould Ileen, who'd just got up to the place, rushed in, with Peg Dwyer and another woman, knee–deep, and clutched a hould of her, and kept her fast, in spite of her struggling, and telling them they were murderers, and calling down curses upon them in her agony. The child wailed again; and Norah, it's thought, would have escaped from them a second time; but Ileen, as soon as she heard the baby begin, clenched her big fist, and, with one blow on the forehead, knocked poor Norah senseless into the arms of Peg Dwyer.

There was a moment of silence, and every one cast an eye of reproach upon Ileen, but no one durst utter a word. "Don't be looking so at me," says she, to them; "wouldn't you suffer a little, any of ye, to save all?— Many's the fine fellow lost his life for want of less than Norah has got! Better a blow on the head, no matter how big the bump that comes after it,—better that, I say, than be drowned. You've seen a boy in a fit, and six couldn't hould him;—and could a fit, think you, give a boy more strength, than the cry of a child where that one is, would give to a mother that loves it?"

All this while,— and it wasn't long,—Ileen was busy tying poor Norah hand and foot.

"Oh! for young Paudrigg, now, or any one that could swim!" cried one of the women; "there's not a boy or a man, —no, nor a bit of a boat even, within sight. What will we do, Ileen?"

"All of you join with me in a loud wail, children and all," replied Ileen; "may be, Jimmy Fitzgerald's boys, or some of the neighbours near him, isn't gone out, and may hear us."

"Is it a tide any of the fishermen would lose such weather as this, think you, Ileen?" asked Peg Dwyer.

"Who knows," says Ileen, "what good God may send us? One of them may be kept back to save that poor baby."

So then they set up such a wail, all of them, that it came to me here, where I was dozing; and if anything could have given me the use of my limbs, it would have been that. I tried to stir, but it was of no use:—so, without losing time, in making more efforts, I pulled open the door with my crutch, and hallooed, and cried "Murder!" five or six times, at the top of my voice. Ileen reckoned upon my doing that; for, as soon as the wail was over, says she, "If that does no good, nothing will;—if one of us ran off for help, before she got near any men and they got back again, the sea would be over the child; and the only chance we'd then have, would be in the wave that floated it bringing it ashore: but that's a poor hope; for every moment the tide drives us back, and leaves it farther away from us. But a scream travels faster than a bird. If no one else heard us, Jimmy Fitzgerald must; for he's always at home:—he's an ould sailor, and won't fail to repeat the signal of distress; it's sure to bring somebody to him, and he'll send every one that comes, away here to us:—so that we save the time of running as far as his cabin, by the wail; and there's hope yet the child won't be lost."

Within a minute or two after I'd done calling out, as I said, there came running in Mick Maguire, and Bat Boroo, and all the lazy–bones of the place: and after them followed Paddy Doolan, ould Malachi Roe, and a power more of landsmen, with women and children at their heels; but not a fisherman, good or bad, ould or young, was ashore. I tould them of the wail I'd heard from the Dillosk–women, and the point it bore from; and off they wint, one following another, as fast as they came in; and it wasn't long before all the place was in arms, and not a soul but me left in it, far or near.

All this didn't take more than the time I'm telling it. Meanwhile Norah recovered: she was now so weak, that Ileen unbound her, but the women still kept a hould of her; and there they were—wailing about her, and she sitting on a stone, with her hands clasped, gazing at the waters, that were just rising towards the top of the land–mark, where the child, that had now cried itself asleep again, lay without knowing its danger. Now and then she turned her eyes along the shore to the men that were running down to the ridge as fast as they well could: though they were landsmen, there was more than one among them that could swim; and Norah, as well as the women about her, had rason to hope bad wouldn't be the end of it.

A man tires, but the rising tide don't, and the waters still kept their pace; but the men slackened, and just as the foremost of them got up,—and that was Mick Maguire, out of breath, and who'd no heart; though his legs was the best,—just as he got up to the women, a great wave came in, and they all saw it a way off, for it was taller, and might be seen above those before it:—it came on slowly, but strongly; and instead of breaking and being divided in two by the land–mark, it swept in a full body above it, and Norah's baby was afloat!

Just then, all set up a shriek; and it was answered by one they little expected: what was it but the scream of the great eagle himself, that came down from the clouds a'most, and gripped up the baby in his mighty claws!—so saving it from one death, for another that was more frightful, and that too, a thousand–fold! He didn't rise at once, but skimmed along the face of the sea for some time, so that the baby dipped in the tops of the waves and scattered a foam round itself and the bird now and then; and it was thought he'd drop it more than once: but no,——he soon began to get higher and higher, and rose, at last, on his strong wings, above the cliffs themselves; and then, making a half circle, wheeled round, and wint over the heads of the women, right away to his nest in the mountain. And all that while, the women looked up silently, and them that was running along the beach stood still, and nobody, breathed; so that the flap of the eagle's wing was heard plainly, far as he was above them.

It would have been well for poor Norah had she swooned off again; but she didn't. When the eagle was gone out of sight, the people turned to look at her; and there she was, standing on tip–toe, with arms stretched out, and her eyes fixed in the air, as though she still saw the bird and her baby, long after they had disappeared to every one else. No one spoke to her,—for what could they say in the way of comfort?—but as soon as they got over the shock of the sight a little, it was just as though they had all been stunned,—they began to ask one another if anything could be done.

"There's but one hope in the world," says Ileen, "and that's to scale the crag."

"And who'll do it?" asked many, but nobody answered. Every one, who'd the heart, had tried before he was twenty, or betuxt that and twenty–five; but no one had ever succeeded. Many of them that was on the beach, had got terrible falls, and two of them broken limbs, in the attempt, and given it up as fruitless. Luke Fogarty was too ould, and Rory too young; Paddy Doolan hadn't the courage to try at twenty; and how could it be asked of him then that he was forty?—Mick Maguire wouldn't venture himself; but he'd go get his gun, and lend it to any one freely that would. One man pointed to his grey locks; another to his lame leg; and a third to his brats of little ones, and seemed to think, that it wouldn't be well of him to risk his life for an other man's child, when he'd six or eight of his own dependent upon him. Bat Boroo flourished about his big stick, and said he'd scale the rock with all the pleasure in life, if it would do any good: "But where would be the use?" says he; "for by this time the poor child is torn to pieces; and if I reached the nest and conquered the eagles that's in it, I'd have nothing but the child's torn limbs to bring back."

"I think," says Malachi Roe,—the ould one, I mane; he didn't spake before, and hadn't been known for a long time to open his lips until a question was asked him;—"I think," says he, "there's no fear of that. Daddy Gahagan, the shepherd, has been telling me, that one of his grandsons came to him while ago, with news of the eagle's mate having just carried off a lamb from the flock he tended. She'll get to the nest first with her prey; and there's a chance—what do I say?—it wouldn't be foolish to lay odds,—no harm comes to the child these two hours."

Every one stared, and wondered if it was indeed Malachi himself that spoke such a speech; they took it, however, for Gospel, and set up a shout: but Bat had turned on his heel, and didn't listen to it. Then all of them began to move off to the foot of the crag, but still nobody offered to venture.

While they wint sorrowfully, but speedily, along,—as though getting near the place would do any good,—they met Misther James Dingle trotting towards them. Two or three—and Mick Maguire was among 'em—had got a–head of the rest; and before they could speak, James Dingle pulled up his horse, and said to them,—"God save ye, boys! I've just seen the big eagle carrying off that in his claw, which I'm sure is a child, by the clothes.

Whose it is, I haven't heard; he may have brought it miles; but I'll give any of you two sparkling yellow boys, that will climb the crag and get it down from him, dead or alive."

Upon this, Mick Maguire tould him the whole story, whose child it was, and how the eagle got it; and before he'd done, the whole cavalcade of them were round him, crying, "Oh! Misther James! what'll we do?" For, next to the Priest, and the lady at The Beg, every one looked up to young Dingle for advice in the day of distress. And such wailing and bothering there was about him, that he couldn't be heard for a minute and more: at last, Father Killala, who had joined the people, got silence for him. The colour had left his cheek, and his lips looked hard and dry; but he spoke out coolly and distinctly, and said, "Though we're told that the crag has been climbed, and the eagle's nest reached, yet no one was ever known, or reported in tradition, to have got down from it again.. Now, Malachi Roe, do you take my horse and ride off to the beach with the best speed you can, and bring a roll of cord back with you, and ropes, if you can get them: but bring the cord away at once, if there's any delay with the ropes; for they may be got after. I'd go for it, but I wouldn't make myself a bit more fatigued than I now am, for that's needless; and while you're gone, I'll be getting ready. Should I reach the nest, I can lower the child to you, if I never come back myself."

"And is it you that's going, sir?" says Mick Maguire.

"It is, Mick," he answered; "no one else will, and so I suppose I must."

And then all of them, that a minute before was dying to meet with any one that would go, began moaning in an under tone, and seemed sorry, and half inclined to persuade James Dingle not to make the attempt. One fellow muttered—and it wasn't well of him— "A man's life is worth more than a child's."

"I don't know that," said James Dingle; "and what if it was? —We were all children once, and not able to help ourselves; but there was then men about, who had strength given them to protect us. Now we're men, we ought to do by the children, the same that others, whose heads he low, did for us,—or would have done for us, if need was,—when we were babies."

"Mr. Dingle," said Father Killala, coming up to him, "we can but ill afford to lose you:—I'd rather another wint who had a heart and body equal to your own; but as no one else offers, go, and God bless you!"

Dingle shook the ould man's hand, and wint on towards the mountain, with all the people following him, and praying blessings on his head.

Malachi Roe this while was far on his way to the fishermen's cabins: he wasn't a man to lose time, or spare horse–flesh when need was; so he came galloping down like a racer, and got back again, with all that was wanted with him, long before he was expected by any but James Dingle, who knew what Malachi was, and what his own horse could do; and, besides that, was impatient to begin. While he was gone, Luke Fogarty, and two or three more that had tried to get at the nest, gave Dingle what advice they could, how to avoid the mishaps they'd met with. Bat Boroo lent him his stick, and offered him a few short instructions in the way of attack and defence with it. But James Dingle silenced him, by saying,— "Bat Boroo, I thank you, but a shillala isn't a broad sword. I've been fool enough to carry a twig to a fair with me, when I was younger and wilder than I've been these seven years past: it was said I knew how to use it then; and though I've had no practice since, I don't think I've forgot which way to flourish it best."

And sure enough there was few that ever could stand up long to James Dingle before he got steady, even while only a stripling. In this place, if I'd a mind to do it, I might keep playing with your feelings, and tell you how young Dingle parted from the people, and what they thought and said, while he was climbing; and how one minute they had rason to hope, and the next to fear for hint:—but I won't do this, for you may imagine it all without any word of mine. I'll come to the point at once:—it was long before James made much way; for the lowest part of the peak was the worst; and when he got higher, he had often to crawl along the ledges a great way to find resting–places above for his feet: but he got on better than he did at the beginning; and after being often lost sight of, behind the pieces of rock that shot up like towers, he appeared again in places where he wasn't expected; and in less than an hour, the people below saw him in the branches of the tree, behind which it was known the eagle's aërie was built. Even then he hadn't done his work:—but you'll hear how he got on.

The eagle's nest rested partly on the tree I spoke of, which grew out of a crevice of the rock, and partly on the floor of a natural cave: it was made of big sticks, and among them was many a white bone of bird and beast, that bad served the eagles for prey, years and years before. James Dingle put aside the branches, quietly as he could, and in no small trepidation, to see what was doing, before he got in:—and he did right, I think; for look before you leap, is a saying that has sense in it, specially when you're going to get into an eagle's nest. So far, all went well; but no sooner had he put his head through the leaves, than he saw a sight that struck him motionless!—Most men have been amazed some time or other; but there never was a man so amazed as James Dingle was. At one corner of the little hollow in the rock,—making himself look less than he was,—who do you think sat then but small Misther Millet?—Misther Millet himself, whiter than the wall,—who had been lost since the day before, as I tould you,— shivering like a mouse within reach of the claws of a cat, with both the eagles opposite, on the brink of the nest, staring at the crature, and seeming to wonder what he was at, and how he got there!—There was two young eagles in the nest full–fledged, and looking mighty frightened at their new friend, Misther Millet. The lamb wasn't touched, though killed; and by its side lay the child, with one of the young eagles' wings over the little darling's face. It seemed as though the birds had all been afraid to begin their meal, with Millet where he was, and hadn't yet made up their minds how to get rid of him. I may as well tell you now, as by–and–by, how he came there, for I dare say you'd like to know.— Well, then, the little man, by his own story, had wandered away the day before, an hour after breakfast, to fetch a romantic walk among the hills, and gather pebbles; and catch butterflies, and draw trees, and make poetry, and do them things he was fond of: but by the time his stomach tould him it was getting on fast for dinner–time, he made a discovery that wasn't singular, considering what he'd been at, and which way he wint. You'll guess he lost his way,—and so he did; and every step he took made matters worse. Night came upon him, in a place where he could see nothing but a few rocks and wild shrubs about, and the sky speckled with stars above him. He chose out the clanest and softest bed he could, took off his coat and turned it inside out; then putting it on again, he lay down, and to his own great surprise soon found himself falling asleep. He had no bad dreams from indigestion that night, you may be sure; but he didn't wake very well in the morning, for all that. At day–break, he began walking again; and, in about an hour's time, upon looking through a few bushes, he got sight of a hole in the rock, which had light at the other end of it. He crawled in upon all–fours, and soon found himself cheek–by–jowl with a pair of young eagles!

Now we knew, from tradition, that there certainly was a long, but not a difficult way to the eagle's nest, through the hills; but though many had

tried that was born and bred near them, none could ever find it out; and
then comes Misther Millet, piping hot from a Liverpool 'counting–house,
and discovers it without trying, and much against his own will, to boot!—
His wonder wasn't well over, before home came the great hen–eagle,
with a lamb; and from that time, he didn't dare stir; for she never ceased
eyeing him, as though she was only waiting until he made a move, to dart
at his face. By–and–by, home came her mate too; and the sight of him
didn't make Misther Millet feel a morsel more aisy, I take lave to suppose;
especially when he saw that the bird had a child in its clutch:—and there
sat the little man, half dead with hunger, and cold, and fear, when James
Dingle looked in upon him.

It was then only, that the birds appeared to know of the approach of
another intruder: they stretched forth their wide wings, and each of them,
at the same moment, seized the lamb with one foot, and stood fluttering
on the other, at the edge of the nest. Dingle reached out his left hand and
dragged the child to him; and with his right, before you'd breathe, struck
the bird that was nearest him—it was the cock—a blow on the head, with
Bat Boroo's oaken cudgel, that knocked him over the edge of the nest;
and down he fell, in a way that made those below think he was killed;
but after falling many yards, he fluttered his wings, and soon recovered
enough to fly to a resting–place. The hen, at the moment her mate got
the blow, screamed so that the rocks rung with it, and got upon the wing.
She wheeled round in the air, and rose, to all appearance, for the purpose
of making a terrible stoop upon her enemy. There wasn't any time to be
lost:—James Dingle pushed both the young eagles out of the nest; they
were able to keep themselves up; and the ould hen, instead of making a
descent upon James, altered her course, flew towards her young, and kept
close to them, until they had reached, and were safe perched upon, the
point of one of the peaks, that grew up by the side of the crag.

While this was doing, Dingle got into the nest, bid Millet crawl back
through the hole with the child, and in a short time followed. He made
up his mind to explore his way through the hills; for, thinks he, Misther
Millet never could have got here, if the road's difficult; unless, indeed, the
eagles carried him up; but that's not likely:—so I'll try; and it's odd, from
this height, if I can't discover the way down, whatever may be said of its
being impossible. The hen–eagle, too, kept hovering about, and would,
no doubt, soon be joined by her mate; and—do you mark?—if he pulled

up the rope by the cord he had, and let down the baby, the great chance was, whether one of the ould birds—to say nothing of the fear he had of its getting hurt against the rocks,—wouldn't pounce upon and destroy it, as it swung mid–way in the air. So he determined to try his luck, and began descending. Misther Millet amused him by his story as they wint: but the gentleman couldn't remember one inch of the way he came; and if Norah Cavanagh's child hadn't been carried off the way I tould you, Jack Dax would have lost a nephew, and the world Misther Millet: for I can't but think he'd have died somewhere about the hills, or been killed by the eagles; and so, one way or other, met with the same fate as the boy did that was seen in the nest long ago, and never got back.

When the people below saw that James Dingle waved his stick triumphantly,—as he did before he left the nest,—and had disappeared for some time, though the eagles hadn't harmed him, they reminded one another of the way to the crag over the hills, and thought he was trying to find it. And when they asked Malachi Roe, he made a speech again,—that is, a speech for the likes of such a one as him:—says he, "I've no doubt but he is; he'd be a fool if he didn't; for look at the eagles above, between this and the nest."

"True," says Mick Maguire; "that didn't occur to us, whin he wint up. Any how, he might have killed the both,—and then there'd be no danger in letting down the baby,—he might have done that, if he'd taken my gun. And I'm thinking that Bat Boroo's stick—"

"What's your opinion, Malachi?" said Father Killala, interrupting Mick;—and it's the only fault he has: for he'd never hear one of my stories half through, without asking two or three hundred questions; and then, may be, he'd go off in the middle of it. But he's a fine man, and that's his only fault, or, I'd rather say, it's a way he has that's not pleasant to some people, though Mick didn't mind it. "What's your opinion, Malachi?" says Father Killala; "do you think James Dingle will find his way back?"

"With the blessing of Providence, I've no doubt of it," replied Malachi;—"no one ever came back from it yet, it's true; but there never was such a man as James Dingle got into the nest before."

"He knows the country as well as any one here, I suppose," observed the Priest.

"Better, Father Killala," said Malachi.

With this, most of the people came back, bringing poor Norah with them; and she was comforted in a great degree. Still she'd terrible fears, and a multitude of bad fancies; but every one strove to console her: those who wouldn't spake to her before, wept for her now; and Norah Cavanagh was grateful to them for it. A few watched the crag; but most of the people, as I said, came away: and they might be seen hanging together in knots about the place, doing nothing the rest of the morning but watch in hopes of seeing James Dingle appear. Some wint up among the hills to scout for him; though that wasn't much use, for nobody knew which way he'd come back.

Hours and hours passed on, but still no news of James Dingle! And his aunt, who heard of what had been done, was almost frantic at the foot of the hill, beyond The Beg. It was long she waited, and often she looked up the crags, but still there was no sign of her nephew:—it was past mid–day, and all the people got round her, and every body began to despair but Malachi.

At last two men was seen coming down from above; and who should they be, as you'll guess, but James Dingle and small Misther Millet! Young Dingle had Norah Cavanagh's child in his arms, and Millet was helping himself on as well as he could by Bat Boroo's big stick.

I won't describe what big Jack Dax,—who was there,—said on seeing his nephew again; I'll rather take up your time by telling you what a better man, and that's Father Killala, did:—though Misther Dax is a good soul, and much liked; but, of course, not to be mentioned with the Priest. And the truth is, big Jack Dax didn't waste much time in words; but, with little or no ceremony, hoisted his poor worn–out little nephew on his own broad shoulders, and so hoiked him off home to The Beg. It was himself—I mane the Priest,—that took the child out of James Dingle's arms, and when he'd seen it was alive and well, he motioned all the people about him to be silent: then, turning to young Dingle, he said, in a tone that those who heard it won't soon forget, "James Dingle, you're the father of this child!"

Every soul stood amazed, and nobody spoke but Dingle himself. "What makes you say so, sir?" said he.

"What?" exclaimed Father Killala: "what but that we've all witnessed to–day?—Your humanity made you offer money to any one that would scale the crag, when you merely knew that a child had been carried off by the eagle; but as soon as you heard the child was Norah Cavanagh's, you prepared to go yourself. None but the father of this babe would have ventured as much for it as you have to—day;—you are that father, James Dingle. In the face of Heaven above us,—before your countrymen,—in the sight of that lost young woman,—and with this unhappy being on your bosom,"—and he placed the child in young Dingle's arms as he spoke,—"with this in your bosom, you cannot—dare not deny it!"

"I don't deny it, Father Killala," replied James Dingle.

It's said the Priest himself looked a little surprised at this; but he wint on:—"Then, Mr. Dingle, as you're a man, I trust it's your intention to follow up this great day's work, by doing right to her that you've wronged."

"He never wronged me, Father Killala,—blessings on him!" said Norah Cavanagh.

Well! how all this would end, no soul could guess. The good Priest looked more astonished than before, and not a little angry at Norah. "And are you so lost to shame," said he to her— "has vice made you so abandoned—"

"She never was lost to shame, and don't know vice;" interrupted James Dingle, rather warmly: "I'll uphould her to be as pure and virtuous as any here."

James Dingle's aunt, who had stood mute with amazement all this time; now broke silence. "What's all this I hear?" exclaimed she:—"Why, he'll say next she's an honest man's wife, and himself her husband."

"That's just how it is, aunt," replied James.

Without repeating more of that part of their discourse, word for word, I may as well tell you, that Dingle owned to his enraged aunt, he'd married Norah secretly, under a promise of getting the aunt's forgiveness within a month or so; but as Norah was a Catholic, and the Dingles were Protestants, and the ould woman herself was as proud as them that was her betters, and so adverse to a Catholic for her nephew's wife, that she'd as soon have done any thing as agree to such a thing;—as, I say, all this was the case,—and James should have thought of it before, shouldn't he?—though his heart was a stout one, he hadn't the courage to mention his marriage to her. When his wife—for so I'll call her now—found he broke his promise, and wouldn't save her from the shame that was fast coming upon her, she resolutely refused to have any— even the slightest—communication with him, and scorned to accept the smallest mite of assistance from his hand: but worked hard and supported herself, and by–and–by her baby too;—bowing down before her bad luck, and taking it as a penance for doing wrong, as she had, by such a marriage; but under all, trusting to Providence for better days.

James Dingle freely confessed how bad he'd acted; and Norah repeated over and over, it wasn't his wish she should work as she had;—but she would. The only excuse he could make was, the situation of his sisters; who, as every one knew, like himself, were quite dependent on his aunt for support. "And though," says he, "I'm strong and able, and could well keep them by the sweat of thy brow, they'd break their hearts in a month, after being brought up the way they have; and I was sure my aunt would turn them out, the day I owned to marrying Norah. But that's but a poor plea for me:—I should have looked to my wife first;—I feel it here!" says he, striking his breast, "I'm a good-for-nothing scoundrel, and them that doesn't despise me is a'most a bad as myself. I made up my mind how I'd act, coming down the crags, with the child smiling up like an angel of goodness in my face, and so telling me, in that mute way, to repent and do right, without more delay. I determined on this, before Father Killala spoke to me;—believe it or no, which way you please.—Norah, I'll go home with you, and in your own little cabin ask your forgiveness; next, I'll beg that of my sisters, who, I suppose, will be sent to me at once;—I begged it from above long ago. Aunt, after the poor return I've made to you for all you did for me and mine before now, it's useless to ask grace of you for myself, I suppose; but my knees wouldn't be stiff, if I thought I could, by entreating, obtain a continuance of your bounty to them who hav'n't offended you;—of course, I mane my sisters. Whether or no, aunt, I'll always be grateful; and do as you will, I'll not repine."

But James Dingle's aunt didn't mind what her nephew said, and wouldn't even listen to Father Killala, but raved and stormed with such violence, that every one thought her passion must soon blow over; but the more she blustered, the better she seemed to be for it. Bat Boroo got his big stick and retired to the rear, seemingly a little frightened or so; Duck Davie rubbed the palms of his hands together, and felt delighted to see the ould lady in such a pucker,—no doubt he did; Mick Maguire stood leaning upon the muzzle of his gun, staring with wonder at her chin going up and down at such a rate; and Luke Fogarty poked his bull's horn as near as he well could to her mouth, to pick up as much of her discourse as his deafness would let him.

At last, as all things must have an end, young Dingle's aunt stopped talking; but without being a bit more contented than when she began. Just then, little Norah knelt down before her, and with tears in her eyes asked, would she forgive her nephew, if she (Norah) left the place for ever with her baby, and wint away to such parts, that none who knew her should ever see sight of her more.

But James Dingle and Ileen stepped up to the little Dillosk–woman as soon as the words were out of her mouth; and one at one side, and one at the other, they raised her up.

"I can't agree to that," says James Dingle.

"No; nor I,—nor any woman here," says Ileen.

"I don't reproach you, Norah," continued James, "for offering to leave me;—but I won't allow it. It's now, perhaps for the first time, I feel how very dear you are to me. I'll give up all for you,—all, Norah; and it's much I shall be in your debt even then."

"The whole that I've to say about the matter, Mrs. Dingle, is this," quoth Ileen; "you've no right to look down upon Norah though she's poor and a Catholic, bekase you're rich and a Protestant: for you were poor yourself, before your husband, that's dead, turned tithe–proctor; and your own uncle is now Coadjutor to the Parish–Priest of Ballydalough. There's not one belonging to you can say his grandfather ever had two chimneys to his house, or more than would buy a day's dinner in his pocket:—that I needn't tell you though, for you know it well enough, Mrs. Dingle. The buttermilk blood will shew itself; but you sha'n't trample upon Norah Cavanagh, while I, that's her own mother's second cousin, can get within a mile of her. She comes of a good family, Mrs. Dingle, and if you won't be a mother to he I will!—I couldn't look upon her while every one had a right to think she'd disgraced herself; but now she's proved to be what she ought, I restore her to my heart."

"Ah! why not be good humoured thin at once?" says Mick Maguire to the aunt; "make no more wry faces at the pill; but, though it's bitter, swallow it at once: why not thin, eh?—and don't be a fool!—If you make any more noise about it, I'll fire away all the powder I have to drown your voice."

"I'll not have my aunt insulted, Mick," says James Dingle: "neither by you, nor any one:—and I'd be better pleased with Ileen had she said less."

"I'm not one for asking lave what I shall say, before I spake, or begging pardon for what I've spoke, James Dingle;" replied Ileen.

"That's true," observed her husband, ould Malachi Roe, in a remarkably positive tone.

Mrs. Dingle seemed to have a mind to begin again, when who should walk up to the place where the people were standing, but my lady from The Beg, leaning upon the arm of Pierce Veogh!—Mick Maguire let off his gun for joy at the sight; the piper played a merry jig; Father Killala and James Dingle shook hands with Pierce, and welcomed him heartily; and almost every body felt delighted: for Pierce, with all his faults, was much loved for many things;—chiefly, though, because he was born among us, and had been unfortunate.

"Thank God!" says he, as soon as he was let speak; "Thank God! I'm here among my people once more; and able to stand a free man on my own ground again. For clearing me of all my miseries,—for recalling me to the right path,—for restoring me to the house of my forefathers,—I am indebted to my wife." The beautiful lady who still kept her arm in his, blushed, and held down her head, as be spoke these words. "My last creditor," continued Pierce, "that rascally mushroom, Mick Purcell, was forced to give me a full acquittance this morning; an hour after that we were married: but it's only since Mr. Dax returned to The Beg with his nephew, that I heard what had happened; and it grieves me to find any one about me wretched at such a time as this. Mrs. Dingle, I don't like to boast of my few good deeds; but, I believe, on one occasion, I had it in my power to grant you an important favour;—did I refuse?"

Mrs. Dingle burst into tears, but made no reply.

"I understand you object to your nephew's choice, little Norah here, because she's a Catholic. My wife," continued Pierce, "was a Protestant; I, as you know, am not: but, with her, the difference of our creeds was no bar to our union."

Well—as I often say—to make a long story short, at last and in the long run, what with Father Killala's preaching, and Pierce Veogh's entreating, and his beautiful lady's winning smiles, and the tears of proud little Norah, James Dingle's aunt agreed to make it up with her nephew. Instead of going home with Norah that night to her own little mud cabin, he took her away to his aunt's house; and she has ever since lived upon good terms with the ould woman, and her nieces to boot.

Pierce Veogh had intended to have made no noise about his wedding that day; but to have kept open house at The Beg, from the next morning, for a whole week. However, as he'd shewn himself to the people, and reconciled his richest tenant to the marriage of her nephew with one of the poorest on the whole domain,—though there never was a better, except my lady, and few so good, upon it as little Norah,—he couldn't but ask every body to come home with him and make merry a little.

And it's merry enough they made themselves, as I can bear witness, for I was among them. They couldn't well get on with out me; so Mick Maguire, and Bat Boroo, with Corney Carolan, and a whole fratarnity of them, came down to fetch me up to The Beg in pomp. But, bad luck to them!—They would have broke my neck if I hadn't a little thought for myself; for they 'd a cup of the crature inside them before they started, and what should they propose but to knock out the head of a large empty cask that had been washed ashore close to my cabin that day week, and, as I couldn't walk, to roll me in it, over and over, right up to The Beg! This, of course, I couldn't allow; but, as there was no other vahicle to be had, I consented,—if they 'd bore square holes through the two ends of the cask, and get a pole to fit them,—to bestride it. So they did as I hinted, and away I wint, with the piper playing before me, and two or three o' them, under Bat Boroo's command, carrying me, straight off to The Beg; where I emptied so many piggins o' pothien to the health of my neighbours, that I know no more how or when I got home, than the man in the moon.

THIRD COURSE:

MY COUSIN'S CLIENTS

MY COUSIN'S CLIENTS

INTRODUCTION

AS executor to my cousin, an attorney who had resided for upwards of thirty years in old Furnival's Inn, it became my duty to look over a quantity of his papers, in order to elucidate some important transactions, to which he had alluded in his will. The mass of documents was too weighty to admit of a removal; and, for some time after his decease, a variety of circumstances prevented me from devoting a morning to their examination at his chambers. At length, the feast of St. Swithin arrived:—the morning was ushered in, as is usually the case, with low and gloomy clouds; and at noon, a heavy shower, of several hours' duration, began to fall. The rain compelled me to abandon the business which I had intended to have done that day, and nothing of interest pressed for my attention at home. I lost an hour in going, alternately, to every window of the house; and, at the expiration of that time, as no symptoms of a change were perceptible, —Furnival's Inn being not far distant,—I resolved on passing the remainder of the morning at my late lamented cousin's chambers. So little inclination, however, had I for my task, that I should scarcely have had courage enough to sally forth in the rain, had I not felt a strong presentiment of an approaching visit from two respectable, but very prosing old ladies,—the poppies of every party in which they appeared,—who invariably took advantage of very wet days, to visit such of their acquaintance as were frequently from home; because, as they said, with some truth, scarcely any one was then out but themselves. Under a laudable fear of the heavy influence which these respectable old gentlewomen would have on my spirits, during such a remarkably dull day, and knowing, from past experience, that when they came, they usually stayed to dine, I glode forth, "like sparkle out of brode," without saying a word to any body; took a hearty lunch at a coffee–house; hurried towards Furnival's Inn; and, at five o'clock, was jocosely reported, to the two old ladies whose visit I had anticipated, as being, notwithstanding the wetness of the day, "absent without leave."

ADAM BURDOCK

ALTHOUGH a very plodding man of business, during the summer and autumn of his life, my cousin Adam had been rather wayward in his youth. After the completion of his articles of clerkship, in the office of an eminent firm in the Temple, he oscillated, for several months, between Mount Parnassus and the Temple of Justice. During that period, he made out a *catalogue raisonné* of above three hundred authors,—most of them men of considerable eminence,—who had deserted law for literature and my cousin Adam would, perhaps, have followed their example, had not a young lady whom he loved,—and of whose taste and judgment he entertained a very high opinion,—treated a copy of verses, composed by him in her praise, and which he considered his poetical *chef–d'uvre*, not merely with coolness, but positive contempt. Her sneers at his rhapsody were so galling, that he set his face for ever against love and literature,—lived an attorney, and died a bachelor.

A good hand at making out bills of costs is an invaluable acquisition to a legal practitioner; a superior statement of charges being, in fact, a concise but clear history, subdivided into items, of the suit to which it refers. Adam Burdock's attendance books were masterly performances in this respect: almost every action, or legal affair, was, as I discovered during my examination of his papers, an interesting little romance; and there appeared to be much of that quality which is, by many modern writers, termed poetry, in the law. My cousin's bills frequently contained moral, as well as pecuniary charges against his clients: for the sake of being explicit, he was evidently compelled, on many occasions, to envelop an accusation in a formal debit. All attornies, as I have since been told, labour, more or less, under this disadvantage: a man acts wisely, therefore, in keeping his legal adviser's bill "aloof from public eye;" it is often a record of follies and offences, for which, perhaps, after they are passed, he blushes and repents. A precise, old–fashioned solicitor's ledger would form a capital volume for the study of human nature: the characters of his clients, their whims, their frailties and their sins, are accurately unfolded in its pages; the sources and consequences of events may therein, without difficulty, be traced; the gradations of a spendthrift, from opulence to penury, are finely marked by the progressive venues from Bond Street to the Bench, in which the attendances against him are laid; and a wholesome moral may, very often, be found in the concluding items of a lawyer's bill.

My cousin Adam's draft sketches of costs, the elaborate marginal memoranda which he had made on them, apparently, for his own amusement,—being, perhaps, under the influence of the *cacoethes* which, in his younger days, he had "scotch'd, not kill'd,"—and the documents to which such sketches and memoranda referred, afforded data for the following tales. Should they prove deficient in interest to the reader, I must either have erred in selecting, or failed in narrating them; for many of my cousin's papers, and especially his briefs, were to me such amusing details of matters of fact, that, for the first time in my life, I heartily enjoyed a wet Saint Swithin's day.

THE MATHEMATICIAN

"A GLORIOUS morning, Hassell," said a spruce middle–aged man, as he walked up one side of the old square of Furnival's Inn, with a small valise under his arm, to a short, pale, elderly gentleman, who was listlessly strolling, in a morning gown, slippers, and velvet cap, on the opposite pathway, and in a contrary direction;—"a glorious morning as ever was seen,—bright—clear—but by no means sultry:—an excellent morning, I protest, and just to my taste."

"Why, sir," replied the pale old gentleman, "I must say it's fine country weather; and, I dare swear, delightful to you, who are just on the brink of quitting the miserable metropolis until the morrow of All Souls."

"No, no," interrupted the first speaker, in a brisk tone; "I shall only be away a month; Trout and Thomas is appointed at bar early in the term, and I must he home after the first three days of pheasant shooting to marshal my evidence. I've a *subpna duces tecum* to produce the papers in Wagstaff's commission at the Cornwall assizes;—*that* carries me clear to Bodmin: and I'm going on a visit to an old client, who lives but eleven miles further; so that the costs out of pocket of my autumnal rustication, this year, will be but a flea–bite."

"Ah! thou'rt a fortunate fellow," said Hassell, with a sigh; "here have I been tied by the leg, ever since Trinity term, with annoyances growing out of Joshua Kesterton's will; and fine weather makes me rabid, because I can't go into the country to enjoy it. Adam Burdock and I will now be the only two principals left in the Inn, except bed–ridden Bailey and poor mad Boyston."

"Burdock does not ruralize, I believe."

"Not he: and if he had a mind so to do, he couldn't just now for he's shackled with the same case as myself."

"But can't you meet each other half–way, and close it at once?"

"Impossible:—it's such an Augean stable, that a regiment of attornies, with a legal Hercules at their head, could not do the needful in a night. We can't get at the facts,—at least we could not until within these few days; and the results of our investigations are so unexpected and staggering, that Adam and I,—and, indeed, all parties concerned,—are well nigh paralysed. Such a case has not come under my cognizance for years: if you were not in such a hurry I'd surprise you."

"I'm not pressed,—not at all. I share a chaise with another witness who picks me up in his way from the city; so I have only to keep my eye on the gates:—pray step across."

"No, hang it! the sun shines there; see how it exposes the clefts and time–worn face of the building, so that the entire side of the Inn looks as though it were in the last stage of decrepitude: it even makes *you* look ten years older than you say you are, friend Waters. An elderly man should always walk in the shade."

"What whims and fancies!" said Waters, stepping lightly across the square. "You're the strangest fellow!—but come, your case, in a few words."

"Thus it is with us, then;—excuse me, but even in the shade you look really past the figure you put yourself at:—let me see, fifty–four, isn't it?"

"Forty–seven! my good fellow! What the deuce—"

"Rely upon it you're labouring under a mistake: it's full thirty years since I first met you in Jay's writ of right.—Speaking of you, I should say, in defiance of verbal statement founded on memory,—which is treacherous, I find, with regard to age, when we are getting grey,—but judging from the date written by the hand of time on the face of the deed, in wrinkles as crabbed as court–hand—"

"I'm sixty. Well, well, be it so; and now for your case."

"No, Waters, you are not sixty; because if you were, by my reckoning, I should be sixty–seven, which I am not: but to resume. This is our case:— Joshua Kesterton came to London with no character, and nothing but a penny loaf in his pocket. Good luck threw him in the way of the well– known Paul Winpennie: Paul had compassion on him, and raised him, by degrees, from an errand boy in his office, to first clerk; and, at last, took him in as joint partner in all his concerns. After some time, Paul retired to enjoy a splendid ease for the rest of his life. At the end of five years, he discovered a secret, namely, that an immense quantity of leisure was the worst stock a mercantile man could possibly have on hand he was suddenly seen in the city again: whether he was not so keen as when he left it, or men had grown keener during his retirement, I know not; but Paul Winpennie, under whose touch every thing used to turn into gold, made ducks and drakes of his money; and, by half–a–dozen unlucky, or, as the world says, mad–cap speculations, was reduced from affluence to comparative beggary."

"Well, all this occurs every day, Hassell," said Waters.

"Ay, ay; but these are only preliminary facts."

"Unfortunately—"

"Hold your tongue, and hear me out. Well, the inquest jury—I omitted to say he was found dead one morning in his room;—the inquest jury returned a verdict of 'died by the visitation—'"

"But I thought it was generally believed that he died of a broken heart, produced by grief."

"We have nothing to do with broken hearts and grief, as a man of your standing on the rolls ought to feel; we can only be governed by the record. But if the coroner's return had been *felo de se*, there would have been little for the crown to take but his wife; and she, I think, from all I know of her, would have been deemed an incumbrance, by most people; although she soon got another husband."

"What! pauper as she was?"

"I said no such thing: if you interrupt me, I shall punish you by being prolix. Joshua Kesterton departed this life very shortly after his friend and benefactor, Winpennie, and, in a spirit of gratitude to the founder of his fortune, bequeathed a legacy of ten thousand pounds to Paul's widow."

"Bravo!"

"No, sir, it was not 'bravo!'—he acted like an ass; for his own daughter, whom he left residuary legatee, was beggared by the bequest. Partly through his own ignorance of the actual state of his affairs,—partly through unexpected but apparently valid claims, made on his estate after his death, and the failure of a firm, who were his principal creditors,— when we obtained a tolerable insight to his affairs, we discovered that, after satisfying the creditors, and paying the, legacy to Mrs. Winpennie, which, you perceive, was a positive bequest, whereby she had a clear claim of priority over his residuary legatee, the poor girl, instead of having, as her father doubtlessly expected, a fine fortune, will scarcely get enough to pay for her mourning."

"A bad case," said Waters; "but won't Mrs. Winpennie do something for the girl?"

"That's a riddle which I can't solve," said Hassell; "for, before she had an opportunity to do so, or, in fact, before she knew that her legacy would make a skeleton of the estate, she got snapped up by a young fellow, who says he's a Dane, but whom I suspect to be a Kerryman. From all I learn, he doesn't feel disposed to forego a farthing; and, as the woman married him without a settlement, he can do as he pleases, you know, with the money, when he gets it. I sincerely wish it may be soon, so that I can get out of town. The investigation of the claims of the principal creditors for whom I am concerned, is now within an ace of being concluded. As soon as the executors get our releases, of course, this gentleman, as he calls himself, who tarried the widow Winpennie, will insist on the full legacy; and however well inclined our friend Burdock, and his clients the executors, may be towards the poor girl, who, I must tell you, was married into a mighty high, but very, poor family, before her father's death, I can't see how they can help her. By George! here she comes,—I dare say, on a visit to Burdock,—and without her husband! That's odd. Poor thing! I'd rather not seem to see her. Let us cross over, and I'll stroll with you to the gate way.—Don't stare at her, and I'll be obliged to you."

The two attorneys walked to the other side of the square, and the lady passed hastily down the Inn towards Burdock's chambers. As she ascended the staircase she heard him speaking, in rather a tender tone, at the door of his office, apparently, to some person who was taking leave of him; and, on reaching the first landing–place, she met a female, attired in a very gaudy manner, and altogether of rather singular appearance, whose handkerchief was held to her eyes as though she were weeping, or desirous of concealing her face. When his fair client reached the office door, which still remained open, Burdock was pacing to and fro within, evidently much vexed and agitated.

"Are you alone, Mr. Burdock?" timidly inquired the lady, after she had stood at the door for a short time without being able to attract the notice of the attorney.

"My dear madam, I ask a thousand pardons," replied Burdock, advancing towards her; "I have been so annoyed that—Did you meet a lady in sulphur and sky–blue?"

"I did, sir: she appeared to be in tears."

"Ah! poor woman! she is much to be pitied; and yet, I protest, her appearance is so questionable, that I sincerely regret that the unhappy state of her affairs led her to pay me a visit. Had she not brought a letter, which I hold in my hand, from a most respectable friend in the country, I should certainly have scrupled to receive her. She's very unfortunate, though, I declare."

"But what are her griefs to mine, sir?"

"My dear Mrs. Wyburn, as I have often told you, bad as your case is, there are thousands who would deem your situation a state of bliss compared with what they suffer. Here, for instance, is this poor woman, forty years of age, at least weak enough to come to me with paint on her cheeks, and dressed in blue and brimstone, but with acute feelings, notwithstanding her folly, who marries a man for love, and, in a few day after the ceremony, is deserted and robbed by him of what should have supported her in old age."

"Wretched woman! like me, then, she is a beggar, I suppose!" said Mrs. Wyburn.

"I fear the poor creature is almost penniless, indeed:—her business with me was to receive a small sum, which my friend, from whom she brought the letter I hold, had confided to me three years ago, to invest for her. I placed it in the hands of your late lamented father; and she holds his note for the amount: but we can't pay her. If she had not told me she had a husband in whom the title now vested, having had no notice from him of the marriage, she must, of course, have had her money:—but now it's impossible. And the woman implored me so not to let her starve, that, in order to pacify and get rid of her, I have been compelled to request her to call again; for which I am now most heartily sorry. I feel ashamed to have her seen go out of my office. But, odso! my dear madam! how is it that I see you alone?—Where is your husband?"

"In prison!"

"At whose suit?"

"In truth, I cannot tell: it is enough for me to know that he is a prisoner, and that I do, not possess the means of setting him at liberty. Kind Mr. Burdock, will you still listen to me?— Will you give me your counsel?"

"I am grieved — heartily grieved," said Burdock; "but I really feel at a loss how to advise—how to benefit you."

"Oh! you can—you can, indeed; or, if you cannot, there is none on earth who will. You know not half of my distresses. I am a thousand–fold more wretched than you imagine. Pity me, sir;—pity me, and I will pray for you."

"I do pity you, most sincerely," said Burdock, considerably affected; "but let me implore you to be calm."

"I will be calm as marble, sir. I have told you my husband is in prison, without shedding a tear;—and now, without a sigh, I will tell you, that my sorrows are of such a nature that I cannot—dare not—must not breathe a hint to him of what I suffer."

"You positively alarm me, my dear madam. I cannot imagine you to have been guilty of any imprudence: and if not, what is there that a wife devotedly attached, as I know you are, to her husband, cannot confide to his bosom?"

"Oh! much, much, Mr. Burdock. I have no friend,—none in the world, to whom I can tell my afflictions, but you; and I have no claim on you to hear them: you have endured too many vexations, in your struggles for my welfare, already."

"I regret that no better success has attended my poor endeavours, Mrs. Wyburn; but, believe me, that as far as prudence will allow, my best exertions are still at your service."

"Then you will hear and advise me?"

"I will, as I hope for mercy, to the best of such judgment as I am endowed with."

"Oh! thank you, thank you!—on my knees I will thank you."

"Nay, nay! I must not be repaid thus: I shall charge the consultation in my bill, and I hope you will one day pay it," said the attorney, with a smile. "Come, again let me entreat you to be calm."

"I am sure I shall be so:—I have overcome the bitterness of bringing my mind to tell you my little tale, and I feel capable of doing so properly. Your kindness gives me additional courage and self–command. I shall endeavour to restrict myself to simple facts, and I will go through the task, unless my heart break in the attempt. Are we free from interruption?"

"Entirely so; my clerks are both out, and I will answer no one until you have done."

"Then I will begin at once. I solemnly enjoin you, sir, not to reveal what I am about to tell you to any mortal; for, alas! It concerns my husband's honour, —nay, even his life. Much as he loves me, I think he would deprive me of existence, rather than let me make you acquainted with his weakness,—I will say his crime: but as it may save us both from being even more wretched than we are, I will trust it to your ear. When George Wyburn married me, he knew I had considerable expectations, and, therefore, did not demand a settlement. My poor father allowed us a handsome income, while he lived; George was high–spirited and gay, but not extravagant; and we had enough, —nay, something to spare, after our yearly expenses were paid, until within a few months before my father's death, when a sad and sudden change came over us. At Harrowgate, my husband,—heaven knows how,—formed an acquaintance with a man, who, after a short time, was our constant visitor and George's bosom friend. In three months, under the influence of his associate, my husband became a gambler and a duellist! He was still kind to me, and I concealed his faults from my father; vain were all my attempts to reclaim him: I had lost my power of persuading him, but yet I feel sure he loved me. I now bitterly lament my folly in keeping his proceedings a secret from my father; for he went on in his evil ways. At last the climax arrived: he lost more than he could pay; and, unable to bear up against the dishonour which his default would have brought upon him, he abruptly quitted Harrowgate with a determination to destroy himself. He wrote to his new friend, stating that, ere the letter reached its destination, he should be numbered with the dead. He declared that he felt unable to address his poor wife; but he warmly recommended her to the care of him to whom he wrote, and begged that her unfortunate husband's fate might be revealed to her as gradually as possible. The wretch came to me as he was desired: he told me a little, and I learnt the rest from the letter which George had sent him. Accompanied by this man, I made all possible haste to the place whence George had written. I found him alive and unhurt. His pistols were lying on the table before him, when I rushed into the room, and he was writing to me: he could not leave the world without bidding me an eternal adieu! He had lingered over the paper, which was damped by his tears; but, from the language of the sentence which he was penning when we entered, his resolution to destroy himself seemed to have been unshaken; and I am convinced that, had we not arrived sooner than he expected, and had not his heart urged him to assure me that he loved and blessed me in his last moments, I should that day have been a widow. He embraced and wept over me, but blushed before his friend, and seemed dreadfully enraged at our arrival. When I, at length, succeeded in soothing him a little, he asked my companion to advise him how he ought to act. The reply I can never forget. It was this:—'Why, truly, Mr. Wyburn, after having stated that you were going to commit suicide, there is but one course to save your reputation, namely,—to keep your word: but as I suppose no one but myself, except your wife, is acquainted with the circumstance, no doubt you will see the wisdom of suffering certain notions, which, perhaps, are rather too rigorously attended to, in some quarters, giving place to the dictates of religion, et cetera;—that is, if you feel satisfied that I can be depended on to keep your secret.' 'Will you swear to do so?' asked my husband. 'Nay,' replied the other, 'if you doubt me, you have your remedy. Were I capable of wronging my friend, I surely should not be prevented from, so doing by the comparatively cobweb fetters of a private oath.' Subsequently, I prevailed upon him, by reproaches and entreaties, to promise me solemnly that he would relinquish all thoughts of carrying his fatal resolution into effect: but he made the most solemn vow, that if either I or his friend betrayed the weakness, or, to use his own words, the cowardice he had shewn, in not completing what he had meditated, he should certainly blow out his brains the first opportunity; for he never could exist under the idea that he was the laughing–stock of the world. Summoning up his fortitude, he returned with us to Harrowgate: and in a few days, a portion of what he had lost at the gaming table was paid; for the remainder, he gave bonds payable on the death of my father; and I firmly believe he has never touched the dice–box since."

"Then I am glad to say all seems to have ended more happily than could have been expected," observed Burdock.

"Not so, sir,—not so, indeed," replied Mrs. Wyburn; "that fatal friend still hovers near him;—my husband still hugs the snake that destroys while he embraces him. Those gambling debts, I am certain, were contracted by my husband with the villain's confederates."

"Then the bonds have been, at length, put in force against him?"

"They have; and I now owe my husband's loss of liberty, as I once almost did the loss of his life, to the machinations of Blennerhagen?"

"Blennerhagen!" exclaimed the attorney, considerably surprised; "you surely do not mean our Mr. Blennerhagen,—he who married Paul Winpennie's widow!"

"He is the man," replied Mrs. Wyburn: "he obtained an introduction to Mrs. Winpennie by means of my husband. Foolish as she is, and lucky as she has been; in one respect,—alas! to my sorrow,—I sincerely pity her; for miserable will be her fate. She is linked to a calm, determined villain, who entertains no spark of affection for her: the possession of my poor father's legacy, and not her person, was his object in marrying her."

"And how do you know this, my dear madam?"

"Oh, Sir, Blennerhagen has thrust his confidence upon me, and I have been compelled to listen to him. Unhappily, he has, or pretends to have, a passion for me; and I have endured the confession from his own lips. He has boldly told me, that, had George committed suicide, he should have offered me his hand, as soon as decency would have permitted him to do so. You find, sir, that I am as good as my word: I tell you this without a blush or a tear, while *you* shudder!"

"Shudder! ay, and I well may. Thou dost not blush or weep, indeed, my poor young sufferer; but thy cheek is deathly pale, and thy eyes seem burning in their sockets. I beseech you, let us postpone this."

"Nay, nay, pray hear me to an end: I have brought my courage to bear it all; if I relapse, I cannot work upon myself to go through the ordeal again."

"But why not unmask this villain—this hypocrite—this wolf?"

"Your honest indignation makes you forget that my husband's life is in his power. That fatal letter, which George wrote to him when he quitted Harrowgate with a determination to commit suicide, is still in the possession of Blennerhagen; I saw him take it from his pocket–book but two days ago, although he protests to George that it is destroyed: and the publication of it would, I fear, hurry my husband to self–destruction at once. I know George's temper so well, that I tremble at the idea of incurring so great a risk; and yet what else to do I know not; for the demon, after persecuting me in vain, for months, now holds that hand–writing before my eyes, and dares me to be virtuous!"

"The monster! I will move mountains, but he shall be defeated,—ay, and punished."

"Thank you, thank you! — my heart thanks you: I knew your will would be good: but, alas! I doubt your power. You know not with whom you have to deal. Blennerhagen prides himself on being impregnable: he talks to me of working like a mathematician: he says that all his plans are laid down with such geometrical precision that they cannot fail. He has thrown such a magic web about me, that I have felt my if to be almost his slave; and yet, thank heaven, I am innocent and loathe him. Save me, Mr. Burdock!—but not at the expense of my husband's life: save me, I implore you!—I have no other friend."

"I will save—I will extricate you, if it be in the power of man. I have worked like a negro for my money, and may soon be past working, and want it. I have debarred myself of every indulgence; but I can—I will afford to gratify my feelings, for once in my life, even at the risk of diminishing some of my hard–earned little hoard. Mrs. Wyburn, I'll back myself, if need be, with a thousand pounds, and,—confound the fellow,—have at him! Excuse me for swearing; but I'm warmed, and feel a pleasure in indulging—"

"Be temperate, sir, in your proceedings, lest you forget that next to my own innocence, my husband's life—"

"Do not fear, madam. Is Mr. Wyburn in prison, or at a lock–up house?"

"At the lock–up house, sir, in Serle's Buildings."

"Then I'll bail him. Hassell may laugh at me, when he hears that I have stepped out of my cautious path, if he likes; but I'll begin by bailing Wyburn: for his liberty, at this time, is of the utmost value. Within a few days the great struggle will come on, which must settle the main question between Hassell's clients and the executors: on the fortunate result of that depends your only hope; and a poor hope it is, I must confess: still, Wyburn should be at large to fight it out, and strive to the last. After to–day, I ought to be in hourly consultation with him.

"Blennerhagen knows all this; and, not expecting God would raise up such a friend to George, has caused him to be arrested. As he boasts of generally making his actions produce double results, he flatters himself, also, that I, being thus overwhelmed with this new misfortune, and deprived of the protecting presence of my husband,—"

"Curse him!—he shall be foiled! I won't put up with it, while I have breath!"

"I must tell you,—for, as you now have heard so much, you should know all,—that one of the threats or temptations he holds out to me, is this:—'Wyburn,' he says, 'will soon, in all probability, be entirely dependent on my bounty; for having, through my marriage with Mrs. Winpennie, an entire control over the ten thousand pounds legacy, which will, apparently, eat up the whole of your father's property, after payment of the debts, I can starve Wyburn, if I like.' This is a specimen of the language which he dares to use to me. Had I my jewels left, I could have raised a sufficient sum, perhaps, to procure George his liberty, without troubling you; but Blennerhagen obtained them from me long ago, without Mr. Wyburn's knowledge, by protesting that he had spent all he possessed to keep the bond holders quiet, and wanted money to enable him to make a figure before Mrs. Winpennie. I have been very weak and very foolish, you will say; but what could I do? Blennerhagen dares me to reveal a syllable of what passes at our interviews, to my husband: he tells me that he should instantly detect my treachery by George's conduct. I am forced to see—to hear him:—he is the worst of tyrants. If I strive to extricate myself from his wiles, I plunge deeper in his toils. To remain passive is to offer up myself a willing victim to a being, whom, of all others, I abhor. Could I have taken counsel of my husband, all might have been well: but I have not dared to breathe a word to him of my sorrows; and Blennerhagen well knows how to obtain advantages over a wife, deprived, as I have been, of her natural supporter."

"It shall be at an end, I tell you: Wyburn shall be bailed, and I'll try if *I* can't play off a few tricks. We'll countermine this scoundrel. I'll insure your husband's life for my security, and then, if he have so high a sense of honour as you think, he won't fix me as his bail by shooting himself; for I shall make him understand that the office won't pay, if the insured perishes by his own hands; so that we're safe until November: and, in the interim, I'll sacrifice a little to those feelings which laudable prudence has taught me, hitherto, to smother. It's hard if a man cannot make a fool of himself once in his life; and, should I lose my time and money both, humanity will be a plea for me, with my own conscience, and that of every honest man in the world. Besides, I'm only fifty, and shall not die a beggar if it comes to the worst, perhaps I will fulfil my promise, madam, be assured! Time is precious:—have you anything more to ask of me?"

"A glass of water," faintly replied Mrs. Wyburn; "a glass of water and a little air; for my strength is gone."

Burdock, with great alacrity, opened the little window of his room, and brought Mrs. Wyburn some water, in a broken cup, time enough to save her from fainting. Some one knocked at the outer door, and she almost immediately afterwards rose to depart. Burdock conducted her to the foot of the staircase, begging her to keep up her spirits, and protesting that he thought he should prove himself as good a mathematician as Blennerhagen: "for," added he, "I have dabbled in the science, and Euclid still affords me amusement in my hours of relaxation from legal business."

The person who had knocked at the office door just before Mrs. Wyburn's departure, was the bearer of a note from Blennerhagen's wife, in which she earnestly requested the favour of a consultation with Burdock, at her own house, on an affair of the utmost importance. The lady stated that she was confined to her room by indisposition, otherwise she would have paid him a visit in Furnival's Inn; and she protested that, if he did not so far indulge her as immediately to obey her summons, she would, at the risk of her life, wait upon him at his office.

"Paul Winpennie's choice was always a fool," muttered Burdock, as he threw the letter on his table, after having. perused its contents; "she was always fantastical, and apt to magnify atoms into elephants; but I don't think she would write me such an epistle as this, if something extraordinary had not occurred: ergo, I'll go to her at once. Perhaps I may glean something which may assist me in extricating Wyburn: I hope I shall; for though I have promised his wife so much, at this moment I can't see my way clear a single inch beyond my nose,—except so far as regards–bailing him, which I'll do as soon as I return. It is possible, that the woman has discovered something; for the most silly of her sex possess an astonishing acuteness on particular occasions. I may meet Blennerhagen with his wife, too:—at all events I'll go, and ponder on the way as to what proceedings I ought to take against this mathematical monster:—for act against him, I will; on that I'm fixed—that is—if I can find out a way to do so, with any prospect of success."

As Burdock concluded this little soliloquy, one of his clerks returned; and the old gentleman, without a moment's delay, set off towards Blennerhagen's house. On reaching the corner of the street in which it stood, he was accosted by a female, who begged him, in a very mysterious manner, to follow her.

"My good woman," said Burdock, "you are in error, I apprehend."

"Not if I am speaking to Mr. Burdock, and if you are going to Mrs. Blennerhagen," replied the woman.

"I certainly am that man," said Burdock; "and you are quite right in supposing that I am on my way to visit that lady:— what then?"

"Follow me and I will conduct you to her. I am her woman, and act by her orders."

"Mighty odd!" exclaimed the attorney; "but lead on;—I'll follow you. I suppose she has her reasons for this; and it matters but little to me which way I go, so that—mark me, woman— so that I am not led a dance: for though I walk slowly, on account of an infirmity in my kneel, time, I assure you, is precious to me. Go forward."

The woman immediately walked on towards a little back street, down which she proceeded a short distance, and then turned under an old arched gateway into a solitary yard. The buildings on one side of this place appeared, by a weather–beaten notice board, to have been long without tenants. Through a low wall, on the opposite side of the yard, there were entrance–doors to the back gardens of a range of respectable houses.

"I perceive," said Burdock, as the woman opened one of the garden doors, "that you are smuggling me in the back way.— Give my compliments to your mistress, and tell her, that I prefer entering in the ordinary manner. If you will step through the house, I dare say I shall be at the front door nearly as soon as you have opened it."

Burdock then turned on his heel, and strode away from his guide at rather a brisk pace. On reaching the front door, he found the woman there waiting for him. Casting on the old gentleman a look of reproach, and significantly putting her finger to her lips, she conducted him up stairs, and silently ushered him into Mrs. Blennerhagen's dressing–room. The lady, who was reclining on a sofa, attired in an elegant morning dress, rose as he entered; and, between jest and earnest, reproached him for not having given a more prompt attention to her note. Burdock protested that he had not been guilty of the least delay in obeying her commands.

"Well, well!" said the lady, "perhaps I am wrong; but to a woman of my nerves, suffering at once under indisposition, and the most agonizing suspense, every moment seems to be an age."

"What's the matter, madam?" inquired Burdock. "Where is Mr. Blennerhagen?"

"Thank Heaven! he is out:—my anxiety has been intense lest you should not arrive before he returned. My dear Mr. Burdock, I'm in the greatest distress."

"Then, upon my honour and conscience, madam, I don't see how I can be of any assistance to you; for my hands are so full of female distress just now—"

"Oh, sir!—but not such pressing—such important distress as mine. Recollect that I'm a wife;—a wife, Mr. Burdock, and not altogether indifferent to my husband."

"Well, madam! there are many wives who can say quite as much, I assure you.—But now for your facts: I am bound to hear, even if I cannot assist you."

"Ah! you're a kind—a dear old gentleman:—I always said so, and now I find that I am right. You have a heart formed to sympathize with those who are in sorrow."

"The world thinks rather differently of me," replied Burdock "my feelings, I know by experience, will bear as much as most men's. Business, madam,—business has hardened them:—but, allow me to ask, what has occurred? You seem to have been ruffled."

"Do I?" said Mrs. Blennerhagen, turning to a looking–glass which stood on the table by her side, and glancing at the reflection of her still lovely face, with a look of anxiety. "Well, now I see myself, I declare I'm quite frightened. I positively look like a hag! don't I?—I ought not to suffer such trifles to affect me so severely."

"Trifles, my dear madam!" emphatically exclaimed the attorney: "I beg your pardon; but I was led to understand, from the tenor of your language—"

"Attribute it to the excess of my womanly fears,—increased, perhaps, by indisposition,—and excuse me. We are weak creatures, as you must know; even the very best of us are agitated into agony, by phantoms of our own creation. My suspicions—"

"Am I summoned to advise you on suspicion, then?"

"Nothing more, I assure you: and, really, I ought to be ashamed to entertain, for one instant, so poor an opinion of Mr. B.'s taste; and, permit me to say it, of my own person. Now I reflect, it was exceedingly wrong of me, perhaps, to be jealous of the woman."

"I wish, with all my heart, madam, you had reflected an hour ago."

"Would that I had! I should have been saved much—much uneasiness:— but I now laugh at my fears," said the lady, affecting to titter.

"I am sorry I cannot join you, madam."

"Ah, Mr. Burdock! I know the interest you take in my happiness; and, therefore, I sent for you to advise,—to comfort me. I look up to you as to my father."

"You do me an honour, Mrs. Blennerhagen, to which I never had an idea of aspiring."

"The honour is entirely on my side, Mr. Burdock," replied the lady, taking one of Burdock's hands in both her own; "I feel proud to be permitted to make free with so worthy and respectable a character. My confidence in you is unbounded, Mr. Burdock: you see, I receive you in my dressing–room—"

"For mine own part," interrupted the attorney, "I should have preferred the parlour; and so, most probably, would Mr. Blennerhagen."

"Don't talk so foolishly, Mr. Burdock: — attorneys, like physicians, are privileged persons, you know."

"True, true, madam," said Burdock, rather hastily quitting his seat; "and now, the cause of our conference is at an end, I will take my leave."

"My dear sir, you surely are not going to quit me in this state:—you have not heard my complaint."

"I thought your mind was easy on the subject."

"Oh! by no means! I am far from soothed,—far from tranquillized: your discrimination may shed a new light upon my mind. I must insist on throwing myself upon your consideration."

"For consistency's sake, don't blow hot and cold in the same moment, Mrs. Blennerhagen. Be in a rage, or be pacified: and if I must hear your tale of woe, the sooner you tell it the better."

"You'll promise not to call me a silly, foolish woman, then, if you think my apprehensions were groundless."

"Of course, madam, I should scarcely call a lady a fool to her face, even if I thought she deserved it."

"How deeply I am indebted to you!—you cannot conceive how much the cast of your countenance, when you look pleasant, reminds me of my late excellent husband,—poor Mr. Winpennie! —Alas! I never was jealous of him, with or without a cause. He was the best—the kindest—"

"Excuse me, madam; but, however I may reverence the memory of Mr. Winpennie, my time is of too much value, and too seriously engrossed just now, by my duties towards the living, to listen to an eulogy on the dead."

"Well! no doubt you are perfectly right: the value of your time, I know, must be great. In a few words, then, about two hours ago, my servant acquainted me that there was a strange–looking creature inquiring at the door for Mr. Blennerhagen: she was painted up to the eyes, and dressed in a vulgar amber–coloured pelisse, with staring sapphire ribbons—"

Burdock here interrupted the lady, by exclaiming, "Hang me if it isn't the woman in brimstone and blue!" and bursting into a hearty laugh.

"Why, Mr. Burdock, you astonish me!" exclaimed Mrs. Blennerhagen; "I beseech you to cease;—my head will split;— you shatter my nerves to atoms. I insist upon your explaining yourself;—I shall scream if you don't cease laughing, and tell me the meaning of this mysterious conduct."

"Oh, madam!" replied Burdock, endeavouring to resume his gravity, "do not be alarmed at that unhappy creature:—I sent her here."

"Is it possible, Mr. Burdock, that a man of your respectability can have such acquaintance?"

"The woman is not what she appears, Mrs. Blennerhagen. I saw her, for the first time in my life, to–day. Her business with me was briefly as follows:—About three years ago, a certain sum was remitted to me by a country attorney, for whom I act as agent, to invest for this woman; and I deposited it in the hands of Joshua Kesterton. Circumstances now compel her to call in her money; but a legal difficulty occurs in paying her off; and I referred her to Mr. Blennerhagen, who, in all probability, will be the party most interested in the matter; thinking that, as the sum was small, he might, perhaps, from motives of charity; relieve the woman's wretchedness, by waiving the legal objection at his own risk. Ha, ha! And so I have to thank the woman in sulphur and blue for my walk, eh?"

"Mr. Burdock, I vow, sir, that you overwhelm me with confusion: but if you were a woman, I am sure you would admit, that when a female of this lady's appearance makes such particular inquiries after a newly–married man, and refuses to tell her business to his wife—"

"Ha, ha, ha!" exclaimed the, attorney again; "that, too, I plead guilty of producing. I told her, that you had nothing to do with the matter: for that the legal estate was vested, by your marriage, in Blennerhagen. I am willing to acknowledge, that the circumstances were suspicious: and, as long as I live, be assured that I will never send a female, in a yellow and azure dress, to a married man again. Hoping you will forget the uneasiness which I have innocently brought upon you, I now, madam, beg permission to withdraw."

Burdock had risen from his chair, and was on the point of taking up, his hat and cane, when Mrs. Blennerhagen's servant entered the room, and said, in a hurried tone, that her master was at the street door.

"Then, I'll wait to see him," said Burdock, placing his hat and cane on the table again, and resuming his seat.

"Heavens, sir! are you mad?" exclaimed Mrs. Blennerhagen. "Unfortunate woman, that I am!—I did not expect him this half–hour. What is to be done, Wilmot?"

"Don't be alarmed, madam," replied the woman; "there's quite time enough for the gentleman to get into the cupboard."

"Is there no other resource left, Wilmot?

"None that I can see, madam!" replied the woman; "he'll meet master on the stairs if he goes down: and though there's time enough, there's no time to be lost. Sir," added she, taking up the attorney's hat and cane, "you'd better slip in at once."

"Slip in!" exclaimed Burdock; "why should I slip in?— What do you mean?"

"Don't speak so loud, sir: —master will hear you," said Wilmot.

"What do I care?" cried Burdock, in a stern tone; "are you out of your senses? Why should I hide like a galivanting beau in a farce?"

"Oh! the wretch! he'll be the ruin of my reputation!" exclaimed the lady.

"Reputation!—What have I to do with your reputation, Mrs. Blennerhagen?"

"This is my mistress's dressing-room, you see, sir."

"Well, you brought me here, woman: and if it is, as your mistress says,—attorneys, like physicians, are privileged persons?'

"Oh! he won't discriminate, Wilmot. Don't you know, you cruel man, that we can't blind others with what we blind ourselves? I am as pure as an angel; but appearance is every thing; and Mr. Blennerhagen is more jealous than a Turk."

"That I am sure he is, madam; for he doats on yon."

"And you, Mr. Burdock, will not be complaisant enough to save our connubial bliss from being wrecked for ever.—If you don't comply, I must scream out, and say you intruded yourself."

"Will you hear me speak?" cried the enraged attorney.

"Hark, how he bawls! And he knows well enough the wife of Cæsar must not even be suspected," said Mrs. Blennerhagen; "let the wretch ruin me;—do, Wilmot."

"Indeed I won't, not if I can help it. Come, sir, if you are a gentleman, prove yourself to be so."

"Bedlamites! will you hear me?—is not my character—"

"Oh! he is a bachelor attorney, and lives in chambers, Wilmot: and you know the character of that class of men is quite obnoxious in cases of reputation: but let him have his way; I must be his martyr, I see."

"Come, come, sir,—right or wrong, be civil to a lady."

"What, do you think I'll make a Jack-pudding of myself?"

"Stop his mouth, Wilmot: don't let him speak; for I hear the creak of Mr. Blennerhagen's boot."

The lady and her woman now seized on the astonished attorney, and thrust him into a closet. The door was instantly closed on him, and the key turned in the lock. Mrs. Blennerhagen returned to the sofa; and Wilmot was applying a smelling-bottle to her nose, bathing her brows, &c., as though she was just reviving from a fainting fit, when the majestic Blennerhagen entered the room.

With a keen and hurried glance he seemed to survey every object around him, while he closed the door: he then approached the sofa, and uttered a few endearing epithets while he relieved Wilmot from the task of supporting her mistress. Anxious to get rid of him, Mrs. Blennerhagen rapidly recovered; and her husband having, apparently by accident, mentioned that he had left a friend in the parlour, she urged him, by all means, to return to his guest, as she found herself comparatively well, and desirous of obtaining a little repose. Blennerhagen kissed her cheek; and after recommending her to the care of Wilmot, passed round the sofa to a writing-desk, which was placed on a table behind it, where he remained a few moments, and then hastily withdrew.

Mrs. Blennerhagen immediately resumed her activity. "Now, my dear Wilmot," said she, "our only hope is to get the attorney down the back stairs, and away through the garden."

"That is how I have settled it, madam, in my own mind," said the woman: "master won't be up again at least these ten minutes."

"If you have any pity, emancipate me from this state of torture," groaned poor Burdock: "I would face a roaring lion rather than remain here any longer; my reflections are most poignant."

"Gracious Heaven!" exclaimed Mrs. Blennerhagen, "I've lost the key?'

"Then, of course, you will permit me to burst open the door," said the attorney.

"Not on any account: be patient, I beseech you. Wilmot, where could I have put it!"

"I don't know, madam; you locked the door yourself: search in your bosom."

"I have; but it is not there:—nor on the sofa,—nor any where. You must have had it."

"Indeed, madam, I never saw it since you took it oft the shelf to lock the door.

"Women!" exclaimed Burdock, whose patience was completely worn out; "rash, mischievous, accursed women! take notice that I am become desperate; and if you do not find the key and release me instantly, I shall certainly break out, and depart, at all hazards."

"For all our sakes have patience, sir," said the lady, in a soothing tone; "be quiet but for a few moments: I hear Mr. Blennerhagen's boot again."

Before his wife could reach the sofa, Blennerhagen strode in, accompanied by a stranger.

"Outraged, injured, as I am," said he, fixing his dark eye indignantly on his wife, "I make no apology for thus introducing a stranger to your apartment. This gentleman is my friend, and comes here with me, at my own request, to be a witness of my shame; so that I may be able to obtain legal reparation, at least, from the unknown assassin of my happiness. Peterson," added he, turning to the stranger, "take the key and open that closet-door."

"Lord! Mr. Blennerhagen," said the lady, with a forced laugh; "don't carry on the joke, by making such serious faces: I told you, Wilmot, he would be too deep for us:—see, now, if he hasn't got the key. 'Where did you find it, love?"

"I took it, madam, from your hand," replied Blennerhagen, "when your mind was occupied in affecting a painful and languishing recovery from syncope. This may be a jest to you, but it is none to me; nor shall it be to him who has wronged me. I have set my mark upon the villain:—perceiving a portion of male attire, which I could not recognise as my own, hanging from the crevice of the closet-door, while I appeared to be busy at the desk behind you, I cut it off: I have it here," added Blennerhagen, producing a triangular piece of brown cloth from his pocket; "let the man who owns it claim it if he dare."

"Adam Burdock dares to claim his own in any place," exclaimed the attorney, bursting the door open with one furious effort: "that's a piece of the tail of my coat."

"Mr. Burdock!" exclaimed Blennerhagen.

"Ay, sir, Mr. Burdock,—heartily ashamed of himself, for being made a ninny by your wife, or a dupe by both of you and my precious friend, Mrs. Wilmot. You all look, astonished; but, be assured, there is no one here half so much astonished as myself. I believe you to be capable of anything, Blennerhagen; but, on a moment's consideration, I think your wife is too much of a simpleton to act as your confederate, in a plot on my pocket; and notwithstanding your skill in mathematics, I am willing to attribute all this to mere accident."

"He calls me a simpleton, Wilmot;—he casts a slur on my intellects, Mr. Blennerhagen," exclaimed the lady.

"In that he is more uncharitable than myself, madam," said Blennerhagen: "it may be an accident, it is true; but I question whether the gentleman, with all his professional skill, will be able to persuade a special jury to think so."

"I am sure my mistress is as innocent as the child unborn," observed Mrs. Wilmot.

"Hold your tongue, woman, and leave the room," said Blennerhagen, angrily.

"Indeed, I shall not leave the room," said Wilmot: "I'll stand by my mistress to the last, and won't leave her for you or anybody else. You're a couple of vile wretches; and there isn't a pin to choose between you."

"Oh! Wilmot, thou art thy poor heart–broken mistress's only friend, after all," sobbed Mrs. Blennerhagen; "she is the victim of circumstances and her own refined feelings."

"Peterson," said Blennerhagen, "I am under the unpleasant necessity of requesting you to remember all that you have just witnessed. You will agree with me, I think, that I ought to make this man quit my house before I leave it myself."

"Unquestionably," replied Peterson.

"I shall do no such thing," said Burdock; "conscious of my innocence, I defy you;—I laugh at you: and, before I quit this 'roof, I will make you wish you had sooner crossed the path of a hungry wolf than mine. I dare you to give me half an hour's interview."

"Ought I to do so, Peterson?" calmly inquired Blennerhagen.

"Not without a witness, I think," was the reply.

"With a score of witnesses, if you will," said Burdock:— "events have precipitated my proceedings: — with a score of witnesses, if you will. But mark me, man, you shall lament, if we are in solitude, that there will be still one awful witness of your villainy. I will unmask your soul; I will shew you to yourself, and make you grind your teeth with agony, unless you are, indeed; a demon in human form."

"Heavens! Mr. Burdock," exclaimed Mrs. Blennerhagen, "what can you have to say against my husband?"

"It matters not, madam; he shall hear me in this place, or elsewhere hereafter."

"I scorn your threats, sir," said Blennerhagen; "and publicly or privately, I will meet any accusation you may have to make against me."

"Privately be it, then, if you dare."

"Dare, sir! Leave the room every body:—nay, I insist;— Peterson and all. Now, sir," said Blennerhagen, closing the door after his wife, Wilmot, and Peterson, who, in obedience to his command, had left the room; "now, sir, we are alone, what have you to say?"

"Blennerhagen," said the attorney, fixing his keen eye on that of the Mathematician, "George Wyburn has been arrested."

"It is an event that has been long looked for. I am rather hurt that, in communicating with his friends on the subject, he should have given you a priority over myself. I lament to say that he has fallen into bad hands."

"He has," replied Burdock; " but I will endeavour to release him."

"I thank you on behalf of my friend," said Blennerhagen, with a malicious smile; "but I would suggest, with great humility, that you will find sufficient employment, at present, to extricate yourself."

"Sir," said Burdock, "I wanted but the key–note to your character: every word you utter is in unison with your actions."

"We are alone," said Blennerhagen, "and I can allow you to be vituperative. Detection renders you desperate: that philosophy which enables me to gaze calmly on the wreck of my own peace, teaches me, also, to bear with those who are so unfortunate as to be guilty. I would not personally bruise a broken reed: I cannot descend to chastise the man, who has injured me deeply, for an insult in words. The highwayman who has robbed us, may defame our characters with impunity; the lesser merges into the greater offence: we do not fly into a passion, and apply the cudgel to his back; we pity, and let the law hang him. If your hands were quite at liberty, pray what course would you adopt to benefit George Wyburn?"

"I am so far at liberty, I thank Providence," replied Burdock, "as to be able to bail him; and I mean to do so within an hour."

"You do?"

"Ay, sir, to the confusion of his enemies, as sure as I'm a sinner. You seem amazed."

"I am indeed,—to say the least,—surprised, and naturally delighted to find fortune should so unexpectedly raise him up a friend."

"I am rather surprised myself; but I'll do it, I'm determined, hap what will."

"It is truly grievous,—a matter of deep regret,—that I cannot fold you in my arms," said Blennerhagen. "How strange it is that the same bosom should foster the most noble and the basest of thoughts. In the human heart, the lily and the hemlock seem to flourish together. If it were possible that your offence against my honour could admit of palliation or forgiveness—but I beg pardon; I must be permitted to write a hasty line, on a subject of some importance, which, until this moment, I had forgotten. It is the miserable lot of man, that, in the midst of his most acute trials, he is often compelled to attend to those minor duties, the neglect of which would materially prejudice some of those about him. I shall still give you my attention.".

"Every syllable—every action of this man, now amazes me," said Burdock to himself, walking towards the window: "he almost subdues me from my purpose."

"I shall be entirely at your service in an instant," said Blennerhagen, advancing to the door with a note, which he had hastily written, in his hand: "I beg pardon,—oblige me by ringing the bell."

Burdock mechanically complied with his request; and Blennerhagen stepped outside the door to give his servant some directions, as Burdock conceived, relative to the note. During his brief absence, the attorney, acting either from experience or impulse, cast a glance on the little pad, consisting of several sheets of blotting–paper, which lay on the escrutoire. Blennerhagen had dried his note on the upper sheet: it was rapidly penned in a full, bold hand: and the impression of nearly every letter was quite visible on the blotting–paper. To tear off the sheet, to hold it up against the looking–glass, so as to rectify the reverse position of the words, and to cast his eye over those which were the most conspicuous, was the work of a moment. It ran thus:—"GILLARD—I must change my plan—let Wyburn be instantly released—contrive that he shall suspect he owes his liberty to my becoming security for the debts—BLENNERHAGEN."

Burdock had conveyed this precious document to the side–pocket of his coat before Blennerhagen returned: he resolved not to act rashly upon it, but to consider calmly what would be the most efficacious mode of using it. He felt highly gratified that he now possessed the means of supporting Mrs. Wyburn's statement as to Blennerhagen's treachery. It afforded him considerable satisfaction, also, that he might, in all probability, not only, in some measure, benefit Wyburn, but, by politic conduct, force

Blennerhagen to desist from giving him any trouble on account of the awkward situation into which he had been placed by Mrs. Blennerhagen's folly.

All these ideas darted through his brain with the rapidity of lightning. He felt pleased; and, doubtless, exhibited some symptoms of his internal satisfaction in his countenance; for Blennerhagen resumed the conversation by saying, "You smile, sir: the prospect of doing a good action lights up your countenance, and makes you forget your personal troubles. Until this day, you have, to me, been an object of respect. What could induce you to act as you have done,—to injure and then brave me? You threatened to unmask me—to make me crouch and tremble before you: I am still erect, and my hand is firm."

"Let that pass, sir," said Burdock; "the novelty—the ridiculous novelty, of my situation, must be my excuse. You can, perhaps, imagine the feelings of an innocent man, labouring under a sudden and severe accusation."

"I can, indeed," replied Blennerhagen. "Do you say you are innocent?"

"I scorn to answer such a question."

"Truly, your manner staggers me;—your character has its weight, too: I should be exceedingly glad to see you exculpated. May I ask what brought you to my wife's dressing-room?"

"To that I will reply: —I received a summons from Mrs Blennerhagen, and was conducted to this apartment by her servant: the idiot wanted to smuggle me in the back way, but I wouldn't put up with it."

"One inquiry more, and I have done. On what occasion, and for what purpose, were you so summoned?"

"Eh! why—gadso! it's very absurd, to be sure; but there I stand at bay. I must consider before I answer your question: I'll speak to Hassell about it, and hear what he says on an A B case, without mentioning names. Perhaps it wouldn't be a breach of professional confidence either; but we shall see."

"Mr. Burdock, I am almost inclined to think, although appearances are powerful, that I have not been wronged. Mrs. Blennerhagen, although I respect and have married her, is not a woman for whom a man, with any philosophy, would carry an affair of this kind to extremities, particularly where the internal evidence is weak. I am willing to give you the full benefit of my doubts: but, sir, at the least you have been indiscreet. Your conduct may cost me much: my reputation is at the mercy of other tongues; which, however, I must admit, may be silenced. Should I consent to smother this matter, will you, in return, comply with such request as I may make, without questioning my motives or betraying my confidence?"

"What if I decline to do so?"

"Then I will accept nothing less than a thousand pounds."

"As hush–money, I suppose, you mean."

"Call it what you please. I shall put you to the test, most probably, within a week. You know the alternative:—if you decline that too, I shall go on with the action, which, in justice to myself, I am compelled to commence immediately. That I may not be defeated, I must also leave my house, or turn my wife out of doors, to wait the result. But do not be alarmed, I will abide by what I have said,—your services or a thousand pounds. After this, I need scarcely say to you, that I do not think I have been actually injured: but the case is clear against you; other eyes have witnessed appearances, which go to impeach Mrs. Blennerhagen's virtue; and I act as any other man would, in demanding atonement, in some shape or other. I shall now send up my friend to see you out."

"*Rem quocunque modo rem!*" ejaculated the attorney, as Blennerhagen closed the door after him. "This fellow is a fearful one to strive with; and I am, unfortunately, in some degree, fettered by the fact he alludes to. But cheer up, Adam!—your cause is good; be courageous, and you shall surely conquer."

Without waiting for the arrival of Peterson, Burdock snatched up his hat and cane, hastily descended the stairs, and, without looking to the right or left, quitted the house. He got into a coach at the first stand he came to, and directed the coachman to set him down, as quickly as possible, in Serle's Buildings, Carey Street. On arriving at the lock–up house, he found that George Wyburn had already been liberated. He was, in some degree, prepared for this intelligence, by Blennerhagen's letter to Gillard, of which he had so luckily obtained a copy. His regret at being thus anticipated by the agent of Blennerhagen, did not make him forget that it was a full hour beyond his usual dinner time: he hastened to Symond's Inn coffee–house; where, notwithstanding the unpleasant scenes of the morning, he ate a very hearty dinner, drank an extra half pint of wine, and perused the daily papers, before he returned to his chambers.

On entering his office, one of the clerks informed him that there was a lady in his private room, waiting, in the utmost anxiety, for his return. Burdock immediately walked in, and, to his great indignation and amazement, beheld Mrs. Blennerhagen. He recoiled from the sight of her unwelcome countenance, and would, perhaps, have fairly run away from her, if the lady had not pounced upon him before he could retrograde a single pace. She dragged him into the centre of the room; where, clasping one of his arms in her hands, she fell on her knees, and implored him to pity and relieve the most ill-starred gentlewoman that ever breathed. "Nothing shall induce me to rise from this spot," continued Mrs. Blennerhagen, "until you promise, at least, to hear me."

"I submit to my fate," replied Burdock. "Pray release my hand; these buildings are old, and I stand exposed to a murderous rush of air. I am naturally susceptible of cold, and have been taught by experience to avoid this spot. Release me instantly, or I must call the clerks to my assistance."

"Promise, then, to hear me."

"Anything madam!—Odso!—have I not already told you I would submit to my fate? And a hard fate it is," continued Burdock, taking up a strong position behind his writing-table as soon as his arm was at liberty; "I consider myself particularly unfortunate in ever having heard of the name of Burdock, or Winpennie either."

"Don't asperse my late husband," said the lady; "call me what you like, but don't asperse Paul. I am a wretched woman, Mr. Burdock."

"You're a very silly, self-sufficient woman, Mrs. Blennerhagen," replied the attorney. "Are you not ashamed to look me in the face, after having, by your absurd conduct, and the assistance of your satellite, your female familiar, brought me into a situation so distressing to a man of my respectability?"

"Don't speak against my poor Wilmot;—don't call her names: call *me* names, if you must be abusive, and I'll bear it all patiently. As to your sneer upon my being familiar with her I can safely say that, faithful as she is, I have never forgotten that Wilmot is a servant. A woman who has seen so much of this vile, odious world, as I have, is not to be told that too much familiarity breeds contempt."

"You misunderstand me, madam;—but to explain would be useless. Allow me to ask you, coolly and temperately,—after what has taken place, what the devil brings you here? You must be out of your senses—I'm sure you must—or you'd never act thus."

"You will not say so when you know my motives: but, anxious as I feel to explain them, I can't help observing, how cruel it is for you to upbraid me with what took place to–day. I can lay my hand upon my heart, and declare that I acted for the best: any prudent woman would have done exactly as I did; for who could expect that ever a man of your years and experience would let the tail of his coat be caught in the closet–door?"

"Pray don't go on at this rate:—go home, my good woman,— go home at once."

"Good woman, indeed, Mr. Burdock! You forget, sir, that you are talking to the relict of the late Paul Winpennie. I hope you do not mean to add insult to the injury you have done me."

"Zounds! Mrs. Blennerhagen, it is I who have been injured, —injured by *you,* madam."

"Oh!' I beg your pardon; if you had only recollected that your coat—"

"Talk no more about it;—it shall be as you please, if you will drop the subject, and come to the point at once. Why do I see you here?"

"I hope I may be permitted to sit."

"Oh! certainly,—I beg pardon," said Burdock, handing Mrs. Blennerhagen a chair, and immediately returning to his position behind the writing–table.

"I am, at this moment, exceedingly indisposed, you will recollect," said the lady; and I ought to be in bed, with a physician by my side, rather than in Furnival's Inn, talking to an attorney."

"You are perfectly right, madam; and I beg to suggest that you should avoid the fatigue of conversation as much as possible."

"I thank you for your friendly hint, Mr. Burdock, and I will endeavour to profit by it. Now I'm going to surprise you. Wilmot—no matter how—contrived to overhear a great part of your conversation with Mr. Blennerhagen. It seems that a thousand pounds was the sum mentioned; but Wilmot thinks, and so do I, that, by good management, with a solemn declaration and her oath, half the money would settle the matter. Now, my dear Mr. Burdock, as you are a little obstinate and self willed,—you know you are, for you've too much sense to be blind to your own little failings,—I thought I would come down at once, and, if you wavered, throw my eloquence and interest into the scale. I need not point out to you how much trouble it will save us both, if you can prevent this little affair from being made public. 'What say you?"

"Why, truly, madam, your matchless absurdity almost deprives me of utterance. You heap Pelion upon Ossa with such celerity, that, before I can recover from the surprise which one ridiculous action has produced, you stun me with a still more prodigious achievement."

"And can you really hesitate?"

"Hesitate, woman! Not at all:—I'm resolute!—Blennerhagen shall never see the colour of my coin."

"Mr. Burdock! are you a man? Can you, for a moment, seriously think of suffering an injured lady's reputation to be placed in jeopardy for the sake of so paltry a sum?"

"Pray hold your tongue, or, vexed as I am, I shall positively laugh in your face. Do you think I am mad, or that I find my money in the streets? But that I can scarcely conceive Blennerhagen is fool enough to think I am such a gudgeon as to bite at his bait, I should certainly be led to suspect what I hinted this morning to be true."

"That I am his confederate? and that we had laid our heads together to entrap you?—I would rather die than you should imagine that I was so vile a wretch! Oh! Mr. Burdock, I could not exist under such an imputation. To prove that I do not merit your odious suspicions, and as you are so ungenerous as not to come forward with your own money on this occasion, I'll tell you what I'll do:—I'll pledge the pearl necklace, tiara, ear–rings, &c., which poor Mr. Winpennie gave me on my wedding–day, and never would let me part with even when he was distressed,—I'll pledge those, and the ruby suite I was last married in, with my two gold watches, and as many little trinkets as will make up the money, which I'll give you before I sleep, if you will promise to keep the secret, and make the matter up with Blennerhagen; so that there may be no piece of work about it.—Now what do you think of that?"

"Mrs. Blennerhagen," said Burdock, advancing from the situation which he had hitherto occupied, and kindly taking the lady's hand, "you are a very weak, imprudent woman;—excuse me for saying so;—it is the fact: and if you are not more careful, you will, in all probability, get into a position, from which you will find it impossible to extricate yourself. The present case is bad enough, in all conscience; but I have some reason to hope, that it is to be got over without the sacrifice of your pearl necklace, or the ruby suite in which you were last married; at all events, let them remain in your own jewel–box for the present. We will not have recourse to either, unless, and until, all other earthly means fail. Let me, however, advise you as a friend, should you escape scot–free on this occasion, to be more careful in your conduct for the future. Now don't say another word, but go home and make yourself easy."

"Oh! Mr. Burdock," exclaimed the lady, "this is, indeed, most fatherly of you. Your words are balm to my agitated spirits; a sweet calm begins to pervade my bosom; —good Heavens! what's that?"

"What, madam?" eagerly inquired Burdock, casting a hurried glance around him.

"As I'm a living creature, I heard the creak of Blennerhagen's boot!— He's coming! I'm sure he's coming!"

As the lady spoke, some one knocked at the outer door; and, immediately after, one of the clerks came in to announce, that the moment Mr. Burdock was disengaged, Mr. Blennerhagen would be glad to speak with him.

The attorney and his fair visitor gazed upon each other in a very expressive manner, at this information: the lady whispered,

"I shall faint; I'm sure I shall!" Burdock, after a brief pause, told the clerk that he should be at liberty in one minute, and the young man retired.

"How exquisitely annoying!" exclaimed the attorney, as soon as the door was closed; "this is the consequence of your indiscretion, madam."

"Don't abuse. me, sir;—don't tread upon a worm!" replied the lady. "We should not lose time in talking, but set our wits to work at once. Oh! if Wilmot were here, now!—That stupid clerk! couldn't he as well have said you were out, or particularly occupied, and told Mr. Blennerhagen to call again?—Where shall I conceal myself? Have you no little room?"

"Not one, I am happy to say."

"Nor even a cupboard?—of course you have a cupboard:—I can squeeze in anywhere, bless you!"

"There is not a hiding–place for a rat; the window is two stories from the ground, and excessively narrow into the bargain: so that circumstances luckily compel you to adopt the plain, straight–forward course, which is always the best. I strongly suspect your husband has followed you here: to conceal yourself would be useless,—nay, fatal. You must face him."

"Oh! Mr. Burdock, you drive me frantic!"

"Nay, nay, madam;—pray be calm: don't tear your hair in that frightful manner!"

"Talk not of hair:—besides, they're only ringlets which I wear in charity to Wilmot; it takes her an hour to dress my own:—I scarce know what I'm doing or saying.—Stay! if I open the upper and lower right–hand doors of that press or book case, or whatever it is, won't they reach to the other wall?"

"Possibly they may."

"Then I can hide myself in the corner."

"Notwithstanding my caution, you are acting as unwisely as ever. I protest against all this, and give you notice that I will be no party to the concealment."

"Do hold your tongue, and be guided by me:—you men have really no brains. There," said the lady, placing herself behind the two doors, which, as the side of the piece of furniture to which they belonged stood within a short distance of the corner of the room, effectually concealed her from observation, "now, if you'll only get rid of him quickly, I'll warrant you I shall be safe."

Burdock immediately rang a little table bell, and his clerk ushered in the Mathematician.

"You are doubtless surprised to see me so soon, sir," said Blennerhagen.

"Not at all; I shall never be surprised again."

"A wise man should wonder at nothing, perhaps. Unexpected circumstances, which I will explain, have led me to visit you this afternoon. In the first place, I understand, from my servant, that a female has been sent to my house by your directions: her appearance and story, it seems, were equally extraordinary. May I be excused for having a natural curiosity to know who she was, and what she wanted? She was sent up, I hear, to Mrs. Blennerhagen: I have no wish that she should trouble my wife again."

"Are you anxious to keep her business with you a secret from Mrs. Blennerhagen?"

"Possibly I may be; but I don't know until I discover what it is:—we have all been young. Why do you ask?"

"Simply because your wife is in this room."

"I don't understand you."

"Mrs. Blennerhagen is now within hearing: she stands behind the doors of that old book–case."

"Excuse me, sir;—you have dined, no doubt;—but I am serious."

"And so am I," replied Burdock. "If you disbelieve what I say, go and see."

"Oh! you vile creatures!" exclaimed Mrs. Blennerhagen, rushing from the place of her concealment:—"you pair of wretches! A plot! a plot! There's a vile plot laid between you to delude—to vilify—to destroy me. I see through it all. And you,—you old, abandoned man," added the lady, addressing Burdock, "to lend yourself to such a scheme!—I'm ashamed of you!—You've played your parts well; but I will be a match for you. Oh! Heavens! is this the way to treat a wife? Mr. Blennerhagen, you may well look confounded."

"Confounded!" exclaimed Blennerhagen; "I'm thunder–struck!"

"Ay! no doubt you are. What, I am to be got rid of, I suppose, by this vamped–up affair between you and your satellite,—as he dares to call poor Wilmot,— to make room for your creature in sapphire and yellow. If I die in the attempt, I will see the bottom of it all, and expose you both!" Mrs. Blennerhagen now bustled out of the office.

"This woman is foolish," said Blennerhagen.

"I think so, decidedly," quoth the attorney.

"What brought her here, pray?"

"Why, as I was a little obstinate and self–willed, she came to throw her interest and eloquence into the scale, (I use her own words,) and induce me to prevent our little affair from being made public. Her woman, who overheard the conversation which I had with you this, morning, seems to think that, although you ask a thousand pounds, with a little management, a solemn declaration of innocence, and her own oath, half the money would settle the matter. Ha, ha!"

Blennerhagen bit his lip. After a short pause, he inquired if the attorney had yet made up his mind to state, on what occasion, and for what purpose, he had visited Mrs. Blennerhagen in her dressing–room.

"I have not spoken to Hassell on the subject," replied Burdock; "but I feel no repugnance, under present circumstances, to say that she sent for me because she was jealous of the woman in brimstone and blue. I have her note, if you wish to look at it. When she heard you coming, I was pushed, *nolens volens*, into the cupboard, by your wife and her maid. That, briefly, is the whole of the matter. By–the–by, I should add, that I acquainted Mrs. Blennerhagen with the lady's business, and I am now willing to do you the same service."

"You are very obliging:—to ascertain that, is partly my object in calling on you."

Burdock now went through the particulars of the poor woman's case with great minuteness. Blennerhagen listened very attentively, and, at the conclusion of the recital, observed, "This is all new to me."

"Of course it is," replied the attorney; "because, legally speaking, you have nothing to do with it. It concerns the executors, in the first instance; and not you, who, by your marriage, merely represent the legatee: their straight–forward course is to send the woman about her business, because she is a *feme covert*, and cannot give a release,—the title being in her blackguard husband. The executors are bound to act strictly; but if you, who are the party beneficially interested, out of motives of feeling think fit to run the risk of consenting to her paltry claim being paid off, out of your enormous legacy, why, of course, they would willingly do it. To give her a chance, I took leave to refer her to you, in order that you might hear the story from her own lips."

"I shall be happy to be guided by you," said Blennerhagen; "but I see nothing, for my own part, in this case that should induce us to go out of the usual course. Were we to put our hands into our pockets to relieve every deserving object that occurs to our notice, we should soon become paupers ourselves. Those who are rich have often as powerful calls on their charity for hundreds—nay, thousands—as pence; but they are compelled to exert their philosophy, and conquer their inclinations to relieve; in fact, for their own sakes, to marshal reason against mere feeling. You ground your appeal on the score of charity; but I could name much greater objects of charity than this woman. She must abide by the consequences of her own folly. She has been stripped of her property, and deserted by her husband, you say: well,—that's hard, I confess; but you know such cases are continually occurring. It would require the exchequer of a Croesus to remunerate,—for that is the proper word,—to remunerate all the women who have been plundered by those whom they have chosen to make legal proprietors,—observe me,—legal proprietors of their property. Besides, we have only this person's own word in support of her strange statement: how do we know but what she was quite as improvident as her husband? And who is to say that, instead of his deserting his wife, the lady herself might not have driven him from his home? It is in the power of some of the sex to do such things."

"That may be true enough," said Burdock; "but I am warranted in saying the contrary is the fact, in the present case, by the letter of a most respectable correspondent, which the woman brought with her. That the husband was a most consummate villain, I have ample evidence. My informant states,—but I will read that portion of his epistle," continued Burdock, taking a letter from his desk: "speaking of the husband, he says, 'during his short stay in our neighbourhood, previously to the marriage, he contrived, by obtaining goods on credit from several tradesmen, to support a respectable appearance; and my unfortunate client, believing him to be a man of some property, nobody knew who he was, or where he came from,—encouraged his addresses.' And then, a little below, it is stated, that 'on account of a sudden indisposition with which she was attacked, the wedding was postponed. The delay thus produced had nearly proved fatal to the hopes of our adventurer: bills, which he had given to some of his creditors, became due, and were dishonoured. Proceedings being hinted at, he called the trades people together, and very coolly requested them to give him time. The creditors said they did not feel inclined to do so, because'—favour me with your attention, Mr. Blennerhagen—'because they had strong suspicions that the bills were forgeries; and that, if such were the case,—and they had but little doubt of the fact,— it was in their power to hang him. This intimation, which would have staggered any man but him to whom it was addressed, did not produce any visible effect on his feelings. He very calmly told them, in reply, that even if the bills were forgeries,—which, of course, he could not admit,—he should feel under no apprehension; said he, I know that you are all too needy to sacrifice your own interests for the sake of public justice: you can not afford to lose your money; and lose it, you certainly would, as you all very well know, if you prosecuted me to conviction. Were I a wretch, without present means or future expectations, I should expect no mercy; but as you are aware that I am on the eve of marriage with a woman of some property, you will act upon that excellent maxim—charity begins at home, and keep the alleged forgeries in your pockets, in hopes that I shall take them up as soon as I am married. You owe a duty to the public, but you owe a greater to yourselves and to your families; and you'd much rather take ten shillings in the pound, than see me, even if I were guilty, dangling at your expense in any devil's larder in the country.'"

"Well, sir, the creditors waited."

"They did; but the deuce a bit did he pay them: he got what money he could together, as soon as he was married, and left them, as well as his wife, in the lurch. They have now sent me up the bills, as there's no hope of his paying them, and begged me to get hold of him if I can: they say he has been seen in London without his whiskers; and that, in a few days, they hope to afford me some clue to his present haunts. They refer me to his wife for a description of his person, which I mean to get of her at our next interview, if I can persuade the woman to be calm enough to give it me."

"What is her name?"

"Tonks."

"Then I am right in my suspicions."

"To what do you allude?"

"Mr. Burdock," said Blennerhagen, "I will not scruple to confess that I know the man. Tainted as his character now is, he has been worthy of esteem. Once in his life, sir, he did me so essential a service,—greatly to his own detriment,—that I have ever since groaned under the obligation, and never, until this moment, did I entertain a hope of being able to relieve myself from its weight."

"This is very odd," said the attorney; "but I am resolved not to be amazed. And, pray, on what do your hopes to help him rest?"

"On my interest with you."

"That is not worth a button; and, if it were, I don't see how you could benefit the man. Professional pursuits have not altogether destroyed my feelings; but I don't think that I should repent having been instrumental in bringing such a villain as this to justice."

"Do not let us be too hasty in consigning a man to infamy," replied Blennerhagen. "Circumstances are often powerful palliatives of guilt; and circumstances, you know, are not always—are they ever?—under our own control. Offences, which, abstractedly considered, appear heinous, would lose much of their odium, were we in possession of the whole chain of consequences, from the first inducement to commit crime, to its final consummation; and it would be but common charity to hope that such may have been the case in the present instance. I stand excused, at least, I trust, for endeavouring to evince my gratitude to this man."

"How can you possibly do so?"

"By procuring the destruction of those bills."

"What did you say?"

"Destroy those acceptances in my presence, and do me a trifling favour which I shall presently mention,—understanding, of course, that you will solemnly assure me I have not been injured,—and the events of this morning shall be buried in oblivion."

"Why, I really thought you had more sense than to make so absurd a proposal," said the attorney: "how am I to account to my clients for the loss of their papers?"

"Oh! every one knows that man is fallible, and may mislay things: clerks, too,—who have access to an attorney's private room,—are poor, and open to temptation: laundresses frequently sweep valuable documents off the floor and burn them: even iron chests are not impregnable; and robberies take place in spite of every precaution."

"I certainly never met with your equal, Blennerhagen: and I'll tell you a piece of my mind presently;—something has just struck me."

"I'll hear you with pleasure; but let us dispose of this little matter at once:—hand me over the bills, pay the woman what she wants, and send her back into the country to-morrow morning. Tonks has many excuses for his conduct, with which, however, it is needless to trouble you. He has acted improperly,—I will even say, criminally,—but I cannot let this opportunity escape of balancing our obligations. I shall feel much more easy after it. I must, therefore, press you to oblige me."

"You stated, just now, that you had some other little favour to ask."

"Had we not better settle this affair first? My plan is always to clear away as I proceed."

"I, on the contrary, when any arrangement is contemplated between parties, like to bring every point into hotch-pot, as a preliminary step."

"Say no more, Mr. Burdock;—I will yield with pleasure. It is rather a disagreeable subject on which I am compelled to touch; but I will go into it at once. Wyburn's wife has been with you to-day;—she stated something to my disadvantage."

"What induces you to suppose so?"

"To be candid,—your threats this morning aroused my suspicions. I have since seen Mrs. Wyburn, and extracted the facts from her."

"What facts?"

"*Imprimis*,—that she has visited you to-day."

"Granted."

"Item,—that she has thrown out hints which, if founded in truth, would not, perhaps, tend materially to the enhancement of my reputation."

"I shall say nothing on that subject."

"Can you deny it?—If I am wrong, why not deny it?—Will you deny it?"

"No, I won't."

"Then it is as I imagined.—Now, sir, as you are kindly disposed towards my friend, I wish to warn you, seriously, against that young woman. She labours under gross delusions: an idea has entered her head, that I am her husband's enemy, and an admirer of her person. Nothing can be more preposterous. She has reproached me, bitterly, for every step that I have taken to benefit George Wyburn, under the impression that my proceedings would be prejudicial to him. I acquit her of malice; but she certainly is very deficient in common sense. Perhaps, how ever, I am uncharitable in saying this; for women, in her sphere of life, are totally incapable of forming a just opinion on the actions of man in mere matters of business. they are like those spectators of a chess–match, who, having obtained only a slight glimmering of the mysteries of the game, consider those moves of a piece which are, in fact, master–strokes of skill, as tending to bring the king into check–mate."

"You are a chess–player, I presume, Mr. Blennerhagen," said Burdock.

"I am, sir; chess is my favourite game. But to proceed with my statement:—George Wyburn himself is by no means a man of business. Proud, and ridiculously affecting independence, although he scarcely possesses a shilling, he would disdain the slightest favour I could offer him; he will not willingly be under an obligation to any man. That assistance, which in extremity he might accept from a stranger, he would scorn if proffered by a friend: I am, therefore, under the necessity of acting in the most circuitous manner, to benefit him. If I do good, in my office as his friend, I must do so by stealth. Mrs. Wyburn has not mind enough to perceive this: a combination of manoeuvres is to her mysterious, and consequently fearful; for she cannot imagine how anything can be fair that is not manifest to! her limited capacity. Now, sir, I have already made considerable progress in relieving my friend from his difficulties, and I do not wish to be thwarted, either by this woman's weakness, her whims, or her delusions. I can convince you, at once, of the honesty my intentions; and I call on you, as at least a well–wisher to George Wyburn, not to countenance his wife's follies, but to put on the wisdom of the adder, and be deaf to her tales;—in fact, not to bring yourself into trouble, by becoming the confidant of another man's wife, and her abettor, without his knowledge, in counteracting such measures as his best friend may think fit to adopt for his ultimate, if not immediate, benefit. I am urged to make this communication; I do it unwillingly, but I think you will feel that I am right."

"And this is your request, Mr. Blennerhagen?"

"It is."

"Have you any thing else to ask?"

"Absolutely nothing:—I require nothing but your promise on this point."

"And the bills—"

"Oh!—of course the bills:—your promise and the bills."

"You have omitted to prove to me the honesty of your intentions towards Mr. Wyburn."

"I will do so in a few words.—Although piqued at George for not immediately acquainting me with the circumstance of his being arrested, the moment I quitted you this morning, I flew to his creditors, and procured his instant release, by becoming security for payment of the bonds on which he had been arrested. You, doubtless, have ascertained that he is discharged: if not, you may do so at once, by sending one of your clerks to the lock–up house. This, you must allow, is a tolerably good proof of my intentions towards him. You will understand, that I do not wish him to know how far I have gone, as it would be needless, at present, to hurt his pride. We should reverence a friend's feelings, although, to our minds, they may appear failings. You are now convinced, I hope."

"I am!" exclaimed Burdock, with unusual energy; "I am convinced that you are an atrocious scoundrel!—Don't frown, or pretend to be in a passion, or I'll shew you no mercy. You're check–mated, Blennerhagen."

"Mr. Burdock! what's the matter? — What has possessed you?"

"A spirit to put out and amove such a monster as you are from honest society. To dumb–founder you, if it be possible, without more ado, know that I am fully acquainted with the contents of the note you wrote in my presence this morning:—'Gillard—I must change my plans—let Wyburn be instantly released—contrive that he shall suspect he owes his liberty to my having become security for his debts—Blennerhagen.' I have the words, your hear, by heart; and what's better, for my purpose, I have them in your own handwriting, in my iron chest. I tore off the impression which you made with the note on your blotting–papers. Now, sir, what say you?"

"Nothing," replied the Mathematician, with his ordinary composure of manner; "nothing, but that I shall be under the necessity of entering into a longer explanation than I could wish at this moment, in order to clear up the circumstance."

"I will hear no more of your plausible explanations:—I have heard enough already. It is time for me to speak."

"With all my heart."

"Where is the letter which George Wyburn wrote to you,— that letter in which he stated he was about to destroy himself?— Be brief in your reply:—where is it?"

"Burned."

"'Tis false! I must be explicit: you shewed it to Mrs. Wyburn very lately;—say within these two days."

"I beg to suggest, that before you gave me the lie, (I postpone the insult for a moment,) you should have reflected that even in two days there is time enough to burn ten thousand letters, and that I have not been deprived of volition during that period."

"Admitted. But I know more than you imagine; and I will not be trifled with. You deem it to be so valuable a document, that you commonly have it about your person. Allow me merely to run my eye through your pocket–book."

"You carry this with too high a hand, Mr. Burdock," said Blennerhagen; "you ask too much, sir; and in a manner, that one who possessed less calmness than myself, would not tolerate. I am not to be intimidated. It would be as well, perhaps, if we postponed this discussion, until you are in a cooler mood."

"Not yet, sir; not yet, if you please. I have something more serious to say."

"You are not going to unmask a battery on me, I hope," said Blennerhagen, with apparent gaiety.

"It may be that I am. Hear me:—I hope I shall be forgiven if I'm wrong: should I, however, be in error, a few hours will set me right. I strongly suspect—I will not call you Blennerhagen, for I have little doubt but that—"

"Hold!" exclaimed Blennerhagen, placing his hand on Burdock's lips;—"hold! I beseech, I entreat you. Before you utter another word, I demand, I implore the favour of being allowed to commune for a few moments with myself."

Burdock intimated his acquiescence by a nod to this request. Blennerhagen rose from his seat, and paced rapidly up and down the room. A multitude of thoughts seemed to be hurrying through his mind; and large drops of perspiration trickled unheeded from his brow. After a few moments had elapsed, he began to recover his composure, and resumed his chair.

"Mr. Burdock," said he, "I am grateful for this indulgence. It is, I believe, an established principle, with professional men, that the confidential communications of a client should be held most sacred."

"So far as regards myself, and many whom I know, that is certainly the case," replied Burdock.

"Allow me to ask—for whom do you consider yourself concerned under the late Joshua Kesterton's will?"

"First, for the executors; next, for your wife and yourself; and, lastly, for Mrs. Wyburn and her husband."

"I have the honour to be your client up to this moment, I believe."

"Of course."

"Then, sir, I beg to acquaint you, in that character, that I am Tonks."

"You don't surprise me at all," said Burdock; "I thought as much, and was just going to tell you so."

"I hope I shall do myself no injury by confessing that I perceived you were; and availed myself of the opportunity of stating the fact, in order to obtain the benefit of your silence, and allow me to add,—your advice."

"Nay, nay," replied Burdock, "I really must decline advising you."

"Well, be it so," said Blennerhagen; "I have sense enough to see that my only safety is in immediate flight. I have been careless in some minute points of my calculations, and my air–built castle topples about my ears; but I must not be overwhelmed by its ruins."

"Understand that I cannot assist you," said Burdock; "understand that most positively. Here's a clear felony;—at least, I'm afraid it would turn out so. And you see, (it has just occurred to me,) although you're my client under Kesterton's will, yet, as the bills have actually been transmitted to me—"

"I have heard you say, Mr. Burdock," interrupted Blennerhagen, "that while you were concerned for a man, you would never act against him."

"I admit it; but, you see, in a case of felony—"

"Allow me to go on:—without my confidential communication, you would, at this moment, have nothing but conjecture to warrant you in calling me Tonks."

"I don't deny it."

"I am under your roof, too."

"Granted."

"Lastly,—villain as you deem me, I am unfortunate as well as guilty. My actions have been culpable, I confess. Money, money, has been my object: I have been compelled to catch little fish, to bait my hooks for great ones. The woman who calls herself Tonks (which is not my real name) has been, unfortunately for herself, one of my victims. I wanted money, and I scrupled not at any scheme that appeared safe, to get it:—the end sanctified the means. I have a father, Mr. Burdock,—a grey–headed man, who has pined in prison during three miserable years: I am the wretched cause of his sufferings. He was convicted, in large penalties, for offences against the revenue committed by me,—by me alone, Mr. Burdock. I attempted to bring the onus of the offence on myself, and to relieve him from the accusation; but justice, in this case, was blind, indeed. My father is in his cell, sir; but, although balked in my designs at present, yet still, while I have existence, in other scenes, in other lands, rather,—for I'm no longer safe here,—I will wrestle with fortune, at all hazards, until I procure a sufficient sum to effect his release."

"Suppose, for a change, as you have hitherto been unsuccessful, you were to adopt some honest course,—I mean, if you escape."

"Perhaps I may:—guilt, however, is but comparative, and—"

"Well, enough of this. What have you to say to your attempt on the virtue of Mrs. Wyburn?"

"I was under the influence of a passion which I could not control."

"You'll be hung as sure as you're born, if you suffer yourself to be governed by such sophistry as you preach."

"I hope not," replied the Mathematician, "for it would break that old man's heart, who has no joy to support him in his captivity but his joy as a father in me. If I had freed him, he must not have known how I obtained the means to do so."

"Another reason for your being honest," observed Burdock; "make a beginning, and you'll find the path pleasant afterwards:—only make a beginning."

"I will; immediately," replied Blennerhagen, taking several papers from his pocket–book, and laying them open on the attorney's table: "there is George Wyburn's letter," added he; "and there are the bonds on which he has been arrested.—Hush! Was not that a knock at the door of your chambers?"

Voices were now heard in the outer office; and, in a short time, Burdock's clerk came into the room to announce the arrival of Mrs. Blennerhagen and Mrs. Tonks.

"My second wife, doubtless, obtained her predecessor's address this morning," said Blennerhagen, "and has been to fetch her. Come in and shut the door, young man," continued he, addressing the clerk:—"I think I heard you close your shutters just now: how many candles have you on your desk?"

"Only one, sir," replied the clerk, "at this moment."

"Oblige me by snuffing it out, apparently by accident, when you return to your seat, and utter some exclamation when you have done it:—do not delay."

The clerk paused for a moment; but, as Burdock made no remark, the young man interpreted his silence as a tacit acquiescence to Blennerhagen's request, and withdrew. In a few seconds he gave the signal: Blennerhagen immediately strode out, rushed across the outer office, and effected his escape.

As soon as the Clerk had procured a light, Burdock informed the ladies, in a few words, of Blennerhagen's villanies; and then left them, weeping in each other's arms, to go in quest of Wyburn and his wife.

Within a week, the claims on Joshua Kesterton's estate were finally determined; and the amount proved. to be so much less than either Hassell or Burdock had anticipated, as to leave a considerable sum after deducting the legacy. Mrs. Blennerhagen,—or, to speak more correctly, the widow Winpennie,—not only paid poor Mrs. Tonks her full claim, but very generously augmented Wyburn's residue, by allowing a handsome deduction in his favour out of her ten thousand pounds. Neither of his wives ever heard of the Mathematician again; and, to quote a facetious entry in the old attorney's private memorandum–book,—George Wyburn was convinced of the folly of his conduct,

> He thought no more of reading Plato,
> And acting like that goose, old Cato.

THE LITTLE BLACK PORTER

SOME years ago, the turnpike road, from the city of Bristol to the little hamlet of Jacobsford, was cleft in twain, if we may use the expression, for the length of rather more than a furlong, at a little distance from the outskirts of the village, by the lofty garden walls of an old parsonage house, which terminated nearly in a point, at the northern end, in the centre of the highway. The road was thus divided into two branches: these, after skirting the walls on the east and west, united again at the south end, leaving the parsonage grounds isolated from other property. The boundary walls were of an unusual height and thickness; they were surmounted by strong oaken palisading, the top of which presented an impassable barrier of long and projecting iron spikes. The brick–work, although evidently old, was in excellent condition: not a single leaf of ivy could be found upon its surface, nor was there a fissure or projection perceptible which would afford a footing or hold to the most expert bird's–nesting boy, or youthful robber of orchards, in the neighbourhood. The entrance gate was low, narrow, immensely thick, and barred and banded with iron on the inner side. The tops of several yew and elm trees might be seen above the palisading, but none grew within several feet of the wall: among their summits, rose several brick chimneys, of octagonal shape; and, occasionally, when the branches were blown to and fro by an autumnal wind, a ruddy reflection of the rising or setting sun was just perceptible, gleaming from the highest windows of the house, through the sear and scanty foliage in which it was embosomed. According to tradition, Prince Rupert passed a night or two there, in the time of the civil war; shortly after his departure, it withstood a siege of some days, by a detachment unprovided with artillery; and surrendered only on account of its garrison being destitute of food. Within the memory of a few of the oldest villagers, it was said to have been occupied by a society of nuns: of the truth of this statement, however, it appears that the respectable sisterhood of Shepton Mallet entertain very grave, and, apparently, well–founded doubts.

For many years previously to and at the period when the events about to be recorded took place, a very excellent clergyman, of high scholastic attainments, resided in the parsonage house. Doctor Plympton was connected, by marriage, with several opulent families in Jamaica; and he usually had two or three West–Indian pupils, whose education was entirely confided to him by their friends. Occasionally, also, he directed the studies of one or two young gentlemen, whose relatives lived in the neighbourhood; but the number of his scholars seldom exceeded four, and he devoted nearly the whole of his time to their advancement in classical learning.

Doctor Plympton had long been a widower: his, only child, Isabel, had scarcely attained her sixteenth year, when she became an object of most ardent attachment to a young gentleman of very violent passions, and the most daring nature, who had spent nine years of his life under the Doctor's roof, and had scarcely quitted it a year, when, coming of age, he entered into possession of a good estate, within half an hour's ride of the parsonage.

Charles Perry, — for that was the name of Isabel's lover,— had profited but little by the Doctor's instructions: wild and ungovernable from his boyhood, Charles, even from the time he entered his teens, was an object of positive terror to his father, who was a man of a remarkably mild and retiring disposition. As the youth advanced towards manhood, he grew still more boisterous; and the elder Mr. Perry, incapable of enduring the society of his son, yet unwilling to trust him far from home, contrived, by threatening to disinherit him in ease of disobedience, to keep him under Doctor Plympton's care until he was nearly twenty years of age. At that time his father died, and Charles insisted upon burning his books and quitting his tutor's residence. On the strength of his expectations, and the known honesty of his heart, he immediately procured a supply of cash, and indulged his natural inclination for horses and dogs, to such an extent, that some of his fox–hunting neighbours lamented that a lad of his spirit had not ten or twenty thousand, instead of fifteen hundred a year.

Young Perry had never been a favorite with Doctor Plympton; but his conduct, after the decease of his father, was so directly opposed to the worthy Doctor's ideas of propriety, that he was heard to say, on one occasion, when Isabel was relating some bold equestrian achievement which had been recently performed by her lover, that he hoped to be forgiven, and shortly to eradicate the evil weed from his heart, but if at that moment, or ever in the course of his long life, he entertained an antipathy towards any human being, Charles Perry was the man. It would be impossible to describe the worthy Doctor's indignation and alarm, on hearing, a few days' afterwards, that Charles had declared, in the presence of his own grooms—in whose society he spent a great portion of his time—that he meant to have Isabel Plympton, by hook or by crook, before Candlemas–day, let who would say nay.

That his child, his little girl,—as he still called the handsome and womanly–looking Isabel—should be an object of love, Doctor Plympton could scarcely believe. The idea of her marrying, even at a mature age, and quitting his arms for those of a husband, had never entered his brain; but the thought of such a person as Charles Perry despoiling him of his darling, quite destroyed his usual equanimity of temper. He wept over Isabel, and very innocently poured the whole tide of his troubles on the subject into her ear; but he felt rather surprised to perceive no symptoms of alarm on his daughter's countenance, while he indignantly repeated young Perry's threats to carry her off. In the course of a week, the Doctor heard, to his utter amazement, from a good–natured friend, that Isabel had long been aware of Charles Perry's attachment, and was just as willing to be run away with, as Charles could possibly be to run away with her. Several expressions which fell from Isabel, during a conversation which he subsequently had with her on the subject, induced Doctor Plympton to believe, that his good–natured friend's information was perfectly correct; and he, forthwith, concerted measures to frustrate young Perry's designs.

Isabel's walks were confined within the high and almost impassable boundary–walls of the parsonage grounds; her father constantly carried the huge key of the entrance door in his pocket, and willingly submitted to the drudgery of personally answering every one who rang the bell. He altogether declined receiving his usual visitors, and became, at once, so attentive a gaoler over his lovely young prisoner, that nothing could induce him even to cross the road. He bribed Patty Wallis with a new Bible, Hervey's Meditations among the Tombs, and Young's Night Thoughts, to be a spy upon the actions of her young mistress; and paid a lame thatcher two shillings a week to inspect the outside of the wall every night, while he did the like within, in order to detect any attempt that might be made at a breach.

But Doctor Plympton derived much more efficient assistance in his difficult task, from a quarter to which he had never dreamed of looking for aid, than either his outward ally, the thatcher, or his domestic spy, the waiting–maid, could possibly afford him. Doctor Plympton had two West–Indian pupils in his house; both of whom were deeply smitten with the charms of Isabel, and equally resolved on exercising the most persevering vigilance to prevent the blooming young coquette,—who contrived to make each of them suspect that he held a place in affections,—from escaping to, or being carried off by, their enterprising rival, Charles Perry. These young gentlemen, one of whom was now nineteen years of age, and the other about six months younger, had been Isabel's play–fellows in her childhood; and Doctor Plympton, who seemed to be totally unconscious of their gradual approach towards man's estate, had as little apprehension of their falling in love with Isabel, at this period, as when they played blindman's buff and hunt the slipper together, eight or nine years before.

Godfrey Fairfax, the elder of the two pupils,—a vain, forward, impetuous young man,—flattered himself that Isabel was pleased with his attentions: he felt satisfied, nevertheless, that the young coquette was of an unusually capricious disposition. He was by no means sure that Perry had not a decided preference over him in her heart; and if his rival did not already enjoy so enviable a superiority, he feared that the consequence of her present state of restraint would be a paroxysm of attachment to the individual of whom she was even forbidden to think. Isabel doated on a frolic; she thought nothing could be so delightful as a romantic elopement; and far from being unhappy at the vigilance with which she was guarded, she lived in a state of positive bliss. Her situation was that of a heroine; and all her father's precautions, to prevent her from passing the garden–walls, were, to her, sources of unspeakable satisfaction. Godfrey was perfectly acquainted with her feelings, and strongly tainted with the same leaven himself. He knew how much he would dare, were he in Charles Perry's place; and, he had good reasons for believing, that any successful exploit to obtain possession of her person, would be rewarded with the willing gift of young Isabel's hand. Charles Perry's reckless character rendered him exceedingly formidable as a rival, in the affections of such a girl as Isabel Plympton: but what created more doubts and fears in Godfrey's breast than any other circumstance, was the fact of a large Newfoundland dog, the property of Charles Perry, obtaining frequent ingress—nobody could conceive by what means—to Doctor Plympton's pleasure–grounds. Godfrey suspected that a correspondence was carried on between Perry and Isabel by means of the dog; and he shot at him several times, but without success.

Of his quiet, demure, and unassuming school–fellow, George Wharton, Godfrey did not entertain the least degree of fear: he attributed Isabel's familiarity with him to their having been brought up together; for that Wharton could really love so giddy a girl as Isabel, he would not permit himself to believe. But the truth is, that George passionately doated on Isabel; and she, much to her satisfaction, had made herself acquainted with the state of his feelings towards her. She had even encouraged him, by a blushing avowal that she esteemed him more than any other human being, except her father; and, in all probability, at that moment, she uttered the genuine language of her heart: but, it is very certain, in less than five minutes afterwards, Godfrey Fairfax was on his knees before her, and kissing her exquisite hand, with an enthusiasm of manner, which she did not appear at all disposed to check. Perhaps she scarcely knew whom she loved best; and trusted to accident for determining on which of the three young men her choice should fall.

While matters remained in this state at the parsonage, the day of Godfrey's departure from the house of his venerable tutor was fast approaching:—the vessel, by which he was to return to his native bland, Demerara, had already completed her cargo, and nearly concluded the final preparations for her voyage.—Godfrey saw that no time was to be lost, if he wished to make Isabel Plympton his own: he was almost constantly with her, and pleaded his cause with such fervour, that, by degrees, Isabel began to forget Charles Perry, to avoid George Wharton, and to feel unhappy if Godfrey Fairfax were absent but for a few moments from her side. Godfrey knew that it would be useless to implore Doctor Plympton for his consent to their union: it would have struck the old gentleman with horror, had a pupil of his,—a youth of Godfrey's immense expectations,—offered to marry Isabel. He would have spurned the proposal as a direct attack upon his honour; and have lost his life rather than suffered such a marriage to take place. It would have amounted, in his opinion, to a breach of his duty towards his employers, to have suffered one of his pupils to fall in love with Isabel. But, even if there were any hopes that Doctor Plympton would give his consent to the match, provided Godfrey obtained that of his father, the young man could not delay his felicity; nor would he run the hazard of Isabel's changing her mind, or being won by Perry, or even young Wharton, while he was sailing to Demerara and back again. Isabel, too, he was sure, would never agree to a mere common–place match with him, when another lover was striving, night and day, to run away with her; and Godfrey, under all the circumstances, deemed it most prudent to carry her off, if possible, without asking any body's permission but her own.

He had made no arrangements for a legal union with Isabel; his sole object was to get her out of her father's custody, and under his own protection. He felt assured that his love was too sincere to permit him to act dishonourably towards her; and a vague idea floated across his mind of carrying her on board the vessel by which he was to leave England, and marrying her at the capstan, according to the forms and usages observed at sea. The principal difficulty consisted in removing her beyond the walls of her father's pleasure–grounds. Doctor Plympton's vigilance was still unabated; George Wharton, although he had scarcely spoken to Isabel for several days past, rarely lost sight of her for a longer period than half an hour; Patty Wallis slept in her room, the windows of which were immensely high; and the key of the door was regularly deposited under the Doctor's pillow. With a heavy heart Godfrey began to pack up his clothes and books, for the day of his departure was at hand,—when the idea of conveying Isabel out of the house in his large trunk, suddenly flashed upon him. He flew to the young lady and communicated to her what he called the happy discovery; and she, without a moment's hesitation, gaily agreed to his proposition,—appearing quite delighted with the idea of escaping in so mysterious and legitimately romantic a manner.

Godfrey passed the remainder of the day in concealing his clothes and books, boring air–holes in the chest, and lining it with the softest materials he could procure. On the morning appointed for his departure, Isabel stole unperceived up to the store–room, where Godfrey was anxiously waiting to receive her, and stepped blithely into the trunk. Within an hour after, it was half a mile on the road towards Bristol, in the fly–wagon, which Godfrey had previously ordered to call at the parsonage for his heavy baggage, a short time before his own intended departure. At length the chaise, in which he was to leave the village for ever, drew up to the garden gate. Godfrey took a hurried leave of his old master and fellow student, leaped into the vehicle, and told the post–boy not to spare his spurs if he expected to be well paid.

In less than an hour, the young gentleman alighted at the wagon–office. Assuming as cool and unconcerned an air as he possibly could, he observed, in a careless tone, to a clerk in the office,—"I am looking for a trunk of mine, but I do not see it: I suppose we must have passed your wagon on the road."

"All our wagons are in, sir," replied the clerk: "we don't expect another arrival till to–morrow morning."

"Oh! very good: then my chest must be here. I hope you have taken particular precautions in unloading it: I wrote 'with care—this side upwards,' on it, in very large letters."

"Who was it addressed to, sir?"

"Why, to me, certainly;—Godfrey Fairfax, Esquire, Demerara—"

"To be left at the office till called for?"

"Exactly;—where is it? I've not much time to lose."

"Why, sir, it has been gone away from here—"

"Gone away!"

"Yes, sir; about,—let me see," continued the clerk, lazily turning to look at the office clock; "why, about, as near as may be, nine or ten,—ay, say ten,—about ten minutes ago, sir."

"Ten minutes ago, sir! What do you mean?—Are you mad? I'll play the devil with you! Where's my chest?"

"I told you before, it was gone, sir."

"Gone, sir! How could it go, sir? Didn't I direct it to be left here till called for?"

"Very well, sir; and so it was left here till called for: it stood in the office for five minutes or more, and then—"

"And then—what then?"

"Why, then, a little black porter called for it, and took it away with him on a truck."

"Who was he?—Where has he taken it?—I'll be the ruin of you. The contents of that trunk are invaluable."

"I suppose you didn't insure it: we don't answer for any thing above the value of five pounds unless it's insured;—vide the notice on our tickets."

"Don't talk to me of your tickets, but answer me, scoundrel!"

"Scoundrel!"

"Where has the villain conveyed it?"

"Can't say."

"Who was he?"

"Don't know."

"Distraction! How could you be such a fool as to let him have it?"

"Why not?—How was I to know?—You'd think it odd if you was to send a porter for your chest—"

"Certainly; but—"

"Very well, then: how could I tell but what the little black fellow was sent by you?—He asked for it quite correctly, according to the address; and that's what we go by, of course, in these cases. And even now, how can I tell but what he was sent by the right owner, and that you're come under false pretences."

"What, rascal!"

"You'll excuse me:—but you don't authenticate yourself, you know; and I've a right to think as I please. If we were to hold a tight hand on every gentleman's luggage, until he proved his birth, parentage, and education, why, fifty clerks couldn't get through the work. I'll put a case:—suppose, now, you are the gentleman you represent yourself to be,—and, mind me, I don't say you are not,—how should you like, when you came here for your chest, for me to ask you for your certificate of baptism?"

"You drive me mad! Can you give me no clue?"

"None in the world;—you ought to have written to us."

"Write to you?—why should I write?"

"Why, to warn us against giving up the goods to anybody except under an order, with the same signature as that in your letter: then even if a forgery were committed, by a comparison of hands—don't you see?—"

"My good fellow!" interrupted the disconsolate and bewildered Godfrey, "you know not what you've done. This is a horrid act: it will be the death of me; and perhaps you may live to repent ever having seen this unlucky day. There was a lady in the chest."

The clerk turned his large dull eyes upon Godfrey, and after a long and deliberate stare of wonder, exclaimed, "Dead or alive?"

"Alive; alive, I hope:—that is,—alive, I mean, of course.—Do you take me for a body–snatcher? If you have a spark of pity in your bosom, you will put me in the way of tracing the villain who has inflicted these agonies upon me. What can I do?"

"Why, if there's a lady in the case—"

"There is, I declare;—I solemnly protest there is."

"Young or old?"

"Young—young, to be sure."

"Why, then, I think you ought to lose no time."

"Pshaw! I know that well enough?'

"If I were you, I should be off directly."

"Off!—S'death, man! you enrage me. What do you mean by 'be off?'"

"Why, off after him, to be sure."

"Which way did he go?"

"Ah! there I'm at fault."

Godfrey could bear no more:—he rushed out of the office, hallooed "Porter!" five or six times, and, in a few seconds, half–a–dozen knights of the knot were advancing, from different corners of the inn yard, towards him. "My good fellows," said he, "did any of you see a little black fellow taking a large trunk or chest from the office, on a truck, this morning?"

Two of them had seen the little black man, but they did not recollect in what direction he went after quitting the yard.

"How dreadfully provoking!" exclaimed Godfrey: "My only course is to ransack every street—every corner, in quest of him. I'll give ten guineas to any one who will discover the wretch. Away with you at once;—bring all the black porters you know or meet with, to the office; and, perhaps, the clerk may identify the rascal among them. I've been robbed!—do you hear?—robbed—"

"And there's a lady in the case," said the clerk, from the threshold of the office–door, where he stood, carefully nibbing a pen; "a mistake has occurred, it seems; and though it's no fault of ours, we should be glad to see the matter set to rights: therefore, my lads, look sharp, and the gentleman, I've no doubt, will come down handsomely. I think I've seen the little black rascal before, and I'm pretty certain I should know him again: if I shouldn't, Ikey Pope would, I reckon; for he helped him to put the chest on the truck.".

"And where is Ikey, as you call him?" eagerly inquired Godfrey.

"He's asleep again, I suppose, among the luggage.—Ikey! —You see, he's got to sit up for the wagons at night, and never has his regular rest. He's like a dog—Ikey!—like a dog that turns round three times, and so makes his bed anywhere.—Ikey!"

A short, muscular, dirty–looking fellow now raised his head from among the packages which lay in the yard, and without opening his eyes, signified that he was awake, by growling forth "Well, what now?"

"Ikey," said the clerk, "didn't you help a porter to load a truck with a large chest, some little time ago?"

"Yes."

"Should you know him again?"

"No!" replied Ikey, and his head disappeared behind a large package as he spoke.

"Well, there's no time to lose, comrades," said one of the porters: "will the gentleman pay us for our time if we don't succeed?"

"Oh! of course," replied the clerk; "away with you!"

The porters immediately departed in different directions; and Godfrey, after pacing the yard for a few minutes, in great anguish of mind, sallied forth himself in quest of the little black porter. After running through some of the adjacent streets, and despatching another half–dozen porters, whom he found standing round the door of an inn, to seek for the fellow who had so mysteriously borne away "his casket with its precious pearl," he hastened back to the wagon–office, hoping that some of his emissaries might have brought in the little black porter during his absence. None of them, however, had yet returned. Godfrey, half frantic, ran off again: and after half an hour's absence, he retraced his steps towards the wagon–office.

"Well, sir," said the clerk, in his usual slow and solemn tone, as Godfrey entered, "I have had three or four of them back; and they've brought and sent in half–a–score of black porters, occasional waiters, valets out of place, journeymen chairmen, *et cetera,* and so forth; but, unfortunately—"

"The little delinquent was not among them, I suppose."

"No, nor any one like him: but I'll tell you what I did—"

"Speak quicker:—consider my impatience. Did you employ them all to hunt out the villain?"

"Why, it was a bold step, perhaps; but—"

"Did you, or did you not?"

"I did."

"A thousand thanks!—I'll be off again?'

"But, I say, sir;—you'll excuse me;—now, if I were you, I'll just tell you what I'd do."

"Well, my dear friend, what?—quick—what?"

"Why, I'd roust out Ikey Pope. He's the man to beat up your game."

"What! The fellow who answers without unclosing his eyelids?"

"Why, to say the truth, he don't much like daylight. Nobody sees the colour of his eye, I reckon, above once a week; but for all that, there's few can match him. He's more like a dog than a Christian. He'll find what every body else has lost; but upon what principle he works, I can't say: I think he does it all by instinct."

"Let us send him out at once, then."

"Not so fast, sir:—Ikey's next kin to a brute, and must be treated accordingly. We must manage him."

"Well, you know him, and—"

"Yes, and he knows me: I have condescended to play so many tricks with him, that he won't trust me: but he'll believe *you*."

"And how shall I enlist him in my service? I stand on thorns: for Heaven's sake be speedy."

"Why, if you only tell him he has a good leg for a boot, and promise him an old pair of Hessians, he's your humble servant to command; for, ugly as he is, he's so proud of his leg, that—"

"Call him;—call him, at once?'

The clerk now roused Ikey, and, with considerable difficulty, induced him to leave his hard and comfortless dormitory.

"The gentleman has a job for you," said the clerk, as Ikey staggered towards young Fairfax.

"I don't want no jobs," muttered Ikey. "Saturday night comes often enough for me. Seven–and–twenty wagons a–week, out and in, in the way of work, and half–a–guinea a–week, in the way of wages, is as much as I can manage."

"They is very temperate, Sir," said the clerk; "very temperate, I must allow;—he eats little and drinks less: he keeps up his flesh by sleeping, and sucking his thumbs."

"Ah! you will have your joke," said Ikey, turning towards the heap of luggage again.

"And won't you earn a shilling or two, Ikey?" said the Clerk.

"No; I'm an independent man: I have as much work as I can do, and as much wages as I want. I wish you wouldn't wake me, when there's no wagon:—how should you like it?"

"Well, but, friend Pope," said Godfrey, "as you will not take money, perhaps you'll be generous enough to do a gentleman a favour. I shall be happy to make you some acceptable little present—keepsake, I mean—in return. I've an old pair of Hessians, —and, as I think our legs are about of a size—"

"Of a size!" said Ikey, facing about towards young Fairfax, and, for the first time, unclosing his heavy lids; "of a size!" repeated he, a second time, casting a critical glance on Godfrey's leg; "I can hardly think that."

Ikey dropped on one knee, and, without uttering a word, proceeded to measure Godfrey's calves with his huge, hard hands. He then rose, and rather dogmatically observed, "The gentleman has got a goodish sort of a leg; but," continued he, "his calves don't travel in flush enough with one another exactly: he couldn't hold a sixpence between his ancles, the middle of his legs, and his knees, as a person I'm acquainted with can, when he likes to turn his toes out:—but I think your boots might fit me, sir."

"I'm sure they will," cried the impatient Godfrey; "and you shall have them."

"Your hand, then; —it's a bargain," quoth Ikey , thrusting out his fist, and striking a heavy blow in the centre of Godfrey's palm. "Now, what's the job?"

Godfrey rapidly stated his case, and, with all the eloquence he possessed, endeavoured to stimulate the drowsy fellow, on whom his chief hopes now depended, to a state of activity. Ikey listened to him, with closed eyes, and did not seem to comprehend a tythe of what he heard. When Godfrey had concluded, he merely observed, "I'll have a shy!" and staggered out of the yard, more like a drunkard reeling home from a debauch, than a man despatched to find out an unknown individual in the heart of a busy and populous city.

"The William and Mary, by which I was to sail, lies at King road," said Godfrey to the clerk, as Ikey Pope departed; "the wind, I perceive, is fair, and sail she will, this evening, without a doubt. Unfortunate fellow that I am!—every moment is an age to me."

"Perhaps you'd like to sit down in the office," said the clerk; "I can offer you a seat and yesterday's paper."

"Thank you, thank you!" replied Godfrey; "but I fear pursuit, too:—I cannot rest here."

The young man again walked into the streets: he inquired of almost every person he met, for the little black porter; but no one could give him any information. At last, a crowd began to gather around him, and he was, with very little ceremony, unanimously voted a lunatic. Two or three fellows had even approached to lay hands on him, when his eye suddenly encountered that of Ikey Pope: breaking through the crowd at once, he hurried back, with Ikey, to the wagon–office.

"I've won the boots," said Ikey , as they entered the yard.

"Which way?—how?—Have you seen him?—Where is he?" eagerly inquired Godfrey.

"I can't make out where he is," replied Ikey; "but I happened to drop into the house where he smokes his pipe, and there I heard the whole yarn. He brought the chest there."

"Where?—where?"

"Why, to the Dog and Dolphin."

"I'll fly—"

"Oh! it's of no use: the landlord says it was carried away again, by a pair of Pill–sharks; who, from what I can get out of him and his people, had orders to take it down the river, and put it toward the William and Mary, what's now lying in King road, bound for Demerary."

"Oh! then, I dare say it's all a mistake, and no roguery's intended," said the clerk, who had heard Ikey's statement: "the person found he was wrong, and, to make amends; has duly forwarded the trunk, pursuant to the direction on its cover."

"A chaise and four to Lamplighter's Hall, instantly!" shouted Godfrey.

"First and second turn, pull out your tits," cried the ostler: "put to, while I fill up a ticket."

"Are you going, sir?" said Ikey, to young Fairfax.

"On the wings of love," replied Godfrey.

"But the boots!"

"Ah! true. There,—there's a five pound note,—buy the best pair of Hessians you can get."

"What about the change?"

"Keep it;—or, oddso! yes,—distribute it among the porters; and be sure, Ikey, if ever I return to England, I'll make your fortune: I'd do it now, but I really haven't time."

In a few minutes, Godfrey was seated in a chaise, behind four excellent horses, and dashing along, at full speed, toward's Lamplighter's Hall. On his arrival at that place, he found, to his utter dismay, that the William and Mary had already set sail. After some little delay—during which he ascertained that his trunk had positively been carried on board—Godfrey procured a pilot–boat; the master of which undertook to do all that lay in the power of man to overtake the vessel. After two hours of intense anxiety, the pilot informed Godfrey, that, if the wind did not get up before sunset, he felt pretty sure of success. Far beyond the Holms, and just as the breeze was growing brisk, Godfrey, to his unspeakable joy, reached the deck of the William and Mary. The pilot immediately dropped astern; and, as soon as Godfrey could find utterance, he inquired for his trunk. It had already been so securely stowed away in the hold, that, as Godfrey was informed, it could not be hoisted on deck in less than half an hour. The impatient youth entreated that not a moment might be lost; and, in a short time, five or six of the crew, with apparent alacrity, but real reluctance, set about what they considered the useless task of getting the trunk out of the snug berth in which they had placed it.

It is now necessary for us to take up another thread of our story; for which purpose, we must return to that point of time when the wagon, which contained Godfrey's precious chest, slowly disappeared behind the brow of a hill, at the foot of which stood the worthy Doctor's residence. Patty Wallis, Isabel's maid and bosom friend, had, for some time past, been bought over to the interest of Charles Perry, to whom she communicated every transaction of importance that occurred in the house. On that eventful morning, she had acquainted Perry with Godfrey's plan,—the particulars of which her young mistress had confided to her, under a solemn pledge of secrecy,—and Perry, from behind the hedge of an orchard, nearly opposite the Doctor's house, beheld young Fairfax consign his trunk to the care of the wagoners. Godfrey entered the house, as the heavy vehicle turned the summit of the hill; and Charles Perry immediately retreated from his place of concealment, to join his trusty groom, Doncaster Dick, who was waiting for him, with a pair of saddle horses, in a neighbouring lane.

"You've marked the game, I'll lay guineas to pounds!" exclaimed Dick, as Charles approached. "I'm sure I'm right;—I can see it by your eyes. Guineas to pounds, did I say?—I'd go six to four, up to any figure, on it."

"I wish you'd a thousand or two on the event, Dick," replied Charles Perry, exultingly; "you'd have a safe book at any odds."

"Well! I always thought how it would be: if there was fifty entered for the young lady, you'd be my first favourite; because for why?—as I've said scores of times,—if you couldn't beat 'em out and out, you'd jockey them to the wrong side of the post."

"I hope you've not been fool enough to let any one know of Godfrey's scheme, or of my being acquainted with it:—'brush' is the word, if you have."

"I'd lay a new hat, sir, if the truth was known, you don't suspect me. You're pretty sure I'm not noodle enough to open upon the scent in a poaching party: I was born in Bristol and brought up at Doncaster to very little purpose, if ever I should be sent to heel for that fault. But won't you mount, sir?"

"I'm thinking, Dick," said Perry, who stood with one foot on the ground and the other in the stirrup;—"I'm thinking you had better push on by yourself, in order to avoid suspicion. Yes, that's the plan:—the high road, and I'll have a steeple–chase run of it across the country. Make the best of your way to old Harry Tuffin's; put up the horse, watch for the wagon, and, as soon as it arrives, send a porter, who doesn't know you, to fetch the trunk:—you know how it's directed."

"But where am I to—"

"Have it brought to Tuffin's:—bespeak a private room, at the back part of the house; and order a chaise and four to be ready, at a moment's notice."

"But suppose, sir, Miss should be rusty?"

"I'm sure she loves me, Dick, let them say what they will: she wouldn't have attempted to run away with this young Creole fellow, if she thought there was any chance of having me. Besides, what can she do?—her reputation, Dick,—consider that: but I'm talking Greek to *you*. Be off—get the trunk to Tuffin's."

"And a thousand to three she's yours; —that's what you mean, sir," said Dick, touching his hat to Perry, as he turned his horse's head towards the high road. In a few moments he was out of sight, and Charles set off, at a brisk pace, down the lane.

On his arrival at Tuffin's, Perry found his trusty servant engaged in deep conversation, a few paces from the door, with a short, muscular, black man, whose attire was scrupulously neat, although patched in several places; his shoes were very well polished; his neckerchief was coarse, but white as snow; he wore a large silver ring on the little finger of his left hand; his hair was tied behind with great neatness; he had a porter's knot hanging on his arm: and, as Perry approached, he drew a small tin box from his waistcoat pocket, and took snuff with the air of a finished coxcomb.

"Is this the porter you've engaged, Dick?" inquired Perry.

"I couldn't meet with another," replied Dick, "besides, sir, he's not objectionable, I think; he talks like a parson."

"But he's too old for the weight, Dick, I'm afraid. What's your age, friend?"

"A rude question, as some would say," replied the porter, with a smile and a bow; "but Cæsar Devallé is not a coy young beauty."

"So I perceive, Cæsar,—if that's your name."

"You do me great honour," said the porter, "and I'm bound to venerate you, Mister—what shall I say? No offence;—but mutual confidence is the link of society. I am so far of that opinion, that I can boast of seven lovely children; and Mrs. Devallé, although full two–and–thirty when I took her in hand, already dances divinely: indeed, I can now safely confide to her the instruction of our infant progeny in the first rudiments of Terpsichore,—graceful maid!—while I teach my eldest boys the violin and shaving. We must get our bread as well as worship the muses, you know; for teeth were not given for nothing."

"No, certainly," observed Dick; "we know an animal's age by 'em:—what's yours?"

"In round numbers—fifty."

"I fear, my learned friend," said Perry, "you are scarcely strong enough for my purpose."

"I am not equal to Hercules," replied the porter; "but I possess what that great man never did,—namely, a truck. I have often thought what wonders Hercules would have done, if some body had made him a present of two or three trifles which we moderns almost despise. Life, you know, is short, and therefore machinery is esteemed: consequently, 'to bear and forbear' is my motto; for nobody can see the bottom of the briny waves."

"You are rather out at elbows in your logic, Cæsar," said Perry; "and your motto seems to me to be a *non sequitur*:—but you read, I perceive."

"Yes, when my numerous occupations permit me,—for spectacles are cheap: but I find numerous faults with the doctrine of chances; and those who pretend to see through a millstone, in my opinion—"

"Keep your eye up the street," Dick, interrupted Charles, turning from the Little Black Porter to his servant; "the wagon must be near at hand, by this time. Allow me to ask you, friend," continued he, again addressing Cæsar Devallé, "are you a regular porter?"

"Why, truly," replied Devallé, "the winds and the weather preach such doctrine to us, that I occasionally shave and give lessons on the violin. All nature is continually shifting;—why, then, should man be constant, except to his wife? Night succeeds the day, and darkness, light; and I certainly prefer practising a cotillon with a pupil, even if she's barefooted, to shouldering the knot. My terms are very moderate: but some people think ability lies only skin deep; to which class you, sir, certainly do not belong;—that is, if I know anything of a well–cut coat."

The Little Black Porter now retired, bowing and grinning, to a little distance, leaving Charles with his servant.

"I'll lay a pony, sir," said Dick, "the wagon isn't here this half–hour."

"Ridiculous!" exclaimed Perry. Dick, however, was right; forty minutes elapsed before the bells on the horses' heads were heard. In another half–hour, Godfrey's trunk, by the exertions of Perry, Dick and the Little Black Porter, was removed from the truck on which Cæsar had brought it from the wagon–office, and triumphantly deposited on the floor of a back room in old Tuffin's house.

Trembling with joy, Charles Perry immediately proceeded to sever the cords. Leaving him occupied with that "delightful task," we shall take leave to carry the reader back again to the residence of Doctor Plympton.

It has already been stated that young Isabel stepped gaily into the chest. She continued to laugh, and actually enjoyed the novelty of her situation, for a few seconds after Godfrey Fairfax had closed the lid. But her courage began to sink, from the moment she heard the bolt of the lock shot, with a noise, that seemed to her at once portentous and prodigious: she even uttered a faint scream; but her pride mastered her weakness in an instant, and her exclamation of alarm terminated in her usual apparently joyous, but, perhaps, heartless laugh. Godfrey, much to his delight, heard her tittering, during the short period he was occupied in securely cording up the trunk. "Now, my dear little heroine," whispered he, through the key–hole, as he fastened the last knot, "keep up your spirits; let the delightful thought of our early meeting, and years of subsequent bliss, support you through this trifling ordeal. Remember, I—mark me, Isabel!—I, who love you better than any other living creature does—I, who deem you the greatest treasure on earth,—I say you are quite safe. Do not forget that my happiness or misery are at the mercy of your courage and patience. I hear some one coming.—Adieu!—Au revoir, my love!"

Godfrey now left the room, and contrived to decoy Doctor Plympton, whom he met in the passage, down stairs to the study, where he amused the old gentleman, by some plausible detail of his future intentions with regard to mathematics and the dead languages, until the arrival of the wagon by which the trunk was to be conveyed to town.

Meantime, an event of considerable importance took place in the store–room. Isabel had made no reply to Godfrey's adieu; for the idea that she was so soon to be left alone, entirely deprived her of utterance; and, as the sound of his footsteps died away on her ear, she began to grow not only weary but terrified. Though incapable of judging of the real dangers of her situation, and blind to the impropriety of her conduct, her spirits were wofully depressed by imaginary terrors, which, however, were not, for a short period, sufficiently powerful to render her insensible to the personal inconvenience which she suffered. She thought of Juliet in the tomb, and felt sure, that were she to fall asleep, she should go mad in the first few moments after waking, under the idea that she was in her coffin, and had been buried alive. Her courage and pride completely deserted her: she moaned piteously, and her senses began to be affected. Luckily for her, perhaps, George Wharton, having nothing else to do, sauntered into the store–room, to see if Godfrey had finished packing up. He was not a little surprised to hear the voice of one in deep affliction proceed from the chest. After a moment's hesitation, during which he almost doubted the evidence of his ears, he knocked on the lid, and inquired if any one were within. It is almost needless to say, that the reply was in the affirmative.

"What trick is this?" exclaimed George. "Who is it?"

"Oh! dear Mr. Wharton! pray let me out," cried Isabel.

"Good Heavens! Isabel!—I'll fly for assistance."

"No; not for worlds! I could not wait for it. Cut the cords and break open the chest this moment, or I shall die."

With the aid of a pocket–knife and the poker, George soon emancipated Isabel from her place of confinement. Pale and sobbing, she sank into his arms, and vowed eternal gratitude to her kind deliverer, whom, she said, notwithstanding appearances, she loved better than any other being in existence.

"If so," said George, very naturally, "why do I find you in Godfrey's chest?"

"Don't I confess that appearances are against me?". exclaimed Isabel, pettishly; "what more would you have?"

"I am not unreasonable, Isabel: but I shall certainly talk to Mr. Fairfax, on this subject, before he leaves the house;—on that, I am resolved."

"No doubt you are; or to do anything else that you think will vex me."

"Nay, Isabel, you are too severe."

"Indeed," said Isabel, "I am quite the contrary: it is nothing but the excess of my foolish good–nature that has led me into this disagreeable situation. My frolic has cost me dear enough. That horrid Godfrey!"

"His conduct is atrocious; and I shall immediately mention it to the Doctor."

"My father would rate him soundly for it, I know; and he richly deserves a very long lecture: but 'forget and forgive,' George, has always been your motto, and I think I shall make it mine. Godfrey has been our companion for years; and it would be useless to make mischief, for a trifle, at the moment of his leaving us; 'twere better, by far, to part friends. Besides, after all, poor fellow, one can scarcely blame him," added Isabel, with a smile, as her eye caught the reflection of her beautiful features in an old looking–glass; "even you, George, who are such an icy–hearted creature, say you would go through fire and water to possess me; and no wonder that such a high–spirited fellow as Godfrey—"

"I feel rather inclined, Miss Plympton," interrupted George, "to shew that my spirit is quite as high as his."

"Then be noble, George, and don't notice what has happened. It's entirely your own fault: you know his ardour,—his magical mode of persuading one almost out of one's sober senses, and yet you never can contrive to be in the way."

"My feelings, Isabel, are too delicate to—"

"Well, then, you must put up with the consequences. I am sure that some people, even if one don't like them much, influence one to be more complaisant to them, than to others whom one really loves; because others will not condescend to be attentive. But, come,—pray don't look so grave: I am sure I was nearly frightened out of my wits just now, and I don't look half so sorrowful as you; although, I protest, I haven't recovered yet. What are you thinking of?"

"I am thinking, Isabel," replied George, "that, after all, I had better speak to Godfrey; for, if I do not, when he discovers what has happened, he will certainly accuse me of the singular crime of stealing his sweetheart out of his box."

"Well, that's true enough: but we must contrive to avoid an eclaircissement. As the trunk is not perceptibly damaged, suppose you fasten it up again with the cords; and, by way of a joke, to make it of a proper weight, put in young Squire Perry's dog as my substitute. Godfrey vowed to kill him, you know, before he left us; and he did so, not above an hour ago, while the horrid creature was in the act of worrying my poor little Beaufidel. Godfrey said he should leave him, as a legacy in the back–yard, for you to bury and bear the blame."

"I must confess," said Wharton, "it would be a pleasant retaliation: I certainly should enjoy it."

"Then fly at once down the back stairs for the creature: no body will see you:—go."

"Will you remain here?"

"Fie, George! Do you think I could endure the sight of the shocking animal?"

"Well, well;—but will you see Godfrey again?" "Certainly not: I shall keep out of the way. It is arranged that he shall say I have the head–ache, and am gone to my room; so he'll insist upon waiving my appearance at his departure. Do as I tell you, my dear George, and we shall get rid of him delightfully."

Isabel now tripped lightly away to her little boudoir, where she was secure from intrusion; and Wharton proceeded to carry her ideas into execution with such unusual alacrity, that he had achieved his object long before the arrival of the wagon. He assisted in bringing the trunk down stairs; but his gravity was so much disturbed, by the very strict injunctions which Godfrey gave the wagoners to be more than usually careful with his property, that, for fear of betraying himself, he was compelled to make a precipitate retreat into the house. As soon as he was out of the hearing of his young rival, he indulged in an immoderate fit of laughter, which was echoed by Isabel, who, peeping through the window of her apartment, heartily enjoyed the anxiety which Godfrey, by his looks, appeared to feel for the safety of his chest and its precious contents. She kept out of sight until young Fairfax had departed; when Patty Wallis was struck speechless, for nearly a minute, at being summoned by Isabel in person, to dress her for dinner.

The indignation and amazement of Charles Perry, on seeing his own dead dog in the trunk, where he had expected to find the fair form of the blooming and lively Isabel Plympton, may easily be imagined. His first emotions of wonder at the sight were quickly succeeded by the deepest regret for the death of his favourite dog: but his sorrow for the animal was suddenly extinguished by a most painful feeling of mortification, at having been so egregiously duped: at last, rage,—violent and ungovernable rage, seemed to master all other passions in his bosom. He raved like a Bedlamite, beat his forehead, tore his hair, stamped up and down the room, vowed to sacrifice, not only young Fairfax, Patty Wallis, Doctor Plympton, but even Doncaster Dick himself; and when his excitement had reached its highest pitch, he lifted the dead dog out of the chest, and hurled it, with all his might, at the head of Caesar Devallé. The force of the blow threw the Little Black Porter on the floor, where he lay with the dog sprawling upon him; and his grimaces, and exclamations for rescue from the animal, appeared so exceedingly ludicrous to Charles Perry, that the young gentleman burst out into a violent and uncontrollable fit of laughter, in which he was most readily joined by Doncaster Dick.

Long before the merriment of either master or man had subsided, Caesar contrived to extricate himself from the dog; and after adjusting his disordered cravat, began to express his deep indignation at the insult he had suffered. He intimated, in a tone tremulous with agitation, but in rather choice terms, that he should be quite delighted to know by what law or custom any person was authorized to hurl the corpse of a huge mastiff at the head of a citizen of the world; and why the alarming position of an inoffensive father of seven children, struggling to escape from an animal, which might, for aught he knew, be alive and rabid, should exhilarate any gentleman, whose parents or guardians were not cannibals; or any groom, except a Centaur. "If we are to be treated in this way," pursued he, "where is the use of tying our hair? We may as well go about like logs in a stream, if gentlemen know nothing of hydrophobia, or the philosophy of the human heart. Even the brute creation teaches us many of our social duties: the cat washes her face, and even the duck smooths her feathers, in order that she may be known on the pond for what she is: but if a man is to embellish his exterior, —if we are to display the character of our minds by outward appearances, and yet be thrown at, for sport, like cocks on a Shrove Tuesday to speak plainly, the Ganges may as well be turned into a tea–pot, and the Arabian deserts be covered with Witney blankets."

"The short and the long of it is," said Dick," he means, sir, that we ought to know, lookye, as how a man who ties his cravat in a small rosette, and shews a bit of frill, don't give or take horse–play. That's my translation of his rigmarole, and I'll lay a crown it's a true one?'

"I suspect it is," said Perry, "and I'm sorry, porter, that—"

"Not a word more," interrupted Caesar, again suffering his features to relax from their state of grave restraint into his habitual smile;—"not a word more, I insist: to evince a disposition to make an ample apology, is quite satisfactory from one gentleman to a—to a—"

"To another, you would say," said Charles.

"You honour me vastly by this condescension, sir; and if ever I compose another cotillon, or Mrs. Devallé presents me with an eighth pledge of our affection, your name shall certainly be made use of. Gratitude is implanted even in stocks and stones; and the acorn that is only half munched by swine, grows into an oak, and, centuries after, becomes a ship, in which our celebrated breed of pigs is carried to the four quarters of the world. Even my namesake Caesar, the Roman, and Hannibal, the Carthaginian—"

"Exactly,—exactly so," said Perry, turning on his heel and biting his lip, as the recollection of the trick which had been played upon him again flashed across his mind.

"I beg pardon," said Caesar, following him; "I don't think you foresaw, precisely—"

"Well, what were you going to say?" inquired Charles, in a tone of impatience.

"I was about to propose, that we should drown all future animosity in a bumper;—that is, if you would honour so humble a member of society as Caesar Devallé, by ordering the liquor. Shall I execute your commands?"

"Dick, get some brandy:—I could drink a glass myself."

"I'll step for a pint or so," quoth Caesar; "I am fond of motion: it exemplifies the living principle, and—"

"No more of your observations, but begone," interrupted Charles. Devallé made a low bow, and immediately left the room. "The fellow's a fool," continued Charles, as the Little Black Porter closed the door. "What say you, Dick, to all this?"

"Why, sir," replied Dick, "I don't like to be over positive; but, to me, it looks rather like a pretty kettle of fish. Moreover, I'll lay a tear's perquisites to half a pound, that Mr. Caesar, the porter, is more rogue than ninny."

"What do you mean? Why do you wink in that manner?"

"Ah! I never winks without there's a notion or two in my head. A sensible horse don't throw his ears forward, unless there's something in the wind he thinks may be worth looking at. I can't make out which way we've been jockied in this form. Where lies the fault, sir?—that's what I want to know. Who put the dog in the box? I wish any one would answer that simple question."

"So do I, Dick, with all my heart."

"Well, then, it's clear there's a screw loose somewhere. I'll lay my leg it don't lie with little Patty.—Then where can it?"

"Ay, that's the point, Dick."

"Why, then, if I'm any judge, this little porter isn't two–pence halfpenny better than he should be He was a long while going for the trunk, you'll recollect: and when I told him that it was directed to Godfrey Fairfax, Esquire, 'Ay, ay!' says he, taking the words out of my mouth, 'Godfrey Fairfax, Esquire, of Demerary.' It did'nt strike me, then; but it seems rather oddish to me, now; and, in my mind, all the roguery was done 'twixt here and the wagon–office: I'll bet a guinea it was."

"Egad, Dick! you're generally right; and there seems some probability. But how shall we act?"

"Why, sir, I recommend that we should make him drunk, and pump him."

"But, suppose his head should prove too hard for ours, Dick."

"Never fear that, sir; I'll ring the changes, so that he shall do double duty."

"You forget, Dick, that all this time he may be making his escape. Run down stairs and look after him."

Dick walked to the door, but returned without opening it. "I hear his hoof on the stairs, sir," said he: "sharp's the word."

The Little Black Porter now entered the room, followed by a waiter with a decanter of brandy and three glasses. Bumpers were immediately filled, and the Little Black Porter and Dick drank young Perry's health: Charles then emptied his glass; more liquor was poured out, the Little Black Porter began to talk, and, in a very short time, the contents of the decanter were considerably diminished. Devallé drank, alternately, and it must be confessed, "nothing loath," to Dick and his master; and the groom, with much ingenuity, contrived to make him swallow at least thrice the quantity that either he or young Perry took. Caesar's eyes gradually grew bright; a slight stutter was perceptible in his speech; he unnecessarily used words of considerable length; and spoke familiarly of persons far above his own station in life.

"You seem to be acquainted with nearly all the residents of this neighbourhood," said Charles, drawing the Little Black Porter to a window; "can you inform me who lives in yonder old brick house, the window–shutters of which always appear closed?"

"The owner, sir," replied Caesar, "is an opulent merchant, old and whimsical,—but age will have its errors; if not, why do we prop a tottering castle, and patch shoes? Nothing is incomprehensible if we adopt the doctrine of analogy; which, as more than one great writer observes, is an irrefragable proof that man is endowed with reasoning powers. The gentleman, whose house you now see, sir, sleeps by day, and dines at midnight. Far be it from me to say that he is wrong: there are quite enough of us to dance attendance on the sun; why should not Luna have her votaries? There's no act of parliament to make man fall asleep at eleven precisely; Spitzbergen does not lie under the tropics, you know; and, perhaps, if I had my choice,—for flesh is grass,—I should prefer that latitude where it is three months day and three months night."

"And why so, Caesar?"

"Why, I need not tell you there's some difference between a rhinoceros and a sugar–cane; and, accordingly, I, for one, seldom or ever want to go to sleep, except when under the influence of a more cheerful cup than I usually take; in fact, when I'm in a state of inebriation, which rarely occurs,—for many mole–hills go to a mountain. But, on the other hand, when I do sleep,—so lovely is nature!—that I never should wake, for three months at least, I suspect,—though, of course, I never tried the experiment,—if Mrs. Devallé did not deluge me with soap–suds. I am told that soap contains alkali; and alkali, to some constitutions, is wholesome;—for fire, you know, will roast an ox;—and the custom of bears retiring into winter quarters, meets with my warmest approbation."

Before Perry and Caesar returned to the table, Doncaster Dick had secretly procured a fresh supply of brandy; with which Charles plied the Little Black Porter so vigorously, that Caesar was soon pronounced by Dick to be sufficiently intoxicated for their purpose. Young Perry and the groom then began to draw Caesar's attention to the dog; and endeavoured, by dint of wheedling, threats, and promises, to elicit from him what had taken place, with regard to the trunk while it was in his possession: but, as the porter had nothing to confess, all their attempts, of course, proved ineffectual; and Caesar, at last, dropped his head on his shoulder, and sank into a profound sleep.

"We have overdone it, Dick," said Perry; "we gave him too much, you see."

"Yes, sir," replied Dick, "you opened too hotly upon him;— that's clear. If you had left him to me, I'd have drawn him as gently as a glove."

Dick and his master, notwithstanding their precaution, had drunk sufficient to intoxicate them: they were ripe for mischief, and heedless of consequences. When Charles Perry, therefore, asked Dick what was to be done with the trunk, it is scarcely a matter of surprise, that Dick proposed packing the porter in it, and forwarding it according to the address on its cover; or that Charles, irritated as he felt, and still suspicious that Caesar had been a party to the trick which had been played off upon him, gaily assented to the proposal. Caesar was lifted into the box, and the cords securely fastened, in a very few minutes. Dick then sallied forth to ascertain where the ship lay. He soon returned with a couple of Pill boatmen, who informed Charles that the William and Mary was lying at Kingroad, and waiting only for the tide to put to sea: they were just about to return to Pill, and they undertook, for a small sum, to carry the chest down the river in their boat, and place it safely on board the vessel before she sailed.

It will, doubtless, he recollected that we left Godfrey Fairfax in a state of delightful agitation, on the deck of the William and Mary, while several of the crew were preparing to hoist his trunk out of the hold. As soon as it was brought on deck, Godfrey, with tears of joy glistening in his eyes, fell on his knees in front of it, and eagerly unfastened the cords. He trembled to find the bolt of the lock already shot back, and with the most anxious solicitude, threw up the cover: instead of the lovely face of Isabel, his eyes fell on that of the Little Black Porter! Uttering a shriek of horror, he leaped upon his feet, and stood aghast and speech less for several moments, gazing on Devallé. The crew crowded round the chest, and Caesar who had been roused by Godfrey's exclamation, raised himself, and stared on the various objects by which he was surrounded,— expressing the utter astonishment he felt at his novel situation by such strange contortions of countenance and incoherent expressions, that the sailors, who at the first glimpse they had of Caesar, in the box, were almost as much amazed as the Little Black Porter himself, began to laugh most heartily. Godfrey, at length, recovered sufficient possession of his faculties to grasp Devallé by the throat, and violently exclaim,— "Villain, explain! What have you done?"

"That is precisely what I wish to know," replied Caesar, as soon as he could disengage himself from young Fairfax. "What have I done?—Why do I find myself here?—And where in the world am I?"

"In de Bristol Channel," chuckled the black cook, who stood tuning a fiddle by the side of the chest. "Him shipped in good order and condition, aboard de good ship William and Mary."

"Consigned, I see," added a sailor, "to Godfrey Fairfax, Esquire, of Demerara,—whither we're bound, direct,— 'with care this side upwards.' "

"Godfrey Fairfax, of Demerara! —consigned to Demerara!" exclaimed Caesar, leaping out of the trunk: "Don't play with my feelings,—don't,—don't! If you are men, don't trifle with me. Your words are poisoned arrows to my poor heart."

"Massa Blackee no runaway slave, eh?" inquired the cook.

"Unfortunate wretch that I am!" replied Caesar; "flesh is frail, and liberty's wand is a sugar–cane. I feel driven by present circumstances to confess, that I certainly did escape in the hold of the Saucy Jane, from Demerara, thirty years ago. Fellow–creatures, do not refund me to my old master:—I was the property of Mr. Fairfax."

"Of my father!" exclaimed Godfrey.

"Miserable me! His son here, too!" said Caesar, "I have been kidnapped,—cheated! I'm a free man, though;—a citizen of the world; a housekeeper, and the father of seven lovely children: do not deprive them of their paternal support. Remember, I stand upon my rights: there are laws even for rabbits; English oak is the offspring of the land of liberty, and consequently I command somebody to put me ashore."

"How can we put you ashore, my good man?" asked a fellow in the garb of an hostler; "we're cantering along at the rate of twelve an hour before the wind; and I've lost sight of land this time."

"I don't care for that:—a kangaroo isn't a cockroach, and I demand my privileges. Put back the ship, I say; I'm here by mistake."

"Put back the ship!" repeated the man in the stableman's dress; "don't make yourself so disagreeable in company. Do you think every body is to be turned to the right–about for you? I've got fifteen mules aboard under my care, and every hour is an object."

"My good sir," said Devallé, with a smile which he deemed irresistible, "think of my wife and family."

"Oh, nonsense! think of my mules."

"If there were but a being endowed with the sublime light of reason, among you," exclaimed Caesar, "I would shew by analogy, —yea, I would convince even any muleteer but this gentleman—"

"Now don't fatigue yourself, nor put yourself out of the way," interrupted the man whom Caesar designated as the muleteer; "we all know, that once free, always free; at least, so I've been told by them that ought to be dead as a nail upon such things: therefore it's only a pleasant trip for you to Demerary and back. Your old master can't take you again."

"But he will," said Caesar.

"But he can't," retorted the muleteer.

"But he will, I tell you: what is the use of your saying a bull can't legally gore me through the stomach, when I know that he will, whether he can or no? I must lift up my voice,—curse that fiddle! it's all out of tune," continued Devallé, snatching the instrument from the cook, who was scraping an old march upon it: "I shall lift up my voice, and protest loudly against this outrage. The downfall of Rome may be dated from the Sabine occurrence; therefore, I warn every body to restore me at once to my adopted land. Retract, I say," pursued the Little Black Porter, almost unconsciously tuning the fiddle, and then handing it back to the cook as he spoke; "retract, and land me, or you'll find, to your cost, that Demosthenes didn't put pebbles into his mouth for nothing."

Caesar, however, was not endowed with sufficient eloquence to get restored to "home, love, and liberty." He appealed in vain to the officers of the ship: they said it was impossible for them to lie to, and land him; for night was coming on—the wind blew a capful—time was of the utmost importance—they touched no where on the voyage—and, unwilling as they were to be encumbered with him,—Jack in the box, (as Caesar was already familiarly termed,) must positively go with them to Demerara.

Leaving the Little Black Porter and Godfrey Fairfax (who scarcely spoke a dozen words during the first week of the voyage) on board the William and Mary, we shall now return to some of the other characters in our tale.

Firmly believing that he had been the dupe of Patty, Isabel, and one or both of his rivals, Squire Perry concealed the circumstances which had occurred at the Dog and Dolphin; and; in a few months, to the great joy of Doctor Plympton, he left the neighbourhood entirely. George Wharton's affection for Isabel in the mean time, had become so apparent, that several good–natured friends alluded to it, at the Doctor's table, in such plain terms, that the old gentleman was, at length, compelled to notice it. He said nothing, however, either to Isabel or George; but wrote to the young gentleman's father, in Jamaica, stating, that, singular to say, the young people had clearly fallen in love with each other, in the opinion of many who were very well qualified to judge in such matters, although, for his own part, he protested that he could scarcely believe it. "I entreat you," he continued, "not to attach any blame to me, on this occasion: I have done my duty to your son, who is as fine a scholar as ever I turned out of hand; although, I must confess, that, latterly, his diligence has visibly decreased. I beseech you, therefore, as he is sufficiently advanced in the classics to enter upon the grand stage of life, instead of suffering him to remain with me another year, which I believe was your intention, to send for him at once, and so blight this unhappy passion for my child in its very bud."

To the Doctor's astonishment, Mr. Wharton wrote, in reply, that nothing could give him greater pleasure than an alliance with so respectable a family as that of his old friend Plympton; that he highly approved of his son's choice; that he was by no means opposed to early marriages; that he had, by the same packet, communicated his ideas as to a settlement, to an able professional gentleman, who would, doubtless, speedily wait upon the Doctor for his approval to a draft deed; and that the sooner the match was made the better.

Adam Burdock, the old attorney of Furnival's Inn, was the professional gentleman alluded to in Mr. Wharton's epistle; and, in a few days after its arrival, Doctor Plympton, who found himself unable to communicate what had transpired to George and Isabel in person, made an excuse to come to London, and thence, by letter, afforded them the welcome intelligence.

The deeds were prepared with extraordinary despatch; and, after an absence of eleven days only, Doctor Plympton, accompanied by the attorney, returned home. On entering the parlour, he was rather surprised to find his own capacious elbow–chair occupied by a stranger of very singular appearance. After gazing for a moment at his unknown visitor, who was fast asleep, he turned to his companion, and muttered a few incoherent phrases, by which the attorney discovered that his host was extremely anxious to disclaim all previous acquaintance with the gentleman in the chair. The stranger still slept. He was attired, in a short nankeen coat and

waistcoat,—the latter lying open from the second button upward, evidently
to display a frilled and very full–bosomed shirt; black small clothes, much
the worse for wear; white silk stockings, hanging in bags about the calves,
and exhibiting an elaborate specimen, from the knee–band to the instep,
of the art of darning: his hands rested on a fine bamboo, and his head was
embellished with a well–powdered wig:—it was the Little Black Porter.

Doctor Plympton coughed thrice with considerable emphasis, moved
a chair with unnecessary violence, and very energetically poked the fire;
but his guest still snored. He inquired of the attorney, by a look, what
he should do. Burdock shrugged up his shoulders, smiled, and took a
seat. Patty Wallis, who had been busy hitherto in receiving the luggage
from the driver, now entered the room; George and Isabel immediately
followed; and the joyous laugh of the latter at once produced the desired
effect on the Little Black Porter. He was awake and on his legs in an
instant; and, while he stood bowing and grinning at Isabel and the Doctor,
Patty informed George, who had just returned with Isabel from a walk,
that the stranger knocked at the door about ten minutes before, inquired
for Miss. Plympton, and, on being informed that she was out, but would
probably return within half an hour, requested permission to wait, as he
had something of importance to communicate.

Although the presence of his unknown guest was particularly annoying
to him, Doctor Plympton addressed the Little Black Porter with his usual
suavity, and begged he would resume his seat. A very awkward silence
of several moments ensued; during which Caesar took snuff with great
self–complacency, brushed away the particles which had fallen on his frill,
threw himself back in the chair, and seemed to be proud of the curiosity
which he excited.

"My friend Doctor Plympton," at length observed the attorney, fixing
his eye on Caesar so firmly—to use his own expression—that he could
not flinch from it, "my friend here, sir, would, doubtless, be happy to know
what fortunate circumstance he is indebted to for the honour of your
company?"

"I dare say he would," replied Caesar, "but my business is with the
young lady."

"With Isabel Plympton!" exclaimed George.

"Ay, sir!" replied the porter; "Cupid, the little blind god of hearts, you
know—eh! Doctor? Ha, ha!—Well! who has not been young?—Cupid

and his bow, and then his son Hymen! My toast, when I'm in spirits, always is—May Cupid's arrows be cut into matches to light Hymen's torch, but his bow never be destroyed in the conflagration."

"Come, come, sir! —this is foolery," said Wharton, who seemed to be much agitated; your business, at once."

"Foolery!" exclaimed Caesar; "I will not suffer the dignity of man to be outraged in my person, remember; so take warning. Foolery, indeed!—but never mind; time is precious; wisdom has been rather improperly painted as an old woman with a flowing beard, and some of us have not long to live: so, as we are all friends, I will speak out my business without delay, provided I am honoured with Miss Isabel's permission."

"I would rather hear it in private," said the young lady.

"Then I am dumb," quoth Caesar. "Venus has sealed my lips with adamant."

"You are joking, Bell;—surely you are joking!" exclaimed young Wharton.

"Decidedly you are, child,—I say, decidedly," cried the Doctor.

"Indeed I am not, father," replied Isabel, with a gravity of manner which, with her, was almost unprecedented. "If he have aught to say to me, and to me alone, I will hear it alone, or not at all."

"You see, gentlemen," said Caesar, "I should be very happy—but Venus has stopped my breath. I have been always a slave to the sex. Mahomet went to the mountain; and it is insolence in a rushlight to rival the moon. Do not entreat me, for I'm inflexible."

"No one entreats you, man," said George: "if Isabel Plympton, and such as you, have any private business with each other, I, for one, will not trouble you with my presence:'

Young Wharton had no sooner uttered these words, than he walked out of the room.

"Good Heavens!" exclaimed the Doctor, "I never saw George so roused. Sir," added he, addressing the attorney, "he's the quietest creature in existence,—gentle as a lamb, — meek as a dove; his enemies, if it were possible for one of his kind disposition to have any, would say he was even too passive. I'm quite alarmed;—pray come with me,—pray do: assist me, sir, to soothe him. I'm quite unused to such events, and scarcely know how to act.—Excuse me, sir, a moment."

The last words of the Doctor were addressed, as he drew the attorney out of the room, to the Little Black Porter. "Don't mention it, sir," said Caesar; "if we can't make free, why should crickets be respected? And now, young lady, as we are quite alone—"

"You come from Godfrey Fairfax," interrupted Isabel. "Bless my soul!" exclaimed Caesar; —"a witch! — the world's at an end! But I ascribe it to Cupid. How do you know—"

"I guessed—I was sure of it:—I dreamt of him last night. Give me his letter."

"His letter?"

"Yes;—have you not one from him?"

"I will not deny that I have; but I was only to deliver it on condition—"

"Don't talk of conditions;—give it to me, at once."

"There it is, then: your commands are my law. I have been a martyr to my submission to the fair, but I don't repent; and, as philosophy and analogy both concur—"

"Not another word," interrupted Isabel, "but leave the house:—go. What! Cupid's messenger, and demur?"

"Never:—I will fly. Wish for me, and Caesar Devallé shall appear. I kiss your fair fingers."

The Little Black Porter perpetrated a bow in his best style, and closed the front door behind him, as Doctor Plympton returned to the parlour.

"He's very obstinate—George is," said the Doctor; "I can't account for it;—he won't come in. But where's the gentleman of colour?"

"Gone, father."

"Gone!"

"Yes; his business with me was brief, you see."

"That may be; but I assure you, Bell, I do not feel exactly satisfied with you. I should like to know—"

"Ask me no questions to–night, papa: I am not well, and I wish to retire, If you will permit me to go to my room at once, I will dutifully answer any thing you please in the morning."

"Well, go, my love;—go, and God bless you! but it's very mysterious for all that."

Isabel retired, and, in a short time, the attorney, followed by George Wharton, entered the parlour. They found the Doctor walking to and fro, with his arms folded across his breast, and evidently absorbed in thought.

Their appearance roused him from his reverie: he advanced, very earnestly shook hands with both of them; and asked pardon for his want of urbanity; as an excuse for which, he protested, with ludicrous solemnity, that he scarcely knew whether he was walking on his head or his heels. "My pupil, too," he continued, looking at young Wharton, but addressing the attorney, "I regret to perceive, still clothes his countenance in the frowns of displeasure."

"Isabel is occupied in privately conferring somewhere with our new friend, I presume," said George.

"No, child—not at all," replied the Doctor, with affected calmness; "she is gone to her room: one of her old attacks of head–ache has occurred, and we may not expect to see her again for the remainder of the evening. The gentleman of colour had departed before my return to the parlour."

"It would have been as well, I think, if you had not quitted it," said young Wharton, angrily: "I remember the time when you made Miss Plympton a close prisoner, and would suffer none but the inmates of your own house to speak to her, in order that she should not hold any communication with a young gentleman of respectable family who was well known in the neighbourhood: now, you leave her with a stranger of the most suspicious appearance, who boldly tells you that he has private business with her, which she refuses to hear even in your presence! But of course, Miss Plympton acquainted you with the purport of his visit."

"No, George, I declare she did not," said the Doctor, with great humility.

"What, sir! did she refuse when you insisted?"

I did not insist," replied Doctor Plympton; "I did not insist, for she told me beforehand that she would answer no questions till the morning,—or something to that effect."

" You astonish me!"

"I confess that I was staggered myself:—but what could I do? She has grown out of her girlhood like a dream; and for the first time in her life, to my apprehension, my child stood as a woman before me. Her look, her, tone, her posture, and, above, all, the expression of her eye–brow, reminded me so strongly, on a sudden, of her majestic mother, that all my energies were suspended: the dead seemed to be raised from the grave, and I was awed before her. But a truce to this; it will not occur again. I was taken by surprise; and, by–the–by, George, on reflection, I feel compelled to observe, that it is impossible that I should submit to the dictatorial air which you thought fit to assume a few moments since. Remember, sir who you are, and what I am; or rather, perhaps, what I was; for truly, I feel that I am not the man I recollect myself to have been:—that, however, is no excuse for you."

"On the contrary, sir," said George, affectionately taking the old man's hand, "it adds to my offence."

"You do not mean to convey, that you are conscious of any visible symptoms of my being unequal to my former self—do you?"

"By no means, sir but—"

"Well, well! once more, enough of this. Let us think of our respectable guest, to whom I owe a thousand apologies, and order supper. Let us postpone all that's unpleasant until the morning; when, I have no doubt, this affair will prove to be a little farce, at which we shall all heartily laugh. The gentleman of colour is, doubtless, an itinerant vender of some of those numberless absurdities for the toilet or the work–box, which run away with a great portion of every girl's pocket–money. The idea did not strike me before, but I am almost persuaded that I am correct in my supposition; and doubtless, Isabel, piqued at your warmth,—which really almost electrified me,—determined to punish you, by affecting to be serious and making a mystery of the affair. Retaliate, George, by sleeping soundly to–night, and looking blithe and debonair, as the young Apollo newly sprung from his celestial couch, to–morrow morning."

In spite of the Doctor's occasional attempts to infuse some portion of gaiety into the conversation that ensued, a deep gloom reigned in his little parlour during the remainder of the evening. Very shortly after the removal of the cloth from the supper–table, the old attorney, much to the satisfaction of the Doctor and George, retired to his bed–room, and they immediately followed his example.

Isabel appeared at the breakfast–table the next morning; but her usual gaiety had vanished: she looked pale and thoughtful, and when addressed, she replied only in monosyllables. George Wharton was sullen, and the Doctor could not avoid betraying his uneasiness: he several times made such observations as he thought would infallibly force Isabel into an elucidation of the mysteries of the preceding evening; but she was proof against them all, and maintained an obstinate silence on the subject. Under the pretence of shewing the beauties of his pleasure–ground, Doctor Plympton drew the attorney, who was breakfasting with the most perfect professional *non–chalance*, from his chocolate and egg, to one of the windows; and there briefly, but pathetically, laid open the state of his mind. "I declare," said he, "I am nearly deprived of my reasoning faculties with amazement, at the conduct of Bell and the son of your respected client. So complete a metamorphosis has never occurred since the cessation of miracles. Each of them is an altered being, sir; they are the antipodes of what they were; and I assure you, it alarms,—it unnerves me. George, who used to be as bland as Zephyr, and obedient as a gentle child, either sits morose, or blusters, as you saw him last night, like a bully. And Bell, who indulged almost to an excess in the innocent gaieties of girlhood, is turned into marble: no one would believe, to look at her now, that she had ever smiled. She has lost her laugh, which used to pour gladness into my old heart, and is quite as dignified and almost as silent as some old Greek statue. How do you account for this?"

"Sir," replied Burdock, whose chocolate was cooling; "make yourself quite easy: such changes are no novelties to me; they must be attributed to the business of the day:—the execution of a deed of settlement, in contemplation of a speedy marriage, is an awful event to those who have never gone through the ceremony before. I have witnessed hysterics at a pure love–match, even when it was seasoned with money in profusion on both sides."

The attorney now strode back to his seat, and began his capital story relative to the great cause of Dukes and Driver. The Doctor reluctantly returned to the table, and seemed to listen to his guest; but his mind was occupied on a different subject; and when the cloth was removed, and the attorney's tale concluded, he was scarcely conscious that he had breakfasted, and knew no more of the merits of the case, than Beaufidel, who sat on a footstool, looking ruefully at his mistress, and evidently disappointed at not having been favoured with his usual portion of smiles and toast.

Immediately after breakfast, Burdock produced, from the recesses of his bag, the marriage settlement, and in a clear and distinct manner, proceeded to read over its contents,—occasionally pausing to translate its technical provisoes into common sense, and enjoining the young people boldly to mention any objections that might strike them to the language of the deed, so is to afford him an opportunity of explaining them away as they occurred. In the course of a couple of hours, he had gone through the drudgery of perusing half–a–dozen skins of parchment; and the gardener and Patty were called in to witness the execution of the deed by the young couple, and Doctor Plympton and Adam Burdock as trustees to the settlement.

It was a moment of interest:—George and the Doctor advanced to lead Isabel to the table; she started from her chair as they approached, hurried towards the deed, and snatched the pen which the attorney gallantly offered for her use. He guided her hand to the seal, against which she was to set her name; but the pen rested motionless on the parchment. After a moment's pause, the attorney looked up: Isabel's face, which had previously been exceedingly pale, was now of a deep crimson; her lips quivered; her eyes were fixed, apparently, upon some object that had appeared at the door of the room; and relinquishing her hold of the pen, she faintly articulated, "Forgive me, George,—Father, forgive me,—but I cannot do it!"

Following the direction of her eyes, Burdock turned round while Isabel was speaking, and, to his surprise, beheld the Little Black Porter, who stood bowing and grinning at the door.

George Wharton said a few words to encourage Isabel, and supported her with his arm; and her father, with clasped hands, repeated, in a sorrowful tone, "Cannot do it!"

"No,—no," said Isabel; "never, father,—never;—while he lives and loves me."

"He, child! Whom mean you?" exclaimed the old man. "Godfrey Fairfax," replied Isabel, tremulously. Her head dropped on her shoulder as she spoke; but though she was evidently fainting, George withdrew his hand from her waist, with an exclamation of deep disgust; and she would have sunk on the floor, had not the Little Black Porter, who had been gradually advancing, now sprung suddenly forward, and, pushing young Wharton aside, received her in his arms. The attention of George and the Doctor had been so rivetted on Isabel, that they were not aware of Devallé's presence until this moment. George no sooner beheld him, than he rushed out of the room; the astonished Doctor staggered to a chair; and the two servants, instead of assisting their mistress, stood motionless spectators of the scene. Burdock alone seemed to retain perfect possession of his senses: he requested the gardener to fetch the usual restoratives, and gently reproached Patty for her neglect.

While Patty, who now became very alert and clamorous, relieved the Little Black Porter from the burthen which be willingly supported, the attorney suggested to Doctor Plympton, the propriety of obtaining possession of a letter, the end of which was peeping out of Isabel's bosom, before she recovered; but the Doctor sat, heedless of his remark, gazing at his pale and inanimate child, Burdock, therefore, without loss of time, moved cautiously towards Isabel, and without being detected even by the waiting–maid, drew the letter forth. At that instant Isabel opened her eyes, and gradually recovered her senses. She intimated that she was perfectly aware of what Burdock had done; and, after requesting that the letter might be handed to her father, with the assistance of Patty she retired from the room.

The Little Black Porter was following Isabel and Patty as closely as possible, and had already placed one foot outside the door, when Doctor Plympton peremptorily ordered him to come back. Devallé returned, bowing very obsequiously; and when he had arrived within a pace or two of the Doctor's chair, with a strange mixture of humility and impudence, he inquired what were the honoured gentleman's commands.

The Doctor had entirely laid aside his usual suavity of deportment, and, in a loud voice, accompanied with violent gesticulation, he thus addressed the ever–smiling object of his wrath:—"Thou fell destroyer of my peace!—what art thou? Art thou Incubus, Succubus, or my evil spirit? Who sent thee? In what does thy influence over my child consist? Why am I tortured by thy visitation?—Speak—explain to me—unfold thy secret—or I shall forget my character, and do I know not what."

"Pray be moderate, my dear friend," said Burdock, interposing his person between the Doctor and Devallé.

"Ay, ay,—that is wisely said,—pray be moderate, my dear friend," repeated Devallé; "we are all like the chaff which we blow away with the breath of our own nostrils. Be calm—be calm: let us be rational, and shew our greatest attribute. A man that is a slave to passion, is worse than a negro in a plantation:—he's a wild beast. I don't wish to be rude, for life is short; and more than one great man has been cut off by a cucumber: but I must observe, that a passionate gentleman is very likely to make holes in his manners.—What says our legal friend? Caesar Devallé will feel honoured in being permitted utterly to abandon himself to the good gentleman's opinion. Arbitration against argument always has my humble voice: and if a man wishes to get well through the world, civility is the best horse he can ride."

"If your observations are addressed to me," said the attorney, "they are unwelcome. Restrict your discourse to plain answers to such questions as I shall put to you. Now attend:—did you deliver this letter last night to Miss Plympton?"

"Why does the gentleman ask?"

"I suspect you did."

"Avow or deny it, sirrah! at once," exclaimed the Doctor.

"Oh, pardon me, there," replied Devallé; "we are all men: the cat expects to be used after its kind; and if a man is to be treated like a dog, he may as well bark, and wear a tail at once. I can bear a blow as well as most people, from a blackguard; but, with gentlemen, I expect a certain behaviour. Resentment is found in the breast of a camel; and there is no doubt but that man is endowed with feelings:—if not, why do we marry?"

"Well, my good friend," said the attorney, changing his manner entirely from that which he had adopted in his first category, "perhaps you may be right: we will not dispute the points you have raised; but you must allow that Doctor Plympton has some excuse for being warm. Appearances are strong; but I doubt not you will, as an honest man, unequivocally answer us, and clear them up."

"Oh, sir," replied Devallé, "I am yours devotedly: ask me no questions; for I do not like to have what I know tugged out of my conscience by an attorney, like jaw–teeth with nippers, or corks from a bottle by a twisting screw; for I have a large family, and am more than fifty years old. I will tell you frankly, that I did give Miss that letter: I was sent on a special mission with it to her from Demerara. I went out in the same ship with Mr. Godfrey Fairfax: on landing, we found that his father had just died, and left him heir to all; then, as flesh is grass, he sent me back at once with orders—if Miss was not married—to give her his *billet–doux*. That's the truth: I confess it freely, for it's use less to deny it; and our heads will be low enough a hundred years hence. Perhaps you will not take it uncivil in me to say, that you would have found all that I have said, and more, in fewer words, if, instead of calling me sirrah, and so forth, you had perused Mr. Godfrey's letter. Excuse me, but the philosopher could not read the stars until somebody told him to buy a telescope. I am for civility, mutual improvement, and freedom all over the world. And now, gentlemen, I hope you will permit me to retire. I must find my wife and family: I have not made a single inquiry for them yet; though they occupy all my waking thoughts, and are the dramatis person of my little dreams. I humbly withdraw, but shall soon be in the neighbourhood again, —for locomotion is salubrious; and, if this present match with Miss be not strangled, I hope to have the honour of seeing you in church, in order, humble as I am, to forbid the banns. You would not smile, perhaps, if it occurred to your recollection, as it does to mine, that lions have been emancipated by mice, and more than one hero has been choked by a horsebean. It is for these reasons, I apprehend, judging from analogy,—a doctrine I reverence,—that cattle pasturing on a common or warren, abhor rabbit–burrows, and we, ourselves, detest and exterminate scorpions and wasps.—Gentlemen, your most humble and very devoted servant, Caesar Devallé."

With his usual multitude of obeisances, the Little Black Porter now left Doctor Plympton and the attorney to peruse the love–letter of Godfrey Fairfax to Isabel. It abounded with professions of the most passionate attachment; the deepest regret was expressed at the writer's present inability to return to England; but he vowed to fly to Isabel, on the wings of love, early in the ensuing summer, if she still considered his hand worthy of her acceptance. He stated, that he was unable to solve the mystery of her escape from the trunk: he feared that something unpleasant had happened, but clearly exonerated his fond, confiding Isabel from having borne any share in the base plot, which had evidently been played off against him.

These allusions to the affair of the trunk, were beyond Doctor Plympton's comprehension; Burdock, however, obtained a tolerably clear insight to the circumstances from Isabel, Patty, George Wharton, and Caesar Devallé, at an interview which he subsequently had with the Little Black Porter in Furnival's Inn. When he communicated the result of his investigations on the subject to the Doctor, that worthy personage protested that he should pass the residue of his life in mere amazement.

George Wharton quitted Doctor Plympton's house, without seeing Isabel again, on the eventful morning when the pen was placed in her hand to execute the marriage settlement; and, with the full approbation of his father's attorney, he sailed, by the first ship, to his native land. Isabel prevailed upon the Doctor to write to Godfrey Fairfax, inviting him to fulfil his promise of paying them a visit. She also wrote to Godfrey herself, by the same packet: but the fickle young man had changed his mind before the letters reached him; and six years after the departure of George Wharton from England, Adam Burdock was employed to draw a marriage settlement between the still blooming coquette, Isabel Plympton, and her early admirer, Charles Perry, who for the preceding fifteen months had been a widower. The Little Black Porter did not think proper to return to Demerara again; and he was seen in a very decent wig, by the side of the gallery clock, when Mr. Wilberforce last spoke against slavery, in the House of Commons.

THE DESSERT

INTRODUCTION

AT a table of three courses, the guests have a right to expect some sort of a dessert; it is the necessary consequence of a certain order of dinners; and, if the host be unable to bedeck the board with choice rarities, he must, at any rate, be provided with a nut, an olive, and, for late sitters, a devilled gizzard. No man is permitted to offend form, or to infringe upon the privileges of diners–out, in this particular. If he cannot furnish what he fain would, he must offer what he can;—it being, properly enough no doubt, conventionally voted sheer cruelty, to give a man nothing to eat after he has had his fill of the best of everything, If no pineapple be present, an apology is peremptorily expected, and some thing must be selected to take the important character which it usually sustains in the festal afterpiece, "for that night only." Mrs. Dousterbattle, my late much lamented friend, considered the tragedy train of Mrs. Siddons, as the *bonne bouche* of her Queen Katherine; and there are many estimable people, who regard the range of dishes at a dinner–table, as merely composing a dull vista, through which they can look forward to the fine prospect of fruit and ices at its termination. However good the by–gone courses may have been,—whatever may be the disposition of the host, whether "civil as an orange," or sourer than a lemon, they sturdily maintain, it must be confessed, with some propriety,—that every man should be treated according to his *dessert*. It occasionally happens, that, notwithstanding his zeal, the founder of the feast caters so unluckily, that some of his friends travel from Dan to Beersheba, among his dishes, and find all barren. A guest so situated, is justified in supposing that there will be, at least, one oasis in the *desert*, to afford him refreshment.

Impressed with the force of his own arguments, the purveyor of the preceding courses has attempted an epilogue to his entertainment; in which, he trusts that he has presumed too much on the usual leniency of after–dinner criticism; and that none of his guests are of the delightful class of censors, who flourish a flail to demolish a cobweb, who indulge in proving, by very elaborate and profound arguments, that there is but little substance in "trifles light as air;" or who occasionally go so far, in fits of ultra fastidiousness, as to cross an author's *t*, and dot an *i* for him.

THE DEAF POSTILION

IN the month of January, 1804, Joey Duddle, a well–known postilion on the North Road, caught a cold, through sleeping without his night–cap; deafness was, eventually, the consequence; and, as it will presently appear, a young fortune–hunter lost twenty thousand pounds, and a handsome wife, through Joey Duddle's indiscretion, in omitting, on one fatal occasion, to wear his sixpenny woollen night–cap.

Joey did not discontinue driving, after his misfortune; his eyes and his spurs were, generally speaking, of more utility in his monotonous avocation, than his ears. His stage was, invariably, nine miles up the road, or "a short fifteen" down towards Gretna; and he had repeated his two rides so often, that he could have gone over the ground blindfold. People in chaises are rarely given to talking with their postilions: Joey knew, by experience, what were the two or three important questions in posting, and the usual times and places when and where they were asked; and he was always prepared with the proper answers. At those parts of the road, where objects of interest to strangers occurred, Joey faced about on his saddle, and if he perceived the eyes of his passengers fixed upon him, their lips in motion, and their fingers pointing towards a gentleman's seat, a fertile valley, a beautiful stream, or a fine wood, he naturally enough presumed that they were in the act of inquiring what the seat, the valley, the stream, or the wood was called; and he replied according to the fact. The noise of the wheels was a very good excuse for such trifling blunders as Joey occasionally made; and whenever he found himself progressing towards a dilemma, he very dexterously contrived, by means of a sly poke with his spur, to make his hand–horse evidently require the whole of his attention. At the journey's end, when the gentleman he had driven produced a purse, Joey, without looking at his lips, knew that he was asking a question, to which it was his duty to reply "Thirteen and sixpence," or "Two–and–twenty shillings," according as the job had been, "the short up," or "the long down." If any more questions were asked, Joey suddenly recollected something that demanded his immediate attention; begged pardon, promised to be back in a moment, and disappeared, never to return. The natural expression of his features indicated a remarkably taciturn disposition; almost every one with whom he came in contact, was deterred, by his physiognomy, from asking him any but necessary questions; and as he was experienced enough to answer, or cunning enough to evade these, when he thought fit, but few travellers ever discovered that Joey Duddle was deaf. So blind is man in some cases, even to his bodily defects, that Joey, judging from his general success in giving correct replies to the queries propounded to him, almost doubted his own infirmity; and never would admit that he was above one point beyond "a little hard of hearing."

On the first of June, in the year 1806, about nine o'clock in the morning, a chaise and four was perceived approaching towards the inn kept by Joey's master, at a first-rate Gretna-green gallop. As it dashed up to the door, the post-boys vociferated the usual call for two pair of horses in a hurry: but, unfortunately, the innkeeper had only Joey and his tits at home; and as the four horses which brought the chaise from the last posting-house, had already done a double job that day, the lads would not ride them on, through so heavy a stage as "the long down."

"How excessively provoking!" exclaimed one of the passengers; "I am certain that our pursuers are not far behind us. The idea of having the cup of bliss dashed from my very lips,—of such beauty and affluence being snatched from me, for want of a second pair of paltry posters, drives me frantic!"

"A Gretna-Green affair, I presume, sir," observed the inquisitive landlord.

The gentleman made no scruple of admitting that he had run away with the fair young creature who accompanied him, and that she was entitled to a fortune of twenty thousand pounds:— "one half of which," continued the gentleman, "I would freely give,—if I had it,—to be, at this instant, behind four horses, scampering away, due north, at full speed."

"I can assure you, sir," said the landlord, "that a fresh pair of such animals as I offer you, will carry you over the ground as quick as if you had ten dozen of the regular road-hacks. No man keeps better cattle than I do, and this pair beats all the others in my stables by two miles an hour. But in ten minutes, perhaps, and certainly within half an hour—"

"Half an hour! half a minute's delay might ruin me," replied the gentleman; "I hope I shall find the character you have given your cattle a correct one;—dash on, postilion."

Before this short conversation between the gentleman and the innkeeper was concluded, Joey Duddle had put–to his horses,— which were, of course, kept harnessed—and taken his seat, prepared to start at a moment's notice. He kept his eye upon the innkeeper, who gave the usual signal of a rapid wave of the hand, as soon as the gentleman ceased speaking; and Joey Duddle's cattle, in obedience to the whip and spur, hobbled off at that awkward and evidently painful pace, which is, perforce, adopted by the most praiseworthy post–horses for the first ten minutes or so of their journey. But the pair, over which Joey presided, were, as the innkeeper had asserted, very speedy; and the gentleman soon felt satisfied that it would take an extraordinary quadruple team to overtake them. His hopes rose at the sight of each succeeding mile–stone; he ceased to put his head out of the window every five minutes, and gazed anxiously up the road; be already anticipated a triumph,—when a crack, a crush, a shriek from the lady, a jolt, an instant change of position, and a positive pause occurred, in the order in which they are stated, with such suddenness and relative rapidity, that the gentleman was, for a moment or two, utterly deprived of his presence of mind by alarm and astonishment. The bolt which connects the fore–wheels, splinter–bar, springs, fore–bed, axle–tree, et cetera, with the perch, that passes under the body of the chaise, to the hind wheel–springs and carriage, had snapped asunder: the whole of the fore parts were instantly dragged onward by the horses; the braces by which the body was attached to the fore–springs, gave way; the chaise felt forward, and, of course, remained stationary with its contents, in the middle of the road; while the Deaf Postilion rode on, with his eyes intently fixed on vacuity before him, as though nothing whatever had happened.

Alarmed, and indignant in the highest degree, at the postilion's conduct, the gentleman shouted with all his might such exclamations as any man would naturally use on such an occasion; but Joey, although still but at a little distance, took no notice of what had occurred behind his back, and very complacently trotted his horses on at the rate of eleven or twelve miles an hour. He thought the cattle went better than ever; his mind was occupied with the prospect of a speedy termination to his journey; he felt elated at the idea of outstripping the pursuers,—for Joey had discrimination enough to perceive, at a glance, that his passengers were runaway lovers,—and he went on very much to his own satisfaction. As he approached the inn, which terminated "the long down," Joey, as usual, put his horses upon their mettle, and they, having nothing but a fore–carriage and a young lady's trunk behind them, rattled up to the door at a rate unexampled in the annals of posting, with all the little boys and girls of the neighbourhood hallooing in their rear.

It was not until he drew up to the inn–door, and alighted from his saddle, that Joey discovered his disaster; and nothing could equal the utter astonishment which his features then displayed. He gazed at the place where the body of his chaise, his passengers, and hind–wheels ought to have been, for above a minute: and then suddenly started down the road on foot, under an idea that he must very recently have dropped them. On reaching a little elevation, which commanded above two miles of the ground over which he had come, he found, to his utter dismay, that no traces of the main body of his chaise were perceptible; nor could he discover his passengers, who had, as it appeared in the sequel, been overtaken by the young lady's friends. Poor Joey immediately ran into a neighbouring hay–loft, where he hid himself, in despair, for three days; and when discovered, he was, with great difficulty, persuaded by his master, who highly esteemed him, to resume his whip and return to his saddle.

CONJUGATING A VERB

DICK ORROD and his brother Giles were fine specimens of the bumpkin boys of the West of England: their father, who was a flourishing farmer, sent them to pick up a little learning at an expensive academy, in a large town about twenty miles from the village where he lived. The master had but recently purchased the school from his predecessor; and, stranger as he was to the dialect of that part of the country, he could scarcely understand above one half of what Dick and Giles Orrod and a few more of his pupils meant when they spoke. "I *knowed*, I *rinned*, and I *hut*," were barbarisms, to which his ear had never been accustomed; and it was only by degrees he discovered that they were translations, into the rural tongue, of "I knew, I ran, and I hit." But there were few so rude of speech as Dick and Giles Orrod.

Fraternal affection was a virtue that did not flourish in the bosoms of either of these young gentlemen. Dick's greatest enemy on earth was Giles; and if honest Giles hated any human being except the master, it was Dick. They were excellent spies on each other's conduct; Giles never missed an opportunity of procuring Dick a castigation; and Dick was equally active in making the master acquainted with every punishable peccadillo that his brother committed.

One day an accusation was preferred against Master Richard, by one of the monitors, of having cut down a small tree in the shrubbery; but there was not sufficient evidence to bring the offence home to the supposed culprit.

"Does no young gentleman happen to know any thing more of this matter?" inquired the master.

Giles immediately walked from his seat, and, taking a place by the side of his brother, looked as though he had something relevant to communicate.

"Well, sir;" said the master, "what do you know about the tree?"

"If you plaze, sir," growled Giles, "if you plaze, sir, I sawed un."

"Oh! you 'sawed un,' did you?"

"Iss, I did:—Dick seed I saw un."

"Is this true, master Richard?"

"Iss," said Dick; and Giles, much to his astonishment, was immediately flogged.

At the termination of the ceremony, it occurred to the master to ask Giles, how he had obtained the saw. "About your saw, young gentleman;" said he, "where do you get a saw when you want one?"

Giles had some faint notions of grammar floating in his brain, and thinking that the master meant the verb, and not the substantive, blubbered out—"From see."

"*Sea*?—so you go on board the vessels in the dock, do you, out of school hours, and expend your pocket money, in purchasing implements to cut down my shrubbery?"

"Noa, sir," said Giles; "I doant goa aboard no ships, nor cut down noa shrubberies."

"What, sirrah! did you not confess it?"

"Noa, sir; I said I sawed brother Dick cut down the tree, and he seed I sawed un, and a' couldn't deny it."

"I didn't deny it," said Dick.

"Then possibly you are the real delinquent, after all, Master Richard," exclaimed the master.

Dick confessed that he was, but he hoped the master would not beat him, after having flogged his brother for the same offence: in his way, he humbly submitted that one punishment, no matter who received it,—but especially as it had been bestowed on one of the same family as the delinquent,—was, to all intents and purposes, enough for one crime.

The master, however, did not coincide with Dick on this grave point, and the young gentleman was duly horsed.

"As for Master Giles," said the master, as he laid down the birch, "he well merited a flogging for his astonishing—his wilful stupidity. If boys positively will not profit by my instructions, I am bound, in duty to their parents, to try the effect of castigation. No man grieves more sincerely than I do, at the necessity which exists for using the birch and cane as instruments of liberal education; and yet, unfortunately, no man, I verily believe, is compelled to use them more frequently than myself. I was occupied for full half an hour, in drumming this identical verb into Giles Orrod, only yesterday morning: and you, sir," added he, turning to Dick, "you, I suppose, are quite as great a blockhead as your brother. Now attend to me, both of you:—what's the past of *see?*"

Neither of the young gentlemen replied.

"I thought as much!" quoth the master. "The perfect of *see* is the present of *saw*,—SEE, SAW."

"SEE, SAW," shouted the boys; but that unfortunate verb was the stumbling–block to their advancement. They never could comprehend how the perfect of see could be the present of saw; and days, weeks, months,—nay, years after,—they were still at their endless, and, to them, incomprehensible game of SEE–SAW.

POSTHUMOUS PRAISE

IF posterity were to judge of us on the evidence of our gravestones, it would certainly pronounce this to be an age of affectionate husbands, tender wives, dutiful children, loving parents, and most sincere and disinterested friends: it would conclude, from the testimony of our epitaphs, that we were all either deeply lamented, universally respected, or the most benevolent and amiable of men. We should have the credit of possessing every talent that can adorn humanity, except that of writing good English;—of being excellent painters, architects, statesmen, and philosophers; but, strange to say, most pitiful poetasters. *De mortuis nil nisi bonum,* is a maxim which no man ventures to offend, either in prose or verse, when composing an epitaph. Many persons who never could obtain a syllable of praise while alive, get very good characters given them after their decease. I always entertained an opinion that Hinks, the attorney, was a low, pettifogging scoundrel, and frequently beat his wife; until one day I discovered, in the course of a stroll round the church–yard, where his remains were deposited, that he was a "tender husband" and "an ornament to his profession." The most impatient patient whose pulse was ever felt by a physician, is described on his tomb–stone as one "who bore afflictions sore," with laudable resignation. The monument–makers, it appears, have always a stock of lettered slabs in their ware–rooms, which, like the skeleton promissory notes sold at the stationers', may be completed at the shortest notice, by filling up the blanks with names and dates. Death's heads have lately been at a discount; but poetical praise on marble is still rather above par; and lines that have been used on more than five hundred occasions, are considered "better than new," on account of their popularity. Hexameters fetch high prices, but Alexandrines are enormous. Those who are desirous of being at once laudatory and economical, are compelled to put the defunct on short commons: in these cases, an hour or so may be advantageously employed in searching for synonyms, and culling the shortest epithets that can be found:—words of above two syllables being generally at a premium. This is the case, also, it seems, in the newspaper obituaries. Some short time ago, a gentleman called at the office of a popular morning paper, with an advertisement, announcing the death of an old lady, for insertion on the following day. He found the person to whom it was necessary to apply on this occasion, rather more gruff, short, snappish, and disagreeable, if possible, than usual. This "brief–spoken and surly–burly" personage, after glancing for a moment at the slip of paper on which the announcement was written, growled "Seven and sixpence." "Seven and sixpence!" exclaimed the gentleman:—"how is that? On the last occasion, when I had the melancholy duty to perform of announcing the death of a person in your paper, I paid only seven shillings." "Seven and sixpence:—if you don't like it, don't leave it," said old Surly–burly. "Well, but allow me to ask, what is the occasion of the difference of price?" "Why," said Surly–burly, frowning severely, "if I must gratify your curiosity, you've put in 'universally lamented;' and we always charge sixpence extra for 'universally lamented.'" "Very well," said the gentleman, "there's the money; and allow me to say, that I am quite certain no one will ever go to the additional expense for *you*."

THE DOS–À–DOS TÊTE–À–TÊTE

MY wife loathes pickled pork, and I hate ham;
   I doat on pancakes—she likes fritters:
And thus, alas! just like my morning dram
   The evening of my life is *dash'd with bitters!*

Old as we are, the ninnyhammer wants
   To teach me French,—and I won't learn it:
My nightly path, where e'er I roam, she haunts,
   And grudges me my glass, though well I earn it.

The other day, while sitting back to back,
   She roused me from my short, sweet slumbers,
By taxing me at such a rate, good lack!
And summing up her griefs in these sad numbers:—

"Though you lay your head thus against mine,
   You hate me, you brute, and you know it
     But why not in secret repine,
     Instead of delighting to shew it?—
You question my knowledge of French,
   And won't believe '*rummage*' is cheese;—
     Why can't you look cool on 'the wench?'
     To me you're all *shiver–de–freeze!*

"When around you quite fondly I've clung,
   You have oftentimes said in a rage,—
     'Such folly may do for the young,
     But I take it to be *bad–in–age!*'
   A reticule–bag if I buy,
   (A trifle becoming each belle,)
     'At Jericho, madam,' you cry,—
     'I wish you and your *bag–at–elle!*'"

"When I had in some cordials, so rich!—
   With letters all labell'd quite handy;
Says you, 'I'll inquire, you old witch,
   If O D V doesn't mean brandy!'
      Whenever I sink to repose,
You rouse me, you wretch! with a sneeze;
      And, lastly, if I *doze—a—doze*,
To *w*ex me, you just *wheeze—a—wheeze*."

A TOAD IN A HOLE

THE Friars of Fairoak were assembled in a chamber adjoining the great hall of their house: the Abbot was seated in his chair of eminence, and all eyes were turned on Father Nicodemus. Not a word was uttered, until he who seemed to be the object of so much interest, at length ventured to speak. "It behoveth not one of my years, perchance," said he, "to disturb the silence of my elders and superiors; but, truly, I know not what meaneth this meeting; and surely my desire to be edified is lawful. Hath it been decided that we should follow the example of our next–door neighbours, the Arroasian Friars, and, henceforth, be tongue–tied? If not, do we come here to eat, or pray, or hold council?—Ye seem somewhat too grave for those bidden to a feast, and there lurk too many smiles about the faces of many of ye, for this your silence to be a prelude to prayers. I cannot think, we are about to consult on aught; because, with reverence be it spoken, those who pass for the wisest among us, look more silly than is their wont. But if we be here to eat—let us eat; if to pray, let us pray; and if to hold council, what is to be the knotty subject of our debate?"

"Thyself," replied the Abbot.

"On what score?" inquired Nicodemus.

"On divers scores," quoth the Abbot; "thy misdeeds have grown rank: we must even root them out of thee, or root thee out of our fraternity, on which thou art bringing contumely. I tell thee, Brother Nicodemus, thy offences are numberless as the weeds which grow by the way–side. Here be many who have much to say of thee:—speak, Brother Ulick!"

"Brother Nicodemus," said Father flick, "hath, truly, ever been a gross feeder."

"And a lover of deep and most frequent potations," quoth Father Edmund.

"And a roamer beyond due bounds," added. Father Hugo.

"Yea, and given to the utterance of many fictions," muttered his brother.

"Very voluble also, and not altogether of so staid aspect, as becometh one of his order and mellow years," drawled Father James.

"To speak plainly—a glutton," said the first speaker.

"Ay, and a drunkard," said the second.

"Moreover, a night–walker," said the third.

"Also a liar," said the fourth.

"Finally, a babbler and a buffoon," said the fifth.

"Ye rate me roundly, brethren," cried Nicodemus; "and, truly, were ye my judges, I should speedily be convicted of these offences whereof I am accused: but not a man among you is fitted to sit in judgment on the special misfeazance with which he chargeth me. And I will reason with you, and tell you why. Now, first, to deal with Brother Ulick—who upbraideth me with gross feeding:—until he can prove that his stomach and mine are of the same quality, clamour, and power digestive, I will not, without protest, permit him to accuse me of devouring swinishly. He is of so poor and weak a frame, that he cannot eat aught but soppets, without suffering the pangs of indigestion, and the nocturnal visits of incubi, and more sprites than tempted Saint Anthony. It is no virtue in him to be abstemious; he is enforced to avoid eating the tithe of what would be needful to a man of moderate stomach; and behold, how lean he looks! Next, Brother Edmund hath twitted me with being a deep drinker:—now, it is well known, that Brother Edmund must not take a second cup after his repast; being so puny of brain, that if he do, his head is racked with myriads of pains and aches on the morrow, and it lieth like a log on his shoulder,—if perchance he be enabled to rise from his pallet. Shall he, then, pronounce dogmatically on the quantity of potation lawful to a man in good health? I say, nay. Brother Hugo, who chargeth me with roaming, is lame; and his brother, who saith that I am an utterer of fictions, hath a brain which is truly incompetent to conceive an idea, or to comprehend a fact. Brother James, who arraigneth me of volubility, passeth for a sage pillar of the church; because, having nought to say, he looks grave and holds his peace. I will be tried, if you will, by Brother James for gross feeding; he having a good digestion and an appetite equal to mine own:—or by Brother Hugo, for drinking abundantly; inasmuch as he is wont to solace himself, under his infirmity, with a full flask:—or by Brother Ulick, for the utterance of fictions; because he hath written a history of some of The Fathers, and admireth the blossoms of the brain:—or by Brother Edmund, for not being sufficiently sedate; as he is, truly, a comfortable talker himself, and although forced to eschew wine, of a most cheerful countenance. By Hugo's brother I will be tried on no charge;—seeing that he is, was, and ever will be—in charity I speak it—an egregious fool. Have ye aught else to set up against me, brethren?"

"Much more, Brother Nicodemus," said the Abbot, "much more, to our sorrow. The cry of our vassals hath come up against thee; and it is now grown so loud and frequent, that we are un willingly enforced to assume our authority, as their lord and thy Superior, to redress their grievances and correct thy errors."

"Correct *me*!" exclaimed Father Nicodemus; "Why, what say the rogues? Dare they throw blur, blain, or blemish on my good name? Would that I might hear one of them!"

"Thou shalt be gratified:—call in John of the Hough."

In a few moments John of the Hough appeared, with his head bound up, and looking alarmed as a recently–punished hound when brought again into the presence of him by whom he has been chastised.

"Fear not," said the Abbot; "fear not, John o' the Hough, but speak boldly; and our benison or malison be on thee, as thou speakest true or false."

"Father Nicodemus," said John o' the Hough, in a voice rendered almost inaudible by fear, "broke my head with a cudgel he weareth under his cloak."

"When did he do this?" inquired the Abbot.

"On the feast of St. James and Jude; oft before, and since, too, without provocation; and, lastly, on Monday se'nnight."

"Why, thou strangely perverse varlet, dost thou say it was I who beat thee?" demanded the accused friar.

"Ay, truly, most respected Father Nicodemus."

"Dost thou dare to repeat it? I am amazed at thy boldness;—or, rather, thy stupidity; or, perhaps, at thy loss of memory. Know, thou naughty hind, it was thyself who cudgelled thee! Didst thou not know that if thou wert to vex a dog he would snap at thee?—or hew and hack a tree, and not fly, it would fall on thee?—or grieve and wound the feelings of thy ghostly friend Father Nicodemus, he would cudgel thee?—Did I rouse myself into a rage? Did I call myself a thief?—Answer me, my son; did I?"

"No, truly, Father Nicodemus."

"Did I threaten, if I were not a son of Holy Mother Church, to kick myself out of thy house? Answer me, my son; did I?"

"No, truly, Father Nicodemus."

"Am I less than a dog, or a tree? Answer me, my son; am I?"

"No, truly, Father Nicodemus; but, truly, also—"

"None of thy buts, my son; respond to me with plain ay or no. Didst thou not do all these things antecedent to my breaking thy sconce?"

"Ay, truly, Father Nicodemus."

"Then how canst thou say *I* beat thee? Should I have carried my staff to thy house, did I not know thee to be a churl, and an enemy to the good brotherhood of this house? Was I to go into the lion's den without my defence? Should I have demeaned myself to phlebotomize thee with my cudgel, (and doubtless the operation was salubrious,) hadst thou not aspersed me? Was it for me to stand by, tamely, with three feet of blackthorn at my belt, and hear a brother of this religious order betwitted, as I was by thee, with petty larceny? Was it not thine own breath, then, that brought the cudgel upon thy caput? Answer me, my son."

"Lead forth John of the Hough, and call in the miller of Hornford," said the Abbot, before John of the Hough could reply. "Now, miller," continued he, as soon as the miller entered, "what hast thou to allege against this our good brother, Nicodemus?"

"I allege," replied the miller, "that he is naught."

"Oh! thou especial rogue!" exclaimed Father Nicodemus; "dost *thou* come here to bear witness against me? I will impeach thy testimony by one assertion, which thou canst not gain say; for the evidence of it is written on thy brow, thou brawny villain! Thou bearest malice against me, because I, some six years ago, inflicted a cracked crown on thee, for robbing this holy house of its lawful meal. I deemed the punishment adequate to the offence, and spoke not of it to the Abbot, in consideration of thy promising to mend thy ways. Hadst thou not well merited that mark of my attention to the interests of my brethren, the whole lordship would have heard of it. And didst thou ever say I made the wound? Never:—thy tale was that some of thy mill–gear had done it. But I will be judged by any here, if the scar be not of my blackthorn's making. I will summon three score, at least, who shall prove it to be my mark. Let it be viewed with that on the head of thy foster–brother, John of the Hough: —I will abide by the comparison. Thou hast hoarded malice in thy heart from that day; and now thou comest here to vomit it forth, as thou deemest, to my undoing. But, be sure, caitiff, that I shall testify upon thy sconce hereafter: for I know thou art rogue enough to rob if thou canst, and fool enough to rob with so little discretion as to be easily detected; and even if my present staff be worn out, there be others in the woods:—ergo—"

"Peace, Brother Nicodemus!" exclaimed the Abbot; "approach not a single pace nearer to the miller; neither do thou threaten nor browbeat him, I enjoin thee."

"Were it not for the reverence I owe to those who are round me, and my unwillingness to commit even so trifling a sin," said Nicodemus, "I would take this slanderous and knave betwixt my finger and thumb, and drop him among the hungry eels of his own mill–stream. I chafe apace:—lay hands on me, brethren!—for I wax wroth, and am sure, in these moods,—so weak is man—to do mischief ere my humour subside."

"Speak on, miller," said the Abbot; "and thou, Brother Nicodemus, give way to thine inward enemy, at thy peril."

"I will tell him,—an' you will hold him back and seize his staff," said the miller,—"how he and the roystering boatman of Frampton Ferry—"

"My time is coming," exclaimed Nicodemus, interrupting the miller: "bid him withdraw; or he will have a sore head at his supper."

"They caroused and carolled," said the miller, "with two travellers, like skeldring Jacks o' the flagon, until—"

"Lay hands on Nicodemus, all!" cried the Abbot, as the enraged friar strode towards the miller;—"lay hands on the mad man at once!"

"It is too late," said Nicodemus, drawing forth a cudgel from beneath his cloak; "do not hinder me now, for my blackthorn reverences not the heads of the holy fraternity of Fairoak. Hold off, I say!" exclaimed he, as several of his brethren roughly attempted to seize him; "hold off, and mar me not in this mood; or to–day will, hereafter, be called the Feast of Blows. Nay, then, if you will not, I strike:—may you be marked, but not maimed!" The friar began to level a few of the most resolute of those about him as he spoke. "I will deal lightly as my cudgel will let me," pursued he. "I strike indiscriminately, and without malice, I protest. May blessings follow these blows! Brother Ulick, I grieve that you have thrust yourself within my reach. Look to the Abbot, some of ye, for,—miserable me!—I have laid him low. Man is weak, and this must be atoned for by fasting. Where is the author of this mischief? Miller, where art thou?"

Father Nicodemus continued to lay about him very lustily for several minutes; but, before he could deal with the miller as he wished, Friar Hugo's brother, who was on the floor, caught him by the legs, and suddenly threw him prostrate. He was immediately overwhelmed by numbers, bound hand and foot, and carried to his own cell; where he was closely confined, and most vigilantly watched, until the superiors of his order could be assembled. He was tried in the chamber which had been the scene of his exploits: the charge of having rudely raised his hand against the Abbot, and belaboured the holy brotherhood, was fully proved; and, ere twenty–four hours had elapsed, Father Nicodemus found himself enclosed, with a pitcher of water and a loaf, in a niche of a stone wall, in the lowest vault of Fairoak Abbey.

He soon began to feel round him, in order to ascertain if there were any chance of escaping from the tomb to which he had been consigned: the walls were old, but tolerably sound; he considered, however, that it was his duty to break out if he could; and he immediately determined on making an attempt. Putting his back to the wall, which had been built up to enclose him for ever from the world, and his feet against the opposite side of the niche, he strained every nerve to push one of them down. The old wall at length began to move: he reversed his position, and with his feet firmly planted against the new work, he made such a tremendous effort, that the ancient stones and mortar gave way behind him: the next moment he found himself lying on his back, with a quantity of rubbish about him, on the cold pavement of a vault, into which sufficient light glimmered, through a grating, to enable him to ascertain that he was no longer in any part of Fairoak Abbey.

The tongue–tied neighbours to whom Nicodemus had alluded, when he broke silence at that meeting of his brethren which terminated so unfortunately, were monks of the same order as those of Fairoak Abbey; among whom, about a century and a half before the time of Nicodemus, such dissensions took place, that the heads of the order were compelled to interfere; and under their sanction and advice, two–and–twenty monks, who were desirous of following the fine example of the Arroasians of Saint Augustin,—who neither wore linen nor ate flesh, and observed a perpetual silence,—seceded from the community, and elected an Abbot of their own. The left–wing of Fairoak Abbey was assigned to them for a residence, and the rents of a certain portion of its lands were set apart for their support. Their first care was to separate themselves, by stout walls, from all communication with, their late brethren; and up to the days of Nicodemus, no friendly communion had taken place between the Arroasian and its mother Abbey.

Nicodemus had no doubt but that he was in one of the vaults of the silent monks: in order that he might not be recognised as a brother of

Fairoak, he took off his black cloak and hood, and even his cassock and rochet, and concealed them beneath a few stones, in a corner of the recess from which he had just liberated himself. With some difficulty, he reached the inhabited part of the building: after terrifying several of the Arroasians, by abruptly breaking upon their meditations, he at length found an old white cloak and hood, arrayed in which he took a seat at the table of the refectory, and, to the amazement of the monks, tacitly helped himself to a portion of their frugal repast. The Superior of the community, by signs, requested him to state who and what he was; but Nicodemus, pointing to the old Arroasian habit which he now wore, wisely held his peace. The good friars knew not how to act:—Nicodemus was suffered to enter into quiet possession of a vacant cell; he joined in their silent devotions, and acted in every respect as though he had been an Arroasian all his life.

By degrees the good monks became reconciled to his presence, and looked upon him as a brother. He behaved most discreetly for several months: but at length having grown weary of bread, water, and silence, he, one evening, stole over the garden–wall, resolving to have an eel–pie and some malmsey, spiced with a little jovial chat, in the company of his trusty friend, the boatman of Frampton Ferry. His first care, on finding himself at large, was to go to the coppice of Fairoak, and cut a yard of good blackthorn, which he slung by a hazel gad to his girdle, but beneath his cassock. Resuming his path towards the Ferry, he strode on at a brisk rate for a few minutes; when, to his great dismay, he heard the sound of the bell which summoned the Arroasians to meet in the chapel of their Abbey.

"A murrain on thy noisy tongue!" exclaimed Nicodemus, "on what emergency is thy tail tugged, to make thee yell at this unwonted hour? There is a grievous penalty attached to the offence of quitting the walls, either by day or by night; and as I am now deemed a true Arroasian, by Botolph, I stand here in jeopardy; for they will assuredly discover my absence. I will return at once, slink into my cell, and be found there afflicted with a lethargy, when they come to search for me; or, if occasion serve, join my brethren boldly in the chapel."

The bell had scarcely ceased to toll, when Nicodemus reached the garden–wall again: he clambered over it, alighted safely on a heap of manure, and was immediately seized by half a score of the stoutest among the Arroasians. Unluckily for Nicodemus, the Superior himself had seen a figure, in the costume of the Abbey, scaling the garden–wall, and had immediately ordered the bell to be rung, and a watch to be set, in order to take the offender in the fact, on his return. The mode of administering justice among the Arroasians, was much more summary than in the Abbey of Fairoak. Nicodemus was brought into the Superior's cell, and divested of his cloak; his cassock was then turned down from his belt, and a bull's–hide thong severely applied to his back, before he could recover himself from the surprise into which his sudden capture had thrown him. His wrath rose, not gradually as it did of old,—but in a moment, under the pain and indignity of the, thong, it mounted to its highest pitch. Breaking from those who were holding him, he plucked the blackthorn he had cut, from beneath his cassock, and without either benediction or excuse, silently but severely belaboured all present, the Superior himself not excepted. When his rage and strength were some what exhausted, the prostrate brethren rallied a little, and with the aid of the remainder of the community, who came to their assistance, they contrived to despoil Nicodemus of his staff, and to secure him from doing further mischief.

The next morning, Nicodemus was stripped of his Arroasian habit; and, attired in nothing but the linen in which he had first appeared among the brethren, he was conducted, with very little ceremony, to the vaults beneath the Abbey. Every member of the community advanced to give him a parting embrace, and the Superior pointed with his finger to a recess in the wall: Nicodemus was immediately ushered into it, the wall was built up behind him, and once more he found himself entombed alive.

"But that I am not so strong as I was of yore, after the lenten fare of my late brethren," said Nicodemus, "I should not be content to die thus, in a coffin of stones and mortar. What luck hast thou here, Nicodemus?" continued the friar, as, poking about the floor of his narrow cell, he felt something like a garment, with his foot. "By rood and by rochet, mine own attire!— the cloak and cassock, or I am much mistaken, which I left behind me when I was last here;—for surely these are my old quarters! I did not think to be twice tenant of this hole; but man is weak, and I was born to be the bane of blackthorn. The lazy rogues found this niche ready–made to their hands, and, truth to say, they have walled me up like workmen. Ah, me! there is no soft place for me to bulge my back through now. Hope have I none: but I will betake me to my anthems; and perchance, in due season, I may light upon some means of making egress."

Nicodemus had, by this time, contrived to put on his cassock and cloak, which somewhat comforted his shivering body, and he forthwith began to chant his favourite anthem in such a lusty tone, that it was faintly heard by the Fairoak Abbey cellarman, and one of the friars who was in the vaults with him, selecting the ripest wines. On the alarm being given, a score of the brethren betook themselves to the vaults; and, with torches in their hands, searched every corner for the anthem–singer, but without success. At length the cellarman ventured to observe, that, in his opinion, the sounds came from the wall; and the colour left the cheeks of all as the recollection of Nicodemus flashed upon them. They gathered round the place where they had enclosed him, and soon felt satisfied that the awful anthem was there more distinctly heard, than in any other part of the vault. The whole fraternity soon assembled, and endeavoured to come to some resolution as to how they ought to act. With fear and trembling, Father Hugo's brother moved that they should at once open the wall: this proposal was at first rejected with contempt, on account of the known stupidity of the person with whom it originated; but as no one ventured to suggest anything, either better or worse, it was at last unanimously agreed to. With much solemnity, they proceeded to make a large opening in the wall. In a few minutes, Father Nicodemus appeared before them, arrayed in his cloak and cassock, and not much leaner or less rosy than when they bade him, as they thought, an eternal adieu, nearly a year before. The friars shouted, "A miracle! a miracle!" and Nicodemus did not deem it by any means necessary to contradict them. "Ho, ho! brethren," exclaimed he, "you are coming to do me justice at last, are you? By faith and troth, but you are tardy! Your consciences, methinks, might have urged you to enact this piece of good–fellowship some week or two ago. To dwell ten months and more in so dark and solitary a den, like a toad in a hole, is no child's–play. Let the man who doubts, assume my place, and judge for himself. I ask no one to believe me on my bare word. You have wronged me, brethren, much; but I forgive you freely."

"A miracle! a miracle!" again shouted the amazed monks: they most respectfully declined the proffered familiarities of Nicodemus, and still gazed on him with profound awe, even after the most incredulous among them were convinced, by the celerity with which a venison pasty, flanked by a platter of brawn, and a capacious jack of Cyprus wine vanished before him, in the refectory, that he was truly their Brother Nicodemus, and still in the flesh. Ere long, the jolly friar became Abbot of Fairoak: he was dubbed a saint after his decease; but as no miracles were ever wrought at his shrine, his name has since been struck out of the calendar.

THE PAIR OF PUMPS

"WHERE is the pumps?" cried Mrs. Jones,
  "Where is the pumps, I say?
They can't be lost; and, by the bones!
  I'll have them found to-day.

"There is but three beneath the roof,
  That's master, you, and I;—
How they has walked I'll have good proof,
  Or know the reason why.

"Your master wore them this day week;
  You knows he did, you jade!
That you're a thief, albeit so meek,
  In truth I'm half afraid.

"Don't answer me, you saucy minx!
  You're lazy as you're long;
At thousands of your faults I winks,
  Although I knows 'tis wrong.

"You looks the baker in the face,
  When he comes with the bread;
You trims your cap with shilling lace,
  And flirts with Butcher Ned.

"You acts as though you thought yourself
  The fairest of the fair;
And seems to think that master's pelf
  You're qualified to share.

"Now don't deny it—hussy, don't!
  For I has watched you long;
But I can tell you, Miss, you won't
  Win master with a song.

"In vain at him you sets your cap;
        He's not the sort of man;
With all your ogles bait your trap,
        And catch him if you can!

"Beneath his roof, for fifteen years,
        Housekeeper I have been;
I cares not if my speech he hears—
        No wrong in me he's seen.

"I slaves like an Trojan Turk;
        I makes his bed and mine;
While you, you hussy! does no work,
        And yet you dares repine!

"Why don't you take a pattern by
        Your master, slut, and me?
We never thinks a thought awry,—
        There is but few like we!

"The pumps was worn but this day week;
        You knows they were, you jade!
That you're a thief, albeit so meek,
        In truth I'm half afraid.

"You stands accused of stealing them—
        A very naughty sin;
And if you're hoity–toity, Me'em,
        I'll call the neighbours in!"

And hoity–toity Kitty was,
        She didn't care a pin!
Says Mistress Jones, "I vow, that's poz!
        I'll have the neighbours in!"

And in she call'd them one by one,
    By two and three, and four;
Such lots came in to see the fun,
    The house could hold no more.

"Oh! what's the matter?" quoth they all,
    "And what is here amiss?"
Says Mrs. Jones, "Pray don't you bawl;
    My friends, the case is this:—

"I keeps my master's house; and he,
    Good soul! is half afraid,
That spite of all precaution, we
    Is robb'd by Kate, our maid.

"Of all the lazy, idle drones
    That ever yet I knew,
Not one could match," says Mrs. Jones,
    "The girl you have in view.

"In all the house three beds we makes,
    For master, she, and me;
Both master's and my own I takes,
    She does but one of three.

"And though she grumbles,—yes, indeed,—
    That she is worked too much;
Yet she can oft her novels read,
    Ay, and the likes of such.

"She won't by me a pattern take,
    Although full well she knows,
In books 'tis said, 'the wayward rake
    Contemns the gather'd rose.'

"I've lost a pair of stockings, and
    About a week ago,
I'd master's pumps in this here hand,
    A–looking at 'em so.

"I hung 'em up upon the pegs,
    I recollects it well;
How they has walked without their legs,
    Miss Kate, perhaps, can tell."

"False Mrs. Jones!" young Kate replies,
    As forward now she jumps;
"She would not ask, were she but wise,
    If I had stol'n the pumps.

"There is but three beds in the house,
    And Mrs. Jones makes two;
We haven't room to stow a mouse;—
    So far her story's true.

"She brags about her virtue, but
    She's got a silly head;
A week ago, the pumps I put
    In Mrs. Jones's bed!"

WANTED A PARTNER

"AH! now, Michael, be quiet,—why can't you?—It brakes the heart o' me, cousin,—so it does thin, and I'll own it,—to see you laugh that way, and the pair of us ruined, as we are!"

"Is it ruined, Thady?—and yourself there with a bull and a hog in your pocket?"

"What's half–a–crown and a shilling? A bull and a hog is but three–and–sixpence.—I'll be starved intirely whin that's gone; for there's no work for us, far or near. I tell you we're ruined."

"Then let's go partners; and who knows but we'll make a fine fortune? What's invention but the daughter of necessity? So now's the time to shew our abilities, if we have any."

"Divil of any abilities have I, Michael; and you know it."

"Ah! Thady, Thady—"

"I'll give you my oath I hav'n't! —so don't be suspecting me. If I'd abilities, do you think I'd be such a blackguard as to consale them? Not I, thin!"

"Well but, Thady, boy, hav'n't you three–and–sixpence?— hav'n't you now?"

"I have,—I won't deny it."

"And hav'n't I abilities?"

"I won't deny that either, unless you've lost them since we last saw one another,—that's two years ago, I think:—I won't deny but you've abilities, Michael; if I did I'd be giving you the lie; for it's often you tould me you had grand ones, if you'd only a field large enough to display them. But where'll we get a field, big or little, for a bull? I would'nt risk more than that of my money upon your abilities,—though it's much I respect them."

"Thady, you're a fool, with your big field and your bull!— Besides, I've a reaping hook, and a long rope."

"I see you have: but tell me, Michael, as we're spaking of reap–hooks and abilities, how did you lose your last place? Wasn't your master a good one?"

"Say 'employer,' Thady, the next time you mintion him. Well, thin, he wasn't so bad, but for two things:—being an Englishman, he hadn't exactly got into our mode of transacting things, don't you see, Thady?—he stuck to the letter o' the law too closely for me."

"You didn't rob him Michael,—did you?"

"Of a little time only, Thady: he'd too many eyes to be robbed of anything else,—if I was dishonest,—but I'm not, you know."

"So I say, Michael, to every one who spakes of you."

"Thank you, Thady, for that:—and, faith! the time I took wasn't worth noticing. He put me into a little patch of peas, and bid me reap them as fast as I could. So I began to work as though I'd the strength often; and he stood by me and tould me I was a fine fellow. I got on well enough till he wint, and a while after even,—so I did. But I'd over-rated my own powers, and was soon obliged to lay down, just by the way of recruiting myself a little, under the hedge. By-and-by, who should be passing that way again but my employer; and, says he, putting his toe in my ribs, 'What did you lie there for,' says he, 'you blackguard?' 'To repose a little, sir,' says I. 'Bad luck to you!' says he, 'didn't I hire you to reap *peas?*' 'Well, sir,' says I, mimicking his way of spaking, 'and isn't sleep a weary man's harvest? and,' says I, quite pleasant, 'if it isn't in sleep I'd reap *ease*, how else would I?' 'Don't be quibbling that way,' says he; 'I'll be obeyed to the very letter.' 'Well, sir,' says I, 'O's and P's ar'n't far apart; they 're next door to one another in the alphabet.' But it wouldn't do for him; he'd have the letter itself; and if he paid me to reap peas, he wouldn't have me repose: so we parted. But don't let's be losing time: there's a rope and a reaping-hook, and they 're mine, ar'n't they?"

"I'd be wrong if I denied that, whin I see them in your hand, and possession is nine points of the law. But what of your rope and your reap-hook, Michael?"

"Why, thin, let them be our stock, and your three-and-six-pence our capital, and us partners and sole and only proprietors. What say you to that? You'll own it looks like business, I hope."

"Yes, Michael; but where'll the customers come from?"

"Don't bother about them; they'll come fast enough when we want them, as you'll see. It's no use to be reckoning our chickens before they're hatched, is it?"

"Not a bit:—what you say can't very soon find one that'll contradict it. It *is* no use to be reckoning our chickens before they're hatched."

"So far, thin, we go on by mutual consint. Now, Thady, would you like to make a great stroke or a little one?"

"The sooner we make money the better, I think."

"But little fishes are sweet, you fool!"

"So they are, Michael: I'm vexed that I didn't think of that; and it's but little we'll risk by way o' bait to catch them."

"But what's the use, Thady,—answer me now, you who set yourself up for a sinsible man—"

"Not I, thin! I'd fall out with you if you said so."

"Well, thin, where's the use, I'll ask you—fool as you are,—of our catching sprats and wullawaughs, when there's sea–cows and whales in the ocean?—A sprat isn't a sea–cow, is it?"

"No, faith!"

"Nor a wullawaugh a whale?"

"How should it?"

"Then why not try for a sea–cow?"

"Bekase I wouldn't like to risk my silver bull, Michael."

"Why, thin, you're a lunatic,—so you are. Suppose you lost your bull— tell me now, where'd your hog be?"

"Gone to try to bring back my bull, may be. I don't think we'll try for a sea–cow, or a whale, Michael."

"Thin you'll be contint with catching wullawaughs and shrimps, is it?"

"Not exactly: I'd like to try for a whale, but not so as to risk what money I have."

"Well, I'll tell you what we'll do:—let us set up a show."

"That plazes me. But what'll we shew, Michael? Is it your reap–hook, that's worn out doing divil a ha'p'orth but going to the grinstone?—or your rope, bekase you found it?"

"No, Thady; that wouldn't do: but I think if you'd tar and feather yourself, I might make something of you, by swearing you were a monster,—a big bird I caught on a furze–bush with bird–lime."

"I'll not consint to that; for if you'd be showman, you'd take all the money."

"And what thin?"

"Suppose you took yourself off one day?"

"And what thin?"

"Suppose you took the money with you, thin what'd I do? Sure, you know, I couldn't run after you in my tar and feathers; if I did, wouldn't the people see me without paying?"

"That would be a loss, I'll admit, if it happened: but I'd have you to know, Thady—"

"Now don't look big, for I'll apologize: but I may spake my mind, I hope?'

"You certainly may."

"Well, thin, I won't tar and feather myself; bekase, how'd we get tar and feathers to do it, without risking my bull, or my hog at the least?"

"Oh! thin, if you've doubts in your mind, I'll abandon the project: but I'll insist upon it that you don't take advantage of my idea, and tar and feather yourself for your own benefit."

"I give you my word, I won't:—but listen, Michael, and I'll tell you what we'll do, and there's no risk in it."

"I'd like to hear:—though I expect you'll be proposing to shoot the stars with a big bow and arrow, and sell them for diamonds."

"That wouldn't be bad, if we'd a bow and arrow that could do it; but I'm afraid we'd find it hard to get one. That's not my plan, Michael; but this is it:—there's a big hole, a stone's–throw from this; dark and deep it is, for I've looked down it; and far below, at the very bottom, runs a stream, that goes under the waters, and under the land, away off to the Red Sea: and it's often a big ould crocodile comes to it, for a day or so, in the summer, by the way of getting a change of air and retirement."

"Well, Thady, and suppose he does?"

"Why, thin, this is my plan:— us fish for the crocodile, and make a show of him if we catch him."

"Arrah! Thady! I didn't think it was in you. But what'll we do for a hook and line?"

"Haven't you your reap–hook and rope?"

"That's true, Thady, so I have; but by way of a bait—you know crocodiles ates man's flesh, Thady."

"I know it: and it's the beauty o' my plan, that we've bait, hook, and line,—all the materials, without a penny expense."

"Oh! I see:—faith! you're a genius, Thady:—you'd have me bait the hook with yourself."

"Not a bit of it, Michael; I couldn't separate you from your hook;—I wouldn't like to part with my money, and why should I ask you to part with your hook?"

"But don't you see, Thady, I run all the risk?—may be I'll lose my property;—the crocodile may carry it off. If we're to be partners, you must risk a little as well as me. I'll be my hook and my rope, with all the pleasure in life, if you'll be yourself,— if you'll let me tie you to them by the way of a bait."

"Nonsinse, Michael! what good would I be? Sure he feeds upon blacks—the crocodile does; and, fair as I am, he wouldn't know I was good to ate. Now, as you've a fine dark complexion—"

"No, I havn't."

"Faith! you have;—and it's what you're admired for, by me among many: I'd like to have it' myself. Why, thin, as you're within a few shades of the raal thing, may be, in the dark, he'd take you for the raal thing."

"Oh! thin, crocodiles ar'n't bamboozled so aisily; we'd better make sure,—and I'll tell how we'll do it:—I'll get some soot, and black you from head to foot."

"I'd be afraid, Michael."

"What harm could happen you, man? When he made his bite, wouldn't my reap–hook stick in his jaws and stop him from shutting them, until I'd pull him up?"

"Suppose he'd nibble and not bite?—suppose, too, he'd untie the cord and make a meal of me, and then pick his teeth with your reap–hook?"

"I'll tie the knot so that he can't: or, I'll tell you what we'll do;—we'll toss up which of us shall be bait."

"With all my heart:—but what'll we toss with?"

"Isn't it with your money? You'll lend me your bull."

"No, I won't lend you my bull, Michael."

"Well! toss your bull yourself, and let me have your hog."

"I won't do that, either; for I couldn't risk my money."

"What! do you suspect me?"

"Far from it; but, as there's grass here, we might lose it, you know."

"But I'll be responsible; and you can't doubt my honour."

"Not a bit; but—what's as bad,—I doubt your means. If I lost my bull, and you couldn't give me another if you would, that's the same thing to me as if you wouldn't give me another if you could,—don't you see?"

"Well, I've another plan: and I think it must plaze you:— did you ever throw a summerset?"

"I tried once, but didn't succeed."

"That's just my own case; so we're even, and it don't matter which does it. Now hark to this, Thady; you'll throw your summerset as well as you can, and while you're throwing it, I'll cry 'head' or 'tail,' just which I like: if I say 'tail,' and you fall on your head, it's you that wins."

"No, Michael; you must toss yourself; for I've no tail to my coat, and you have."

"Arrah, man! won't I lend you mine? Sure, we'll exchange."

"Well, but suppose I lost?"

"Thin you'd strip yourself, and I'd black you."

"But why strip myself, Michael?"

"Don't the crocodiles always catch people that's swimming? And suppose they didn't, don't the blacks go naked? They do, Thady: so that if you were in your clothes, the crature couldn't know you were a man, and we wouldn't catch him. If there was a fish that ate apples, you wouldn't bait your hook with a dumpling, would you?"

"I wouldn't: still, I couldn't leave my clothes."

"Why not, thin, eh?"

"Bekase there's my bull and my hog in the pocket; and I'd not like to risk them, with nobody on the bank, but yourself, to take care o' them."

"I don't know how it is, Thady, but nothing plazes you;— you're too particular by half."

"I'm fool enough to be too fond of my money, I'm afraid."

"I'm afraid you are:—but will I tell you what you'll do with it,—once for all now?"

"What, Michael?"

"Why, thin, you'll just lend me two–and–sixpence, and I'll go and do something in the way of speculation with it; so that, whin we meet again, I'll be able to give you back your bull, with some thing handsome to the tail of it."

"That's not bad, Michael: but I'd be afraid we wouldn't have the luck of meeting whin we'd wish. Who knows but one of us might be looking for the other, all over the wide world, like a needle in a bundle of hay?"

"Thady, is it trash your trying to talk? People meets where hills and mountains don't, you know."

"That's true: but I've found out that though one meets with them one don't want to see nine times a week, one goes a whole year, and more, without getting a sight o' them one wishes to come across. Who knows but, if I lent you my bull, the sight o' you would be good for sore eyes?— For that rason, I'll not lay you under the obligation, I think, Michael."

"Oh! bad luck to you, and every bit of you! Get out o' that, for I don't like you;—giving people trouble, by making believe you're a fool, whin all the while you ar'n't!"

"I'm beginning to think you'd bad intintions, Michael."

"Do you think I'd chate my cousin?"

"You would thin,—I'll say that for your abilities,—if you could get anything by it. Ar'n't you trying to bully me out o' my bull?

"Get out o' that, I tell you!—go away intirely:—I dissolve the partnership. Go at once, for I'm in a passion."

"Who cares for you, Michael? Go away yourself. I'll engage you'll find many's the one who wants a partner that's active, and won't mind about capital; but I don't think he'll be a man of property. Why should you crow over me, I'd like to know? is it bekase you've a cock in your eye?"

HANDSOME HANDS

AN elderly bachelor of my acquaintance is one of the warmest admirers in the world of a beautiful female hand. "A fine hand," he will say, "is a vastly fine thing, sir. As I always turned my attention very particularly to that part of the person, and have been king's page, and this, that, and t'other about a court, during many of my best years, the very finest of hands have fallen under my notice. Believe me, I am not at all captious, but merely critical, or in a trifling degree historical, when I say, that your fine hands of the present day, are very different from the fine hands of the old school. My father was convinced that hands had degenerated since Charles the Second's time; but he could not help confessing that, in my time,—I mean, when he was seventy, and I was thirty—hands were still handsome. And, mark me, he spoke of hands generally:—but, adad! *now,* if you meet with a fine hand once in a year or so, you're in luck, and ought to sacrifice a kid to Fortune. The fact is, that fine hands are very much talked about, but they are not properly cultivated; true beauty of form is no longer understood or appreciated; and the classical style of hand is, I fear, almost out of fashion. I am acquainted with two or three exquisite pair in town, and one,—its fellow, unfortunately, is deformed—one matchless hand at Putney. But nobody else admires them; I have them all to myself; and what is most provoking, these treasures,—these living and lovely reliques of a former age of grace and beauty,—these symbols of glorious pedigree,— these aristocratic heir–looms, are thrown away upon persons, who, if it were not for a spice of self–love, and that they're their own, would deem them but middling specimens. They positively try to coax them out of a beautiful into a barbarous style, so as to make them look like those of their neighbours, which the senseless young fellows of the modern school have the bad taste to admire. There never, perhaps, was a woman with such delightful hands as the charming Aurelia Pettigrew, afterwards Mrs. Watts, of Grange Hill, subsequently Mrs. Jervis, of Eton; whom I attempted at once to console and immortalize, by a copy of verses, written on the occasion of her having met with an accident, from an awkward waiting–woman's scissors, which produced a slight, but, in the opinion of many, a pleasing and piquant obliquity of the visual organ. These are the stanzas:—

"'When Chloe wandered o'er the mead,
To pluck the grateful flower;
Strephon and every shepherd swain,
Confess'd her beauty's power.

Enamour'd Colin, gazing knelt,
And soon resign'd his breath;
While each fond youth ambitious sighed,
To die so sweet a death.

Two suns the earth could ne'er endure,
Nor man her double glance;
So nature bade the right blaze on,
And turn'd the left askance.'

"I did not sing the charms of her hands, for they were above all praise:—small, plump, and graceful, with tapering fingers, and dimples where the knuckles lay, which, to the eye of fancy, seemed to smile like those in Love's own cheek. Miss Pettigrew was not of a very excellent figure; nor had she, with the exception of her eyes, particularly beautiful features; but her hands were matchless! They won her one husband, and many hearts,—my own among them,—at nineteen; and another husband with more than one suitor,—I was among 'em, again— when she was a widow, at forty. There are some Goths and Vandals, who would have their nails half as long as the fingers:—filbert–nails, I think is the term for such pretended beauties; which, in my opinion, bears striking resemblance to the convex side of the bowl of a horn spoon. But, though I consider a deep margin to a nail vulgar in the extreme, and would never, on any account, suffer its disk to peep over the Aurora–tinted horizon of the finger's summit, yet, understand me, I am no advocate for cutting them down to the quick. Of the two extremes,— a woman who pares her nails to the skin's edge, and a Chinese lady, who suffers hers to shoot forth into talons, I know not which is the more provoking. The Chinese female has at least the custom of the country in her favour; her, therefore, I have no right to blame, because it occurs that I am not a Chinese: but if I meet with one of my countrywomen, with claws at the ends of her fingers, I always long to call in a gardener or a sheep–shearer, with the necessary implement to prune or clip them down to a state of decorum. I do not possess sufficient talent to invent an appropriate and adequate punishment for a lady who is so enamoured with ugliness as to bite her nails. For her friends' sake, she ought to cannibalize in private, and conceal the revolting relics of her feast by wearing gloves, even in the presence of her most intimate friends. Those little machines which look like old gloves cropped to the knuckles, are gross outrages upon taste: they are called, I believe, mittens; and many excellent young ladies wear them, particularly in the country, during cold weather. The sight of a hand in one of these things invariably produces an emotion of pity in my bosom for the four long, cold, naked fingers, which protrude from the sockets of the stalls. In the matter of gloves, women are frequently so rash and inconsiderate, as 'to make the judicious grieve.' I have told every lady, with whom I have the honour to be intimate, and who has happened to have large, ignoble hands, that she ought not to wear tight gloves; I have declared, on the honour of a gentleman, that they increase rather than diminish the apparent size of the hand: but my preaching has never proved of much effect. A lady with an excellent, or even a good hand, should never have a wrinkle in her glove; but it is an absurd notion of many, that mere tightness is perfection: on the contrary, a glove that is well adapted to the hand never appears tight, but fits smooth and unwrinkled as the fair skin which it conceals. The kid should he close against the palm of the hand; the fingers should have no awkward bags at their extremities, and no bridges between their bases; indeed, the glove should fit as though it were an admirable mould, endowed with such elasticity as to assume every variety of form into which graceful action can possibly throw the hand. It, doubtless, has been to many persons, as well as to myself, a matter of astonishment, that the thousand and one elegant and delicate pieces of workmanship, in various materials, which seem to be fashioned by the exquisite fingers of a Belinda, are found, on inquiry, to be the productions of huge awkward paws, apparently fit only to wield flails and pull about blocks of granite. A celebrated frizeur, whose name I won't mention, has a very laudable antipathy to what he terms 'huge–ous hands':—he is a little lax in his language, but a very good frizeur for all that. Some years ago, he wanted a few assistants in his hair–cutting rooms; and inserted an advertisement in the paper to that effect. Among other applicants there was a good–looking youth, whose appearance, and answers to the preliminary questions put on such occasions, were highly satisfactory. 'Will your last master give you a character for civility?' inquired the hair–dresser. The boy answered in the affirmative. 'Well, and where are your gloves, young gentleman?' 'I don't wear any, sir!' 'Not wear gloves! I protest, I never heard of such a thing in all my born days. Take your hands out of your breeches pockets, then, boy, and let me inspect them.' The boy, with some difficulty, produced a pair of rather large and very high–coloured hands, and artlessly exhibited them to the frizeur. 'Oh! go away, boy—go away,' exclaimed the latter, recoiling three paces from the spectacle; 'you won't suit me at all: the advertisement particularly said, Wanted a few *good hands*, you know. It's not possible for me to take a young man into my establishment with great, large, red bits of beef, hanging out at the ends of his coat sleeves.—Go along!'"

MISLED BY A NAME

IT was my fortune to pass a portion of my youth at a celebrated watering–place, to which it was the fashion, at that time, with the faculty, in all parts of the kingdom, to consign their patients, usually in compliance with the desires of the latter, when medicine could be of no more avail; and there was such a constant influx of pale people of fortune, who were buried within so brief a period after the announcement of their arrival, that I sincerely pitied persons of opulence, because they seemed to be Death's favourite prey. Burials occurred so frequently, that at least a tithe of the inhabitants were undertakers.

It was really laughable to witness the intrigue that took place in the event of a death. The funeral was generally bespoke, even before the patient had been given over by the resident physicians: the sick gentleman's grocer, his tailor, his shoemaker, the master of the inn where he had put up on his arrival, the person in whose house he was expiring, the barber who shaved him when be was no longer able to shave himself, his butler, who had become tainted with the mania of the place, and the man over the way, whose wife was a laundress, were all undertakers in disguise, and sighing for his dissolution. This is a true sketch of the state of things some years ago, at ——, and, doubtless, at many other equally celebrated resorts of the afflicted. The various candidates for "a black job,"—that was the technical term,—frequently formed a coalition of interests. One of the party was nominated to bury the deceased, and divide the profits among all. Bribery to the domestics, in these cases, was carried on to a shocking extent; for the resident tradesmen of the place, rendered callous by custom, purchased the votes of every individual who was likely to have any voice in the election of an undertaker. Humorous mistakes frequently occurred in the ardour of the pursuit, and in the rivalry existing between the real gentlemen of the hearse, and those who were constantly on the alert to obtain a share of their profits. A case occurs to my recollection, which may, perhaps, be deemed not altogether devoid of interest.

An undertaker, who had received intelligence from one of the numerous jackals of the place, that the doctors had received their last fee from the friends of a patient, who lodged at Mr. B.'s house in a certain crescent, immediately repaired to the scene of action. He knocked at the door, but the footman (having received a bribe, and very particular instructions from a rival undertaker, who bad purchased the same intelligence a few moments earlier from the same identical jackal, and who was then in the pantry, trying to buy over the butler,) told him that he had mistaken the number; that his master was perfectly well; and that, in all probability, the gentleman who was dying, lived at Mr. B.'s other lodging–house, No. 7, in the same crescent.

"Do you know his name?" inquired the undertaker.

"The Reverend Mr. Morgan," replied the footman.

"Do you know his servant?"

"Yes; he's a thick–set man, with a slight cast in his eye."

"In or out of livery?"

"Out."

"May I use your name?"

"With all my heart, on your tipping the usual."

"There's a crown; it's all speculation,—neck or nothing; so I can't afford more. What's your name?"

"I am Sir Joseph Morgan's under–butler."

"Thank you;—good day:—but stop, allow me to trouble you with a dozen of my cards; a judicious use of them may pay you: I come down handsomely, and you may make it worth your while, as well as mine, should anything occur in your family. Will you do what you can?"

"With pleasure."

"Much obliged: and,—d'ye hear?—here's another: if you know of any house where the ravens roost,—you understand me— stick it in the frame of the house–keeper's looking–glass. Good morning!"

The Reverend Mr. Morgan, to whose lodgings the under–butler had referred the undertaker, was a middle–aged gentleman, lately married, and in daily expectation of having an heir to his name and the little freehold which his uncle had devised to him in the county of Brecon. He was just the sort of man that the under–butler had in his eye, when describing his servant. As the undertaker approached the door of No. 7, the reverend gentleman, in his usual neat, but homely dress, made his appearance. The undertaker, suspecting that he was the servant, accosted him the moment be had closed the door behind him, and the following dialogue ensued:—

"Your most obedient, sir."

"Yours, sir;—I ask pardon, but as I am in a hurry—"

"One moment—"

"Really, sir, if you knew the situation of affairs—"

"I do, sir;—I do, indeed."

"No!"

"Yes!"

"Well, it's rather odd. But I cannot stand here gossiping. Mrs. Morgan—"

"Ah! poor dear creature! but these things will happen, you know:— transitory life—sublunary world—sad mortality—tale of tears!—Going for the doctor?"

"No, not just yet; but—"

"Ah! still the event is pretty certain, I believe."

"Why, yes; I flatter myself it is."

"Good. Pardon me for being intrusive; my dear friend; but it lies in your power to do me a favour, I think: will you?"

"Oh! yes,—anything;—provided it costs me nothing."

"Not a penny:—you'll be in pocket by it. But, before I explain, allow me to ask,—have you any interest with, or influence over Mrs. Morgan? Be candid."

"Why, sir, I think I ought to have."

"Oh! I see:—a managed matter;—a candidate for dead men's shoes, eh?—Ah! you sly dog!"

"Sly dog!"

"You'll soon be master, I guess."

"I hope so; I have been long trying for it."

"Ha, ha! I know it. Oh! I can see things. But now to business:—the fact is, I'm a professional man."

"Oh! are you?"

"Yes,—you understand:—and a soon as any thing occurs, call me in; and I'll make matters agreeable to you."

"But Mrs. Morgan,—she must be consulted: I'm just going to see a gentleman on this very business."

"To be sure Mrs. M. must be consulted! Far be it from me to think of intruding myself without her permission. But you can use your influence. A word in your ear: I'm empowered to mention the name of Sir Joseph Morgan's under-butler. Manage it well, and I'll tip you a five pound note."

"Sir Joseph Morgan's under-butler! Me? Tip me?"

"Oh, honour! honour among thieves, you know. Ha, ha! Harkye;—the moment he goes off—"

"Goes off! Who?"

"The parson.—I say, the moment he goes off—"

"Ah!"

"Smuggle me up to his wife."

"To Mrs. M.? Smuggle you?"

"Oh! these things must be done with decorum, you know."

"Well, but—"

"Leave me to manage the rest. I flatter myself that my talent and experience will ensure us the desired success. Act well your part, and depend upon it I shall be the happy man."

"The happy man!"

"Ay; see him home, as we say."

"See who home?"

"Why, M., to be sure."

"M.?"

"Yes. Really, though, now I look at you, you don't seem to follow my ideas exactly."

"Not with that precision which I could wish."

"Psha! In plain English, then,—the parson being about to kick the bucket—"

"Kick the—"

"Ay,—hop the twig,—or pop off the hooks:—pick and choose, I've a variety."

"And pray, sir, what may his kicking the bucket be to you?"

"Thirty pounds, at least, if his widow's a trump, and things turn out kindly."

"I'm quite in a fog!—Pray, sir, who and what are you?"

"Didn't I say I was a professional man—an undertaker?"

"Oh! you're an undertaker, are you?"

"At your service."

"Thank you. And so you think of seeing M. home, do you?"

"Yes; box him up, as we say;—Ha, ha!"

"And I'm to have five pounds—"

"Exclusive of the usual jollification on the occasion, with the mutes and mourners; and an additional guinea, if you think proper to officiate with a black stick and hat–band. Pull your hat over your eyes, hold a white pocket–handkerchief to your face, and nobody will know you:—that's the way to manage. Ha, ha!"

"Very good; very good, indeed. Ha, ha!"

"Ha, ha! But come—what say you to a cheerful glass on this melancholy occasion? Sorrow is dry, you know;—I'll be a bottle."

"You're very good. And so you're an undertaker, after all, are you?"

"To be sure I am:—come along."

"And I'm to smuggle you up to Mrs. M., eh?—Ha, ha!—I must say I admire your mode of doing business much."

"Tact, my dear fellow,—tact and decorum; I display no other talents."

"Your gay manner, too—"

"Yes; 'we're the lads for life and joy,' as the song says. I'm naturally cheerful; but when I feel pretty sure of my man—as I now do—oddsheart! I'm as merry as a grig. Take my arm."

The undertaker marched off in triumph with his supposed prey leaning on his arm, towards a neighbouring tavern; but whether the reverend gentleman blighted his hopes by an early explanation, or forgot Mrs. M. for a few moments longer, and partook of the proffered bottle, "the chronicler cannot state."

THE LAST MAN

IN my little parlour, where,
Seated in an easy chair,
At the dull decline of day,
Oft I doze an hour away;—
Yester–eve I had a dream,
Of such seeming misery,
That, at last, my own loud scream,
Roused me to reality:
And, though strange my say may seem,
Sleep I'd rather never more,
Than hear again what then I bore.

Time, methought, was journeying fast:
Years, like moments, fleetly passed;
Still on they flowed,—behind,—before,—
Across what seemed a dismal sea,
To break like billows on the shore
Of measureless Eternity.

From all his leaden clogs releas'd,
Anon, the speed of Time increas'd;
Till even light could scarcely vie,
With the speed of a passing century.
The hills were grey,—the world was old;
Its hour was come, its sands were told;
The knell of a million years had rung;
And I, alone, continued young.

And, now, the work of woe began,
Despair through every bosom ran;
Death stalked abroad in open day,
And, visibly, attack'd his prey:
No more by slow disease he work'd,
Or in the cup of nectar lurk'd;
No host was now in battle slain,

No man set up,—a butt for Pain
To shoot her lingering arrows through;
No more the earth devour'd a town;
But Death walk'd openly in view,
And, with his scythe, mow'd myriads down.

I clos'd my eyes,—I saw no more,
Until a voice close to my ear,—
A voice I ne'er had heard before,
(So dismal that I quail'd with fear,
And utter'd that wild horrid scream,
Which rous'd me from my wretched dream;)
Bade me awake, methought, and see
Him, whose doom it was to be,
The last of human kind!

An awful form before me stood,
Whose aspect boded aught but good:
His looks were grim, his locks were grey;
He seem'd like one near life's last goal
And thrice, methought, I heard him say,
That he came to cast my soul!

My sight grew dim, I gasped for breath;—
(For who can brave a sudden death?)—
A moment's fearful pause ensued,
Then he,—the object of my dread,—
Address'd me thus in accents rude;
I listened, less alive than dead.

"I've said it once, I've said it twice,
I've raised my voice, and said it thrice:
My time is short,—I've much to do;—
I've lately lost my brother;—
I cannot wait all night on you,
For I must cast another.
To make your boot fit well, a tree

You've ordered, as I told;
And, once again, I say, in me,
The last–man you behold."

ALSO AVAILABLE FROM NONSUCH PUBLISHING

Reflecting the enormous changes wrought by the Industrial Revolution, John Halifax is a poor orphan who raises himself up from his humble beginnings, triumphing over his poverty-stricken start in life to become a respectable member of 'society'.
448 pages
ISBN: 1-84588-027-7
£6

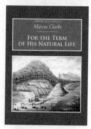

Forced to conceal his identity and forego his inheritance, Rufus Dawes is unjustly implicated in his father's murder, convicted of theft and sentenced to be transported to Australia, where he encounters the brutality of the penal system.
544 pages
ISBN: 1-84588-082-X
£6

Set against the backdrop of the Eureka Stockade of 1854, Jack Wainwright, Harry Coates and Michael O'Donoghue, the 'three diggers,' face everything from highwaymen to broken hearts in the harsh and unforgiving landscape of colonial Australia during its Gold Rush.
224 pages
ISBN: 1-84588-084-6
£6

Sam Slick, the Clockmaker of the title, is the embodiment of straight-talking. Witty and irreverent, often satirical and sometimes downright scandalous, Sam's shrewd observations on 'human natur' mark him out as one of literature's greatest comic sages.
576 pages in 3 volumes
ISBN: 1-84588-050-1
£10

For sales information please see our website:
www.nonsuch-publishing.com